Praise for Chloe Neill's
Chicagoland Vampires Novels

'These books are wonderful entertainment'

Charlaine Harris, *#1 New York Times* bestselling author

'Neill creates a strong-minded, sharp-witted heroine who will appeal to fans of Charlaine Harris's Sookie Stackhouse series and Laurell K. Hamilton's Anita Blake' *Library Journal*

'A wonderfully compelling vampire heroine'

Julie Kenner, *USA Today* bestselling author

'If you loved Nancy Drew but always wished she was an undead sword-wielding badass, Merit is your kind of girl' *Geek Monthly*

'Between the high stakes, the intense romance, and the fabulous cast of characters, I cannot recommend this book any higher!'

A Book Obsession

'Chicagoland Vampires is one of my favourite series, and with each instalment, I'm reminded why I keep coming back for more'

All Things Urban Fantasy

'Delivers enough actin, plot twists, and fights to satisfy the most jaded urban fantasy reader' Monsters and Critics

'A fast and exciting read' Fresh Fiction

A descriptive, imaginative, and striking world . . . roughly fantastic from beginning to end, with one of the best endings in urban fantasy history' *RT Book Reviews*

'The pa͟   ͟ance fans
alike' *Booklist*

Also by Chloe Neill:

Chicagoland Vampires series

Some Girls Bite

Friday Night Bites

Twice Bitten

Hard Bitten

Drink Deep

Biting Cold

House Rules

Biting Bad

Wild Things

Blood Games

Dark Debt

Midnight Marked

Howling for You (eBook only novella)

Lucky Break (eBook only novella)

Dark Elite series

Firespell

Hexbound

Charmfall

THE
VEIL

A DEVIL'S ISLE NOVEL

CHLOE NEILL

Copyright © Chloe Neill 2016

First published in Great Britain in 2016
by Gollancz
An imprint of the Orion Publishing Group
Carmelite House, 50 Victoria Embankment,
London EC4Y 0DZ
An Hachette UK Company

This edition published in Great Britain in 2016
by Gollancz

1 3 5 7 9 10 8 6 4 2

A CIP catalogue record for this book
is available from the British Library

ISBN 978 1 473 21534 4

Printed in Great Britain by Clays Ltd, st ives plc

To my remarkable editor, Jessica Wade

ACKNOWLEDGEMENTS

Thanks, as always, to my wonderful agent, Lucienne; my assistant Krista; my mostly patient husband, Jeremy; and Baxter and Scout, who are always (literally) by my side. Thanks to Debra Fiala for assistance with medical and anatomical knowledge. Special thanks to all my readers who've given me the opportunity to explore New Orleans.

'Hell is empty, and all the devils are here'
William Shakespeare

CHAPTER ONE

The French Quarter was thinking about war again.

Booms echoed across the neighborhood, vibrating windows and shaking the shelves at Royal Mercantile—the finest purveyor of dehydrated meals in New Orleans.

And antique walking sticks. We were flush with antique walking sticks.

I sat at the store's front counter, working on a brass owl that topped one of them. The owl's head was supposed to turn when you pushed a button on the handle, but the mechanism was broken. I'd taken apart the tiny brass pieces and found the problem—one of the small toothy gears had become misaligned. I just needed to slip it back into place.

I adjusted the magnifying glass over the owl, its jointed brass wings spread to reveal its inner mechanisms. I had a thin screwdriver in one hand, a pair of watchmaking tweezers in the other. To get the gear in place, I had to push one spring down and another up in that very small space.

I liked tinkering with the store's antiques, to puzzle through broken parts and sticky locks. It was satisfying to make something work that hadn't before. And since the demand for fancy French sideboards and secretaries wasn't exactly high these days, there was plenty of inventory to pick from.

I nibbled on my bottom lip as I moved the pieces, carefully adjusting the tension so the gear could slip in. I had to get the gear into the back compartment, between the rods, and into place between the springs. Just a smidge to the right, and . . .

Boom.

I jumped, the sound of another round of fireworks shuddering me back to the store—and the gear that now floated in the air beside me, bobbing a foot off the counter's surface.

"Damn," I muttered, heart tripping.

I'd moved it with my mind, with the telekinetic magic I wasn't supposed to have. At least, not unless I wanted a lifetime prison sentence.

I let go of the magic, and the gear dropped, hit the counter, bounced onto the floor.

My heart now pounding in my chest, the fingers on both hands crossed superstitiously, I hopped off the stool and hurried to the front door to check the box mounted on the building across the street. It was a monitor with a camera on top, triggered when the amount of magic in the air rose above background levels—like when a Sensitive accidentally moved a gear.

I'd gotten lucky; the light was still red. I must not have done enough to trigger it, at least from this distance. I was still in the clear—for now. But damn, that had been close. I hadn't even known I'd been using magic.

Boom.

Already pumped with nervous energy, I jumped again.

"Good lord," I said, pushing the door open and stepping outside onto the threshold between the store's bay windows, where MERCANTILE was mosaicked in tidy blue capitals.

It was mid-October, and the heat and humidity still formed a miserable blanket across the French Quarter. Royal Street was nearly empty of people.

The war had knocked down half the buildings in the Quarter, which gave me a clear view of the back part of the neighborhood and the Mississippi River, which bordered it. Figures moved along the riverbank, testing fireworks for the finale of the festivities. The air smelled like sparks and flame, and wisps of white smoke drifted across the twilight sky.

It wasn't the first time we'd seen smoke over the Quarter.

On an equally sweltering day in October seven years ago, the Veil—the barrier that separated humans from a world of magic we hadn't even known existed—was shattered by the Paranormals who'd lived in what we now called the Beyond.

They wanted our world, and they didn't have a problem eradicating us in the process. They spilled through the fracture, bringing death and destruction—and changing everything: Magic was now real and measurable and a scientific fact.

I was seventeen when the Veil, which ran roughly along the ninetieth line of longitude, straight north through the heart of NOLA, had splintered. That made New Orleans, where I'd been born and raised, ground zero.

My dad had owned Royal Mercantile when it was still an antiques store, selling French furniture, priceless art, and very expensive jewelry. (And, of course, the walking sticks. So many damn walking sticks.) When the war started, I'd helped him transition the store by adding MREs, water, and other supplies to the inventory.

War had spread through southern Louisiana, and then north, east, and west through Alabama, Mississippi, Tennessee, Arkansas, and the eastern half of Texas. The conflict had destroyed so much of the South, leaving acres of scarred land and burned, lonely cities. It had taken a year of fighting to stop the bloodshed and close the Veil again. By that time, the military had been spread so thin that civilians often fought alongside the troops.

Unfortunately, he hadn't lived to see the Veil close again. The store became mine and I moved into the small apartment on the third floor. We hadn't lived there together—he didn't want to spend every hour of his life in the same building, he'd said. But the store and building were now my only links to him, so I didn't hesitate. I missed him terribly.

When the war was done, Containment—the military unit that managed the war and the Paranormals—had tried to scrub New Orleans not only of magic but of voodoo, Marie Laveau, ghost tours, and even literary vampires. They'd convinced Congress to pass the so-called Magic Act, banning magic inside and outside the war zone, what we called the Zone. (Technically, it was the MIGECC Act: Measure for the Illegality of Glamour and Enchantment in Conflict Communities. But that didn't have the same ring to it.)

The war had flattened half of Fabourg Marigny, a neighborhood next door to the French Quarter, and Containment took advantage. They'd shoved every remaining Para they could find into the neighborhood and built a wall to keep them there.

Officially, it was called the District.

We called it Devil's Isle, after a square in the Marigny where criminals had once been hanged. And if Containment learned I had magic, I'd be imprisoned there with the rest of them.

They had good reason to be wary. Most humans weren't affected by magic; if it was an infection, an illness, they were immune. But a small percentage of the population didn't have that immunity. We were sensitive to the energy from the Beyond. That hadn't been a problem before the Veil was opened; the magic that came through was minimal—enough for magic tricks and illusions but not much else. But the scarred Veil wasn't as strong; magic still seeped through the rip where it had been sewn back together. Sensitives weren't physically equipped to handle the magic that poured through.

Magic wasn't a problem for Paras. In the Beyond, they'd bathed in the magic day in and day out, but that magic had an outlet—their bodies became canvases for the power. Some had wings; some had horns or fangs.

Sensitives couldn't process magic that way. Instead, we just kept absorbing more and more magic, until we lost ourselves completely. Until we became wraiths, pale and dangerous shadows of the humans we'd once been, our lives devoted to seeking out more magic, filling that horrible need.

I'd learned eight months ago that I was a Sensitive, part of that unlucky percentage. I'd been in the store's second-floor storage room, moving a large, star-shaped sign to a better spot. (Along with walking sticks, my dad had loved big antique gas station signs. The sticks, at least, were easier to store.) I'd tripped on a knot in the old oak floor and stumbled backward, falling flat on my back. And I'd watched in slow motion as the hundred-pound sign—and one of its sharp metallic points—fell toward me.

I hadn't had time to move, to roll away, or even to throw up an arm and block the rusty spike of steel, which was aimed at the spot between my eyes. But I did have a split second to object, to curse the fact that I'd lived through war only to be impaled by a damn gas station sign that should have been rusting on a barn in the middle of nowhere.

"No, damn it!" I'd screamed out the words with every ounce of air in my lungs, with my eyes squeezed shut like a total coward.

And nothing had happened.

Lips pursed, I'd slitted one eye open to find the metal tip hovering two inches above my face. I'd held my breath, shaking with adrenaline and sweating with fear, for a full minute before I gathered up the nerve to move.

I'd counted to five, then dodged and rolled away. The star's point hit the floor, tunneling in. There was still a two-inch-deep notch in the wood.

I hadn't wanted the star to impale me—and it hadn't. I'd used magic I hadn't known I'd had—Sensitivity I hadn't known I possessed—to stop the thing in its tracks.

I'd gotten lucky then, too: The magic monitor hadn't been triggered, and I'd kept my store . . . and my freedom.

Another boom sounded, pulling me through memory to my spot on the sidewalk. I jumped, cursed under my breath.

"I think you're good, guys!" I yelled. Not that I was close enough for them to hear me, or that they'd care. This was War Night. Excess was the entire point.

Six years before, the Second Battle of New Orleans had raged across the city. (The first NOLA battle, during the War of 1812, had been very human. At least as far as we were aware.) It had been one of the last battles of the war and one of the biggest.

Tonight we'd celebrate our survival with colors, feathers, brass bands, and plenty of booze. It would be loud, crazy, and amazing. Assuming I could manage not to get arrested before the fun started . . .

"You finally losing it, Claire?"

I glanced back and found a man, tall and leanly muscled, standing behind me. Antoine Lafayette Gunnar Landreau, one of my best friends, looked unwilted by the heat.

His dark brown, wavy hair was perfectly rakish, and his smile was adorably crooked, the usual gleam in his deep-set hazel eyes. Tonight, he wore slim dark pants and a sleeveless shirt that showed off his well-toned arms—and the intricate but temporary paintings that stained his skin.

"Hey, Gunnar." We exchanged cheek kisses. I cursed when another *boom* sounded, followed by the sparkle of gold stars in the air.

I smiled despite myself. "Damn it. Now they're just showing off."

"Good thing you're getting into the spirit," he said with a grin. "Happy War Night."

"Happy War Night, smarty-pants. Let me check your ink."

Gunnar obliged, stretching out his arms so I could get a closer view. New Orleans was a city of traditions, and War Night had its own: the long parade, the fireworks, the spiked punch we simply called "Drink" because the ingredients depended on what was available. And since the beginning, when there was nothing but mud and ash, painting the body to remember the fallen. Making a living memorial of those of us who'd survived.

The intricate scene on Gunnar's left arm showed survivors celebrating in front of the Cabildo, waving a purple flag bearing four gold fleurs-de-lis—the official postwar flag of New Orleans. The other arm showed the concrete and stone sculpture of wings near Talisheek in St. Tammany Parish, which memorialized one of the deadliest battles of the war, and the spot where thousands of Paras had entered our world.

The realism lifted goose bumps on my arms. "Seriously amazing."

"Just trying to do War Night proud. And Aunt Reenie."

"God bless her," I said of Gunnar's late and lamented aunt, who'd been a great lover of War Night, rich as Croesus, and, according to Gunnar's mother, "not quite there."

"God bless her," he agreed.

"Let's get the party started," I said. "You want something to drink?"

"Always the hostess. I don't suppose there's any tea?"

"I think there's a little bit left," I said, opening the door and gesturing him in.

Gunnar was a sucker for sweet tea, a rarity now that sugar was a luxury in New Orleans. That was another lingering effect of war. Magic was powerful stuff, and it wasn't meant to be in our world. Nothing would grow in soil scarred by magic, so war had devastated the Zone's farms. And since there were still rumors of bands of Paras in rural areas who'd escaped the Containment roundup and preyed on humans, there weren't many businesses eager to ship in the goods that wouldn't grow here.

There'd been a mass exodus of folks out of the cities with major fighting—New Orleans, Baton Rouge, Mobile—about three weeks after the war started, when it began to look as though we weren't equipped to fight Paras, even on our own soil.

There were plenty of people who still asked why we stayed in the Zone, why we put up with scarcity, with the threat of wraith and Para attacks, with Containment on every corner, with Devil's Isle looming behind us.

Some folks stayed because they didn't have a better choice, because somebody had to take care of those who couldn't leave. Some stayed because they didn't have resources to leave, anywhere to go, or anyone to go to. And some stayed because they'd been through hard times before—when there'd been no electricity, no comforts, and too much grief—and the city was worth saving again. Some stayed because if we left, that would be the end of New Orleans, Little Rock, Memphis, and Nashville. Of the culture, the food, the traditions. Of the family members who existed only in our memories, who tied us to the land.

And some folks stayed because they had no choice at all. Containment coordinated the exodus. And when everyone who'd wanted to get out was out, they started controlling access to the Zone's borders, hoping to keep the Paras and fighting contained.

No, staying in the Zone wasn't easy. But for a lot of us—certainly for me—it was the only option. I'd rather make do in New Orleans than be rich anywhere else.

We'd tried to make the best of it. In the Quarter, we'd solved the scorched-earth problem by planting things in containers with "clean" soil. I had a lemon tree and a tomato plant in the courtyard behind the store, and I got more fruit and produce from the small roof garden shared by a few of us who still lived in the Quarter. We'd taken over the terrace that had once been a fancy pool and cabana at the abandoned Florissant Hotel, turned it into a community garden. Containment had done the same thing at the former Marriott to provide supplies for the agents.

War made people creative about their survival.

Owning one of the few stores left in the Quarter also had some advantages. Because so many of my customers were Containment personnel, I'd been able to get goods from the military convoys that crossed the Zone. It also helped that Gunnar worked for Devil's Isle's Commandant. Of course, that had unfortunate personal implications, too. Gunnar didn't know about my magic, and I had no intention of telling him. That would be bad for both of us.

Gunnar followed me inside to the small curtained area behind the front counter. It was the building's "kitchen," and held a small blue refrigerator that had lived (thank God) long past its prime, a gas stove, an old farmhouse sink, and a few stingy cabinets.

I sighed with relief at the burst of cold air from the fridge. Gunnar moved beside me, and we stood in front of it for a moment, savoring the chill.

"All right. Let's not waste the cold while we've got it." Consistent power was another rarity in the Zone. Magic and electricity didn't mix, which made the electrical system unstable. Keeping the lights on and the city dry were constant battles.

Considering that, it made sense to finish the tea while it was still good and cold. I grabbed the cut-glass pitcher and poured the rest of the tea into two plastic hurricane cups.

The pitcher had come with the store; the cups were my contribution.

Gunnar sipped, closed his eyes in obvious pleasure. "You could steal a man's heart with this."

I took a drink, nodded. "It's good, but it hasn't done much heart stealing so far." My last go-round hadn't been successful. Rainier Beaulieu had been tall, dark, and handsome. Unfortunately, when he told me I was the "only one," he'd forgotten to mention "right now."

I'd been in a lull since that little mistake. The Zone wasn't usually a draw for the young and eligible.

Gunnar grinned. "It's War Night. Everything could change."

That was the best part of it: Anything seemed possible. "My fingers are crossed. Feel free to keep an eye out."

"I love playing your wingman."

"I can wing my own men. You're just the scout. How are the crowds?"

"Emboldened by the heat," Gunnar said with a grin. "And embiggening. It's gonna be a helluva night out there."

"War Night always is," I said, but knew exactly what he meant. New Orleans could never be accused of shyness, and War Night would be no exception.

He glanced at the wall clock. "Tadji's meeting us at the start. How much longer till you close up?"

Tadji Dupre was the third in our friendship trio. "Fifteen minutes if I keep her open until six."

"Be a rebel," he said. "Close early."

Funds were hard to come by these days, and I wasn't one to turn down even fifteen minutes of business. On the other hand, I probably wouldn't be missing big sales tonight. People would be thinking about jazz and booze, not dried fruit and duct tape.

Some of that jazz bloomed outside, and we walked back into the front room, drawn by the music.

Half a dozen men in brilliantly colored suits, the fabric and elaborate headpieces covered in feathers and beading, filled the sidewalk. They were the Vanguard, New Orleanians who'd served in the war and organized the first War Night parade six years ago. A few had been the feathered performers known as Mardi Gras Indians, and they'd brought some of those traditions into this celebration.

One of members stopped, tapped a dark fist against the window. I grinned back at Tony Mercier, a silver whistle between his teeth, a black patch covering the eye he'd lost in the Second Battle. Tony had fought with the Niners from the Ninth Ward. And now he was the Vanguard's Big Chief.

He pointed down the street, signaling their destination, and then back at me. That message was obvious: They were heading to the starting line, and it was time for me to join them.

"I'm leaving soon!" I called out, and waved them on. They shuffled down the sidewalk, followed by a second line band that grooved to notes wrought through worn brass. A tuba marked the beat, a trombone and trumpet pushed the rhythm and melody, and half a dozen men, women, and children with tambourines, silver whistles, and homemade drums danced behind them.

The song, the instruments, and the parade were bittersweet reminders of life before the Veil had opened. But they were also reminders of what made New Orleans so amazing: its creativity, its traditions, its willingness to band together and face down a common enemy.

I rejected the idea that I was part of that common enemy. And besides, tonight wasn't about fear or regret. Tonight was about life, about experience, about celebration.

"All right," I said, grinning at Gunnar. "Lock the door. Let the good times roll."

"Laissez les bon temps rouler," he agreed.

CHAPTER TWO

Blacks, grays, taupes. There weren't many civilians left in New Orleans these days, especially in the Quarter, and we tended to wear neutral colors. Military colors. Our clothes blended with theirs, and that was fine by me.

Stay quiet; work hard. That was my motto.

But this was War Night. War Night deserved more than camouflage, so I'd donned a pale violet dress sprigged with white flowers. While Gunnar waited downstairs, I changed from black and gray into NOLA-appropriate purple that worked pretty well against my green eyes and long red hair. Fortunately, I was happy with it straight, because it wouldn't hold a curl if you begged it.

When Gunnar finished off the tea and the store was locked up tight, we followed Royal Street past brick buildings still half-destroyed, then turned onto Canal. As Gunnar had reported, the crowd was already huge.

The few remaining palm trees swayed, the air cooling as the sun dropped toward the horizon. The sounds and smells of War Night were carried on the breeze—the rhythms of brass-heavy jazz, the fruity scent of tonight's Drink, lingering smoke from the fireworks.

The Vanguard stood at the head of Bourbon Street, scepters waving beneath a homemade arch of metal scraps, paper flowers, beads from prewar Mardi Gras parades. This year's War Night theme was "paradise," so they'd also stuck in palm fronds, Spanish moss, and flowers made of cut soda cans.

The parade would zigzag through the Quarter, down Bourbon to St. Anne, and then over to Jackson Square, a gorgeous park even war hadn't managed to destroy. At the Square, the parade would turn into a block party that would last until the band got tired, the booze ran out, or Containment shut us down.

"Claire! Gunnar!"

We looked over, found Tadji waving from a spot in the middle of the street. She was tall and slender, with velvet-dark skin and curly hair that framed a face dominated by enviable cheekbones and a wide mouth. Tonight she wore a gauzy purple tunic over a saffron bodysuit, and a dozen thin golden rings on her fingers that sparkled in the light. The ensemble—fluid fabric over her long, strong form— made her look like a pagan goddess.

She was absolutely gorgeous, crazy focused on her work, and usually unflappable.

Except when it came to magic.

Tadji was a couple of years older than me. She'd been born in a small community in Acadiana, the French-speaking part of Louisiana, but left the state after high school. Her mom and aunt, and her grandmother before them, had practiced voodoo, preparing gris-gris and cure-alls for neighbors, helping them summon loa and saints.

Tadji thought they were con artists, and had been angry and embarrassed that they'd wanted to bring her into the family business. It wasn't until the Veil opened that we learned magic really did exist, that some of the voodoo and hoodoo practitioners, psychics, and magicians really did have some power. I wasn't sure whether Tadji's relatives fell in that category.

She'd eventually made peace with her mom and aunt. But she didn't talk about them much, except to say they moved around a lot. She never wanted to discuss them, or magic.

Tadji was now in grad school, studying linguistics at Tulane, the only college still operating in southern Louisiana. She was interviewing survivors in southern Louisiana to investigate how war affected language in the Zone.

I hadn't gone to college, but I knew how to make do. I read as much as I could on my own, and I'd learned some things on the streets that couldn't be learned in a classroom. But I was still in awe of how much Tadji knew about so many things. Jealousy bit me sometimes, even though I knew I'd made my choice to focus on the store.

We exchanged hugs, and she and Gunnar exchanged cheek kisses.

"Hey, guys!" she yelled over the booming drum. "Happy War Night!"

"Happy War Night!" we shouted back at her. She pulled paper cups and a recycled lemonade bottle from the khaki messenger bag around her shoulder, distributed the Drink.

"To New Orleans," Gunnar said. "May she be forever strange."

I sipped, my eyes widening at mouth-puckering tartness that warred with sinus-clearing alcohol.

Tadji was good with words. Tadji was not good with chemistry.

"That is . . . strong," I said as Gunnar wheezed beside me.

"Is it gasoline?" he asked.

"What?" Tadji blinked in surprise. "What do you mean?" She took another drink, tasted. "It's good, right? It's good."

"It's definitely *almost* a beverage," Gunnar said, then pointed toward Bourbon Street. "Ooh! Fire-eaters."

When Tadji turned to look, he took my cup and tipped both his and mine into a planter box overgrown with weeds. I doubted the plants would survive the night.

"Gumbo," he whispered, the word a warning.

I loved Tadji. But as we'd learned during Sunday night dinners—our weekly ritual—she could not cook. As far as I could tell, she didn't taste things the way other people did, and didn't have much interest in food anyway. I didn't consider myself a foodie, but I preferred edible to gummy cardboard. Which generously described the "gumbo" she'd made for us one evening. Gunnar and I had worked to keep her away from the stove after that.

Since there was no point chastising someone who literally didn't have a taste for cooking, Gunnar just kept smiling.

"So good," he complimented after handing my cup back to me, but shook his head when she held up the bottle in invitation. "Don't want to push things too early."

The look in her eyes said she didn't buy the excuse, but she didn't argue about it. "Suit yourself. I like your dress," she said to me.

I glanced down. It was probably a little old-fashioned for War Night, but that made it feel more appropriate. That was why we were there, after all—to remember traditions and luxuries we couldn't afford anymore.

"Thanks," I said. "You look amazing."

Tadji shrugged off the compliment. She wasn't great with them, which I thought was residual guilt about coming home with more than she'd had when she left. And probably more than her family had now.

The music grew louder as the Vanguard prepared to move. Gold fireworks arched over us, sending my heart stuttering again as the crowd's roar grew to a thundering crescendo.

"*Nous vivons!*" we shouted together. It meant "we live," and was our mantra of remembrance, of grief, of joy that we'd survived war, even as we lived in its shadow.

The Vanguard stepped forward, feathers and sequins flashing in the gaslights that had replaced streetlamps. We were a few dozen feet from the front of the crowd, and we could take only tiny steps forward. It took ten minutes for us to reach the arch, which was guarded on both sides by a pair of Containment agents in gray fatigues and black boots. Their gazes passed over the crowd, looking for troublemakers.

One of the agents made eye contact with me. I forced a vague smile and pretended to be nothing more than a red-haired girl in the crowd.

Gunnar, Tadji, and I linked our hands as we passed beneath the arch, the soda can flowers glittering as they shimmied in the breeze.

Gunnar squeezed our hands. "Let's make this a War Night to remember, ladies."

Even in the heat, people were damn certain they'd enjoy War Night. A party was a luxury they wouldn't give up.

There weren't many wrought-iron balconies left on Bourbon Street. But people still filled them because you couldn't have a parade in New Orleans without throws. Beads were expensive and not exactly a priority for military convoys, but paper was still easy to come by, so necklaces of twisted paper and folded flowers had become another War Night tradition. Folks on the balconies wore dozens of necklaces on their arms, and they tossed them over the parade as it passed, filling the air with paper petals.

I snatched two as they fell, handed one to Tadji, and we slipped them over our heads. The twisted necklace and its flowers, big as old-fashioned peonies, were made from folded phone book pages. Not that we needed them—war had destroyed most of the phone, cable, and fiber-optic lines and towers. The Paras had learned quickly enough to target them.

We were six blocks into the parade, and the sweaty crowd had bunched together again, any sense of personal boundaries completely abandoned. Gunnar had found a dance partner a few people away, so when the fourth sweaty person in a row bounced against me, I decided it was time for a break. I grabbed Tadji's hand and maneuvered through jostling bodies to the edge of the crowd.

The breeze felt like a miracle.

"Oh my God, that's better," Tadji said, flapping her tunic to cool herself. "Good call."

I nodded. "I was about to punch the next sweaty person who elbowed me in the stomach."

"The next person who *elbowed* you in the stomach, or you were going to *punch* them in the stomach?"

Sometimes it didn't pay to be friends with a woman obsessed with words. "Har-har. The point is, there are a lot of sweaty people in that crowd." I glanced back, surveyed the mass of people. "I think the party's even bigger than last year."

She nodded. "The population's actually gone up a little in the last few years. Some people think it's safe to come back, that there's no chance the Veil will open again. And some people are fascinated by what happened, really hope that it will."

Her voice had gone quiet, and I glanced at her, found her gaze on the high wall that surrounded Devil's Isle, visible at the other end of Bourbon Street, the sky orange above it from the glow of the electrified mesh that covered the neighborhood and kept the Paras from escaping upward.

"Do you ever wonder what it's like in there?" she asked.

I had wondered, and hadn't liked what my imagination had come up with. A few thousand Paranormals and Sensitives interned for our protection—and because the government had no idea what else to do with them. We'd closed the Veil, after all. That made them prisoners of war from a world we could no longer access.

That made me think of uncomfortable things. I wasn't bad, and Containment still would have tossed me into Devil's Isle. If I wasn't bad, what about the other Sensitives who'd been locked in?

"I try not to think about it," I said honestly.

"It's a complicated issue. But man, what I wouldn't give to get in there. Can you imagine the vocabulary they've developed? The Paranormals probably had to create a completely new language just to describe what they're going through."

She was probably right, and I could admit it was intriguing. But I still didn't want any part of Devil's Isle, and I had no interest in going in there. Not when the odds were good that they wouldn't let me out again.

While Tadji watched the parade, bouncing to the music, I checked out the street. There was a former walk-in daiquiri shop on the corner. It was missing a front wall, but an off-duty Containment agent—a man I'd seen in the shop—stood behind the bar and poured red liquid into plastic cups. His version of Drink, probably, and an opportunity to make a little extra money. Couldn't fault him for that.

A handful of his uniformed Containment colleagues looked on from the sidewalk, gazes moving suspiciously between the parade and the patrons in the make-do Drink shop.

Most of the agents who worked in the Quarter had been in the war. They'd seen its horrors, and knew about its tragedies. Others came from outside the Zone, or were too young to remember battle. They'd missed the fighting, the injuries, the sweet and bitter smells of death and battle. Maybe because they hadn't seen the horrors for themselves, there was fervor in their eyes. They'd learned to hate Paras, and wanted their own chance to fight magic.

I looked away, torn as usual between who I was and what magic would have made of me, and let my gaze skim the rest of the revelers. The couple whose pale skin sheened with sweat, whose eyes were filled with love as they drank greedily from plastic cups. The friends who sat in a line on the curb, shirts soaked through, but all of them grinning. A man who stood alone, arms crossed, watching the party.

He was tall, with a long, taut body, and wore jeans and a short-sleeved shirt that snugged over muscled arms and chest. His hair was dark and short, his eyes sharply blue and topped by thick eyebrows, his nose a sharp, straight wedge. He blinked long, dark lashes that fell like crescents across his tan skin.

"Handsome" didn't seem nearly a good enough description. His attractiveness was nearly visceral, bladed and sharp, like a weapon he could draw. He probably had women at his beck and call, probably had every romantic skill a woman might imagine.

And because I lived in a war zone, I had a very active imagination.

A casual glance would have said he was bored by the shenanigans. But boredom hadn't tensed his body like a panther posed to attack, or put that intense gleam in his eyes. He was coiled energy, and his gaze was on the crowd, tense and watchful, as if he was waiting for something big to happen.

His gaze suddenly shifted, those sapphire eyes streaking toward mine and locking on.

Something settled low in my gut, like my soul had rearranged itself, changed and shifted to account for him. For this man I'd never seen before.

Each dull thud of my heart ticked off another second, and still he didn't move or look away. The intensity of his gaze didn't diminish, and that made cold sweat skitter down my spine. Why was he focused on me?

A group of men and women shaking tambourines and maracas

passed between us, breaking our eye contact. There were nearly twenty of them, dancers with plastic coins sewed to their bodysuits, feathers braided into their hair. And when they finally cleared the block, he was gone.

I turned in a circle, scanning the street and crowd for him, half annoyed to find him gone, half relieved. He apparently hadn't been watching me. But he had been . . . interesting. Hard edges, serious eyes, beautiful body. I wouldn't have minded if he'd ambled toward me, asked my name. And I didn't say that very often.

"Did you hear what I said?"

I blinked at the sound of Tadji's voice. "Sorry. What?"

"You were staring again."

It was a bad habit. Like the man with blue eyes, I was a watcher of the world.

"Guilty as charged," I said, putting a smile on my face, rolling the sudden tension from my shoulders. "What were you saying?"

"I was asking if you were ready to get back out there."

"Absolutely." I put an arm through hers. "Let's get back to the parade."

Three hours later, we stood in front of the Cabildo, where the parade had turned into a party.

The Cabildo had been a city council building, a court, a museum. After the storm, the Louisiana State Police set up there. Now it was the headquarters for the Devil's Isle Commandant—and Gunnar's tidy desk sat outside his office. Its former buildings-at-arms, St. Louis Cathedral and the Presbytère, had been destroyed in the war, leaving the Cabildo as the lone sentinel in front of Jackson Square.

Magic had mostly skipped over the Square itself. The plants had survived the war, providing a gorgeous spot of green among the gray of the Quarter. But the statue of Andrew Jackson, the hero of the first Battle of New Orleans in 1815, hadn't made it through the second one. Jackson could beat back the British. He wasn't as good with Paranormals.

Around the Square and inside its gates, War Nighters abandoned paper flowers and costumes in the heat, switched from booze to bottled water shipped in by a snack food company outside the Zone that had apparently been feeling charitable—or wanted to market its goods to the folks who came into the Zone for a good party.

We'd danced so long I was almost deliriously tired. But it was the right kind of tired—the kind of exhaustion that made troubles seem far away. War Night was about unity and debauchery, and we were taking full advantage, like hedonism on this one night could make up for a lot of want the rest of the year.

Tadji and I sat in front of the fence that surrounded the Square, our feet stretched in front of us.

"I am starving," Gunnar said, hand on his stomach as he leaned against the fence. Bodies and sweat had smeared the paint on his arms, blurring the figures and landscapes into hazy stripes.

He glanced speculatively at a pushcart on the corner selling unidentified meat chunks on skewers. The grill filled the air with the slightly gamey scent of swamp critters.

"No," I said.

"What if I dared you?" Gunnar asked, poking me with the toe of a boot.

"I've had my share of questionable meat," I said. "And I don't need to relive it." Times had been even leaner during the war, when even FEMA had trouble finding food in New Orleans. Dealing with wars on American soil was politically complicated, and it had taken nearly a week for the feds to mount a response to the invading Paranormals. In the interim, before FEMA brought in the trucks, we did what we had to survive. If that meant nutria for dinner, so be it.

"Our little scavenger," Tadji said, patting my arm. "You know what would do us all some good right now?"

"A bottle of very old Scotch?" Gunnar suggested.

"That, too," Tadji asserted. "But I was thinking good, old-fashioned yaka mein."

Yaka mein was another New Orleans specialty that took off during the war, but tasted a helluva lot better than gamey swamp critter. It was supposed to be hot broth over noodles with hard-boiled egg and green onions. Nowadays, it was bouillon cubes and dried, reconstituted eggs. Not exactly the same, but it still hit the spot, when you could find it.

We probably could have wandered into one of the more residential neighborhoods, found someone selling bowls from the back of a truck. But I was running out of energy to find anything.

I yawned hugely.

"Lightweight," Gunnar teased.

"Guilty as charged. I think it's time for me to head home. Who wants to carry me back to the store?"

"I've got a little party left in me yet," Tadji said. "But even if I didn't, I'm not carrying you anywhere."

I looked at Gunnar, who shook his head. "You're not a helpless damsel. Rescue your own damn self."

I couldn't really argue with that. "In that case, my friends, this is where I leave you. I'll drag my tired, old bones back to the store." I held out a hand to Gunnar. "If you'll at least help me up."

Tadji clucked her tongue. "She always gets so dramatic when she's tired."

"I know. She's twenty-four, acts like she's eighty-four."

"I have customers who are eighty-four," I pointed out, "and I'm sprightlier than at least some of them."

Gunnar offered both hands, helped pull me to my feet.

Tadji stood up, too. She looked a little guilty, and I half expected her to give in and walk back with me.

But before she could speak, a shadow fell over us. We looked up. The shadow belonged to a very well-built man. His skin was dark, and his eyes were brown and amused beneath slightly pointed eyebrows. His chest was bare, his abandoned T-shirt tucked into one of his back pockets. And across his gloriously broad chest was a black tattoo in a Gothic font: WORK HARD, PLAY HARD.

I could relate.

"Hey," he said with a smile.

"Hey," the three of us said simultaneously. We all held out hope.

The man grinned, a flash of white teeth, but it was all for Tadji. He put a hand on his chest. "I'm Will Burke," he said, then hooked a thumb toward the band, currently offering us a lively rendition of "Tipitina." "But everybody calls me 'Burke.' Would you like to dance?"

"Oh, well, I—" Tadji looked at me, eyebrows lifted in obvious hope.

"Don't mind me," I said with a smile. "I was just leaving. The store is calling my name."

Burke snapped his fingers, pointed at me. "I knew I'd seen you before. You run Royal Mercantile?"

"I do." The Marriott was only a few blocks away, and the soldiers who lived there bought sundries at the store, so I knew a lot of agents by sight. But Burke didn't look familiar. "Have you been in?"

"Only once. I haven't been in the city very long. I'm with PCC Materiel. Just transferred." He grinned. "I hear you've got the best store in the Quarter."

PCC was the Paranormal Combatant Command, the Defense

agency that managed the entire war effort. Containment was one of its units, as was Materiel.

"It's easy to be one of the best when you're one of the few," I said, returning the smile, and deciding I liked him. And not just because he'd complimented my store. "But don't let us interrupt you. You were going to dance?"

"Thank you," Tadji mouthed, and took Burke's extended hand. They walked toward the crowd, began to move and sway to the music.

"I like him," Gunnar said.

I snorted. "That's because he's your type: gorgeous and well connected."

"And apparently skilled at the art of materiel."

"And in civilian terms that means what, exactly?"

"That means he has access to the good stuff. Food. Furniture. Uniforms."

I knew an opportunity when I heard one. I turned to him, linked my hands together pleadingly. "See if he can get me some cheese. The real stuff, not cheese-flavored product, not 'cheeselike' spread. Actual, real cheddar."

"You know refrigerated trucks don't do well in the Zone."

I knew—it was another electricity problem—but I didn't care. "I'll give you a million dollars if you can get me some real cheese."

"You don't have a million dollars."

"I have a million walking sticks."

Gunnar grinned. "I don't want your walking sticks." He pursed his lips, considering. "But I do need to make sure he's on the Commandant's visitor list." He pulled out a small notebook and pencil to scribble a note. Gunnar took his job seriously, and wasn't going to miss an opportunity to tell the Commandant about a material (or materiel) advantage.

That's precisely what made my friendship with Gunnar tricky. But he was too much my family to give up on him now.

"Come on," he said, shoving the notebook away again. "I'll walk you back to the store."

I didn't mind the offer, but I knew the Quarter better than I knew the guy who'd just asked Tadji to dance. I didn't get any bad vibes from Burke the materiel guy, but better safe than sorry. And besides: cheese.

I shook my head. "Don't worry about me. You stay with Tadji. Keep an eye on her. And when they're done dancing, find out which materiel he's responsible for. Use your copious charm." I spread my hands in a dramatic rainbow. "Think dairy."

"That's my hilarious girl," he said, but concern flashed on his face. "There were three wraith attacks last week. Are you sure you'll be okay walking back alone?"

He'd told me about each attack to warn me, to keep me on my guard. He hadn't realized the irony.

"It's only four blocks," I said, "and there are Containment agents everywhere." That was a blessing and a curse. "I'll probably have to push them out of the way just to get inside the store."

Gunnar didn't look thrilled, but his pressed his lips to my temple. "Be good, Claire. And be safe."

I told him I would.

And I really had meant it.

CHAPTER THREE

Instead of heading down Royal Street, I walked around the Square to Decatur. It was only a block out of the way, and I liked the route better—I liked seeing the river and imagining the world hadn't really changed, that life as we'd known it hadn't really ended. That my father and I still lived in a house in Central City, and I was worrying about dating and getting a good job. That a giant prison wasn't lurking behind me.

When I was younger, I'd roam through the store's antiques, making up adventures. I'd always thought it was cool that so many people who lived or worked in the Quarter knew my dad, considered him a friend. It was like being part of a secret club—the secret guild of folks who weren't just tourists but who *knew* New Orleans. I guess I had a little of that now—Burke seemed to know who I was, for example. But it wasn't the kind of familiarity I'd expected. And now it was dangerous.

I turned up Conti, reached the building that held the Louisiana Supreme Court, an enormous marble structure that took up an entire block between Royal and Chartres. It was square on the Royal side, and rectangular on the Chartres side with rounded towers on each end.

I'd heard the city had spent tons of money restoring it in the late nineties, only to have most of the back half destroyed in the war. Now the building was abandoned, and the few surviving palms and magnolias around it overgrown. The windows were supposed to be boarded over, but plywood was a valuable commodity, so it disappeared more often than not. This time, someone had gotten creative, removing the plywood from enough windows in one curved flank that the dark holes looked like a grinning skull.

You could take the people out of New Orleans, but you'd never get all the crazy.

I rounded the corner, saw movement near one of the magnolias. From the very unfortunate groans, War Night or Drink or both had gotten the best of someone.

I nearly smiled in sympathy before she burst out of the foliage. She couldn't have been more than eighteen or nineteen, and she was screaming like a maniac.

She didn't see me in front of her and hit me full on, so we struck the sidewalk together like felled trees. Pain sang through the elbow I'd inadvertently used to break my fall, and the skin scraped against still-hot asphalt. She tried to get to her feet, kneed me in the stomach.

I grunted, tried to help her up, but she wore only shorts and a tank top in the heat, and her skin was slicked with sweat. "What the hell?" I asked.

She didn't respond, and she was panting when she finally crawled off me, climbed to her feet, and loped into the street. She was limping.

I sat up to watch her, confused. Did she need help, or was she just walking off the effects of a long and boozy night?

But when her gaze met mine, her eyes were wide and terrified. She hadn't been drunk, I realized; she'd been afraid.

She knew had been my first paranoid and totally irrational thought. She'd somehow realized I had magic, thought of war and terror and death.

But it wasn't me she was afraid of.

He emerged through the darkness like a horrible ghost, whipping past me like a raptor and leaving behind the scent of something sour and spoiled. The magic had left him desiccated and skeletal. He looked brittle, with pale, nearly translucent skin and hair that had gone white.

He was a wraith. And he wasn't alone.

A second monster, another male, streaked after him, joined the first one as they followed the woman into the street.

Their withered and angular bodies were partially covered by dirty scraps of cotton and denim, probably the remnants of the clothes they'd been wearing when they finally crossed the line between Sensitive and wraith.

Fear flooded me, and with it, memories of war. Of the blood-hungry Valkyrie I'd killed with my own two hands. Of the angel I'd seen standing atop the Superdome, calling out to his troops with a golden horn, his ivory wings streaked with blood.

I glanced up at the building on the corner. The light on the magic monitor that hung ten feet above the street blinked green, activated by the wraiths' abundant magic, the energy they'd absorbed from the Veil. Containment had been notified. Agents would be on their way, so I shouldn't get involved. That was always my father's advice.

One night, a few weeks before the Battle of New Orleans, he'd stood beside me while we watched a Containment vehicle rumble down Royal. In the back, clutching each other with obvious fear, were male and female Paras whose naked skin glowed pale green in the twilight.

"Will-o'-the-wisps," he'd said. "Or what we'd call will-o'-the-wisps, at any rate." That had been before the gaslights were turned on again, and it didn't take the truck long to disappear from sight.

"They look scared," I'd said. They hadn't looked like the enemies we'd faced, the Paras who'd threatened us with weapons and death.

"It's better not to get involved. What's our motto?"

He'd said the words a thousand times. "Stay quiet. Work hard."

"Good. You worry about the store, about the citizens of the Quarter, and let Containment take care of the rest." He'd looked up at the stars that dotted the sky over New Orleans, visible when the power was out, and put a hand on my shoulder. "Someday, things will be back to the way they were before. Only hard work will get us there."

He told me that six weeks after he'd helped the army personnel who were left in New Orleans fight a battle it didn't look like we could win. But he'd jumped into it anyway, because, his warnings to me notwithstanding, that was the kind of guy he was.

He'd died two weeks later.

The woman screamed, pulling me from the memory and back to the present. She'd moved into the empty street, shrieking wildly as she tried to scurry away from the wraiths. Her ankle crumpled, and she hit the ground again.

All the while, the wraiths were getting closer, their eyes focused on her. And they weren't going to wait. The surplus of magic short-circuited their brains' impulse-control centers, made them extra aggressive. They'd kill her without hesitation, without remorse, because they existed to feed their hunger for magic. And damn anything that stood in their way.

I knew my father had wanted me safe, that he'd told me not to get involved because life in New Orleans was too precarious now. But the woman was in danger, and Containment wasn't here. This was my street, my Quarter, my city. That made it my responsibility.

I had to keep her safe—or at least keep the wraiths away from her—until help arrived.

I couldn't use magic—not with Containment cameras all around. I looked around, found a fallen limb beneath one of the gigantic magnolias. Hands shaking with adrenaline, I grabbed it up and ran back toward them, holding the branch like a baseball bat.

"Hey! Get away from her!" I hoped yelling would scare them away and bring out people with actual weapons—assuming anyone was sober enough to hear us, or that the sound could carry over the horns and drums that still echoed from Jackson Square.

One of the wraiths turned back to me, a man with arms painfully pulled toward his body, skinny fingers tipped with long nails. He seemed to sniff the air—recognizing the magic I absorbed like him—then opened his mouth, screamed with a sound that was somewhere between fingernails on a chalkboard and the scrape of rough metal against metal. It was a horrible noise, pitiable and terrifying at the same time, and it made my stomach tighten with nerves.

Head bobbing, he began to lope toward me.

I pushed down fear. If he was moving toward me, he was moving away from her.

"Yeah, that's right!" I yelled. "Over here!" I waved the stick in the air, ran back and forth across the street, trying to get the other wraith's attention, too. Not that I knew what I'd do if I got it—but I was at least mobile, stick in hand, with solid lungs.

But it didn't work. The second wraith grabbed the woman's ankle, lunged at her.

This time, I didn't think, I didn't remember, I didn't debate. I ran forward, wound up, and slammed the branch across the wraith's spine. He screamed and reared back, looked at me with furious, watery eyes that were equally pitiful and terrifying.

I wasn't thrilled about hurting something that I could so easily become. But he didn't seem to care about my struggle. He shrieked, took a step forward. I moved backward and swung the limb in front of me to make sure he was giving me space.

I caught movement from the corner of my eye, realized the other wraith was also moving toward me. I'd managed to get their attention off the girl, but that might not serve me well in the long term.

I realized I could have used one of those walking sticks about now. Maybe one with a pop-up bayonet.

I looked back at the girl. She still looked wan, but she'd survive, if she could get up and run.

"Go!" I told her, and she climbed to her feet, limped down the street.

I looked back at the wraiths, trying to keep them both in front of me so I wouldn't be surrounded, so they couldn't trip me up.

One of them reached out to grab, skinny fingers like painted bones, tipped in thick, pointed nails. I swung the limb to bat the hand away, but he was faster than I'd anticipated. He snatched it, wrenched it from my hands, and tossed it down the street.

He swung out with his free hand. He might have been skinny, but he was strong, like his strength had been honed and concentrated into what was left of him. His arm hit me like an iron bar, and I flew backward through the air, a doll thrown by a spoiled child.

I hit the asphalt on my back. Pain burst through my body as the air seemed to fly out of my lungs. I tried to breathe, wheezed roughly.

They were both moving toward me. I sat in the middle of Royal, with not a soul in sight. Drums echoed down the street, the rhythm growing faster as the song rose to its crescendo.

Just like Gunnar had said, I had to be my own hero.

I climbed to my feet, still woozy, and paused to let my brain catch up with my body. But that only gave time for the fear to settle into my bones.

The wraiths opened their mouths, their high-pitched wails shuddering through my body. One of them darted forward and scraped claws along my arm, the scratches burning like he'd poured salt into them. Instinct had me slapping back, pushing him away.

The other one stepped in, ready to take over. I ran down the street to the other corner, putting space between us, but they followed quickly, eyes darting back and forth as they closed the distance.

I moved to the right, and they dodged.

They might have moved like animals, but there was something very human in the way they looked at each other, in the way their eyes met, as if silent communication passed between them. Silent agreement.

They made a deep and guttural sound. The one who'd first followed the woman into the street stayed where he was. The other moved to cut off my exit, as though they were executing a careful plan.

Were they working together? *No.* That was impossible, just fear and panic making me paranoid.

Either way, they were getting closer. I looked for escape. I glanced around, remembered the alley that ran between two buildings to my left. The fire escapes for both ended there, and a gate halfway down the alley kept people from playing around on them. Well, prewar, anyway. Now the gate was always unlocked; folks who lived in the Quarter used the alley as a shortcut.

I didn't think wraiths could climb. So if I could get into the alley, I could get behind the gate and close it, putting iron bars between me and them.

I ran for it.

I could hear them lumbering behind me; they sounded more excited. I turned sharply into the alley and barreled toward the gate. I hit the wrought-iron fence, pushed . . . and nearly ran into it when it didn't budge.

"No, no, no," I murmured, pushing the gate to force it open, before realizing a shiny new lock had been installed, the gate solidly locked. Of all the damn days for someone to be careful about the damn lock.

I looked up, around. The fire escape was on the other side of the fence, and there was no way to scale it. It was at least seven feet tall, with vertical balusters and nothing to climb.

Like they'd realized victory was near, the wraiths lurched forward.

I was trapped.

I glanced up at the brick walls. There was a monitor at the edge of the alley, the light green like the one down the block. Containment was on its way, but that wasn't all. The monitors had cameras that would begin filming when the sensors were activated. If I did magic here and now, they'd have me on tape.

"Damn," I murmured. Talk about a rock and a hard place—or two wraiths and two brick walls and an iron fence. We were down to magic or die.

I decided I'd rather be alive and running from Containment than dead on the street.

"To everything there is a season," I murmured. I had to hope this wouldn't be the reason for my incarceration in Devil's Isle.

Through the alley, behind the wraiths, was an empty building that had once held an art gallery. The gallery was gone, but its sign still hung from hooks in front. NOLA ARTWERKS was painted across the square of wood in curved purple script around a fleur-de-lis.

A sign could be a weapon, as I'd learned.

Moving something wasn't difficult in itself—I'd proven that enough in the shop today. But there was a big difference between moving something accidentally and consciously getting it to go where you wanted. There was a gap between those things I hadn't learned how to bridge—mainly because I wasn't allowed to practice.

I blew out a breath. I was going to have to be very careful, and since Containment was supposed to be on the way, I was going to have to be fast.

I focused on the sign, its warped and beaten edge, and thought of the magic that hovered in the air. I tried to clear my mind, to imagine gathering up all that power, using it to force the sign off its hooks and pull it toward me. Frankly, I had no idea what I was doing; this was a best guess.

The wraiths crept forward, drawn by the buzz of energy in the air. But I made myself ignore them, concentrate, set my gaze on the sign, apologize to the person who'd crafted it. Using all that magic in the air, sweat sheening across my skin with the effort, I pulled.

The sign popped off its hooks and hurtled through the air toward us. But that's where the easy part ended.

The sign was only a couple of feet across. But moving it was like guiding an elephant across a piece of dental floss a thousand feet in the air. I drew it toward me, but the sign barely wanted to obey. It barreled across the street, bumping into the brick at the edge of the alley and ricocheting backward.

I didn't have time to be excited I'd gotten it this far, because I was going to have to thread the elephant-laden dental floss through a needle.

I narrowed my eyes with purpose, imagined the alley growing bigger, the sign shrinking until it was the side of a postcard. And when I had them lined up, I tugged the sign toward me.

One of the wraiths reached out, and I dodged to the side to avoid him. The thread between me and the sign jerked, too. It barreled down the alley, cracked against the wall like thunder, splintering in half. I spun, standing straight again, clasped my hands in front of me, and then wrenched them apart so each hand pointed at the wraiths.

With that motion, I hurled the two pieces of the broken sign toward the wraiths, nailed them both on the back. They screamed, arching and rolling in pain.

But they weren't deterred. If anything, I'd made them angrier, more intent on getting to me and punishing the hurt I'd caused. I wouldn't be able to use the power much longer, and could already feel exhaustion settling into my bones. I had to make this count.

I sucked in air, still hot and humid, and jerked the signs forward with the leash of magic I'd created. They moved toward me, and I hit the wraiths again—one across the back, the other on the shoulder.

They were still furious. But they were in pain, and their hearts weren't in the fight any longer. Howling in frustration, they loped back down the alley and into darkness again.

I held my breath, counting to five just in case they changed their mind. But the street was quiet and still. I let the rest of the power go, felt it flow through the alley like a brutal wind. The remains of the sign hit the ground with a clatter, and silence fell again.

I didn't have much time to savor my victory. I had been on camera, filmed working magic in violation of the Magic Act. I'd be locked into Devil's Isle, where I'd sit behind bars and wait to become a wraith. There was no way in hell I was going to let that happen.

Unfortunately, I didn't have any magical endurance, so using it left me starving and dizzy. I took a breath, made myself concentrate, remember what I'd told myself to do, the list I'd made myself memorize just in case worse came to worst. That's how I dealt with the real possibility I'd be found out: I had an escape plan. A bag and a goal. I'd head west into the country, across southern Louisiana toward Texas. That was the closest Zone border, and if I could get out of the Zone, I'd have a chance.

Follow the steps, I reminded myself. "Step one," I quietly said, then repeated it again until the words made sense. "Step One: Go home."

Easier said than done. I crept to the end of the alley, saw two flashlights bouncing up from the river end of Conti. I dodged down the street into the next doorway, pausing while the agents looked into the alley, and then hustled around the corner to Royal.

I hauled ass back to the store, nearly tripping over the uneven sidewalk as I reached the door. I pulled the keys from the dress's pocket, but my hands were shaky, and it took three tries to get the right key and shift the tumblers home. When the lock snapped, I shoved the door open, slammed it shut behind me again, and ran to the narrow staircase that led to the building's second and third floors.

Step Two: Get the go bag.

I climbed the stairs to the second floor, opened the antique armoire near the door, grabbed the change of clothes waiting for me. I yanked the dress over my head, wincing as the fabric touched the scrapes on my arm, kicked off my shoes, pulled on the jeans and black T-shirt I'd set aside, and stuffed my feet into low boots. I shoved the discarded clothes into the back of the armoire. Containment might find it, might wonder. But it wouldn't matter, because I'd be gone.

Next to the waiting pile of clothes was the black leather valise I'd cleaned and outfitted with a cross-body strap. It was packed with necessities: a perfect copy of my identification papers, a few changes of clothes, money. My hands shaking with need, I pulled it out, unfastened it.

Step Three: Fuel.

I grabbed one of the energy bars I'd packed inside, tore at the wrapper like a fiend. I wouldn't be able to think or run if I was still dizzy from post-magic hunger. I ate the entire thing in two bites, mouth full and chewing as I fought to ease the screaming need in my belly. I swallowed, paused to breathe and suck in air. And when my vision wasn't shaky, I closed the bag again, rose, and pulled the strap over my body.

I'd gotten to my stash, gotten nutrition. There was only one step left.

Step Four: Say good-bye.

I looked around the room, blinking back tears. Hatboxes, tins, suitcases, books piled in columns around the room that stretched to the rafters. Vintage clothing hung from racks, vintage oil and gas signs—including that damn star—leaned against a brick wall. There was a labyrinth of French secretaries, chests, and armoires brought to New Orleans once upon a very different time to outfit majestic homes.

My chest ached with the heavy sense of failure. I hadn't managed to hold on to the stuff, to the store—to my family—for nearly long enough. Not enough to keep my family's memories alive, to safeguard the treasures they'd found. Maybe someday, when Containment wasn't looking for me, I could return. Maybe—if they didn't take the shop.

I shook my head, fighting back tears. It couldn't be helped now. It couldn't be changed. War had taught me enough about that.

"I'm sorry," I whispered to the ghost of my father, and walked out of the room. It was time for Step Five.

Run.

CHAPTER FOUR

I crept down the stairs, ears straining for the sound of sirens that would signal Containment's arrival, and the official end of the life I'd known. But the world was quiet, the only sound from the first floor the steady tick of antique clocks. War Night must have kept them busy tonight.

I rounded the stairwell, stepped into the store's first floor, decided the back door and alley were a better bet than the front. I stopped short when I realized a large body filled the doorway.

My heart hammered against my chest like a frightened bird, which wasn't much different from my own emotional state.

"Going somewhere?" he asked.

Damn.

The man was backlit by the bright shard of moon, so I couldn't see his face. But he was a big one. Broad-shouldered, easily six foot two or three. Larger and probably stronger than I was. I wouldn't be able to best him physically, and I'd have to wait to recharge before I could move something again. That meant I'd have to talk my way out of this. Fortunately, I had eight months of fibbing under my belt.

I schooled my expression into nonchalance and walked toward the counter. My gaze was on him, but I was thinking about escape, about making it to the back door, then the alley, then Royal, where I'd run until my legs couldn't carry me anymore.

"The store's closed."

"Be that as it may, the door wasn't locked." His voice was deep, strong, and just a little accented. Cajun, I guessed.

I cursed myself silently for failing to lock the door. "My mistake. But we're closed for War Night. Open again tomorrow."

He took a step forward, slipping into the spear of light, and I stared at him. He was the man from Bourbon Street, the blue-eyed guy who'd looked at me before disappearing into the crowd.

The impact of that dark hair, those vivid eyes, was even stronger up close. Not just because he was handsome, but because he now seemed to be a threat. I pushed down the warring attraction and fear. Neither would help me.

His gaze dipped to the valise. "You taking a trip?"

Concentrate, I demanded, my brain beginning to unknot as nutrition moved through my body. As casually as I could manage, I pulled off my bag, put it on the counter.

"Just moving some things around." I crossed my arms, gave him the rudest look I could manage. "But since that's none of your business, and we're closed, why don't you get the hell out of my store before I have to call Containment?"

"Since you're a Sensitive, I seriously doubt you'll do that."

I froze, hoped he hadn't seen my body jerk. "I don't know what you're talking about."

I didn't think he was Containment. Anyone here to arrest me wouldn't have bothered with coy questions.

He could be a bounty hunter, a freelancer who hunted down fugitive Sensitives, wraiths, and Paras, who had decided I was his next bounty. There were plenty of bounty hunters in the Zone—folks who'd stayed behind because they wanted to live in a new version of the Wild West.

Or he could be a run-of-the-mill crazy asshole.

I wasn't sure any one of those options was better than the others.

"I saw you disappear into that alley, and then I saw the sign." He glanced at the bag. "I suppose your plan was to run away."

No point in lying about it now. He'd clearly seen something. "That's what I was trying to do. Until someone got in my way."

"You better be glad of that. You can't run from Containment."

"You're one of them?"

"Containment?" He said the word with enough derision that I felt a little better. "No."

My anger flashed. "Then I'm none of your business. You want to report me, report me. Otherwise, get out of my store and out of my way."

His mouth twitched. I wasn't sure if it was anger, frustration, or amusement. It wouldn't be the first time I'd given someone one or more of those feelings.

"You've got a smart mouth, *cher*."

Definitely Cajun. "That's what I hear."

Cold sweat began to slide down my back as my gaze snapped between the front door—the figures moving outside—and the back. He was bigger than I was, but I had magic, and enough time might have passed that I could use it again without hurting myself.

He must have guessed my plan. "Don't even think about it," he said, lifting his shirt enough to show muscled abs and the gun belted at his waist. It was the same model carried by Containment agents, and I hoped I hadn't made a huge mistake.

"I don't want to use this," he said, "but I will if you try to use magic against me."

He cast a glance behind me at the store windows, at the bobbing flashlights that signaled Containment's arrival.

"Damn it," I said, panic rising, but I pushed it down. I'd been in trickier situations before, and probably would be again. As much as I hated to admit that my father had been right, that it was better not to get involved, the evidence was piling up. "This is your fault. I'm going."

The man stepped in front of me, his big body completely blocking mine. "It's too late. They're outside, and they'll have seen us in here. This is the only store in this part of the Quarter, and we're probably the only sober people in a three-block radius. They'll want to talk to you, see if you saw anything."

"They got me on camera," I said, pleading with him to understand. "If I don't leave, I'm screwed."

I'm Isle-bound/and there I'll stay/wear the devil's crown/till the end of days. That was how the song went. And if I wasn't careful, it would become autobiographical.

His eyebrows lifted, concern obvious on his face. Even he knew how bad the situation was. "You're sure?"

"I know how to recognize an activated Containment camera."

He considered for a moment, shook his head. "Containment agents are dispatched based on the detection of magic—the triggering of the sensor. These agents will probably have been rerouted from the party, so they won't have reviewed the tape yet. If you run now, they'll think you're guilty of something, and they'll stop you. And if they stop you, they'll check the film."

Hope shone like a distant star, then faded. "Then I have to get to the video."

And how was I going to do that? Gunnar, I thought queasily. I'd have to ask Gunnar to do it, to get into Containment's video system and delete the evidence.

"We'll deal with the video. But right now you need to calm down and do what I say."

I lifted my eyebrows. "Do what you say? I don't even know you."

"And you don't have a reason to trust me," he admitted. "But the other choice is worse. PCC doesn't like Sensitives. They don't fit into its tidy little worldview. They'll put you in Devil's Isle, and as you probably know, Sensitives don't have much to hope for in Devil's Isle. They'll wait for the magic to destroy you."

He didn't look any happier about that than I felt. But that still didn't give me much comfort.

"Maybe they won't catch me."

"You'll still become a wraith, and you'll hurt people."

I opened my mouth to object, but he shook his head. "You won't have a choice, not when your body begins to break down, when your mind begins to go. You'll kill, and that's a fact." His voice grew rougher. "And it would be my job to hunt you down. It would have to be my job to hunt you down. I don't want to have to do that."

So he was a bounty hunter. He'd probably delivered plenty of wraiths and Sensitives to Devil's Isle. And that explained how he knew the worst of what could happen to me.

"I'm a Sensitive," I reminded him. "You could just take me in now."

"I don't trade in Sensitives," he said. "You aren't a threat to anyone, at least not yet. And that's the point. If you want a chance to keep from becoming a wraith, to live outside the Marigny, to keep your store, you'll follow my lead."

I didn't have to trust him. I could still try to grab my bag, slip out the back door. But there were a lot of flashlights outside, and a lot of moving bodies. I'd never make it. And he was right—running would make it look like I'd done something wrong, and they'd take me in. If they saw the video? Same result.

I swallowed hard, looked around the store like it could offer guidance, like my father might emerge from the shadows to give me advice that, this time, I wouldn't ignore.

"I'm sorry," he said.

I nodded, gathered up all the bravery I could manage, because I was putting all my trust in a man I'd seen exactly twice in my life. "Okay," I finally said, looking back at him, hoping I was doing the right thing. "We'll try it your way. At least tell me your name?"

His expression softened. "I'm Liam Quinn."

I swallowed, nodded, waited to be sure my voice wouldn't shake. "I'm Claire Connolly. This is my place."

Liam nodded. "Then turn on the lights, Claire Connolly, and let's get this over with."

I'd been sweaty at the party, but that was nothing compared to the cold sweat that slicked down my back when two Containment agents walked into my shop in gray fatigues and boots, guns and batons strapped to their belts.

I'd turned down the lights and moved behind the counter. Liam leaned casually against it, flipping through the day's *Times-Picayune*. There wasn't much to it these days—more a community bulletin than newspaper, a few sheets of thin, handmade paper run on a hand-cranked letterpress. They were delivered to the store every week or so, less often if the printer ran out of ink.

"Gentlemen," Liam said, folding the paper and standing straight when they walked in. The simple act of repositioning his body showed off his physical power. It would be an advantage against wraiths, probably a necessity, given his job. "Took you long enough."

One of the agents, broad-shouldered, with dark skin and eyes and a gleaming bald head, moved in front of the others. I'd seen him in the shop before. Phelps was his name.

Phelps glanced at me, then Liam. "Quinn. What are you doing here?"

"Same thing as you, I imagine. Chasing monsters."

The second agent nodded. "You saw them?"

"We both did," Liam said.

Phelps looked at me. "You're Claire Connolly, right?"

My heart thudded in my chest and ears so loudly it seemed impossible they didn't hear it. I wanted to answer the question, but was afraid to open my mouth, afraid of what I might accidentally say, or what they'd be able to glean from anything I did say.

Liam glanced back at me. "Wake up, Claire," he said, then looked apologetically at Containment. "Sorry. The wraiths freaked her out."

Phelps looked instantly sympathetic. "First time seeing one?"

"Second time, actually." A few months ago, I'd seen Containment agents capturing a wraith outside the door, binding it in what had looked like an old-fashioned straitjacket.

My voice sounded rough, so I cleared it, made myself fake nonchalance. "But it's still freaky. And yeah, I'm Claire. I've seen you in here before."

He nodded. "You get that pasta MRE I like."

I grimaced, knowing which one he meant. "Ugh. That so-called pasta is not good."

"It's not great, but it's better than the blue cheese meat loaf. Why would they put blue cheese in meat loaf? Sorry. I'm getting off track." He pulled a small black disc from his pocket, put it on the counter. "I'll need to get your statements about what happened. Do you mind if I record them?"

Stay calm, I demanded, and shrugged. "No. Although I don't know how helpful I can be."

"We just need to hear what you saw. It's procedure." He touched the glossy surface, which flashed green.

"Agent Phelps, investigating Sector Twenty-seven combatant attack."

It hadn't occurred to me that they thought of wraiths—humans who'd succumbed to the magical infection—as just another type of combatant, just another evil Paranormal. That wasn't the whole story, but it backed up what Quinn had said about PCC.

"Interview with Connolly, Claire," Phelps continued. "And Quinn, Liam. Now, you said wraiths, plural. There was more than one?"

Relief rushed through me. If Containment didn't know how many wraiths had been there, Liam had been right—they hadn't watched the video. Yet.

"Two," Liam confirmed.

"Where'd they come from?"

Liam gestured toward me, the move utterly casual and mildly bored. "She saw them first. I was behind them."

"Near the Supreme Court," I said. "They were in the foliage on the south side. They were attacking a woman. She got away, ran me over, and then moved into the street. The wraiths followed her there."

"Wraiths don't hunt together." The second agent had stepped forward. He was older, with pale skin, shorn silvering hair, and a dark mustache over a wide mouth. His eyes were deep-set and brimming with suspicion. "Thomas" was the name on his uniform tag.

I shrugged. "I don't know about that. Just telling you what I saw."

"And then what happened?" asked Phelps, sounding irritated by his partner's interruption.

It would have been too easy to get lost in lies, so I decided on the truth, or at least as much of it as I could tell.

"They started to attack her. I yelled to scare them off, but it didn't work. So I grabbed a tree limb and tried to scare them away. When *that* didn't work, I hit them with it."

Phelps's eyebrows lifted. "You beat two wraiths with a tree limb?"

"I didn't *beat* them. I hit them. And they ran away." And a few things in between about magic that I didn't really want to mention.

Phelps gestured at my arm. "They gave you those scratches?"

I looked down. Fear of Devil's Isle had numbed the pain, and I'd forgotten about the scratches. "Yeah. One of them had pretty long nails."

"What about the sign on the ground?" Thomas asked.

The back of my neck went hot. "The sign? What sign?"

"There was a store sign on the ground, pretty well cracked."

"Oh, I don't know. Maybe one of the wraiths knocked it down? They were moving all over the place. They kind of"—I hunched my shoulders over—"lurched around when they moved?"

"And where did they go?" Phelps asked.

"Uptown, toward the CBD." We let the Central Business District keep the acronym, even though there wasn't much business there these days.

"And the girl?"

I shook my head. "I don't know about her, either. I told her to get up and run, and she did. I didn't see the direction. I was watching the wraiths."

Phelps nodded, glanced at Liam. "And when did you pop into this fight?"

"After it was over."

"You looking for a bounty?"

"Always," Liam said coolly. "But it wasn't to be this time."

"You could have chased them," Thomas said. "Why are you still here?"

"Because right now I want information more than I want bounties."

"Information about?"

"Why two wraiths attacked a human together."

"They didn't." Thomas's tone was flat. "That's not something that happens."

Liam lifted his hands. "Like Claire said, I'm just telling you what I saw. You can watch the tape yourself. Matter of fact, I'd appreciate a copy of it when you're done."

Just the mention of the tape made my stomach twist with anticipation. I thought I knew what Liam was doing—acting just the way a bounty hunter might act in this scenario—but the request still rankled.

Phelps nodded. "You know there's a procedure for that. Put in the request with the Commandant."

"Sure," Liam said. "In triplicate, undoubtedly."

Phelps made a vague sound of agreement. "Bureaucracy."

"Bureaucracy," Liam agreed.

Apparently satisfied with the information he'd gotten, Phelps touched the recorder, which turned red as it disengaged; then he pocketed it. "That should be all for now, but stay around in case we have more questions."

I nodded. "Sure."

He looked at Liam. "You'll be around, too?"

"Here and there. I can be found."

Phelps nodded. "Then we'll finish up outside so we can get our report in. Y'all have a safe night." He paused at the door, glanced back. "Oh, and happy War Night."

"Nous vivons," Liam and I said together.

It wasn't until the bell signaled the door's closure that I took a full breath. I put my elbows on the counter, put my head in my hands, cursed. This wasn't exactly how I'd thought War Night would go. I hadn't had nearly enough Drink.

"You're a pretty good liar."

I slid my gaze to Liam, didn't especially enjoy the smirk on his face. "I've had practice."

"So I see."

I stood up straight again, tried to compose myself. "God, what a mess."

"It is," he agreed. "And right now we need to move so you get to those tapes before Containment does. Our window to minimize the damage is closing."

I nodded. "Okay. Where do we do that?"

"Devil's Isle."

I stared at him. Sensitives didn't go into Devil's Isle if they ever wanted to come out again. "What do you mean, 'Devil's Isle'?"

"That's where my mechanic lives. He's the only man I know who can do it."

"My life's goal is to stay out of Devil's Isle. I'm not going to just walk in there under my own volition."

"If you want to take care of the video, you do it in Devil's Isle."

"You can't do it on your own?"

"No, because the mechanic is only our first stop." He moved a step closer so that I had to look up at him.

"I promise you, Claire—tonight, you'll enter Devil's Isle of your own free will, and you'll walk right back out again. But if you want to keep it that way, if you want to keep your free will intact, then you need to learn to regulate your magic."

"That's not possible."

"Becoming a wraith isn't inevitable, Claire. You aren't the only Sensitive in New Orleans. Hell, you probably aren't the only Sensitive in the Quarter."

I stared at him. "There are more of us? Sensitives who aren't in Devil's Isle? How many?"

"Enough. And, like them, you've got to learn to normalize your magic, to keep the infection at bay. That can be done, with diligence."

"How do you know that?" I asked.

"Friends and experience." His eyes darkened. "If you don't learn soon, there'll be no turning back. Once you become a wraith, there's no reversal. There's no pill, no cure, that can fix that damage. If you don't learn, I'll have to drag you to Devil's Isle."

Liam Quinn had a crappy bedside manner, and he clearly wasn't one to pull a punch. On the other hand, I wasn't sure anything else would have been so effective. No, I didn't want to walk into Devil's Isle as a Sensitive . . . but I certainly didn't want to go in as a wraith. I hadn't known there were more of us—Sensitives who'd learned to deal with their magic, who'd kept from becoming wraiths. If there was a possibility I could have a life—a real life—then I'd have to take a chance on Liam Quinn.

For the first time in a while, I felt a little bit of hope. But that didn't make me reckless.

"Even if I agreed to go, I couldn't get in without a transit visa. And I don't have one."

"You don't need one. You're going with me."

"You said you weren't Containment."

"I'm not. I'm a bounty hunter. Containment pays the bounties."

I mean, it wasn't the same as actually being a Containment agent, but it still seemed like a pretty thin line.

"Do you kill the wraiths you capture?" The question wasn't very diplomatic, but then again, I was potentially one of his bounties.

"My job is to capture, not to kill. I promise you that we can discuss the details of my career later. Look," he said, "I get that you're still processing what's happened, but if you want to deal with the video *before* they watch it, we have to go—now. We're already cutting it close."

Final question, just for posterity's sake. I narrowed my gaze at him. "This isn't a trick to get me into Devil's Isle without a fight?"

He snorted. "If I'd wanted to take you in, I'd have taken you in." There was no doubt in his voice, or in the steadiness of his gaze. And, in fairness, he'd already lied to Containment about my being a Sensitive, when he could have just turned me in for the money.

"Taking you in like this doesn't do me or you any good. I promise, Claire, you'll be back in your bed before the night's over."

I strapped that courage on a little tighter. "Okay," I said, and looked up at him. "Let's go to Devil's Isle."

CHAPTER FIVE

Seventeen minutes later, I was staring up at the concrete panels that rose high into the sky around the Marigny to the steel grid that curved above it like the Superdome's roof.

I'd never been this close to the wall, to the prison. The store was nearly a mile from the gate, and it wasn't something most of those who'd stayed in the Zone wanted to focus on. Tourists occasionally would trek through the Zone to look at the walls, at the gates. They hadn't seen the war, and they were curious about it, grim as that was. But we'd seen more than enough.

The Marigny was shaped like a triangle, if someone had sheared off the bottom point. It was a wedge of a neighborhood. Peters Street, which was riverside, made up the short side of the wedge. A wall had once separated the neighborhood from the New Orleans Public Belt Railroad tracks that ran along the river, but most of it had been trashed during the war.

Lakeside, Devil's Isle stretched up to St. Claude Avenue. The Quarter bordered it on the west, Bywater on the east. And the Containment wall surrounded the entire neighborhood, made of what looked like a Hoover Dam's worth of concrete.

The wall panels must have been poured into wooden molds, because they'd kept the whirls of the wood's grain. I reached out, touched one, expecting to feel the rough grit of concrete. But it was smooth to the touch, even where it looked like the wood grain had changed the texture. And it was warm enough that I yanked my lingering fingers back after a few seconds.

The gate was in the middle of Peters Street. It was the only part of the Devil's Isle that wasn't surrounded by concrete, or at least not completely. A tall black fence had been mounted into a couple of feet of concrete barrier. The fence had been "requisitioned" by Containment when the wall was being built, from an architectural salvage place in Bywater. It had come from a plantation on River Road, and was incredibly ornate, with ROSEVILLE in gold capitals across the front.

Only in New Orleans would a prison get a Gothic revival.

The gate was closed, a sleek guardhouse sitting outside it, guards standing at attention around it.

I blew out a breath, clenched and unclenched my fingers against very sweaty palms. My body felt suddenly heavy, like it was rooting in place to stay outside those walls. My escape plan hadn't had a sixth step. And if it had, it wouldn't have been "walk into Devil's Isle of own accord."

But the fear wasn't all about me. Part of it was about *them*. About the images that lived in my mind about the war, about the beings who'd fought it, and the prison I'd imagined. I thought of military barracks, utilitarian buildings, sad faces. Beyond that, I had no idea what to expect, and that was as scary as anything else.

"You do what I tell you, and nothing more, and you'll be fine."

It was the tone of Liam's voice that had me looking up, hoping it had been a good idea to follow a man I'd only just met into a supernatural prison that wanted to add me to its rolls.

I nodded. "I'm not afraid of many things, but this place is one of them." The intimacy of the admission had me looking back at the concrete, at all the things it kept in, and the things it kept out. "Of being locked away because of something I didn't choose," I said. "Something that came to me, and not the other way around. I tried to help someone tonight, and that's threatening to tear my world apart."

I swallowed, looked into his shockingly blue eyes. "I didn't run—because you asked me not to. You were straight with me about the Containment agents. I'm going to trust that you're being straight with me now."

"And if I'm not?"

"I'll tell Containment you lied to them about a Sensitive and let them sort it out."

His eyebrows lifted in appreciation. "That's a pretty good threat. I consider myself duly warned."

"Okay," I said, and fell into step beside him. Because sometimes a girl had to take fate into her own hands.

A Containment agent stood inside the guardhouse, his gun strapped to one side of his belt, a stick on the other. He looked at us mildly.

Liam seemed utterly cool and composed.

"Hawkins," Liam said.

"Quinn," Hawkins responded. He was medium height with brown hair and blue eyes. Every bit of him seemed precise: bluntly square jaw, perfectly shorn hair, an immaculately pressed uniform that he filled out with heavy muscle.

Liam pulled a leather wallet from his back pocket. Hawkins scanned his ID with a small wand, and the comp inside his station beeped with approval.

"Who's she?" he asked.

"Trainee."

Hawkins looked me over. "She doesn't look like much of a trainee."

"You tryin' to insult me, or her?"

"If the shoe fits," Hawkins said. "You hear about the wraith attack tonight? Some girl in the Quarter fought them off with a stick."

I decided it wasn't a good idea to take credit for that. But Liam didn't have any qualms.

"She's the girl," he said, and tucked the wallet away again.

Hawkins's eyebrows lifted. "You don't say."

"It was me," I said. "But it was a tree limb. Not a stick."

Liam looked at me with amusement. It was the first time I'd seen him put on anything close to a smile, and it highlighted dimples in each cheek. They transformed his face, made him seem a lot less disquieting.

"Making sure you get full credit?" he asked.

"I earned it."

"T'as raison," Liam murmured.

"He says you're right," Hawkins translated with a smile. "I'm thinking you've got a handful with this one."

"Which one of us are you talking to, Hawkins?" Liam asked.

He smiled at Liam. "Weapons?"

Liam pulled up his shirt, showing the gun belted at his lean hip. He removed it, handed it over.

Hawkins nodded, scanned it, placed it in a locked box beneath his console. "You know the drill. You can retrieve it on the way out."

When Liam nodded, Hawkins brushed fingertips across his control panel, and the security grid disappeared.

"You're about to leave the city of New Orleans and enter a territory of the United States government," Hawkins recited. "The U.S. government makes no guarantees regarding your health, welfare, or safety while you are inside Devil's Isle. Magic is prohibited inside the walls. If you observe magic, report it immediately to the nearest Containment agent. Other than that, have a good night, and be careful in there." Hawkins leaned back into the gatehouse and pressed a button, and the gate began to slide open.

I followed Liam through the gate, into the area that had once been the Marigny. And just like that, I was inside Devil's Isle.

I tried to calm my ragged nerves. "Anything you want to prepare me for?"

"You haven't been in the Marigny since the war?"

I shook my head.

"It looks a lot different now. That can be hard for people who lived here, or have memories of here, so just plan on being surprised. As for Paras, keep your eyes ahead of you. Don't stare at anyone, don't talk to anyone. Stay beside me. If someone approaches us, let me handle it."

The sun had long since set. "It's late. You think we'll have issues?"

"Some Paras are nocturnal, and most aren't too fond of humans. Guards will be posted everywhere, and you don't want to stare at them, either. And don't do magic. Like Hawkins said, it's banned, and there are monitors everywhere."

"We're already in Devil's Isle," I murmured. "What else could happen?"

He didn't seem to appreciate my sarcasm. "Gunshot wounds from a guard's service weapon, or solitary confinement in a jacket." He glanced down at me. "You've seen those before? The ones they capture wraiths in?"

"Yeah." I nodded. "I have."

"Basically, you don't want to draw any undue attention to yourself. You want to blend."

The warnings aside, that actually calmed me. "Blending I can do," I assured him, and blew out a nervous breath. "Where are the wraiths and Sensitives kept?"

"There's a clinic. It's on the other side of the neighborhood. We won't be going near there tonight."

That made me feel a little better.

"You do what I say, and get this done, and you'll be fine. I promise. And try to keep an open mind."

I glanced at him. "About what?"

Hands on his hips, he settled his gaze on the streets and buildings in front of us. "About everything."

The Marigny had been a mostly residential neighborhood with blocks of Creole cottages and shotgun houses. The streets were in pretty much the same place as they'd been before, but half of those buildings were gone.

War had knocked some of them down. Containment had left some of the lots empty, probably to improve their lines of sight from the tall guard towers in the middle of each wall and on each corner. Other lots had been refilled with long metal temporary buildings.

There were uniformed guards every few hundred feet in familiar gray fatigues, guns belted at their waists. And above them, mounted on the buildings, were the magic monitors.

Liam let me look around for a moment, get my bearings, before gesturing me toward a sidewalk that led deeper into the neighborhood. "This way."

It might have been late, but it was also hot, and it looked like Containment wasn't spending money on air-conditioning. Paras stood outside, in small groups in the empty street, in doorways of the Containment buildings, or on the porches of the occasional cottages. Short and tall, horns and wings, feathers and fangs. The street was a catalogue of Paranormals, of the diversity created by magic and biology.

Their expressions were just as diverse, but equally grim. Some looked sad, others numb, and some stared at me with obvious loathing, as if I were the personification of their oppression.

We passed a woman who stood in a doorway, one hand on the frame, her lithe body silhouetted by candlelight. She was pale, with a long neck atop a slender body. Her hair was platinum blond and pulled into a knot, pale tendrils dusting high, round cheekbones. Her long, slender fingers were red, as was the line of deep crimson that ran down the bridge of her nose, then across her lips to her chin. She wore a simple dress of white cotton that fell from a straight neck to the ground below, the hem stained with dirt. She watched us as we walked, her body perfectly still, her face expressionless, but her wide almond eyes flicking to follow us.

"Seelie," Liam whispered, his gaze on the street.

I nodded. That's what we'd once believed was a "good" fairy. A Seelie was one of the many supernatural creatures humans had imagined, just as we had imagined angels and fae, demons and nymphs. We still called them the names we'd given them, because that was how we'd understood them *before*. But we'd gotten the names and the stories very, very wrong. Paras didn't care about us. They didn't grant wishes, or make us immortal, howl at the moon, or watch over us like benevolent guardians. They were invaders, plain and simple.

Or maybe not so simple, I thought, as we passed the doorway. Ahead of us, a little girl with vibrantly green skin and lavender eyes hummed to herself while she played with a set of old-fashioned jacks—except that the jacks floated in the air like oversized molecules.

"I thought they weren't allowed to use magic," I whispered.

"They aren't." Liam's eyes narrowed with concern. "And the penalties are stiff."

The closest magic monitor was across the street. It hadn't signaled yet; maybe the girl's magic wasn't strong enough. Clearly, the technology wasn't as consistent as Containment liked to think.

A human guard was closer, a woman with a long face, hair slicked back into a low bun. She slanted her gaze toward the girl, the spinning jacks, and started toward us.

"Damn," Liam muttered, and walked toward the child, putting his body between her and the Containment agent.

The little girl's eyes grew enormous as she looked up at him. The jacks fell back to the ground like Newton's proverbial apple.

He winked at her. "Yeah, I've always been interested in history," he called back to me, obviously playing off what he was doing—protecting the little girl.

A door opened in the ratty shotgun house behind him, and a woman in a long dress darted outside, grabbed the girl's arm with her own green hand.

The woman looked up at Liam with round lavender eyes. She nodded at him, then pulled the girl inside, and closed the door with a resounding thud.

Liam scooped up the jacks and the little red rubber ball, placed them in a pile near the door through which the woman and child had disappeared.

The Containment agent reached the sidewalk. I hadn't done anything (other than exist), but the determined look in her eyes still gave me cold sweats.

"There a problem here?"

Liam looked back at her, smiled. "Not at all. But I think we scared the kid. I was showing my friend here the plaque," he said, pointing to a metal square bolted to the building. It explained the history of Fabourg Marigny—and showed Liam was a very quick thinker.

But Containment agent's gaze shifted back to the closed door. "She was using?"

Liam frowned. "Using?"

"Magic?"

"Oh. No." He put his hands on his hips, looked back at the door. "I mean, she's a little kid. But I did notice you've got a monitor out." He pointed to the box across the street. He was right—the light hadn't turned green, but it also wasn't in its "Ready Red" state, as Containment liked to call it.

The Containment agent nodded, pulled out her walkie-talkie. "Appreciate the heads-up," she said, and walked back across the street to the monitor.

"Let's go," Liam whispered, putting a hand at my back. He had big hands. Warm hands.

"That was a nice thing you did," I said when we'd put half a block of distance between us and the agent.

"Like I said, she's just a kid," Liam said. "Sins of the father aren't the sins of the child. And things are always more complicated than they seem."

"She probably didn't even know she was doing it. It happens."

He looked surprised. "To you?"

I nodded. "First time was how I found out I had magic. I got lucky—the monitor wasn't signaled. But it was still terrifying—to become an enemy of the state in a snap of the fingers, and not because you did anything at all wrong."

"Yeah," Liam said. "I get that."

We kept walking. I'd seen photographs of neighborhood's in New York and Chicago during the Industrial Revolution, when everything seemed dark and gritty and horribly depressing. This was pretty much the same, right down to the color scheme.

Those old photographs had been black-and-white, and everything was gray, covered with what looked like a fine covering of dirt. I reached out, swiped a finger across a street sign, rubbed my fingertips together. The residue was dark and gritty, and left a sooty stain on my fingertips.

"Ash from the security grid," Liam said as I wiped my fingers on my pants and glanced up at the metal web that covered the Marigny.

"It's electrified, except when it's not. Motes, dust get singed, fall down again as ash. Containment didn't think about the ash when they developed it. It was freakishly expensive, as you'd imagine when you put a lid on an entire neighborhood. There wasn't money to fix it."

"Why bother prettying up a prison for enemy combatants?"

"That's the theory."

I wasn't sure what I'd expected to feel. Probably to be scared, intimidated. To remember violence and war. Maybe even to feel hatred. To see in the things that lived here as the reason my family was gone. As the source of some of my pain. All of those complicated feelings would have been normal. They would have been expected.

And they were there, in part. So was fear, since I could feel angry and suspicious eyes on us as we walked down the street.

But so was pity. And I hadn't expected that. Not when we'd spent so much time hating them, fighting against them, being absolutely sure they were our mortal enemies. Because they had been.

We reached another shotgun house still surrounded by a low fence. There were remnants of bright paint on the clapboards. It was "haint" blue, once one of the city's favorite colors, a pale, chalky blue used to scare away "haints"—restless, wandering ghosts. Now the house was mostly a dingy gray.

MOSES MECH was scrawled on a piece of torn ruled paper taped inside the front window. Liam walked up the steps to the small concrete porch, knocked on the door. I followed him, waited.

There was a buzz, then a click, and the door unlocked, opened. We stepped inside.

In shotgun houses, the front door directly faced the back door, and each room daisy-chained the next along the way. This front room wasn't big—maybe ten feet square. But every single inch was filled with shelves, and every inch of shelves was filled with electronics. Old, bulky television sets. Radios. Toasters. Lamps. Electronic toys. Receivers. Clocks. Every row was stacked at least three deep, and the shelves extended all the way to the room's ten-foot ceilings. Video players were crammed up to the acoustic ceiling tiles, pushing some of them off-kilter.

For all the stuff, there wasn't a speck of dust or ash in the place. It was clean as a whistle.

A counter had been built at the opposite end of the room, making a barrier between the front room and the door that led to the rest of the house.

A man sat behind the counter. He was small and pale, with green eyes, and a receding line of dark hair. Two glossy black horns popped from each temple. They gleamed like lacquer, and it took several seconds to realize I'd been staring.

It hadn't occurred to me that Liam would be bringing me to a Paranormal. He hadn't said one way or the other, but I'd figured he had a friend in some Containment office. I guess I'd been wrong.

"I need you, Mos."

This must have been Moses, from the sign in the window. Which meant this was his shop.

"And what brings you to Devil's Isle today?" He looked up, nearly smiled at Liam before sliding that glance to me. His expression became very unfriendly very fast. "You brought someone in here?" His voice was low, gravelly, and utterly pissed.

"She's with me," Liam said. "And I need a favor."

The man snorted, tossed his head, light catching the horns like they were made of glass. "I don't help clueless humans."

"You'd be helping me. And she's not a clueless human. She's Sensitive."

Moses looked at me again, head tilted with interest. "I'm listening."

"She took down a couple of wraiths in the Quarter using magic."

"She got firepower?"

"Telekinesis," Liam said, then glanced at me with a smile. "Not that she knows how to use it."

"She regulating?"

"She is not. She's pretty much ignorant of everything magic. Containment got her on video," Liam added. "We need that video cleaned up."

Moses snorted. "She's too skinny to take down wraiths."

"I most certainly am not."

Both of them ignored me. "She took them out," Liam said. "My word on it."

Moses looked at Liam. "You trust her?"

Liam's blue-eyed gaze was cool and appraising. "I'm not sure yet. But I know Containment's gonna make trouble if we don't take care of her *Candid Camera* problem." He reached into his jeans pocket, pulled out four shining silver discs about the size of a quarter, laid them on the counter, where an image of St. Louis Cathedral, destroyed in the war, gleamed.

They were Devil's Isle tokens, created to allow Paras to buy supplies and food from the commissary. I had a dozen in the store's lockbox, most given to me as souvenirs by agents and officers. Too bad I hadn't thought to bring them.

"You got cash, you're the boss," Moses said, then spun around on his stool. He pulled a keyboard from beneath the counter behind him, rapped his palm hard against one of the monitors.

It whirred to life, a blue screen flickering with white symbols that looked like text. Moses raced his fingers, each tipped by a long, triangular nail, over the keys with audible *clicks*, and the images on the screen blurred by.

CONTAINMENT-NET scrolled across the top in block letters.

I took the opportunity to be amazed that someone from a world I assumed was completely different from our own had become so skilled that he could hack into a Containment database.

And then I thought about what he was doing.

"You can't break into a government computer," I said. Gunnar, at least, wouldn't have been breaking in. He'd have been using his access improperly, yeah, but that at least seemed like a *slightly* grayer area.

"How else did you think we were going to alter the videos?" Liam asked.

"I don't know. But that's not exactly legal. They find out I was involved in altering it, it's only going to make the whole thing worse."

Liam gestured toward Moses, stepped back. "Let her have it, Mos."

Moses grinned, cracked the knuckles on his small fingers like a boxer preparing for a brawl. "Happy to." He put his hands over the counter, leaned over it, glared at me. "You wanna talk about legal, honey? I been sitting in this goddamn neighborhood for six and a half years. Can't go anywhere else. Can't see anything else. Can't get home again. And why? Because your government is too stupid to tell the good guys from the bad guys. And you want to whine about what's *legal*? You think *this* is legal? Interning people for nearly a decade? You think this is due process?"

I wasn't sure what to say to that, so I just stayed quiet.

"Well," Mos said after a few seconds, "at least she's smart enough to keep her trap shut."

He turned back to the keyboard and screen, began typing. A moment later, a list of files began scrolling across the screen.

"Is their security that bad, or is he that good?" I whispered.

"He's that good," Mos said, whapping the monitor again when it dimmed, waiting while it flickered to life again and the file list appeared on the screen.

"Where did it happen?" he asked.

"Royal and Conti," Liam said. "Near the Supreme Court."

"Containment says that's Sector Twenty-seven. When?"

"About an hour ago."

Mos whistled. "Cutting it close, Quinn. Cutting it close. They could have accessed it by now." He kept clicking.

"But you're in luck," he said. "They haven't." And when the wraith's image filled the screen, activated by his emergence, he shifted to the side so we could all watch the video.

The wraith dodged out from the trees around the Supreme Court building, followed seconds later by the second one.

"There aren't cameras around the building," Liam said. "It's too dark, and there's too much greenery. So the camera would have been triggered when they emerged into the street."

"Why not just clear out the brush?" I wondered.

Liam crossed his arms, eyes narrowed on the screen as the camera jerked and followed the wraiths' movements toward the girl. "The state owns the building and the land. They don't have the money. Containment didn't want to get into a big federalism argument, so they left it alone."

The camera panned out, caught me at the edge of the frame hitting the wraith with the limb, then getting flattened by his backhand. A little interim fighting, and then I disappeared into the alley.

"Hold on," Mos said. "There are two other cameras that track that sector." He flipped through files until he found the right one, then loaded the video. The camera was across the street. It wasn't close enough or high-quality enough for a lot of detail, but the wraiths moving toward me were plenty visible.

I watched carefully, wondering whether I'd imagined that moment of communication I thought the wraiths had shared. But if it was there, I didn't see it on the tape.

Liam hadn't spoken, and I glanced at him, found his gaze intent on the screen as I pulled the sign toward the alley. Not just watching, I thought, but measuring. My abilities, my performance, my style.

It was an odd feeling to be judged for something I'd been hiding for so long.

When the wraiths ran off, the video stopped. Mos tapped a few more keys, looked back at us. "So here's the deal: I could borrow clips from earlier that don't show wraiths—just the empty street. I can splice 'em in. But Containment'll be expecting to see the fight, and when they don't see one, they're going to ask questions about the tapes being altered."

Liam frowned. "So what do you suggest?"

"Better to introduce some noise, make it look like an electrical failure. Cameras are on the regular grid, not the gennies. Both fail, but the grid fails more often. So it's a possible scenario."

"Do it," Liam said. "Probably better get the sign, too, if you can."

"If I can," Mos muttered.

It took him less than a minute. He pulled up all three videos, found the fight, tweaked a small panel of dials and knobs until the images waved and fuzzed on screen. He replaced the files, got an answering beep.

And just like that, my criminal past was erased, the evidence I'd used magic, that I was anything other than a normal human.

I closed my eyes, felt some of the tension finally sliding from my shoulders. Now I could get back to the store and back to work. Life would go back to normal again. That was a definite mood lifter. "Thank you, Mos."

"Sure. That was entertaining. Feel free to call me again for your future hacking needs."

"Let's hope there won't be any. Come on, Claire."

Liam headed for the door, but I stopped, smiled back at Moses. "Can I tell you something?"

Moses's eyes narrowed, and I could feel Liam's concern at my back. His fear that I'd do something completely asinine to insult the man who'd just helped me.

"Okay," Mos said carefully.

"You've got a really great shop. Thanks for letting me see it."

His face blossomed with pleasure, which was as disorienting as his horns. I guessed he hadn't had much practice at it, because it looked really awkward. The smile was lopsided, his eyes slightly bulging, too much tooth on display. But that he'd tried so hard to do something that hadn't come naturally made me like him even more.

"You take care out there, Red."

I nodded, and we left Mos to his electronics.

CHAPTER SIX

"You handled that well," Liam said when we were on the sidewalk again. "About the store, I mean."

"It was the truth. He's got a lot of cool stuff in there. Scavenged from the houses around here?"

"Some scavenged, some traded. There's a pretty extensive bartering system."

I stopped, looked at him. "It doesn't bother you that he's fighting against Containment? I mean, by doing what he does? By breaking into their computers, or whatever else he can do in there."

"You wouldn't be safe if he hadn't done it."

"I know. And that's what's bothering me. It's just—I've been told for seven years that Paras—all of them—are the enemy. There weren't shades of Paranormals. There weren't good and bad. They were just the enemy. And I certainly didn't meet any Paras who laid down their weapons, who tried to help us. I lost friends, most of my city, my family. They tried to annihilate us."

"The enemy who just helped you."

"Exactly. And I don't know what to do with that. Moses said we were too stupid to tell good guys from bad. What did he mean by that?"

"That it's easier to pretend humans are good and Paras are bad.

That makes dealing with threats easier. It makes housing them easier. And it makes killing them easier."

That explained part of why he'd made me come into Devil's Isle. He didn't really need me to fix the video, but he'd wanted me to meet Moses. To see the neighborhood. To get a sense of it, and the people who lived there. Had he showed me some exceptions? Sure. On the other hand . . . "They did attack us."

"As you've seen tonight, there's more to it than that. Humans aren't good because they're human. And Paras aren't bad because they're Paras."

"And Sensitives?" I asked, looking up at him. "What are they?"

He looked at me steadily. "That depends on the Sensitive. The point is, there are options."

When he didn't say anything else, I figured he was done playing Devil's Isle tour guide and it was my cue to say good night.

"Thank you for helping me with the videos. If you'll point me back toward the gate, I'll get out of your way."

"You're not leaving. Not until we find someone who has time to deal with you. To teach you."

I nearly stumbled. "Wait, you mean tonight?"

"This is serious magic, Claire. Serious and potentially deadly, to you and others."

I managed to control my temper, but only just. "I know how serious it is. I live and work in the French Quarter, surrounded by monitors that make sure I don't accidentally use magic I didn't even know I had. That I shouldn't have in the first place." *That I'm my own enemy for having.*

"And how did it feel tonight after you dealt with the wraiths?"

The question, and the intensity in his eyes, made me shift uncomfortably. But I kept my gaze on him. I wasn't about to look away. "I refueled."

"A snack isn't going to fix the problem. Long term, you'll keep absorbing magic until it destroys you. Until it is a cancer that knows only how to grow and destroys you from the inside out. Being in denial isn't going to help you."

"I'm not in denial. I'm—I just need a minute." I shook my head, trying to clear it. I was feeling overwhelmed, trying to reorient myself in a world that had just completely flipped on its head. "This is just happening really fast."

Liam paused. "Why did you help the girl, when you could have been spotted?"

"I didn't have a choice. She knocked me over."

Liam just kept looking at me, his silence saying he wasn't buying my answer.

I sighed. "Because she needed help."

"So she did, and you helped her. You made a choice. Now you face the consequences." His voice softened. "Do you really think you can go back to living in denial after what you've seen tonight?"

I looked away from him, trying to get my bearings, trying to center myself again. I wasn't entirely sure what I had seen tonight. So yes, I did want to go back. I wanted to crawl into bed, sleep for ten or twelve hours, and wake up in the morning to a dull day with nothing but MRE shipments to worry about.

On the other hand, MRE shipments weren't interesting on their best day. In pretty important ways, life had all but stopped for me when my dad died. I'd kept the store running. That had been my focus, at least until I met Tadji and Gunnar. They'd brought me out of my shell, but there still wasn't much to life in the Zone. Except, at least right now, a lot of fear.

Hell. Maybe if I could learn how to deal with the magic, keep myself from becoming a wraith and being locked into Devil's Isle, I wouldn't have to worry about it anymore.

I looked back at Liam. "What, exactly, do you have in mind?"

"Come on," he said. "I want to show you something."

We walked deeper into the neighborhood in silence, down a narrow street of film-covered buildings, with residents huddled pitifully in doorways. There were more temporary shelters in this part of the Marigny, more Paras milling around with vacant expressions—or clear hatred in their eyes. A man with cragged gray skin leaned against a wall, small, dirty wings folded behind him, peeking through a dirty gray trench coat. His copper eyes, pupils slitted like a snake's, watched us warily as we moved.

This was a prison, and we were the captors, which made us the enemy.

Liam stopped at a town house surrounded by a chain-link fence. There was a long two-story building on one side with a balcony that wrapped around the second floor, and on the other side a pile of rubble that no one had bothered to clean up.

Liam unlocked the gate, pushed it open, gestured for me to go inside. He looked around warily before closing and locking it again. I followed him into the building, which smelled like cinnamon and smoke—and up a narrow staircase to the second floor. The stairs dead-ended in a door, which he unlocked with a series of keys.

The door opened into a long, narrow apartment. There was a living room with a couch and bar at one end, a kitchenette and small table and chairs at the other in front of a large bank of windows. A doorway in the exposed brick wall probably led to a bedroom or bathroom.

There wasn't much furniture, and it was an odd mix of styles. An old-fashioned cane-backed couch sat opposite the bar and brick wall, its cushion a deep emerald velvet. The wall behind it bore the remnants of a landscape mural, heavy on the greens and blues. The bar had a counter in front and cabinets behind of gleaming wood, topped by a wood-framed mirror. The bar and the bottles of rum and bourbon on the shelves had probably been salvaged from a watering hole that hadn't survived the war.

I glanced back at Liam, found his eyes on me. "This is your place," I realized.

"It is."

But he was human. "You live in Devil's Isle?"

"I lived in the Marigny before the war. Didn't see any reason to stop."

"And Containment didn't object?" I still felt I needed to understand his connection to them.

"They like keeping an eye on me."

I walked to the painted wall, crossed my arms as I looked over the scene someone had carefully painted onto plaster. It looked like an afternoon in Regency England. A dozen men and women in white lounged near a lake, baskets and blankets spread on the ground for a picnic, a large house in the background. The paint was faded, the house partially chipped away, some of the partygoers missing their painted limbs.

There was probably a metaphor for war in there somewhere.

"You live in the Quarter?" Liam asked.

"Above the store," I said, glancing back at him. "I was seventeen when the war started. I didn't know my mom. I lived with my dad, helped him run the store. Now he's gone, and it's mine."

"I'm sorry."

I nodded. "There are happier stories, sadder stories. War does that."

"Yeah, it does."

I turned around. "What about you? Your family? Are you close to them?"

"Some more than others," was all he said.

I nodded, and in the silence that followed, asked, "Why are we here?"

He looked at me for a long time, judging, evaluating, appraising. He did that a lot. "Come here. I want to show you something."

He walked to the other end of the apartment, disappeared through the doorway. He didn't wait to see if I'd follow, but I did. I was curious to see what kind of sanctuary a man like Liam Quinn needed.

And when I stepped through the threshold, I wasn't sure if it was a sanctuary so much as an ode to the biggest bed I'd ever seen.

This room ran nearly the entire length of the apartment. The bed faced another wall of windows, its carved headboard situated against a half wall that, I guessed, probably hid entrances to a bathroom and closet. The footboard was nearly as long and just as ornately carved, both of them curved around the edges of the thick mattress.

I walked toward it, ran fingertips across glossy wood.

I looked up, found him staring at me, felt warmth creep up my neck. It wasn't often I was caught staring at a man's gigantic bed.

"This is beautiful," I said, like a confident appraiser.

"Thanks. My paternal grandfather was a furniture maker. But that's not what I wanted to show you. Come here."

I nodded, followed obediently around the half wall. As I'd guessed, it hid doors to a bathroom and closet, and a small office area. And that was what he'd wanted me to see.

The office held a long desk with a pencil cup and a notebook. Above it, the wall was covered with dim photographs, news-sheet clippings, handwritten notes, all radiating from a map of the city stuck with pins of different colors. Colored twine connected them in a very grim art display.

The largest photographs were of a girl with long dark hair and shining brown eyes. In one, she was a toddler with dark pigtails and a dress that poofed with crinoline. In another, she was an adolescent wearing jeans and a vintage purple LSU shirt, her long hair in a ponytail.

"Her name was Gracie. My baby sister. She was sixteen."

I looked back at him. He ran a hand through his hair, and I realized as he stared at the pictures, the mementos, that he looked tired, like a man who'd been fighting for something, or someone, for a very long time.

Pity tightened my chest. "I'm so sorry. What happened?"

"She was killed by a wraith."

My mouth went dry, and my stomach went cold. A wraith—the thing I could become—had killed his family. No wonder he'd wanted me off the streets. And probably part of him hated me to the core.

I tried to stay cool, nodded. "When did she die?"

"Seven months ago." He moved forward, stood beside me as he looked over the board he'd created. "She was only ten when the war started. She survived that, only to be killed by a wraith." He pointed to a star near in the Garden District. "She was killed here. The rest of the black dots represent other wraith attacks. I've been tracking them."

They were scattered randomly across the city, with no pattern that I could see. "And what have you learned from that?"

"We're supposed to believe wraiths don't think. That they're violent, aggressive, and will attack whoever's closest. But attacks are increasing. There have been twenty-four attacks in New Orleans in the past four months alone. And they're becoming more complicated."

The hair on the back of my neck lifted, his words spurring a memory. "What do you mean 'more complicated?'"

"I think they're showing more independent thought. More planning. Scoping out prey. Attacking in pairs, like the wraiths tonight. Killing together."

I opened my mouth, nearly said what I'd seen, but couldn't get past the fact that it seemed insane.

But Liam didn't miss much. His gaze narrowed, evaluated. "Did you see something?"

"I don't know," I said. "I watched the tape, and I didn't see anything. So maybe I just imagined it."

"Just tell me."

I felt ridiculous saying it, but made myself put it out there. "Before I went into the alley, they looked like they were communicating—verbalizing, I mean—about strategy. Making a decision of some kind, and then acting on it. One going one way, one going the other."

Liam frowned, crossed his arms. "I didn't see that on the video, either."

I nodded. "Maybe I imagined it. I don't know. It happened really fast."

"Do you think you imagined it?"

I sighed. "No." I paused. "I think they were communicating. But doesn't that sound crazy?"

"Unfortunately, no. It doesn't. Something is changing. I just don't know what."

I nodded, feeling a little bit less ridiculous, and looked back at the board and the picture of the girl who'd lost her life before it really began.

"You were a bounty hunter before you started looking for her killer." I looked back at him. "But now you have a different reason to understand them."

His eyes were the color of a dark and deadly sea. "She shouldn't have died." His voice carried a hard edge of guilt. "I want it to matter that she did. That's what I can do for her. I can find out what's happening, and I can stop it."

And here he was, consorting with a Sensitive. The root of the evil that had taken his sister.

We'd both known love and loss, had fought through it. I worked in the store every day to remind me of what had been, to keep that reality alive. He worked every day to give some meaning to her loss.

"I really miss my dad, too."

I didn't mean to say the words. Certainly hadn't meant to say them to him, to this man I'd only known for a few hours, on a night that was meant for living, not grieving. But there they were.

I felt Liam's gaze on me, but I kept my eyes on the lines and squares that made up the French Quarter on the map in front of me.

"He died?"

"Right before the war ended. He was hurt the night of the Battle of Port Allen. There was a second, smaller attack in the Quarter."

"I remember. It was near the Old Mint."

I nodded. "He wasn't a fighter, but the troops were spread thin because of Port Allen, so he and some others went down to help. The battle was chaotic. He was shot."

"With an arrow?"

I looked up at him. "With a bullet."

Liam's eyebrows lifted. He understood quickly. Paras didn't use guns; why bother, when you had magic? Which meant he'd been shot by a human.

"Friendly fire," I said. "There'd been no power, no moon, no lights, and the troops were surrounded. Things got confused. Anyway, they treated him for the gunshot wound, and he seemed to be healing just fine."

"And then?" he asked when I paused.

"Blood clot, they thought from the shot. There weren't many doctors left in the clinic then."

"I'm sorry."

I nodded. "He's the reason why I stay in the store." I glanced back at the wall. "And she's the reason why you're making sure I get help."

"That's part of it." He reached out, adjusted a photograph so it hung levelly. "Sensitives, on their own, aren't inherently dangerous, any more than Paras are. They're only potentially dangerous. Containment doesn't care for that distinction." He glanced at me. "I do. That's why I don't take them in." He paused. "The first time I met a Sensitive, I was expecting a monster." There was amusement in his voice.

"And that's not what you found?"

He smiled now, turned to face me, leaning a hip on the desk. "No. Forty-two-year-old husband and father of six. Lived with the mom, the kids, in an abandoned house uptown. His crime? Green thumb."

"That was his power?"

Liam nodded, spread his hands. "Fourteen-foot-high corn. Watermelons big as a microwave."

I grinned, equally impressed and jealous. "Damn. I have a plot at the Florissant garden, but my thumb is barely green. So what happened?"

"Unfortunately, he'd attracted attention. Containment was aware of him, so he couldn't stay in New Orleans without being in Devil's Isle. I helped him pack up, drove him and the family into the bayous." Liam paused. "He wasn't the only one."

"That's technically treason."

"It was treason," he agreed, looking at me. "But sometimes it's worth it."

For a moment, we stood beside each other in silence, shoulder to shoulder, with death staring back at us. And for the second time that night, something shifted. Something between us—like we'd crossed that barrier from strangers to friends of some type. The link forged, and the moment passed, and the air seemed to clear again.

"Anyway, that was before I started hunting. Once I did that, I met other Paranormals, other Sensitives. They weren't wraiths—or anything close to it—so I figured there must have been a reason for that. They told me magic could be regulated, controlled."

It was information Containment could have gotten, had they bothered to try. That was the most frustrating part.

Liam sighed. "You ever wonder why we didn't leave? Start over outside the Zone?"

"Because memories are the most powerful chains," I said.

He looked surprised by my answer. "That's right on the mark."

"Between stocking batteries and dusting antiques, I have a lot of time to think." I nodded toward his display. "So you think something's up with the wraiths. If they're changing, why?"

It took him a moment, but he turned his attention back to the wall. "Well, maybe different people are becoming wraiths. Or they're becoming wraiths differently."

I frowned. "Is that possible? I mean—it's just a biological process, right? It's the effect of too much magic breaking down the mind, the body."

Liam shook his head, rolled his shoulders and neck to relieve tension. "I don't know. Every theory is really just a guess about what's happening. I just don't have enough information. It doesn't help that Containment won't pursue it—because that would require the feds to acknowledge it's possible to regulate magic."

He looked at the wall for another moment. "Well, standing around here isn't going to do anything. Let's get down to business."

"Which is what, exactly?"

"I've got someone else for you to meet. The first step on your road to successful magical maintenance."

Well, I did like steps, at least.

Liam grabbed a paper bag from his kitchen, then locked up the apartment and headed downstairs again. I followed him outside, and to the building next door—the one with the long balcony.

"The person we're going to see lives next door?"

"She does."

"It's late," I said, the sky still dark, although morning would be dawning soon enough.

"She doesn't sleep much."

I followed him up the sidewalk and to the black front door with a large brass knocker in the shape of a fox's head. He opened the door, held it open for me to follow him.

The first floor, several large rooms with oak floors and wallpapered walls, was empty of furniture. The walls were marked by dark shadows of smoke and ash, the floor smeared with it. Long streaks and smudges, as if battle had taken place there.

I left Liam in the foyer, walked into the front room. It was a large parlor, had probably once held fancy sofas for visitors, uncomfortable armchairs.

A whimper sounded somewhere deeper in the house.

My first instinct was to crouch. I had no idea why—what would crouching do if an unfriendly Para was pounding down the hallway?

I heard the click of nails on wood, and a big yellow dog—a Lab, probably—trotted onto the threshold, froze there, and stared at me.

It had been months since I'd seen a dog. There wasn't much food to go around in the Zone, so having a pet to feed wasn't easy. I liked dogs, but I was smart enough to be careful around them. Slowly, I crouched, offered a hand for sniffing, and waited for him to come to me.

He padded carefully forward, one step at a time, until he reached me. He sniffed my hand with a rough, wet nose, then nuzzled his head against my palm. And just like that, we were friends.

"Hey, boy. Are you an ear man or a neck man?" I scratched his neck beneath his faded collar, grinned when his rear foot began to slap rhythmically at the floor. "And we have a winner."

"Foster, you are a fickle friend."

Foster's head came up at the sound of Liam's voice. He saw him, galloped forward, and sat down, head on his paws. He whimpered.

"Don't let him fool you," Liam said, bending down to offer a scratch. "This is a ploy for attention."

Liam opted for Foster's ears, and the dog's tail thumped heavily on the worn oak floor.

Maybe there was more to Liam than the gruff exterior. After all, a dog this nice couldn't like a jerk, could he?

When Liam stood up again, Foster rolled onto his back, scratched it against the wooden floor with little piggy grunts of pleasure.

"He is a dog, right?"

"Forty percent Lab. Thirty percent cat. Thirty percent porcine something or other."

Foster rolled over again, stood, and shook from nose to tail with a delicious shiver. Then he sat down again and stared up at Liam, waiting for affection, instructions, or snacks. He caught sight of the paper bag, made a low whine.

"He's a clever one."

"He's a spoiled one," Liam said. "You have any pets?"

"No." I shrugged. "Although I do feed a stray cat in the Quarter now and again."

"'That hardly counts."

I couldn't argue with that.

"She's upstairs," Liam said. He pointed toward the front door. "Keep an eye on the door, Foster."

Foster made a sound that was a cross between a grunt and howl, but he rose and trotted to the door, nails clicking, and sat down in front of it.

"He's a good dog," I said.

"He is. And part of the family."

"Do you think there'll be trouble? I mean, do we really need a guard dog?"

His eyes darkened again. "There will always be trouble. The only issues are where, when, and how well you're prepared for it."

"You're such an optimist, Liam."

I looked up at the new voice, found a woman standing in the hallway with an empty plastic pitcher. She was trim and fit, with short, dark hair and brown eyes and high cheekbones. Her dark skin contrasted against bright blue scrubs.

"Victoria."

She smiled at him. "Good to see you today."

"This is Claire. Claire, Victoria. She's one of Eleanor's nurses."

Without hesitation, Victoria walked forward, offered a hand. "It's nice to meet you."

Her hand was cool, her handshake firm. "You, too," I said.

"How is she?" Liam asked.

"Today's been a good day. She's tired, but she ate some soup." She chuckled. "There weren't any good pears in the market today, so we didn't have any at the clinic, and she didn't get any for lunch. She was most displeased."

Liam chuckled. "Typical."

"Yep."

"She up for visitors?"

"As much as ever. You know she loves to chat."

Liam nodded. "You heading back to the clinic?"

"Yeah. Finishing up a double, then off tomorrow. I'm actually leaving a little early, but Maria will be here in half an hour or so."

Liam nodded. "You want an escort back?"

She lifted her shirt to reveal the gun clipped to the waistband of her pants. "Official issue. Drops a peskie at twenty paces."

"Then stay twenty-one paces ahead of them," he said. "Have a good night."

"You too, Liam. You, too."

Foster didn't move from his spot in front of the door, so Victoria stepped over him to get outside, and he sat down morosely when she closed the door again.

"The Devil's Isle clinic," Liam explained. "She's on staff."

That explained why another human seemed to have free rein in Devil's Isle. Maybe that was precisely the tone the Commandant was trying to set—humans will always be here, and will always be watching.

"What's a peskie?" I asked him as I followed him to the staircase, which was covered by a tired running carpet.

"Small, flying Paras. Irritating little assholes that like to bite."

The hallway at the landing led to several closed doors, I guessed bedrooms from the layout of the house. Liam walked to the last one, knocked on the door.

"Come in," said a soft and faded voice.

CHAPTER SEVEN

Compared to the rest of the house, which was empty and scarred, the room was a palace. It was a large bedroom with high ceilings and large windows. The floors were wood, and nearly every inch was covered in gorgeous woven rugs. The plaster walls had high crown moldings and were painted a warm, dusky green. Gilded frames held portraits of aristocratic men and women Dad would have wept over, and they were still outshone by gorgeous French empire antiques. There was a small bed, a high chest of drawers, and a round table with chairs. Although it was October, the house was still in summer dress, and gauzy white fabrics covered the furniture.

In a high-backed chair near the window sat a woman in a blue dress, a woven shawl in a rainbow of colors draped around her shoulders. Her skin was warmly colored and well wrinkled, her hair cropped and gray, her eyes hauntingly blue. She was a beautiful woman even now, and had probably been stunning in her youth. And I recognized her.

She was Eleanor Arsenault. The Arsenaults were old New Orleans from an even older Creole family. They'd had a mansion on Esplanade and threw big krewe parties every year. Or at least they had before the war ended those traditions.

She looked toward me, then Liam, and she smiled broadly. Her gaze fell near us, but not upon us, as if she couldn't see precisely where we were. If she could see, it didn't look like she could see very well.

"Hello, Eleanor," he said, walking toward her, and pressing his lips to her cheek.

"Hello, darling. How are you?"

"I'm good. I brought you some tea."

So that's what had been in the paper bag. I should have snooped. And I should certainly find Quinn's dealer.

"And how's your friend?" Eleanor asked. "Your Blythe?"

"She's . . . fine."

I guessed Blythe was his girlfriend.

"Mm-hmm," Eleanor said, and looked at me. "And who is this?"

"Claire Connolly. She works in the Quarter. She's Sensitive."

"Ah," she said, and looked toward me with those hauntingly blue eyes. Toward, but not quite at. Her eyes were focused on something, but I didn't think it was me.

"I'm Eleanor," she said with a smile, and patted the arm of her chair. Come sit by me, Claire Connolly."

I walked toward her, sat down on the small footstool in front of the chair. She held out a hand, and I offered mine. Her skin was cool and soft, and felt as fragile as a bird's.

"Tell me about yourself, Claire."

I looked hesitantly between her and Liam. "I'm not sure there's much to tell."

"There's always something to tell. You're from New Orleans. I can tell from your voice. It's a lovely voice."

"Thank you, ma'am. I'm from New Orleans. My father's family is from here. The Connollys."

She smiled softly. "No ma'ams are necessary here, dear. We're already friends if you've gotten past Liam, Victoria, and Foster."

"Liam barked the most."

Eleanor threw back her head and laughed with gorgeous melody. "So he does, dear. So he does. Now, you said you're a Connolly. That's not the Michael Connolly family, is it? The one who ran Royal Mercantile?"

"Michael was my great-grandfather." He'd emigrated from Ireland. "My father's name was Mark."

She nodded. "I believe my family knew both of them. Bought from the store frequently." Her voice softened. "And is your family still living?"

"No. I mean, not the Connolly side. My dad was the only one left. He's gone. I didn't know my mother."

She made a soft sound of acknowledgment or understanding. "I see. And that makes you the last of your line. Is the store still open?"

"It is. For as long as I can keep it."

And then it hit me. Because of Liam, I hoped I'd be able to continue running the store, to look forward to a "normal" life, something I thought was impossible only a little while ago.

I looked at him, found his eyes already on me. "Liam helped me tonight. The store will be open tomorrow because he helped me."

Liam nodded. "Least I could do."

"Well," Eleanor said. "Well. I'm glad to hear he's doing his part for this city. It's a good city, where we live." She patted my hand, still in hers, and looked just over my head. It occurred to me that perhaps she couldn't see at all.

"You can call things," she said. "Move them."

I blinked. I hadn't thought of it as "calling" things before, but yeah—that's pretty much exactly what I did. "Yes. You can tell that?"

"I'm only blind in this world, dear. Not the other one."

Startled, I looked at Liam.

"Eleanor was struck by a *sharur*, an enchanted mace, during the

Second Battle. She began to lose her vision—in our world—and she became able to see magic."

"You're Sensitive?" I asked.

"Not really," she said. "At least, not in any way that activates the magic monitors. We believe Sensitives are born, that their Sensitivity is part of their makeup. I wasn't born this way, but received my new sight—that's what I like to call it: my new sight—because I was hit by magic. And perhaps because of where I was hit by magic." She touched her forehead gingerly, where a pale scar crossed her forehead at an angle.

"Prefrontal cortex," Liam said.

"The impulse-control center," I said, and Liam nodded with approval.

"That's basically where she was hit," he said. "We think that might be the reason she's been affected this way."

"And not affected the other ways," Eleanor said. "But enough about me. What brings you by?"

"Claire needs a teacher."

I didn't like the implication—that I was doing it wrong currently—but I couldn't exactly disagree with him.

"We all need teachers in our lives," Eleanor said soothingly. "Different times, different lessons to learn." She smiled, and I could see a hint of wickedness that had probably gotten her into trouble as a teenager.

"My husband taught me how to tango," she said. "He was very handsome. Nearly as handsome as Liam here. And he was a wonderful dancer. He'd take me to dances on Friday nights—because Saturday night was for Mass, of course—and we danced up a storm."

She lost herself in the memory for a moment, her smile so happy. And then she seemed to shake herself out of it. "I do sometimes get lost in the past. It's the danger of growing old, I'm afraid."

"Better to grow old than not," Liam put in.

I couldn't argue with that.

"Every person we meet can teach us something. What's harder is to find the perfect teacher for the very thing you need to learn. All magic has a color," Eleanor continued. "The best person to train you isn't someone whose magic is precisely like yours, but one whose magic complements yours, not unlike colors on a color wheel. Yellow and purple are complementary, for example. Each brings out the best qualities of the other. Yellow and green are not. They clash, create tension. We do not need more tension here."

With her free hand, she gestured elegant fingers toward the rest of the room. "Bring me the quartz, please. It will be on the sideboard beside the alabaster."

Liam nodded, rose, walked to a dark wooden buffet with several drawers with silver knobs, the top cluttered with trinkets and memories. No—not cluttered, because Eleanor probably knew where everything was. But definitely full. He carried back a clear, angular rod of quartz about the size of a candle.

"Thank you, dear," she said, and placed the quartz on the table beside a taper candle stuck into a blue and white tea saucer. She slid a long match from a small box, and with an elegant flick of the wrist that sent the nose-ticking scent of sulfur into the air, she set fire to the wick.

The light bloomed through the quartz, sending a rainbow of color across the table in front of it. I'd always loved rainbows. There was something soothing about them—about the ordering of color, I guess. Every shade in its place.

"Now," Eleanor said. "Your hand, child."

I offered it to her again.

"First," she said, "we find your color." Her soft, cool hand guided mine in front of the quartz.

As soon as skin touched light, the rainbow of light shattered, and split, all colors fading except a line of faint orange.

Eleanor smiled. "Interesting. That's a lovely shade. I'd call it 'pumpkin.'"

"You can see the color?" I asked carefully, hoping not to offend.

"It's not just a color," Eleanor said with a smile. "It's a reflection of magic—the trail that's left behind in our world from the magic that comes from theirs. In their world, it's magic. In our world, it's electrons."

"Eleanor enjoys science," Liam said with a smile.

"All women of intellect must," she said, "or at least be conversant in it. That's how I've managed to learn of their world what I've learned so far. Reading, experimenting, vigorous note-keeping. Learning as much as I can from the Paras I've met here."

"Have you met many?"

"Quite a few. Most of them are lovely people; some of them are not. Not unlike humans, in my experience. Now, keep your hand there, if you would. Liam, will you please bring me my notebook?"

Liam walked back to the bureau, pulled open a door on the buffet, and slipped out a red leather book, its pages held together with brass posts. He extended it toward Eleanor, who felt the air for it with seeking fingertips before settling it into her lap.

She opened it, revealing what looked like a ledger of color. One half of the page held small painted squares of translucent color, each only slightly different from the last. It looked a little like one of the antique watercolor swatch books I'd seen in the store. The other half was a list in small and tidy handwriting too small for me to read.

Eleanor flipped through the pages quickly, the colors blurring into a rainbow from red to orange to something akin to the pumpkin I matched. She slowed, stopped on a square that looked remarkably like the light that still slitted through the prism, and lifted the small pencil attached to a chain around her neck.

She scribbled, paused. "What's your middle name, dear?"

"Bridget," I said. "It was my grandmother's name."

"And a lovely one. Claire Bridget Connolly." She wrote my name, then let the pencil fall again. "And I've marked you down. Not your actual name, of course. I use my own code for your protection."

"Sure. Are those all Sensitives? Each color?"

"Sensitives and Paras both. It's a collection of colors, and their magical echoes in the Beyond. I fill in the names when I find them. And over seven years, there've been a few."

Satisfied I'd been recorded in her journal, she moved through the pages until green turned to blue, which faded to deep indigo. Finally, she paused, touched her fingertips to the page as, brow furrowed, she seemed to gaze into middle distance. "This, I think. The names, Liam?"

She gestured to the scripts beside each square.

Liam leaned over, read the first name. "Michael Temperly."

"Dead, unfortunately, rest his soul," Eleanor said, and crossed herself.

"Elizabeth Conyers Proctor."

"Quite dead," Eleanor said. "But not unfortunately. She was a horrible person. Wife of Senator Ellis Proctor. We invited her to a party—this was before the war—and she had the gumption to decline because we were 'too Creole for her.'" Eleanor made a sound that hovered between disbelief and disgust, but managed to be lady-like. "As if that's possible. Well, too late for her at any rate. Who else?"

Eleanor frowned, ran her fingers over the book. She hovered over another square, brow furrowed again, before moving back a row. "I'm afraid this as close as we're going to get. Liam?"

As he read the words, Liam's smile faded quickly. "Nix."

Quiet descended over the room at the bombshell of the name, whatever it meant.

"Gavin is not going to like that," Liam said into the lingering quiet.

Eleanor made a sound of disapproval. "Whether he likes it is no matter. She's the right choice. It is what it is. There's no point arguing with complementary magic."

Liam grunted. "Like magic's ever stopped him. I don't disagree Nix's a good choice, but he's going to take some convincing." He scratched absently at the back of his neck. "I'd be happy to let you handle that, Eleanor."

I wasn't sure who Liam was talking about, but Eleanor seemed to get it. And this time, her response was closer to a snort. "Liam, dear, I'm sure you'll find a way."

Maria was another no-nonsense nurse, which I guess was probably a job requirement, considering where she worked. With dawn nearly breaking, we left Eleanor with Maria and promised to visit her again. That I was hoping to avoid returning to Devil's Isle made me feel a little guilty. But Liam could pass along a message to her.

Telling him I wanted to be done made me feel guilty, too.

When we'd said our good-byes to Foster, which took more scritches than it probably should have, we walked into the night again. The sky was still dark above the wall, but it wouldn't be dark for much longer. I'd have to open the store in a few hours. The length of the night, of everything that had happened, was beginning to weigh on me. I was tired.

"So, how did you meet Eleanor?" I asked Liam as we walked back toward the main gate and the freedom I was really looking forward to.

"She's my grandmother."

"Your . . . ," I began, but stopped, thought back about what he'd told me of his family. "Your grandmother is Eleanor Arsenault?"

"She is."

Since the last names didn't match, she must have been Liam's maternal grandmother. "And the man who taught her how to tango?" I asked with a grin.

"That would be my Arsenault grandfather. And a mildly uncomfortable conversation."

I smiled. "So where did the Cajun come from?"

"My father," Liam said, and there was much less enthusiasm in his answer.

I nodded, and we walked a few feet more. "Was Eleanor incarcerated here?" I asked the question softly, as if that would give me a secret defense against it happening to me.

Liam shook his head. "No. I brought her here after my parents died. It wasn't an easy decision, but sometimes it's better to be strange among strangers. In the outside, even if Containment didn't sense her magic, didn't find her, she'd be on her own. She'd be different from everyone else. She needs people who understand her."

"People—you mean Paras?"

He nodded. "Moses knows, and he visits her. They're actually pretty good friends. He's taught her a few games from the Beyond." Liam chuckled. Amusement looked good on him. "He told me she cheats when she thinks she can get away with it."

I couldn't help laughing, too. "I like that idea."

"So do I, especially since he was probably doing the same thing. 'It ain't cheating if you don't get caught,' " he said, in a pretty good imitation of Moses's thick drawl.

"Not a bad impersonation," I said. "You ever do that in front of Moses?"

Liam snorted. "Hell no. He'd blow a gasket."

Yeah, that seemed about right. "What about Containment? Don't they care that she's here?"

"Being an Arsenault has its advantages," he said. "I have a couple of allies in PCC, which helps. And she has allies, friends, across the country. Her money doesn't go far in the Zone, but it matters to the rest of the world. She has, let's say, protectors. Containment thinks she's here so I can keep an eye on her. That's right, in part. They know she's blind, and that she's getting older. They think that makes her harmless. They'd be very, very wrong about that."

I kicked a pebble down the sidewalk, then again, watching it skitter in front of us. I accidentally sent it too far to the left, but Liam caught it with a toe, sent it moving again. It was a little thing, but I put it in Liam's "win" column. Finding whimsy in a war zone wasn't any easy thing to do.

"I like her. She seems very formidable."

"She is. You remind me a little bit of her, actually. You're both recklessly brave."

I snorted. "Liam Quinn, I don't think you mean that as a compliment."

"Claire Connolly," he said, my name slipping softly from his lips. "I'm not sure I do, either."

I stopped to look at him, to check his expression against the sudden thoughtfulness in his voice. His eyes were stormy, his expression intense, considering.

"Come on," he said. "Let's get you home. Then I'll talk to Nix."

"She doesn't live in Devil's Isle?"

"She moves around," Liam said cryptically.

"And what, exactly, will she be doing?"

"Teaching you not to become a monster."

"That's a good goal. Also, could you be a little more specific?"

"It involves regulating the magic," he said. "I'm not sure about the details. That's pretty far outside my wheelhouse."

"And what's in your wheelhouse, exactly?"

"Being a warrior and general badass."

"And humble soul, barely aware of his own strength?"

"Well, obviously that, too."

I had a thrill of surprise when Liam bent his mouth to my ear. But his interest wasn't romantic.

"I'm going to tell you something, and I want you to keep your eyes on the street in front of us."

His tone was flat, all-business, and I was smart enough to realize he meant it. I nodded, just a little.

"There are two Paras following us, and two more in front of us watching. The two behind us are at my seven o'clock. The ones in front are at your two o'clock. The ones in front want to talk to us. The ones behind want to cut off our exit. Take a quick glance, if you want, but like you're taking in the architecture."

I did, glancing casually ahead, but not to look at the architecture. I was looking for the Containment agents who were supposed to be at their posts . . . but weren't.

"The guards?"

"Probably paid for a few minutes of privacy. It's not hard to bribe folks in the Land of Unplenty."

"Sounds like this isn't your first experience in a situation like this."

"I don't know these guys in particular, but they probably belong to Solomon. He's the friendly neighborhood crime lord. A coward, but very good at giving favors—and extracting payment."

"He did you a favor?"

"No. But he thinks he did. And that's enough for him. I'm going to handle this. I need you to stay behind me."

I'd been in war, knew how to fight, could hold my own, as the wraiths should have proven. "I'm not going to stand by and just—"

"You can't use your magic," he reminded me. "And I brought you into Devil's Isle—that makes you my responsibility."

I didn't have time to argue. They stepped into the street. Two in front of us, two behind. They looked generally like humans, but their patterned skin gleamed like an amphibian's. Their eyes and ears were large and round.

"Cave dwellers," Liam whispered. "They tend to flee instead of fight." That explained why I hadn't seen them before—and why Liam didn't sound very impressed.

The Para on the right stepped forward. His teeth were small, white, pointed. I'd seen other Paras with teeth filed to points, and the memory made my heart flutter. But looking scared wasn't going to help. I made myself stand a little straighter.

"Solomon wants a word," the Para said.

Liam's expression chilled. "I don't see him here, and I don't speak to men who are too cowardly to deliver their own messages."

The Para bared his teeth. "Only an idiot insults Solomon."

"Only an idiot works for Solomon," Liam corrected. "He was captured by Containment, lives in Devil's Isle, and uses errand boys. Not exactly great leadership."

It happened simultaneously—the Paras behind moved forward to grab me as the ones in front moved toward Liam.

Liam's gun—the one he'd handed over to Containment—sure would have been handy right now.

The first guy who came at me smelled like rancid water. I sidestepped him and, when he paused to pivot, smashed a boot heel into his instep. He swore, stumbled, staggered back.

The second one came in lower. I reached out to hit him, but my fingers skidded off slick, rubbery skin. It was like trying to punch a stingray.

The Para roared, lunged forward. I tried to dodge, but he was faster. He wrapped an arm around my waist, hauling me into the air.

"Let go, you asshole!" I kicked backward, trying to land my heel between his legs, but he kept dancing away from my feet.

The sound of bone and flesh connecting punched through the air. I looked for Liam, saw the first Para howl and stagger back as Liam's uppercut landed.

Liam was built like a boxer—solid and lean—and he moved like one. Light on his feet, quick to move, and quick to dodge.

The Para tried to hit back, but his swing went wide when Liam ducked to avoid it. He came up again, landed a blow to the Para's stomach, which put him in a crouch.

With his partner down, the next Para stepped up, and he didn't look nearly as excited to fight now.

I squirmed, trying to get free, but the Para's arm tightened around my waist. He was stronger than me, and I didn't have a weapon that I could actually use. Not with cameras potentially engaged.

I needed a distraction.

I went for the obvious. "Containment!" I yelled.

He started, dropped me. I hit the ground and, when he leered over me, nailed him in the crotch.

He might not have been human, but he was human enough. He made a strangled sound, fell to his knees.

I looked back. Liam took a hard punch to the side, but stood straight again, eyes gleaming. Liam Quinn clearly enjoyed a good fight—and battle looked pretty good on him.

The time Solomon had managed to buy ran out. An air raid siren began to howl, just like the kind Containment had used to warn us of incoming attacks.

Agents hurried out of buildings and alleys toward us, batons raised and ready to meet unyielding flesh.

Curtains snapped closed as Paras who'd stopped their business to watch ducked inside again, made themselves invisible. They were interested in this human skirmish, but didn't want any part of a Containment investigation.

The agents rushed forward, surrounding the Paras and yelling orders until they were on the ground facedown, hands behind their heads.

"Solomon will hear about this!" the first Para muttered.

"Yeah," Liam muttered. "From me."

A few Containment agents escorted Solomon's men to some unseen part of Devil's Isle too depressing for me to even imagine. Two others asked us questions about the fight—who'd started it, what it was about. Not surprisingly, Liam didn't give them much, and they sent us on our way pretty quickly.

We didn't see a single Para on the walk back. Either it had gotten too late even for them, or they'd decided they were better off inside—away from Solomon's men and Containment.

When we reached the gate, Liam retrieved his weapon. I expected to say my good-byes, but as we passed through the gate, and even as I felt some of the pressure in my chest loosen, he fell into step beside me.

"You don't have to walk me home," I said halfheartedly. It had been a while since I needed to fight someone, and now I'd done it twice in one night. I didn't need protecting, but that was enough to push me off balance. I wouldn't mind the company.

Liam didn't buy the bravado—or didn't care about it. "Tonight, you have an escort."

We walked silently down the street. "Will Solomon give you more trouble?"

"Solomon always gives me trouble. He's a long-term problem."

"Why doesn't Containment handle him?"

"Because he's an asset. He has information. And when you're dealing with enemies on your own soil, you'll put up with a lot to get good information. Someday, he'll run his mouth off to the wrong person. Until then, I'll deal with it."

I didn't doubt that one bit. Liam Quinn didn't seem the type to shy away from conflict.

"Probably not the way you expected War Night to go," he said.

"No, not exactly. I spent time with my friends before the wraiths, at least." I stopped, looked at him. "I saw you in the Quarter. We took a break, and you were on the sidewalk."

He went silent, and I would have given a handful of District tokens to know what was spinning around in his head.

"You came out of the crowd like a dervish," he finally said. "All that red hair flying around."

"You have a way with words. I'm not saying it's a good way, but it definitely could be described as a 'way.' "

He grinned. "Dervish," he said again. "I think that would make a good nickname for you."

"No." And since I'd enjoyed his manly grin a little too much, I changed the subject to something that would definitely keep my mind off it. "So, Blythe. She's your girlfriend?"

"Not anymore." He ran a hand through his hair, biceps flexing with the move. "But it's a long story, and I didn't want to get into that with Eleanor. She worries."

"Ah." I suspected Eleanor didn't have anything to worry about where Liam Quinn was concerned, but I kept that to myself.

And when he lowered his arm and that muscle flexed again, I ignored that, too.

The night had been so weird I half expected to find the shop door open, the shelves looted. It wouldn't be the first time. A few months after the war ended, we had an unusually cold December. It was too cold to plant anything, and there were virtually no shipments into the Zone. One night, someone broke in, ransacked the store for the few MREs that were left. They'd shattered one of the front windows, knocked over antiques, left a general mess in their frustrated search for food. It being the Quarter, half a dozen folks showed up the next morning to get things in order again. And it wasn't long after that that the convoys began moving supplies through the Zone.

Tonight, the store was intact, locked, and quiet. The tree limb and broken sign were gone, as was any sign of the wraiths I'd fought.

"I'll let you know about Nix," Liam said. "I'm going to try to get her here sooner rather than later."

"Yeah. Okay."

We looked at each other for a few seconds. I found it suddenly so odd that I hadn't even known this man existed a few hours ago. A wraith attack, his intervention, a Containment interview, a trip into Devil's Isle, and everything that had gone on there. We'd gone from strangers to strange allies. And considering how we'd done it, it wasn't as horrible as it could have been.

"Thank you for your help tonight. But maybe next time you could just knock on the door instead of breaking in?"

One corner of his lip curled. "The door was unlocked."

"So you say."

"I do say." He crossed his arms, his muscles cording with the movement.

I nodded. Silence fell, and it fell awkwardly. I had no idea what to say or do.

"Well," I said, breaking through the quiet when I couldn't stand it anymore. "Good night, Liam Quinn."

He looked at me, blinked those long lashes. "Good night, Claire Connolly."

One last look, one last sweep of coal over cobalt, and as dawn broke over New Orleans he turned and began the walk back down Royal, back toward the prison at the other end of the street.

It had been an important night. A night that I knew would change everything.

I was no longer on the outside of magic—pretending to be just the same as everyone else. I'd stepped across the line. I wasn't yet sure how far I'd stepped, but I was certain I'd find out soon enough.

I thought of Liam's steel-eyed stare, the straight jaw and broad shoulders, the relaxed smile he'd shared only with Eleanor, and wondered what he thought about as he walked through the breaking dawn. I wondered if the night had been important to him, too.

I turned back to the door, unlocked it, and pushed it slowly open. Just in case, I stood quietly in the threshold darkness for a moment, ears straining for Containment agents in wait, or wraiths looking for their next battle.

But the store was wonderfully, gloriously silent.

I locked the door, grabbed the go bag, and trudged up the steps to the second floor, where I tucked it back into the armoire.

I made it to the third floor just as a rectangle of sunlight began to creep across the floor. Today was Sunday, so the store wouldn't open until noon. Unfortunately, Sundays were also convoy days, so I'd have to sign and unpack boxes earlier than that.

I'd probably end up looking like I hadn't slept a wink. But since War Night meant most of the people left in New Orleans wouldn't have slept much, at least I wouldn't have to explain anything.

The third-floor apartment was a studio, with old oak floors and brick walls, the bathroom in the middle, floor-to-ceiling windows on both ends. The front windows opened to a balcony that faced Royal; the back opened to the courtyard behind the building.

I'd kept the furniture simple: a tufted daybed with tall wooden ends, an armoire, a chest of drawers, an oak table and chairs. I'd put candles and hurricane lamps on the window ledge near my bed, stood a ten-foot-tall antique mirror along one wall in front of an antique rug that had been worn as soft as silk.

In times like these, I was living in luxury.

The apartment was stuffy. Night hadn't managed to burn off the heat of the day before, but I was too tired to care. I pulled off my clothes, slid into a nightgown, and fell face-first onto the bed.

I was asleep in an instant.

CHAPTER EIGHT

My wake-up call came too quickly, and with a slap of sound. The War Night cleanup crew was brushing paper flowers and Drink cups off the streets by ten a.m.

Thankfully, that was two hours later than usual. But they were singing, and not very well, and the sound rumbled through the old windows.

I wasn't a morning person on the best of days, and today I was exhausted all the way around.

"Damn it," I murmured, and pulled the quilt over my head. I was just drifting back to sleep when Gunnar's voice echoed up the stairs.

"Claire? Are you up there?"

I damned myself for giving him an emergency key. "Go away. I need my beauty sleep."

There was clomping on the stairs. I uncovered my head, pushed the hair from my eyes. Gunnar walked in, perfectly groomed in the gray fatigues the Commandant preferred of his civilian employees. For a man who'd probably gotten as little sleep as I did, he looked pretty amazing. No swollen eyes, no slightly nauseated post-Drink tint to his skin.

"Do you know what day it is?" I grumbled.

"It's Sunday."

"Yeah. So I should be sleeping late. Why are you here so early? And why do you look so good?"

"Beauty sleep. And I need to get some things done at the office today." No one had told Gunnar the pace of life had slowed in the Zone after the war. If there was work to be done, he'd by God do it early.

"You're crazy."

"I'm busy. And in case you weren't aware, there's a line of eligible bachelors outside your front door with luxurious bubble bath and scented candles."

I groaned, considered burrowing into the blankets again. "Your cruel, cruel lies won't get me out of bed."

"Yeah, that was mean," he said, and sat down on the edge of the daybed. "You got home okay?"

I hadn't had time to decide what to tell Tadji and Gunnar about last night. I couldn't tell them I'd been in Devil's Isle without telling them about the magic. And I didn't want to tell them about the wraiths, because they'd freak out. I loved Gunnar like a brother. But he could be a smidge on the overprotective side.

On the other hand, Containment had interviewed me. I was in the official record, and it was probably better that he hear it from me.

I sat up, pushed my hair behind my ears. "You have to promise not to freak out."

"Your saying something like that guarantees I'm going to freak out."

"Two wraiths attacked a girl near the Supreme Court building. I chased them off, and Containment came to the store to talk to me and a bounty hunter named Liam Quinn."

Gunnar blinked. "Slow down, and give that to me again from start to finish."

I ran him through it again, from War Night to wraiths. And when I was done, he did not look impressed.

"What in God's name convinced you to hit a wraith? You should have run. God, I should never have let you walk home alone." He looked stricken.

"The girl needed help. I wasn't about to leave her there helpless. And it was War Night. Containment wasn't exactly in a hurry." Which worked out just fine for me.

"They probably thought it was a false alarm," Gunnar said. "Someone in costume, or too drunk to tell fact from fiction." He sighed, looked at me. "I'm glad you're okay."

"So am I."

"Unfortunately, the wraith situation clearly hasn't improved."

I managed not to grimace. "Does Containment think it's getting worse?"

Gunnar frowned. "I haven't seen any official numbers, but it does seem like we're hearing about them more often. Two wraiths together are definitely rare. Maybe I'll take a look at the investigation report."

I nodded. "I'd like to know if they found the wraiths. I'd feel safer." That, at least, was absolutely true. "Maybe let's talk about something more pleasant. How's Burke?"

Gunnar shrugged. "I'm not really sure. He and Tadj got along, but you know she's guarded. I'm not really sure what she's feeling, and she certainly didn't confess anything to me. He seems like good people, though. Very old-school gentleman vibe. Corny sense of humor. I don't think she's sold on him yet. But I don't know."

"I'll talk to her tonight." It was Sunday night, which meant it was dinner night. "Now go away so Cinderella can get into her gown."

"Cinderella didn't wear taupe. And she had fairy godmothers and a Prince Charming."

"I have a store, a lemon tree, and the Commandant's chief adviser."

"That is true." He stood up. "I'll see you tonight. I invited Burke, if that's all right."

"Wait—why did you invite Burke if Tadji's not into him?"

"Because I like him." He frowned. "I don't have many male friends. I need more male friends."

"Because Tadji and I only want to talk about princesses and ponies?"

Gunnar grunted. "You know what I mean. And he offered to bring red beans and rice. I couldn't exactly say no to that."

I looked at Gunnar suspiciously. "He's not from New Orleans. Does he know how to make it?"

Gunnar shrugged. "He says he can. I say we give him a chance. And since it was your turn to cook, and it doesn't look like you've started anything . . ."

He had a point there. "Fine," I said. "But if this dinner goes sideways, it's your responsibility to turn it around again."

He made a gallant bow. "At your service, ma'am," he said, and disappeared into the stairwell.

I got dressed. Today's ensemble was ankle boots, a short skirt, and a flowy button-down shirt, all of them in taupe. Gunnar's opinion aside, it was about blending. Especially now, when blending seemed like the best course.

I walked downstairs, flipped on the lights in the kitchenette . . . and nothing happened. I rolled my eyes, checked my watch, made a mental note to try again in ten or fifteen minutes. Power outages usually didn't last very long. It was the frequency that was irritating. There were members of Congress who'd suggesting moving everyone out of the Zone, bulldozing the area, and layering on new soil from consecrated grounds. That, they assured us, would fix the problem, and we could all get back to normal.

The idea was stupid. And I guess, in a way, we'd gotten used to it. I'd been a normal teenager before the war, and I'd had my own share of gadgets. And yeah, they'd been a crutch, a way for me to tune in or zone out instead of thinking about whatever high school angst I'd been dealing with. In the beginning, it was weird not to have them anymore. But you learned to adjust. And you certainly learned to focus on the stuff in front of you.

I found my usual delivery guy, Trey, outside the back door in his fatigues, fanning himself with his clipboard in the heat. He worked for Containment, distributing across the Quarter the goods that had arrived in the Containment convoy. He stood beside the old mail truck Containment had refashioned into a delivery vehicle that could easily maneuver through the Quarter's narrow alleys.

"Already a scorcher today," he said.

"Extra hot this year," I agreed. "You get to take War Night off?"

"Whole city took the night off. Wife and I had a great time. A little too much Drink, not enough water yet this morning to shake it off."

"I always forget you're married," I said with a grin.

"Fourteen years of bliss. Ida hates me today as much as she hated me the day we were married."

The truck's back door was open. He looked over the boxes and their Containment seals, counted them, filled in something on his clipboard.

"What have you got for me today?"

"MREs, big surprise. Nutrition bars. Water. Powdered milk. Soap. Nylon cord. Batteries. Duct tape." He looked up at me. "You know what they say."

I grinned at him. "The French built New Orleans; duct tape rebuilt it."

"That's it," he said, nodding. "Looks like also some oatmeal, dried potatoes. Oh, and a treat."

My eyes lit up. "A treat?"

He handed me the clipboard, climbed into the truck. I signed my name on the line at the bottom, promising to pay Containment for the goods within thirty days.

A minute later, he emerged with a small foam cooler.

That meant something cold. And that meant something perishable.

I squealed when I exchanged the clipboard for the cooler. It was heavy. Cold, perishable, heavy. These were good signs.

"Give me one more box," I said. "I can carry two, and I want to get this inside."

Trey set another box on top of the first, grabbed his own, and followed me into the store. I put them both on a library table near the door, slipped the tape on the foam with a fingernail. I lifted the lid, felt the cool rush of ice.

"What is it?" Trey asked, almost reverentially. Containment, being military and feds, had access to plenty of food and supplies. But treats were rare—and that much more awesome.

I pulled out the frozen gel pack, felt around for the contents, and grinned. I pulled out eight boxes of unsalted butter.

"It's a War Night miracle," I said, nearly tearing up with excitement.

"Damn," Trey said. "I haven't seen that much butter in a long time."

A memory tickled, of my father baking cookies in our small kitchen for some holiday or other. There were mounds of pale yellow butter in a wide crockery bowl, and he was stirring it with a wooden spoon. If we had butter, life was almost normal. And these days, almost normal was pretty exceptional.

In the silence that had fallen across the store, I put the butter back in the box, stuffed in the gel packs.

"More reliable than the fridge," Trey said quietly.

"Sad, but true." I glanced at him, took in the dark skin, round face, brow now furrowed with regret. Trey was in his forties, so he'd seen even more of prewar life than I had. He'd had more to lose.

"I can put aside a stick or two for you if you want to grab it when you get off shift."

Something crossed his face, like he was trying to shake off the melancholy, and he smiled a little. "Too rich for my blood. The taste," he clarified before I could make him a better offer. "Don't want to get used to something like that these days. I nearly prefer not to have it than for it to be taken away."

"I can respect that."

"Better get the rest of the boxes," he said. "Still a few deliveries to go."

We left the cooler on the table, walked back into the heat.

"Heard there was a wraith attack last night," Trey said, stepping into the truck again and handing me a box.

It didn't look like I'd be able to avoid the wraiths. "Yep. Right down the street. Two of them."

"They get away?"

"As far as I'm aware. They were trying to attack a girl. I understand she got away, too."

"Good. Good for her. Quite a damn thing, ain't it? New Orleans thinks it's well and done with monsters and magic, and they just keep popping back up."

"Indeed they do."

"So," he said as we moved another load into the building, "did you hear about old man Lipscomb? Got into it last week in the middle of the street with Hoyt Bauer—accused him of stealing his woman."

I smiled. "I did not. Tell me all about it."

That story, as it turned out, was a good and sordid one, with plenty of deception, passion, betrayal. New Orleans gave good gossip.

I'd gotten just the last of the stock put away when the cuckoo clock in the front of the store began to chime noon. It was shaped like a small cottage and was dark brown with age. At the first chime of noon, a small girl in a red cape would move along a track in front, basket in hand. When the sixth peal sounded, a tall gray wolf with glinting yellow teeth emerged from the other side to follow her. He chased her into the cottage, and at the peal of noon, Little Red Riding Hood kicked the wolf out the door.

"She's almost as brave as you are," my father had said.

My dad had brought the clock back in several pieces from a scouting trip to Germany. I was proud that I'd been the one to put it back together, to fiddle with the gears and springs and screws until it chimed again.

Noon meant it was time to open the shop. I walked to the door, found Liam Quinn on the sidewalk, arms crossed and staring at an arrangement of Limoges snuffboxes in the window. Not a lot of demand for snuffboxes these days, but they made a pretty display.

He wore jeans and a snug black V-neck T-shirt, and there was dark scruff on his cheeks. He probably had slept as little as I had, but on him the effect was more roguish, more dangerous.

He said he'd talk to me about Nix, but part of me was still surprised to find him there. He was a strange new chapter in my life, and the thread between those pages and the others still seemed fragile and thin.

I flipped the CLOSED sign over, then unlocked and opened the door. "Liam."

"Claire. Can I come in?"

I moved aside, gestured grandly. "Store's open. Cash and tokens accepted. You break it, you buy it."

He snorted, moved inside.

I walked back to the counter, unlocked the metal cashbox from the small safe under the counter, and set it out, along with a receipt pad and pen.

Liam took his time moving through the store, his gaze slipping over furniture, antiques, supplies. After a moment, his gaze shifted to mine, like he'd felt my stare, realized I'd been watching him. He was in my store, on my turf, so I didn't look away.

"Nix is willing to meet with you tonight," he said, cutting to the chase.

I winced. Bad timing. "Is there any way we could do it at any other time?"

He just lifted his brows, obviously not impressed by the question.

"I know you're both doing me a favor," I said, holding up my hands. "It's just, on Sunday nights I have dinner with some friends." I knew the explanation sounded weak—sounded like an excuse—but dinner was my weekly ritual, a dose of normalcy I needed. I had to hold on to normalcy, to Gunnar and Tadji. "It's important to us. It's just—"

"It's normal," he said.

"Yeah," I said, relieved. "It's normal."

"What time is it?"

"Seven thirty."

"We could come at six o'clock. That would give us an hour and a half. It's not ideal, but it will work for the first meeting."

"Thank you. That would be great. But how are we going to do whatever we'll be doing here? There are monitors everywhere."

"We'll leave that to Nix," Liam said. "Maybe she'll want to walk somewhere else."

"You're sure she's trustworthy?" I was putting a lot of faith in Liam, in what we were doing, in his ability to keep me out of Devil's Isle. Nix was an unknown.

"I'm not sure anyone's trustworthy when push comes to shove," he said. "But I don't have any reason to doubt her. I've known her for years."

It wasn't a rosy worldview, but it was practical. I could appreciate that.

"Six o'clock," he said again.

He looked at me for a moment, lips drawn into a near smile, daring me to argue with him. But I knew when to pick my battles, and this wasn't a fight worth waging.

"Okay."

He nodded, the deal done.

"And since I was in the neighborhood, I went by the Supreme Court. I wanted to check out the grounds in daylight, see if there was any sign of the wraiths, anything they might have left behind."

"What did you find?"

"Looks like they've been sleeping in the building. The ground was pretty soft, and I found footprints back to one of the boarded-over windows. No longer boarded over, of course. There's a corner where it looks like they bedded down. Couple of blankets, some food wrappers. They've probably been foraging."

That made sense. There were probably still a few houses in New Orleans that hadn't been cleaned out of food and supplies.

"That doesn't necessarily mean it was wraiths," I said.

"It could have been humans," Liam allowed, "but I don't think so. There aren't many tracks, and the few that are there lead to the spot where the wraiths emerged."

"Does that mean Containment didn't check it out?"

"Why would they?" Liam asked. "Their resources are limited. If they think wraiths are animals, and their only goal is to bring them in or take them down, there's nothing to investigate."

The bell rang, and we both glanced back at the door. I was expecting Mrs. Proctor, one of my regulars, who always came by on Sundays to see what the convoy had brought.

It wasn't her. Instead, a man walked in—tall, light skin, dark hair—and he searched the store, ultimately settling his blue-eyed gaze on Liam.

But Liam was facing me, his back to the door. "Behind you," I warned quietly, keeping my gaze on the stranger, waiting for him to reveal whether he was friend or foe.

Liam turned back, his shoulders stiffening at the sight of the man who strolled toward us like he was on a personal mission. He reached Liam, then punched him square in the face with a cruel right cross.

"Son of a bitch," Liam roared, and jumped forward. They met like rams battling for territory: arms pushing, fists swinging, and mouths bleating with anger and four-letter words.

I rushed around the counter, one hand on the wood to keep my balance, ducked to avoid a swinging elbow. When they made a dive toward a lawyer's bookshelf that held antique canning jars, I jumped in. I'd rather have a black eye than lose the merchandise. I'd foraged those myself.

Besides, Liam had saved my bacon the night before. We were practically friends now.

"Jesus, break it up!" I said, putting an arm around Liam's waist—the devil I knew—and yanking him back. Or trying to—it was like trying to move a mountain.

"What the hell is wrong with you?" I said, a half grunt with one arm still around Liam's waist. "Step back! There's no fighting in my place. And definitely no sucker punches."

The man dropped his double-fisted grip on Liam's T-shirt. Liam stepped back, the anger pulsing off him, hot as sunlight on the August asphalt.

Chests heaving, muscles tensed, they stared at each other.

"It's only a sucker punch if you don't know the entire story," said the new guy. I wasn't sure if there was amusement or challenge in his eyes. "And if you're smart, *cher*, you'll step aside and let me and your man handle this little dispute."

"He's not my man."

"I'm not her man."

Our answers had been quick, simultaneous. Not flattering for either of us.

The man lifted his gaze to Liam's. "Ouch. Haven't yet convinced her, have you, Liam?"

Liam curled his lip, winced at the cut. "Shut up," he said, lifted the back of his hand to his mouth, pulling back to see blood. "You split my lip."

"I owed you one."

"I think your memory has taken a turn for the worse, *frère*."

Their eyes were narrowing at each other, fists curled and ready for another strike. Which I was not going to allow. I grabbed an old cowbell from the bookshelf, shook it to send a metallic *clang* in the air.

"Everybody shut up!" I yelled.

This time, they both jumped back. I returned the bell to the shelf, glanced back to realize Mrs. Proctor stood in the doorway, her petite frame in soft pants and a matching top, a silk scarf knotted around her neck. She always dressed up for a trip to Royal.

I rushed forward. "I am so sorry, Mrs. Proctor. We're just—"

She grinned, white teeth against dark skin. "Oh, don't stop on my account, dear." She gave Liam and the interloper a very naughty grin. "That's the best thing I've seen in seven years."

I put a gentle hand on her arm, pointed her toward the display of new merch. "Yes, ma'am. Maybe you could check out the soap we just got in while I take care of this?"

She didn't look thrilled that I was taking away her entertainment. She walked into the right-hand part of the store, but kept her admiring gaze on Liam's butt.

It wasn't a bad butt, I thought, before snapping back to attention and striding back to the guys. I put my hands on my hips. Since I didn't want to jump in the middle of whatever this was, I hoped it made me look authoritative. "Are you done being idiots?"

"You don't mince words," said the stranger.

"This is my place. I don't have to mince words."

"It's all right, Claire." Liam had pulled a bandanna from his jeans, daubed it against his mouth before pocketing it again. "This is Gavin. My younger brother."

"Yeah, I had enough high school French to get '*frère.*'" And it made sense physically. They both had the same dark hair, the same blue eyes. Gavin would have had the same nose, but for the spot on the bridge where it had obviously been broken, probably in another fight.

But that didn't explain what had just happened—and was currently being enjoyed by Mrs. Proctor, who was peering at us from behind the bookshelf, eyes wide.

"Mrs. Proctor," I warned, and she disappeared again.

Gavin choked back a laugh.

I skewered him with a glance. "Why did you punch your brother?"

Gavin kept his gaze on Liam. "There's not enough time for that list of grievances. Who are you?"

"Claire Connolly," Liam said. "It's her store."

"That's what I hear. Hello, Claire Connolly."

"Hi."

"How did you find me?" Liam asked.

"A mutual friend," Gavin said.

"Nix?"

"Maybe." Gavin's gaze shifted to Liam, then back to me. "And how did you two meet?"

"Wraith attack last night. Couple of blocks from here."

"She looks healthy," Gavin said.

"I'm right here. And I'm fine."

Liam lowered his voice. "She fought back. She has some . . . skills."

He'd used the code word, I guessed, because we weren't alone. But Gavin seemed to get it, and nodded.

"You've been gone for nearly a year this time," Liam said.

That explained the animosity. Maybe Liam was pissed his brother had bailed on New Orleans, or maybe on their grandmother. And if the punch was any indication, Gavin had bad feelings toward Liam, too.

"I had a job," Gavin said.

"Oh, I'm sure you did."

"Bec mon tchu."

I didn't recognize the Cajun, but I got the gist from Gavin's spitting tone, and it wasn't polite.

"Where'd the wraiths come from?" he asked.

"Near the Supreme Court building," I said. It was my story to tell, after all. And I was getting pretty good at telling it.

Gavin smiled grimly. "Demons in the Supreme Court. Seven years ago, that would have been a pretty good joke."

"It was a pretty good one last night," Liam said. "How long will you be here this time?"

Gavin's face went blank. "I'm here for a job. Then I'm leaving."

"Commitment never was your forte."

Gavin glowered. His voice, quiet given Mrs. Proctor's apparent interest, was still fierce. "Some of us have lives in the real world."

"The Zone is the real world," I said. "And we have lives."

"All evidence to the contrary." He glanced at me, gaze appraising. "One day under your tutelage and she's already insulting me like a pro."

"I'm not under his tutelage."

"No," Liam said, and I caught the gleam in his eye. "But she needs tutelage from someone. We talked to Eleanor, and she brought out the catalogue."

"How is Eleanor?"

"Good, not that you'd know. You should visit her."

Gavin shook his head, looked away. "My being there doesn't do her any good."

"You're more of an idiot than I thought if you truly believe that. In any event, you'll want to talk to her. She matched Claire with Nix."

Gavin's gaze snapped back to Liam. "*No*. I won't put her at risk."

Liam had guessed right about Gavin's reaction. His brows lifted. "It's not your choice. It's hers. And she's already agreed to meet."

Gavin's voice went quiet, cold. "She didn't mention that. And she won't understand the danger. She never does."

"I don't want to be in danger, either," I offered with a raised hand, but they both ignored me. This was a brotherly testosterone battle that clearly had nothing to do with me.

"There has to be someone else."

"There isn't."

Gavin opened his mouth to retort, changed his mind. He walked to the front window, crossed his arms, gazed outside.

"I presume Nix is a love interest?" I asked quietly.

"Not at present."

"Ah," I said. "Not at present" could cover any number of sins or breakups or infidelities. "He doesn't seem to be happy about that result."

"He is not. And he's jealous. It's an awkward combination."

"I would imagine so."

Gavin walked back, anger tightening his shoulders. He moved with a swagger, and I wondered who Nix was to have knotted him up so tightly—and what had happened with them.

Mrs. Proctor emerged from a set of secretaries with a box of powdered milk.

I waved a hand at the Quinn boys, brushing them aside. "Customers, gentleman." This time, the grumbles were unanimous. That was probably progress. Anyway, they moved over.

I took the milk from her, marked my receipt pad, put it in a small paper bag with a handle. "Mrs. Proctor, we got butter today. Would you like some?"

Her eyes widened. "Oh, I'd love to say yes, but I don't have any ice, and that nice boy from the icehouse—what's his name?"

A shop down the road, formerly a bookstore that had been burned out during the war, sold blocks of ice. When the convoy delivered fresh goods to my store, he usually had good days. People didn't want to trust rare treats to the whims of electricity.

"Clark. And he's not quite a boy. I think he's seventy-eight."

She waved a hand. "I'm ninety-eight, dear. And I don't look a day over seventy-two."

"Not a day over," Gavin agreed, and winked at her.

She winked back. "He won't be back around until tomorrow. Which is fine by me. I don't mind the heat. But I don't think the butter could take it."

"Well, I'll keep a stick aside, and if you decide you want some after you visit with Clark, just let me know."

She nodded. "I will do that." She unsnapped her coin purse and handed me several tightly folded dollars.

I gave her back her change and put the receipt in her bag. "Thank you, Mrs. Proctor. I appreciate your business."

She smiled at me. "You know I love your store, dear. It makes me feel young to walk around, see all of your . . . beautiful things." Her eyes settled on Gavin, and he smiled grandly.

"The merchandise isn't the only beautiful thing in the store," he said.

But Liam wasn't about to be outdone by his baby brother. "Ma'am, can we help you with your package?"

Mrs. Proctor looked slowly up at Liam, who towered over her by nearly two feet, her grin spreading. "As much as I would like to say yes, young man, I'm afraid you wouldn't be able to handle me." She patted his hand. "The day I stop being able to carry my packages is the day they put me in the ground."

"Yes, ma'am," Liam said, with a glint of appreciation in his eyes.

Mrs. Proctor nodded, took her package, and shuffled back to the door.

"I like her," Liam said. "She's got spirit."

"She's fantastic. Gets lonely, I think. I visit her sometimes, take her a book or two." I gestured to a bookshelf on the opposite wall, where I'd made a small lending library, including two full shelves of paperback romances. In times of crisis, people needed a good love story.

"When are you planning to introduce her to Nix?" Gavin asked, when Mrs. Proctor was safely out the door.

Liam's lips tightened. "Tonight."

Gavin pushed off the counter he'd been leaning against. "I'm going to talk to her again."

"You do that," Liam said. "But go see Eleanor first." He looked at me. "I'll see you at six."

I nodded, and without another word for me, both of them focused on their irritation with each other, they headed for the door.

"And thank you for your business," I mumbled as the door closed behind them.

CHAPTER NINE

Word traveled fast (delivered by Mrs. Proctor), and the butter all but disappeared in a few hours. I traded two of the sticks for a bar of goat's milk soap dotted with lavender, which would feel a lot better than the industrial-strength stuff that usually arrived on the convoy. I had one bar left, which I'd save for an emergency or special occasion. Or to trade for honey, if I could find some. I'd heard a woman in what was left of Metairie still kept bees, and honey had a thousand uses. Maybe I could convince Gunnar to give me a ride out there.

In the lulls when business was slow, I tried to work on the owl again. But my mind kept drifting, and I couldn't let that happen during daylight hours, when the store was open and Containment agents were in and out. And I certainly couldn't take another chance with the monitor.

At ten till six, the sun finally sunk behind a bank of heavy clouds that signaled rain was on the way. Good. The Quarter could steam in the heat instead of just baking.

The bell rang, and the door opened. For the second time today, Liam Quinn crossed my threshold. His lip was still swollen, but it looked a little better.

He'd brought a brown paper bag and a very petite woman.

She was a slip of a person, barely five feet tall and delicate. She had long, wavy blond hair, her eyes round and green beneath darker brows and above a slightly upturned nose. She wore a long, sleeveless, gauzy dress in mint green with a darker ribbon around the waist.

"Nix, this is Claire. Claire, Nix."

"Hello," she said, looking me over.

"Hi," I said, doing the same. She was the woman who stood between me and monsterdom. I wanted to be sure of her.

Liam held out the paper bag. "This is for you."

"For me?"

"Bread. I brought it for you."

I wasn't sure I could have been more surprised. I wouldn't have figured a bachelor bounty hunter for a baker. "You bake?"

He grinned. "Do I look like I have the patience for that? Eleanor made it. She trained in France."

I opened the bag, looked inside. A crusty round loaf of bread sat inside, just like the kind my dad had sometimes brought home from a patisserie on Ursulines. It smelled like flour and yeast. If there were gifts involved, maybe this Sensitive-training gig wouldn't be so bad.

I looked up at him. "It looks amazing. Seriously, thank you, and thanks to Eleanor, too. I really appreciate it." Maybe Eleanor should be the recipient of the Glorious Final Stick of Butter.

"Where should we work?" Nix asked.

"Why don't we go discuss that upstairs?" Liam suggested. "Fewer eyes curious about an after-hours meeting with a bounty hunter."

"Containment does think I'm your trainee."

"That's a point."

I held up the bag. "Let me just put this in the kitchen."

I left the bread on the counter, closed the curtain behind me, and led them upstairs to the second floor. There wasn't as much room here as on the third, but I wasn't ready to invite either of them into my personal abode. Besides, people usually got a kick out of seeing the inventory.

We reached the second floor, and I opened the door, gestured them in. "The storage room."

Liam looked over the furniture and antiques with wistfulness in his eyes, but it was shielded by his masculine brow and pursed lips. Nix didn't worry about hiding her emotions. She walked right in, began moving from item to item, trailing small, slender fingers over everything.

"No Gavin?" I asked quietly as Nix pulled open a drawer in a tall chest, checked the contents, closed it again.

"He has a previous engagement."

She flipped through a shoe box of postcards.

"What does he do?" I asked.

"Most of the time, whatever he wants."

That was all Liam said, but his tone made it clear that he wasn't thrilled about it. Not that he told me what "it" was. If I ever needed a man to keep a secret, Liam Quinn was the obvious choice. I could fill a book with what I *didn't* know about him.

"And more specifically?" I asked.

"He's a tracker. He travels mostly in the Zone, finds things, people who don't want to be found."

"For PCC?"

"Sometimes. Not always. He's got good skills, but he's . . . unsettled."

"Yeah. I got that from your talk with him. Bad blood between him and Eleanor?"

Liam shook his head, eyes tracking Nix as she made her way through the room. "No. Just a little war guilt. Feels like Eleanor was hurt because of him. Puts off visiting her because that's how he copes. *Tête dure.*"

"What's that mean?"

Liam chuckled, glanced down at me. "It means he's got a head as hard as yours."

"And yet you're intrigued by me."

"That's one of the possible ways to describe it."

"There you go with the flattery again."

Nix walked back to us before Liam could reply. "I like your inventory."

"Thank you. I do, too."

"You can move things?"

I nodded. "Yes."

"How long ago did the magic appear?"

"Eight months."

"Sudden or buildup?"

"Um, sudden. I stopped something that was falling on me."

"And since then?" Her questions were quick, businesslike. It took me a moment to realize I was being interrogated. Maybe I wasn't the only one who needed assurance about this partnership. She was putting herself in a really dangerous position, too.

"It happened once when I wasn't thinking about it. Other than that, I haven't really tried much."

"And how do you feel afterward?"

"Dizzy. Hungry."

She nodded. "Humans weren't built for magic. It takes a toll on your body, which grows exponentially the more you absorb."

"Your body is a sponge," Liam said. "That's your little biological gift."

"And I'm so grateful for it."

Nix ignored the jokes. "You have to learn to get rid of the magic, but in a way that won't make the situation worse, or expose you publically. You have to learn to cast and bind it."

"Wait. So if the thing that saves me is getting rid of the magic, and actually using it gets rid of it, why can't I just do that? Why do I have to do something else?"

"Both methods discharge a certain amount of magic, yes. But not in the same way. It's the difference between opening a dam on the Mississippi River and blowing up a levee. Water moves both ways, but one is much safer than the other.

"This is a process," she continued. "A requirement for the rest of your life, if you want to stay sane."

I had a friend in elementary school who'd been diabetic. Every day, she monitored her blood sugar levels, gave herself a shot of insulin. She acted as though it was no big deal and for her, by that point in her life, it probably wasn't. That was the attitude I needed—positive resignation.

"I don't want to become a wraith," I said, and glanced at Liam. "And I certainly I don't want to hurt anyone—there's been too much of that already. So yeah. I'll learn. It won't hurt, will it?" I wasn't big on pain.

Nix's smile was sympathetic. "Not nearly as much as magic destroying your body from the inside out."

I couldn't argue with that. "Then let's get started."

She nodded. "Let me just get comfortable." She shook her shoulders, and the image of the long-haired girl human who'd walked into the store fell away like curling bark. It left behind a woman with delicately tipped ears, long fingers, and a faintly green cast to her skin.

I figured Liam would bring a Sensitive skilled at hiding her magic and who'd learned how to keep her levels balanced. But that wasn't who Nix was . . .

"You're a Paranormal." I heard the anger in my voice, was embarrassed by the judgment in it. But this wasn't a visit to Devil's Isle, where Paras were supposed to be. This was my home, and Liam had brought a Para here without so much as a word.

I slid my gaze to him, let my lifted eyebrows ask the obvious question: *Why is she here?*

"I'm what humans might have called a wood spirit or a dryad," Nix said. "And, contrary to popular belief, not all Paranormals hate humans. And not all of us chose war."

"You had a funny way of showing it."

"Perhaps you aren't trustworthy enough to know the truth."

I kept my steady gaze on hers. "Two Paranormals, a bounty hunter, his brother, and his grandmother now know that I'm a Sensitive. I've walked into Devil's Isle, and I've outright lied to Containment."

Then I shifted my gaze to Liam. "You have enough information to put me away for the rest of my life. You wanted me to keep an open mind, and so far, I have, because I don't want to hurt anyone, and I don't want to go to Devil's Isle. But if you want me to keep believing in you, trusting you, then you need to explain what's going on."

Liam and Nix shared a look, and he nodded.

"Tell her."

Nix sighed, clasped her hands in front of her. "Very well," she said, then looked at me.

"Humans like to see the world as black and white, good and evil. It's a lot easier to wage a war against magic when you've decided everyone with magic is your enemy. But that's not how it happened.

"An assembly of Paranormals we call the Consularis ruled the Beyond peacefully for many millennia. That is no longer the case. There is rebellion—those who want to overthrow the Consularis, no matter the cost to law, to order, to peace. They call themselves the Court of Dawn, and their power has been growing stronger with each new generation. But they are still dwarfed in number by those aligned to the Consularis. When the Court determined they would not be able to rule the Beyond—"

"They decided to take our world instead," Liam said.

Nix nodded. "The Court broke the Veil. But that is not all—they used power and magic to compel others to fight. They conscripted loyal citizens of the Consularis into the battle to help them take your world."

"What do you mean 'conscripted'?" I asked.

"Magical compulsion," Liam said. "The Court decided there weren't enough of them to fight humans. So they built their army with Paranormals who didn't want to fight."

Something settled hard and heavy in my stomach, weighted by the sudden possibility I'd hurt Paras—killed Paras—who hadn't actually been our enemy. "Containment didn't tell us that."

"Containment didn't know until the war was over," Liam said. "For most, the compulsion didn't end until the Veil closed again. By then, most remaining Paras were in Devil's Isle."

"So now they're all in there together," I realized. "The Court and the Consularis."

Nix nodded. "Yes."

"It's almost impossible for Containment to know now who was conscripted and who wasn't," Liam said. "If they asked the Paras in Devil's Isle if they were Consularis, and the Paras thought saying yes would get them freedom, they'd all say yes."

Still. "So why don't the conscripted Paras rebel now? Why don't they break out of Devil's Isle?"

"Where would they go?" Liam asked. "The Veil is closed. They can't go back to the Beyond. And some of them don't want to leave. There's war in the Beyond, or so we assume. Devil's Isle isn't the nicest place to be, but it's home for a lot of them. It's relatively safe, and it's relatively stable. I'm not saying they're thrilled about being there, but they understand the grass isn't always greener."

"You're talking about Moses?"

Liam nodded.

I walked to a church pew made of gleaming oak, sat down. I needed to digest this. To think about what they'd said—and measure it against what I knew and what I'd seen of war.

I sat silently for a few minutes, until the worst of my guilt had subsided a little. "How many?" I asked, glancing over at them. "How many Paras were conscripted?"

"The estimate is four thousand," Liam said.

Damn. Four thousand people forced to fight against their will, some of them undoubtedly killed in battle, even though they hadn't really wanted to hurt us. Or they'd survived like Moses, been locked away in Devil's Isle without a way to claim their innocence.

I blew out a breath, ran my hands through my hair, tugged like it would clear the doubt out of my brain, the new and sharp-edged guilt.

When I could breathe again, I sat up, looked at Nix. It wouldn't help to drown myself in pain that belonged to someone else.

"You said 'they' couldn't surrender, not 'we.' You weren't one of those who had to fight?"

She shook her head. "I was fortunate. My people take many forms. Some are connected to water. Others, like me, to wood. I came through the Veil near Bogue Chitto."

Bogue Chitto was a park and wildlife refuge north of Lake Pontchartrain, surrounding the Bogue Chitto River. Or it had been before the war. Now it was an unmonitored wilderness.

"It was the best possible luck," she said. "The wood eventually gave me strength, allowed me to fight the compulsion, although it was a struggle. I stayed there for many years with others, hoping to find a way home, a way through the Veil. That hasn't happened yet. But we have found friends, made new lives for ourselves."

She was a wonder. "I don't think I could be as gracious as you."

"I wasn't always gracious. There were times when I wanted to fight for my freedom." Nix's gaze narrowed, flashed with something sharp and dangerous. "But not against humans. They may be naive, but they are not my enemies. They did not bring me here."

"You live as a human?"

She nodded. "I can pass when necessary, but I do not stay in the city often. We have a community. It is hidden, and it is safe."

She walked to a rolltop desk, trailed fingers across the ridged shell. "There is a lot of wood in here. Cherry. Mahogany. Oak. It is happy to be appreciated, to be loved. And there was much love here."

She glanced my way, and the expression of utter certainty on her face brought quick and surprising tears to my eyes. By that look, she acknowledged my family and remembered them.

"Yeah," I said, blinking to keep the tears from falling. "There was. Thank you for that." I looked away, embarrassed by the sudden emotion.

"Thank you for caring for these things." She smiled. "But we should get started."

She picked up a Newcomb vase—a tall, narrow design in pale green with deep blue flowers—and checked the mark on the bottom like a seasoned pro, set it down again.

"What are you looking for?"

She looked back at me, hair falling over one shoulder. "A casting and binding object. Ah," she said, and picked up a small black-lacquered box. She opened it, peered inside. A moment later, apparently satisfied with whatever she'd found, she nodded.

She brought it back, handed it to me. "Magic is energy, yes?"

I smiled thinly. "That's what I hear."

"You must regulate that magic. You will cast the extra magic into this box—remove it from your body so that it does not harm you. Later, you will learn how to bind it. That's too much for one evening."

I glanced down at the box. It was pretty—layers of gloss over black, with a pattern of thin, waved lines in gold beneath—but not that big. Maybe four inches by six. "It doesn't look like it would hold a lot."

Nix laughed, the sound as bright and happy as silver bells. "Magic doesn't have mass. Not in the way you'd define it. It will fill and infuse the box many times over before you need another container."

She put the box on the floor, gestured to it. "Sit comfortably."

If my dad could see me now, I thought, and lowered myself to the floor.

"She didn't mean on the box," Liam said with a grin.

"Yeah, thanks. I figured that out." I sat a few inches from the box, crossed my legs.

Nix took a seat on the floor on the other side of the box. She sat as beautifully and effortlessly as a dancer, folding her legs beneath her, delicate hands in her lap.

Liam, who'd become silent as he watched us, moved closer, leaned against the edge of a console table.

"Tell me how you move things," she said.

"Accidentally?" I said, and explained the star and the owl. "If I'm doing it on purpose, I just imagine the air is full of magic, and I try to gather it together. Then I pull. But not very well. Are we going to work on that? My aim is not good."

"It really isn't."

I glanced up at Liam, prepared to give him a dour look. But he was grinning, and it was a pretty good smile.

"No," Nix said, drawing my gaze to her again. "That is for you to practice. I am here to keep you alive." She gestured to the box. "Imagine, as you gather up magic, that you're taking the extra magic inside of yourself and putting it in the box."

"How will I know if I did it?"

Liam lifted a hand. "You won't become a wraith."

I was clearly encouraging him by snarking back. So this time, I ignored him.

"Liam is right, in his fashion," Nix said. "As you become more sensitive, pardon the expression, you will learn to gauge the level of your magic and adjust it as necessary. Now," she added, nodding toward the box, "you try."

I leaned over a little, focused my attention on the box, blew out a breath. I was about to perform a magical act in front of an audience.

I was nearly to the point of feeling out the magic in the air when my brain started working.

I bolted upright. "Wait. *Wait*. I can't just pour magic into a box in here. We're, like, forty feet away from a Containment monitor."

"You think I did not consider that?" Nix sounded entirely unimpressed with me. "I would not have dropped my human shadow if the building was not insulated."

It hadn't even occurred to me that dropping her guise actually expended magic. It clearly had occurred to Nix, given the indignation in her voice. "The—wait. What? What do you mean, it's insulated?"

Frowning, Liam rose, moved through the labyrinth of furniture to the window. He pushed it open, climbed onto the balcony outside. I waited, nerves firing and body prepared to run again, if he found the light outside had changed.

After a moment, he climbed in again, closed and locked the window. I waited impatiently for the verdict.

"The monitor hasn't been triggered."

I blew out a breath through pursed lips, tried to slow my racing heart. And I thought of the falling star, of the lifted gear, of the fact that neither of those little bouts of magic had signaled the monitors outside. It wasn't because there hadn't been much magic, or I'd gotten really lucky. It was because they *couldn't* have. Because someone had fixed it so magic couldn't be detected here.

"I said that already," Nix said. "Someone has insulated the house for magic—made it impermeable."

"That's not possible."

She lifted her eyebrows. "I would not have dropped the shadow if it wasn't."

"Someone would have had to perform magic on the building," Liam said, joining us again.

"Like I said, that's not possible. This store has been in my family for more than a century."

"Are any members of your family Sensitives?" Nix asked.

"No."

"Then they must have had a friend who was."

She said that as if it was the simplest thing—that my father had had friends who were Sensitives. But that wasn't likely. My dad didn't involve himself in magic, although there had been times when it was unavoidable.

"The building took a hit from a flaming sword during the Second Battle," I said. There was still a dark streak of soot across the brick wall that faced the alley. Soapy water and elbow grease hadn't made a dent. "Maybe that's why."

"Maybe," Nix said.

"So, what does this mean?" I asked. "I can do magic in here and Containment won't know it?"

"Theoretically," Liam said. "But that doesn't make it a good idea. You don't want to make the problem worse."

"No," Nix said. "She does not. The house is insulated. Your body is not." She pointed to the box. "Try."

I wiggled on the floor, adjusting my seat, and leaned forward again.

To put the bystanders out of my mind, I closed my eyes, imagined everything in the world was dark—except for the glimmering magic that had situated itself in my body, an irritating cancer that would eventually destroy who I was.

I reached in, grabbed a handful of those stars, and yanked.

Dizziness racked me, and cold sweat trickled down my back, while everything inside my body felt cold, heavy, and completely disorganized—as if every organ were in the wrong place.

"Oh, crap," I said, bearing down hard against a wave of nausea that almost had me tossing my lunch in front of Liam Quinn. Which I didn't think I'd ever live down.

I tried to ignore it. I opened my eyes, squeezed my palms tight against the magic I'd metaphysically grabbed, and imagined pushing the magic into the box.

It worked as well as stuffing my previous tightrope-walking elephant into a water bottle. Neither one of them would be super-psyched about the idea.

The magic flashed back, sparks arcing through the air—and this time, they were real. Liam stamped a few out, looked back at me with obvious concern in his eyes. But I couldn't worry about him. Not right now.

I tried again, winced as magic flashed back again, stinging me like a shock of static.

"Damn it," I said, shaking my hand, bracing against another wave of nausea. "This isn't working."

"Maybe she needs a break?" Liam said.

"She doesn't need a break. She needs to focus. If she can gather magic to move things, she can gather magic to do this. She just needs to concentrate."

"I don't know how to concentrate," I growled. I could feel irritation growing. I was hungry, tired, and running on fumes.

"Come on, Claire." This time, Liam's voice was harder. "You can do this. I know you can. Get it together and get it done."

I nodded. Tried to center myself. Thought about the box, how I wished the box was bigger. Big enough to encompass the entire building, so I could shove a lifetime's worth of magic in there . . .

That was when I realized I was going about this completely wrong. If magic didn't have mass, the size of the box didn't really matter. *It didn't matter.*

I gathered up the magic again, pulling at the twisting filaments that crowded my body even now. I imagined the box was the red dot in the middle of the target and shoved. Cold spilled over me again as the magic twisted, fought back, tried to slip through my fingers like wriggling fish. But I ignored what it wanted and settled my mind on where I wanted it to be.

Slowly, carefully, I moved it toward the box, the box that could be as big as a room. And then I released it.

Nix reached forward and slapped the lid closed.

Dizziness hit me again. I closed my eyes and counted backward from ten, just as I'd done on car trips as a kid when I was a few miles away from barfing all over the backseat.

"Are you all right?" Liam's voice sounded far away.

"She'll be fine," Nix said. "She has pulled magic away from herself. It has left her disoriented. The feeling will pass."

It might pass, but I wasn't thrilled it existed at all—or that I'd need to do this for the rest of my life. "Will I get used to it?"

"Possibly."

Not the ringing endorsement I was hoping for.

I opened my eyes again, blinked. "Did I at least do it right?"

"If you hadn't, you wouldn't feel like that. But if you want to know, look for yourself."

I growled, wished I knew a few Cajun curses, and closed my eyes again. This time, instead of imagining the magic in me was the source of light, I ignored everything except for the box's eight corners and its small, shiny interior.

The light was faint, like a far-off star, but if I relaxed just enough, I could see it pulsing with magic and energy. Satisfaction filled me. I'd done it.

And I was going to sleep like a baby.

CHAPTER TEN

Thirty minutes, three attempts, and one more successful round of casting later, the bell clanged downstairs, followed by the sound of shuffling footsteps.

"Claire? You up there?"

Damn. I glanced at a grandfather clock that stood in the corner. It was seven thirty, and Gunnar was prompt as usual. I was a little dizzy and a lot ravenous.

"I'll be down in a minute," I called out, then looked at Liam and Nix, waited for their images to come into focus. "They're here for dinner. You might want to put the—what did you call it? your human shadow?—back on."

Nix sighed, but waved a finger, and her disguise whirled and re-formed around her body like bark replacing itself again.

"Who is it?" Liam asked.

"Tadji Dupre, Gunnar Landreau, Will Burke. Gunnar's the Commandant's adviser. Tadji's a grad student. Will works for Materiel."

Liam whistled. "That's a lot of Containment in one place."

"Yeah. So be careful," I said, glancing between them. "I don't want either of you getting into trouble."

"More trouble, you mean," he said, and we headed toward the stairs. "A Sensitive, a dryad, and a bounty hunter walk into a bar," he murmured.

Gunnar, still in his dark fatigues, stood with Burke and Tadji in the store's front room. Burke had a large enamel pot in hand, and he'd worn fatigues, too. Tadji had opted for snug jeans, a T-shirt, and boots today. And based on the body language, she didn't look especially thrilled about Burke's presence. Not a love match, I guessed. We'd have to talk.

"Dinnertime!" Gunnar said. "And you have . . ." He trailed off as Liam and Nix appeared behind me. "Company."

"Yeah," I said brightly. "Company. This is Liam and his friend Nix. They're, um . . ." Damn. I hadn't actually though that part through.

"I'm a bounty hunter," Liam said.

I guess he didn't see the point in easing into it. Everyone's eyebrows lifted with interest.

"For wraiths?" Gunnar asked, and Liam nodded.

They looked at Nix like they were daring her to say something even more interesting.

"I don't do anything nearly so exciting," she said. "I'm a gardener."

I wasn't sure if that was the truth. But if so, it made sense for a wood spirit.

"Cool," Gunnar said. "I'm glad to hear there's still ground that can be planted. You have to stay for dinner. Burke brought plenty of food." He glanced at me for support, and I felt bad that I hadn't thought to ask them in the first place.

"Absolutely," I said, glancing at Liam, then Nix. "We'd love to have you. Liam brought us some bread," I added. "Homemade."

Not surprisingly, Nix begged off—all the better to keep her away from two PCC agents—and Liam walked her to the door. When he made it back to the table, he paused beside me.

"Please be careful," I whispered.

He leaned forward, his breath just a whisper. "I'm not the one with skills. Keep yourself in line, Claire." He'd meant magic, obviously, but there was still something in the rumble of his voice that sent a spark down my spine.

I slipped an arm into Tadji's. "Tadj, maybe you could help me in the kitchen? And, Gunnar, can you please set the table?"

I gestured to the cypress table on the left-hand side of the store. It was absolutely beautiful, with a bumpy edge of raw bark. A shame it hadn't sold, but there weren't many who needed a fifteen-foot-long table these days, or could afford it. I took advantage and used the store as a dining room when Gunnar and Tadji came over.

Gunnar grinned. "She says 'set,' but she means put away the price tag and find some chairs."

"The less furniture I keep, the more furniture I can sell," I reminded him.

"Like that's ever stopped you before."

I left them to their sarcasm and hustled Tadji into the kitchen, snapped the curtain closed again.

"Details," I whispered as I pulled out a tray to carry necessaries to the table. "Gunnar says you aren't feeling it with—" Since the curtain was thin, I pointed toward the room where Burke stood.

"He's a nice guy," she said. She'd let her hair curl into ringlets today that bobbed when she moved her head. "But I'm just not sure there's chemistry. I don't think we have that much in common. He's a football kind of guy. I'm an OED kind of girl."

I nodded, moved to a drawer, pulled out a bread knife and spoons. "That might be the nerdiest thing you've ever said."

"Grammar isn't nerdy," she said with a grin. "It's important. And my point still stands." She shrugged. "He's not going to be here forever, so it wouldn't even make sense to get into something."

"You aren't going to be here, either," I pointed out. When she finished her research, she wasn't likely to find a job here. There weren't a lot of professorships in the Zone. "If that's your standard, you can't date anyone."

"And I'm okay with that, Claire. I've always been an introvert, and I'm not afraid to be alone. Besides, I'm focused on my work right now. I don't really have time for dating."

Those were perfectly legitimate reasons. She was entitled to be happy, whether with or without other people. And if being alone made it easier to track the "Etymological Origins of Paranormal Designations in Post-War French Louisiana"—I think I had the title right—more power to her. But I still worried she was making excuses. Because of her childhood, she'd never felt like she fit in anywhere, and she hated that feeling. I hated to think she was avoiding a potential love interest because of it.

"Your call, Tadj. As long as you're happy, it's your life to lead. But I'm still a smidge bummed. He seems so nice. *And* he brought dinner."

"So why don't you date him?"

I smiled. "Because he only has eyes for you."

She patted my arm. "Let it go."

"It's gone. Will you grab some napkins?"

While I searched for enough bowls and cups, she pulled out a long drawer, took out a stack of folded napkins. Good food might have been hard to come by, but in an antique store, good linens weren't. The monograms and embroidery didn't match, but that hardly mattered now.

She put the napkins on the tray next to the glasses I was gathering. "And who are the new kids?"

"The bounty hunter or the gardener?"

"Let's start with the bounty hunter. Is this related to the wraith thing? Gunnar told me about that."

Good. Saved me trying to remember what I'd told him and match up the stories. Lying was filthy, complicated work.

"Yeah," I said.

"He's gorgeous."

"Yeah, he is."

"And you two are . . . ?"

I frowned. "Friends. Kind of." I pulled the bread from the sleeve, placed it on the tray. "But he brought bread. And it looks really good."

The tray assembled, we looked down at it. Mismatched silver-ware, mismatched bowls, mismatched cups. Linen napkins, bread, bread knife.

"It's not awful," she said. "I'd call it artistic."

I picked it up. It was heavy, and it had been a long time since my prewar high school job at Berger's Burgers. But I managed to keep it balanced. "I'm guessing everyone is hungry, and as long as they get a bowl and a spoon, they probably won't care."

"That's life in the Zone," Tadji said, moving the curtain aside so we could head back into the main room. "A little chaotic, but on the better days, there's spicy food and good company."

Dinner was pretty damn delicious. The food was brilliant, and so was the conversation.

Burke, Gunnar, and Liam seemed to hit it off, shared stories about their weirdest experiences in the Zone. Between them, they'd seen a giraffe, two alligators in bathtubs, a drunken man on a unicycle, and a riot over a doughnut truck. There were grim stories, too, of death and sadness. But we'd all known too much of that. It was part of our shared history, and not something we needed to say aloud to understand.

The best part of dinner was the watching, the listening. I nibbled the crusty end of the loaf while the stories were passed around like good wine (which was hard to come by) and hot sauce (which Liam kept in a small pocket flask for "emergencies").

I watched Tadji and Burke, and tried to figure out if the problem was chemistry or timing. A little of both, I decided, bummed on Tadji's behalf.

I watched Liam eat, grin, pour enough hot sauce on his dinner to set his mouth aflame, and seem totally unbothered by it. He glanced my way, realized I'd been watching him again. His expression swung from surprise to amusement to male satisfaction.

I could feel the heat rising in my cheeks, but looked away casually, as if our gazes had just coincidentally met while I scanned the table, and not because I was finding my eyes drawn back to him over and over.

But I was. Maybe it was those eyes. Maybe it was his obvious strength. Maybe the fact that he'd helped me, or that I'd watched him try to protect that child in Devil's Isle. We'd gone from strangers to mostly friends in twenty-four hours. And part of me wondered if we could be something more. That was probably a dangerous thought.

Liam opened his mouth, probably to say something sarcastic, but before he could speak, there was a loud pop. The lights went out, leaving us in darkness.

"And now we can get the party started!" Gunnar said, and we laughed as he'd meant us to do.

"Life in the Zone," he said with resignation, pushing back his chair. "Claire, I'll help you get the candles."

It said something about the Zone and Gunnar that he was practiced enough at this to know what to do, where to find what he needed. Or maybe we'd all spent too much time in this building.

I rose, moved carefully through darkness to the counter and the shelf where I kept the candles and matches. I pulled them out—two silver candelabras with long white tapers, four hurricane lamps with butter-yellow beeswax candles I'd traded for several packs of batteries. I flicked a match against the side of the box, and the flame took. I protected the flame with the cup of my other hand, brought it to the candles' wicks. A soft glow filled the room.

"At least moonlight is flattering," Gunnar said as we carried the candlesticks back to the table, set them down the middle in intervals.

"There is something to be said for it," Burke agreed, with a smile that Gunnar reciprocated.

"When we were kids," Gunnar said, "Dad would take us to this cheap motel on Pensacola Beach. Cinder block walls, tile floor. It was not fancy. This was before he made his money."

Gunnar's father, Cantrell Landreau, had been a very successful surgeon. His practice had bought the family's house in the Garden District. (The Arsenaults were an old family with old money. The Landreaus were relatively new to New Orleans and newer to money. Even after the war, that difference still mattered to some.) Cantrell had been a field doctor during the war, and had refused to leave the city when the war was over.

"We'd buy groceries when we got into town, fill a mini fridge with hot dogs and milk so we wouldn't have to eat out. The beach was gorgeous then—white sand. Blue water. Absolutely amazing.

They had these little grills on the patio. Just a firebox on a pole with a grate on top. Anyway, at night, after we'd spent the day on the beach, we'd walk down to the shore, with the moon hanging above us. The sand would have cooled off by then, and it would feel so good between your toes. We'd sit down on these wooden beach chairs, watch the moon and stars, listen to the waves rush in."

We sat quietly for a moment, thinking about the scene.

"A beach vacation would hit the spot right now," Burke agreed. "Man, or even just zoning out in front of the television."

"Best way to spend a weekend afternoon," Gunnar agreed.

"What about you, Claire?" Tadji asked. "What do you miss?"

"Oh, I got this," Gunnar said with a grin. "She misses cheese, good tea, and air-conditioning."

"Nearly nailed it," I said, raising my glass to him.

"Sweet tea?" Burke asked.

"Earl Grey, if I can get it." I looked at Liam, lifted my eyebrows. "I understand you may have a supplier."

"I am a man of many talents," he said with a grin, which made Tadji whistle.

"You know why she loves Earl Grey?" Gunnar asked, shifting in his seat to look at me. "She discovered something awesome."

"And what's that?" Liam asked, smiling at me.

"It's silly," I said, "but if you put honey in Earl Grey, it tastes a little like Fruity Rockers."

"The breakfast cereal?" Liam asked, and I nodded.

"Saturday mornings with television and Fruity Rockers," Burke said. "Now, that was bliss."

It had been bliss for me, too. Were we possibly better off without sugary cereals and zombifying television? Maybe. But it would have been nice to have the choice to ruin myself. If I could have gone back in time—something I thought about a lot at the beginning of the war—I'd have smacked my younger self for not appreciating the small conveniences.

"That's not the only thing I miss, though," I said. "My grand-mother was a Peretti. Very Italian, but also very Southern. She'd lived in Mississippi before she came to New Orleans. I didn't know her very long—I was only five or six when she died—but we'd go to her house on Sunday for lunch. She'd make this enormous Italian-Southern meal. Fried chicken, fried okra, mashed pota-toes. That would all be one half of the table," I said, using my hands to illustrate. "And on the other side would be this Italian feast. Ziti with sausage, and red gravy. Mussels. Carbonara. There was so much of it, and it was all phenomenal. I mean, honestly, it was an obscene amount of food. Not that anybody was complain-ing about it."

"What about you, Liam?" Burke asked. "What do you miss?"

There was a pop, and the overhead lights blinked, buzzed on. Without missing a beat, Gunnar leaned forward, blew out the can-dles.

"So much for the romantic evening," he said with a grin, settling back again. "We'll assume consistent power is one of the things Liam misses."

"It didn't hurt," Liam said. "I miss Abita beer. A cold beer on a humid day was pretty remarkable." He was quiet for a moment, lost in the memory, before he tipped his chair back again. "My family had this place on Bayou Teche. It was a cabin, and hardly that, but it snugged up next to the bayou, or at least as close as you could get. Had a dock, and you could sit out, watch pelicans land, see gators slinking through the water while you drank a beer. It was pretty damn exceptional." He smiled at us. "Not that this fine feast you've assembled isn't spectacular. Because it is."

The compliment was interrupted by hurried pounding on the store's front door. Liam, Gunnar, and Burke went on immediate alert.

I stood up, and Liam did the same. I walked toward the door, could feel him moving protectively behind me. I held up a hand to call him off, unlocked the door.

It was Campbell, Gunnar's blond, lanky cousin. And he looked absolutely panicked.

"Campbell," Gunnar said, rushing around furniture to the door. "What are you doing here?"

"It's Emme." That was Gunnar's younger sister. "She was attacked by wraiths."

"Jesus," Gunnar said, putting a hand on Campbell's arm. "Is she all right?"

"She's got a couple of pretty bad lacerations. Your father was at home when she was attacked. He stitched and bandaged her, gave her morphine. There was a Containment patrol in the neighborhood, so we flagged them down. I knew you'd probably be here."

"Can I get you a bottle of water or something, Campbell?" I asked.

He shook his head. "I'm good. Thank you."

"She's at the house?" Gunnar asked.

Campbell nodded. Without cell phones or landlines in the Zone, the only way to communicate quickly was to play Paul Revere—you hauled ass to wherever someone was and then you hauled ass back again.

"We'll go," I said, putting a hand at Gunnar's back. "We'll go to your house, make sure she's all right." I glanced at Liam, who'd moved behind me, watched with a serious expression. "Maybe you could come, too?"

His expression had gone serious. "Already planning on it."

Gunnar looked back at Liam, nodded. "I'd appreciate it. You'll know more about them than any of us. And you're welcome to the bounty if you can find them."

Liam shook his head. "Don't worry about that. We'll make sure your sister is safe, and go from there."

"Why don't I stay here," Tadji suggested, "get things cleaned up? I can lock up the store or stay until you get back."

"I could stay, too," Burke said. "I'd be happy to help."

I could see Tadji's internal war—she'd rather be alone than deal with an uncomfortable assistant—but she was gracious enough to know that this wasn't about her, but Gunnar and his family. And it probably wasn't a good idea for her to be here alone, just in case.

She nodded. "That'd be great, Burke. Thank you."

So as Burke and Tadji began to clear things from the table, we worked out the transportation. Campbell had driven, so he'd take me, Gunnar, and Liam to the house.

For now, that was plan enough.

Campbell had an old-fashioned, military-style jeep. Two seats in front, a bench in back, the doors open. The vehicle had been stripped of most electronics since they weren't reliable anyway. It wasn't pretty, but it was as solid as you could get in the Zone.

"Tell us what happened," Liam said when we'd climbed into the back, and Gunnar and Campbell had taken the front.

"Emme was on her way home from school. She's a sophomore at Tulane," he added, glancing in the rearview mirror to meet our gazes.

"She has a car, gets home around the same time most days, and Zach keeps an eye out for her."

"Zach?" Liam asked.

"My younger brother," Gunnar said.

Campbell nodded. "He checked the window, saw them—two male wraiths."

Liam and I exchanged a glance. It didn't take much to imagine they were the same wraiths I'd fought the night before. But we wouldn't know that for sure unless we found them.

"They attacked her when she got out of the car. Zach ran out to help her, used a flare gun to scare them off, but not before they got violent."

Flare guns were popular in New Orleans during and after the war. When phones didn't work, you could send up a flare to signal emergency or to alert Containment crews.

"He got her inside, and your father helped her."

Campbell turned the vehicle onto St. Charles Avenue. Before the war, St. Charles had been the primary street on the New Orleans star tour—the street where the famous writer had lived, the actor, the chef, the former senator. They'd celebrated their money with architectural grandeur, not that it was worth much now.

It was a four-lane road separated by a median of streetcar tracks, what we called the "neutral ground." Both sides of the street and the neutral ground had once been lined with trees, including tons of live oaks planted after the storm. Some had been knocked down in battle. Others had died when magic seeped into the soil, or when humans had cut them down to make firewood.

The neighborhood's mansions, businesses, and high-rises hadn't fared much better. Many had been leveled, especially near Lafayette Cemetery No. 1, where there'd been heavy fighting during the Second Battle.

"What happened to the wraiths?" Liam asked.

"I don't know," Campbell said. "I guess Zach scared them off?"

If it was the same two wraiths that I'd seen in the Quarter, that was two nights in a row they'd attacked and been scared off. I didn't think we'd stay that lucky for much longer.

The Landreau house was two stately stories in creamy yellow fronted by porches and marked with columns. The main house had once been surrounded by palm trees, so tours had referred to it as the "Palm Tree House." I'd passed it a dozen times as a teenager. I hadn't known Gunnar then, but I'd known the house. Now the trees were mostly gone, and so were most of the Landreaus' neighbors.

We parked and climbed out of the jeep. There was a Containment vehicle at the curb, a few agents milling around. Even the sight of them made me nervous.

"You'll be fine," Liam murmured. "They'll have already interviewed the family."

Gunnar jogged to one of the agents, nodded at whatever information he got, then joined us again.

Campbell's wife, Sloane, met us at the front door. Gunnar embraced her, and we followed them in silence through the house.

It looked, as it always did, untouched by war. No soot on the walls, no smears from magical fire on the antique carpets. The furniture was expensive and immaculate, the crown molding pristine, pretty little art objects and framed photographs on nearly every surface. The house blazed with lights, and the air was frigid. The Landreaus had two generators, and they'd donated several dozen to the city's remaining schools. They'd also paid a small fortune to repair their house after the war. But the city needed it. We needed normalcy. We needed hope. That was, after all, why we'd all stayed—because we believed regular life in New Orleans would be possible again someday.

We walked into the living room, where beautiful lamps cast shadows along walls papered with toile. Emme lay on a long sofa in the living room, her skin pale, white bandages across her neck and forehead. She was tall, nearly six feet of slender girl, but tonight she looked as small and delicate as a doll.

Liam stood beside me a few feet away, and I felt his body jerk, probably with the sharp and painful memory of his sister. I reached out, squeezed his hand. That made him jerk, too, so I pulled my hand away again and focused on standing there awkwardly.

"Damn it," he murmured. "I'm sorry."

I shook my head. Of course he didn't want sympathy from me. I was a Sensitive. If it wasn't for people like me, his sister would still be alive.

I tried for a nonchalant smile, but I wasn't sure if I pulled it off. I made myself focus on what was in front of me.

Gunnar knelt on the floor beside the couch, replacing Zach, who stood up, wincing. I guessed he'd been there for a while. He walked toward us. He was clearly a Landreau, with his crooked mouth and dark hair. Tonight, he looked exhausted.

He reached out, gave me a hug.

"How are you doing?"

"Not great."

I nodded. "I'm so sorry. She's stable?"

Zach nodded. "For now, yeah. Dad has her on some pretty stiff painkillers." He rolled tension from his shoulders. "I never saw a wraith before. It was—not good. I was here during the war, and I'm not sure I've ever been so scared."

"They're pretty horrible," I agreed.

His gaze fell to Emme again, heavy with guilt. "It took me a moment to move—if I'd gotten there faster, maybe . . ."

Zach suddenly realized Liam was standing there, blinked. "Who are you?"

"God, I'm sorry," I said. "Zach Landreau, this is Liam Quinn. I don't know if you heard, but I happened upon a wraith attack last night. Liam helped me. He's a bounty hunter."

Gunnar looked back at me. "The wraiths you saw—weren't there two of them?"

"Two males," I said with a nod. "They were headed uptown."

"So it could be the same ones," he said.

Liam nodded. "It's a possibility. They could have bedded down in the meantime, then gone out again tonight."

"And had Containment done a damn thing to stop them, this wouldn't have happened."

The voice was deep, Southern, and very, very angry. Cantrell Landreau stood in the beautifully arched doorway, fury and worry warring on his face, in the deep lines around his mouth and eyes. He'd been a handsome man, was still handsome in his way, but the war had taken a toll on him, put bags beneath his eyes. But he still wore pressed khaki pants, an immaculate button-down shirt. He wasn't a man to let war come between him and the finer things— things he'd undoubtedly worked hard to achieve. And a house in the Garden District was a long way from a cinder block motel.

Gunnar's mother, Stella, stood behind him. She had dark, frizzed hair and wore a belted robe over long pajamas. I guessed she'd woken up to find her daughter injured.

"Dad," Zach said, moving to intercept Cantrell. "Not tonight. This isn't the time or the place."

"It's my house," Cantrell said. "And if not tonight, when? We *gave* this city to Containment. We gave it to them because they promised to make things normal again. Because they promised to give our city back to us. Bullshit. What has Containment done? Squandered it. Let Paranormals roam free." Gunnar might have been on his knees on the floor beside his injured sister, but Cantrell didn't care.

Gunnar's expression was nearly mutinous. "If you think we don't try to stop this, try to prevent it in every way that we can, you're insane."

"Then why did my daughter nearly die tonight?" Cantrell asked. "Containment certainly didn't stop this."

I knew he didn't mean Gunnar personally, but since Gunnar was the only Containment agent in the room, it would have been difficult not to take the remark that way.

I'd seen arguments like this all the time during the war. People wanted to believe there was a reason for everything horrible that happened. There was no such thing as being in the wrong place at the wrong time; everything was someone's fault, traceable back to that bad person or bad decision.

Life didn't usually work that way. But since Liam was on the same type of quest, I had to hope he'd have better luck.

"You know there aren't enough people to have a Containment agent on every block. That just couldn't happen. But they're here now, investigating, and so am I. I'll do everything I can," Gunnar replied.

When they started yelling over each other, Liam put two fingers in his mouth, whistled. The crowd quieted, heads snapping to him.

"I'm very, very sorry for what's happened," he said. "It's a horrible thing. But blaming each other isn't going to help."

"Who the hell are you?" Cantrell demanded.

"He's a friend," Gunnar said. "A friend with experience." That Gunnar had called him a friend so quickly made me want to reach out and hug him.

Cantrell spat out a curse. "If Containment isn't responsible, then who is? Who else got us in this situation, hurt my daughter?"

"I'm not sure," Liam said. "And that's what I'm trying to find out. But there's no reason to believe it was your own family."

Gunnar looked as grateful as I felt for the words.

Emme stirred. "Gunn . . . ," she said, voice hoarse, and Gunnar turned back to her.

"I'm here, Emme. You all right?"

"The monsters."

"They're gone. Zach took care of them, and he took care of you. You're in the house, and safe now."

Her eyes were still closed, but her lips curved upward. "Zach did good."

"Yeah," Gunnar said, smiling at Zach. His body shifted, relaxed with Emme's forgiveness. "He did real good." He'd done what he could, and gotten Emme to safety.

Now if we could just keep her there.

CHAPTER ELEVEN

Gunnar, Liam, and I walked outside to take a look around. The air was thick and still and nearly silent, fog softening the house's hard edges, hiding what remained of the landscaping. The Containment vehicles were gone. Either they hadn't found anything or they hadn't bothered to check very hard. But as Liam had said, if Containment thought wraiths were animals, why bother?

"Remind me what we're looking for," Gunnar said as we took the sidewalk toward the street.

I didn't answer. I wasn't sure how much Liam wanted Gunnar to know about his suspicions, and figured it was better for him to make that decision for himself.

"Indications of intelligence, complex thinking."

Gunnar stopped. "What?"

"Does Containment track wraith attacks?" Liam asked.

Gunnar stopped in the junction between the sidewalks, where the Landreaus had planted smaller palms in giant terracotta urns, faced Liam, then looked at me, gaze thoughtful. I'd asked Gunnar almost the exact same question, and he'd have realized there was something bigger going on.

"Why?"

"Because I do track them," Liam said, letting the cat out of that particular bag. "Attacks have been increasing, and wraiths' behavior seems to be becoming more developed."

Gunnar's eyebrows lifted. "Elaborate."

Liam didn't answer, but checked the street for traffic (there wasn't any) and jogged across to the neutral ground. We followed him, watching as he pulled a small flashlight from his pocket, began checking the ground.

"Recent patterns suggest they pick their victims, track them, and possibly coordinate their attacks."

"We haven't seen any evidence of higher-level thinking."

Liam glanced at him, his face bland. "Haven't seen it? Or weren't looking for it?"

"I wasn't aware there was anything *to* look for."

"There could be evidence they camped out, waited for her." His beam flashed back and forth across the ground, but didn't settle. After a moment, he flipped off the flashlight—all the better to save the batteries—and glanced at Gunnar. "Are you good at your job?"

Gunnar's look could have iced over Lake Pontchartrain. "Not at all. You just have to walk in and smile to be the Commandant's chief adviser."

I bit back a grin. It was fun to watch Liam Quinn get the business for a change—and nice not to be on the receiving end of it.

"I wasn't implying. I was asking. Wraith behavior is changing. There are more of them, and they're acting more intentionally."

Gunnar frowned, crossed his arms. "You're talking about evolution?"

"I don't know," Liam said. "But I'd bet you've got more access to information than nearly anyone else in New Orleans, including me. It would be worth your time to check it out. It would be worth Containment's time."

Gunnar slanted me a glance before looking back at Liam. "Because you're apparently friends with Claire, I'll spare you the lecture about bounty hunters telling me how to do my job. Instead, I'll just say I appreciate the heads-up."

"Don't thank me yet. I don't see anything here."

"Check around the house?" Gunnar suggested, and Liam nodded. He swung the flashlight back and forth across the road; then we moved into the front yard.

"I'll check the side yard," I said to them.

"Be careful," Liam said. "Yell if you need us."

I promised I would.

There was a stone patio on the side of the house beneath a pergola still covered in leafy vines. Once upon a time, the patio would have been decked with flowers, surrounded by blossoming shrubs. And on a warm night like this, probably fancy people in fancy clothes holding even fancier drinks. But that was all gone now.

I walked around to the side lawn, then the back. It was big for New Orleans, with plenty of space on the sides between the neighbors' houses. Patches of grass were black where magic had struck like lightning, but a few live oaks had survived the war. They were gorgeously creepy, Spanish moss hanging down from long, gnarled branches.

Fog swirled in a sudden shift in the wind, rising in a column that spun like a dervish until it sank to the ground. And in that moment, before the fog lifted again, I saw a dark figure move across the lawn between the arching branches of the oaks.

My heart began to pound. I hadn't actually expected to see anything out here. Not after my run-in with the wraiths, and the fact that Zach had chased them off tonight. And maybe it was nothing. My very overactive imagination. Or someone from the family who wanted fresh air.

But what if it wasn't? I ran through the possible options. One, a wraith, waiting for another chance to attack. Two, a nosy neighbor. Three, someone else doing their own investigation about the wraiths who'd attacked Emme.

I thought about yelling for Liam, but that might have scared the person off. And I didn't want to do that. If someone was spying on the Landreaus, or if the wraiths had come back for another bite, we'd need to know.

My boots, thankfully, were silent and soft, and didn't make a sound as I snuck around and into the grass. I darted to the closest tree, waited for a moment in case I'd made too much noise, ears straining for sound.

I knew I wasn't as scared as I should have been. It wasn't that I thought I was invincible; I wasn't naive. But I was being careful, and I figured the odds were better that whatever was out here would run away as soon as it saw me.

As slowly and quietly as I could manage, I looked around the trunk of the tree I'd been sheltering against. There, at the other end of the alley of oak trees, maybe forty feet away, stood a man. He was tall, broad-shouldered, with light hair. The darkness had dulled colors to black and white and gray, so I couldn't tell much else.

Then the wind shifted again, moving fog and shadows, and revealing the arch of wings at his back.

I froze, and my bravado wavered. There was a chance it was an innocuous Para—a cloud nymph, maybe, what we'd have called a Nephele.

But most things with wings were things to be avoided. Angels with their golden bows, Valkyries with their deadly spears. Both were ferocious fighters.

Memories rushed me, made my hands shake with adrenaline and fear. But like I'd done so many times before, I put them away. There wasn't time to be weak, to be afraid. Especially not if one of them had managed to avoid Devil's Isle and was hunting again.

I shook my head. After last night, I didn't have the right to assume all Paras were enemies anymore, no matter how terrifying. I had to be more open-minded. And I had to be very, very careful.

I moved around the tree, took one step forward, then another, until I stood in the middle of the trees, nearly in line with him.

If he'd had a bow and arrow, I'd be a straight and easy shot.

"No," I mouthed. I wasn't allowed to think about that.

I screwed up my courage, took a breath. "Who are you?" I called out.

The man turned back to me. I still couldn't see his face, but his eyes shifted golden in the pale light that sifted through the trees.

"Golden eyes, better be wise," went the war song that warned children to stay away from angels.

There was a shift of light as his wings retracted, disappeared. That was one of the reasons angels had been so terrifying during the war: You didn't know they were angels until they were preparing to fly.

Darkness engulfed him again. I couldn't tell if he was friend or foe, if he was waiting for a moment to strike—or looking for the same information we were. After all, the wraiths' violent existence only strengthened the idea that Paranormals were bad, dangerous, and always our enemies.

"Claire?"

I jumped at the sound of Liam's voice, glanced back in surprise. And when I looked at the tree line again, the man was gone. "Damn."

"What are you doing?"

"There was someone out here."

His gaze shifted to the oaks, scanning back and forth. "Where?"

I pointed out the spot. "I think it was an angel."

"I haven't seen any angels outside Devil's Isle. You're sure you saw wings?"

I nodded. "Yeah. And I've seen Nephelai and Valkyries. I know how to tell the difference, even in the dark." Especially in the dark. "It was an angel."

"I'm not sure getting closer to it was a great idea."

"And you'd have let him fly away?"

"Fair point."

"Damn right it is." I walked forward, both of us searching for a clue about who the angel had been, and what he'd been doing here.

Liam crouched, hands folded in front of him. "Here," he said, pointing at a shoe print in an area just soft enough to hold the impression.

"Why would he be out here?"

"I don't know," Liam said, and I didn't like hearing that tight, concerned tone. He was worried. He rose again, and we stood in the dark for a moment.

"Thank you for coming here tonight. For Gunnar. And for me."

"You're welcome."

"We should get back inside," I said. But neither of us moved. We stood there together, the only sounds our breathing and the hum of cicadas, the soundtrack of a warm Southern night. When I started toward the door, Liam reached out and took my wrist.

His skin was hot against mine, his eyes dark and intense, and just as heated. There was need there, I thought, but that wasn't all. Need was a simple emotion. And there was nothing simple about the desire in his eyes.

"You guys in there?"

I blinked at the sound of Gunnar's voice on the other side of the tree line. And just as the fog had lifted and rolled away, the moment passed. Liam's fingers slipped away.

"We're on our way out," Liam called back.

Cantrell might have had issues with Containment, but Stella ignored them. By the time we returned to the house, she'd put together a dish for us to take home. The meal wasn't nearly as fancy as her house—MREs doctored into a casserole—but the thought was nice.

Gunnar decided to stay the night at his parents', so he borrowed Campbell's jeep and took us back to the store. Liam and I didn't say anything to each other for the entire ride.

Tadji and Burke met us at the door. A board game was spread out on the table. Tadji didn't look overly irritated, so I took that as a good sign.

"How is Emme?"

"Conscious, so that's good," I said, placing the dish on the table. "And Mrs. Landreau gave us an MRE casserole."

No one volunteered to take it home.

"What about the wraiths?" Burke asked with a frown.

"There were two of them, males," Liam said.

"Same wraiths as the Quarter attack?"

"We don't know," Liam said. "There's no evidence that confirms that yet. Claire did see someone outside, and we found a footprint."

He didn't mention the wings, so I didn't, either. There was no telling yet if the winged individual was friend or enemy, so might as well not raise the alarm and put a target on his back until we knew more.

"They were with the wraiths? Or watching the house?" Burke caught on quickly.

Tadji crossed her arms, glanced between us with concern. "Why would someone be watching the house?"

"We don't know," Liam said. "Could be another hunter looking for a bounty, trying to track the wraiths."

"Poor Gunnar," she said. "And what a nightmare. That's two nights in a row of wraith drama."

"It's not been my favorite week so far," I agreed. "And it's late." I gestured to Gunnar, still at the curb, busily making notes in his tiny notebook. Undoubtedly making Containment plans for tomorrow. "He's going to give you a ride home."

Tadji nodded. "Good. I've got three interviews tomorrow. I'd like to be awake for them."

Tadji and I exchanged hugs, and then Burke moved in for one. He might have been new to the group, and maybe wasn't a match for Tadji, but he certainly wasn't giving up easily.

The long night ended again with wraiths on my mind and Liam Quinn at my store again. But tonight, there was a new emotion layered over it. A new kind of interest.

"This is becoming a bad habit," I said, moving to the table to put game pieces back in the box. "Me and you and wraiths."

"Yeah. It's the world we've got, I guess."

"I guess. Not an optimistic thought, though."

"No, it isn't. I'm sorry about Emme. If you find out anything else, or if she remembers any other details . . ."

"I'll let you know," I promised. I put the top back on the box, walked back to its shelf, and stayed there for a moment. "If this was my fault—if she was hurt because I didn't kill them—"

"You don't control their behavior," Liam said. "They could just as easily have attacked you, killed you."

"Yeah, but if I'd killed them last night—"

"Don't," Liam interrupted, moving closer. "Don't ever wish you'd killed something."

I turned back to face him. "I have."

I hadn't often said the words aloud. I said them because I knew he'd understand. Because killing shouldn't be easy or expected or just part of life, just part of the chain of war. Because I didn't think he'd judge.

Because I wanted to feel something.

Liam's expression softened. "How?"

I paused. "I was home alone. School had been canceled by then, but I was seventeen. A Valkyrie came in through the front door—threw it off its hinges. A handful of Containment soldiers had been chasing her. She was probably looking for a place to hide. She said something—I didn't understand the language—and then gave me this ferocious smile. Her teeth were filed to points, and she wore that golden armor."

They'd all worn golden armor, the Paras who'd fought us. It was shockingly bright, polished to a high gleam, and absolutely effective. The military had spent a lot of money trying to figure out how to penetrate it. They eventually learned that iron cut through that particular Beyond alloy like butter. That had been another lesson that human myths—in this case, about the power of cold iron against supernatural creatures—often had a grounding in the Beyond.

The fear rose, cold and biting. I swallowed it back, made myself finish telling him.

"I had a gun. My dad had given it to me, taught me the basics of handling it." I paused. "I killed her. She didn't give me a choice. By that time, we were on the front lawn. Containment caught up, found me, and took her. A soldier named Guest, Sandra Guest, helped me clean up. Called my dad. I killed two more after that. Goblins or dwarves. I'm not sure which."

"I'm sorry."

I nodded. "Me, too. I know I did it because I had to. And I know I may have to do it again. But I don't want to. I don't want death to be normal. I don't want death to be usual."

Liam crossed his arms. "My first Para was a Seelie. It was right after the Veil opened. The power was gone by then, but the house hadn't been destroyed yet. We were all in the house—the extended Arsenault family—just waiting for something to happen."

"That was the house on Esplanade?"

Liam nodded, crossed his arms. "Yeah. One of my cousins said, 'There's a girl on the lawn.' I went to look, and sure enough, there she was. She was beautiful—so beautiful. Long limbs. Pale dress. I saw the streak of crimson across her face, but I thought she was human, that she was hurt. That was before they put out the Guides."

PCC had eventually created Guides to help us identify Paras, especially those who looked so human.

"I went outside and asked if she needed help. She gave the signal, and they attacked the house. There were a dozen of them, maybe sixteen. I shot her, killed her. The Seelie were enraged. They torched the house before Containment arrived. We got everyone out, but that was the beginning of the end of the Arsenault kingdom in New Orleans." His tone was rueful. Sad.

"War is the worst."

I hadn't been joking, but the sentiment made him smile. "Yeah, it is. It really is."

"So what do we do now?"

"You keep working with Nix. I need to get back to work. I didn't go out tonight, and we know how last night turned out. I'll need to go out tomorrow, so I may not be around."

Liam meant wraith hunting. I made a quick—and potentially deadly—decision. "I want to go with you."

His brows lifted. "Why?"

"Because they attacked me and my best friend's sister. Because I believe you—that they're changing. That something's happening.

And if there are more wraiths, if something is making more of them, that means I'm at risk, too. I can't stand around waiting for that to happen."

Liam looked pleased that I'd offered, but not convinced. "You could get hurt."

"So could you. I could also help."

"You can't use magic. Not with monitors around."

"No, but I know how to shoot," I said grimly. "And I have what they want."

"Which is?"

"Magic. The wraiths in the Quarter sensed it. It managed to take their attention away from the girl they were chasing."

"In fairness, you were also waving around a really big stick."

I couldn't help but grin. "Effectively, I might add."

He chuckled, shook his head. "So basically you're proposing to use yourself as bait?"

I didn't really like the way that sounded—"you're proposing to be the fierce, redheaded warrior that you are" would have been better—but it was an accurate summary of what I'd said. "In a manner of speaking, I guess I am."

He took a step forward. "I said you were recklessly brave, didn't I?"

He was close enough that I had to look up to see his face. And God, what a face. I could have said Liam Quinn wasn't the most beautiful man I'd ever seen. But that would have been a lie. And I could have said I didn't want to step forward and sink into his arms. That would have been a lie, too.

"Yes."

He stared down at me, brow furrowed. His eyes had darkened again, emotions warring against the background of deepest blue.

And while he looked at me, while we looked at each other, time slowed, and the moment seemed to stretch in front of us, full of promise.

Liam dropped his head, lashes falling as he moved toward me, stepped into me, his hands suddenly on my cheeks, thumbs stroking my face, the line of my jaw.

My heartbeat stuttered, sped. I closed my eyes, lips parted with wanting, waiting for that moment of electricity, of connection. His lips hovered, only a moment away from mine. Anticipation and desire built, rose, spun together.

He dropped his forehead to mine. "Jesus, Claire." His voice was rough with desire, and I braced myself for the onslaught.

But then he stepped back.

My eyes flashed open. The loss of his body chilled me; I felt like I'd been doused with ice.

He pulled a hand across his jaw, his breath rough with unsatisfied longing.

"Liam?"

He shook his head, but not quite steadily. "I'm sorry, but this can't happen. I just can't afford you. But if things had been different . . ."

I stared at him. "What does that mean?"

The clock struck two. Liam lifted his gaze to the clock, then looked at me. "It's late. You need sleep, and I need to go. Now."

And with that, Liam Quinn slipped into the Quarter again.

CHAPTER TWELVE

So much of living after a war was adapting to what remained, figuring out how to build things you were familiar with out of what you had.

There was a brass mail slot in the store's front door. Since it was so hard to keep in touch without phones or computers, and mail delivery wasn't exactly efficient in the Zone, I let folks use the slot and a vintage cubby to share messages, trade goods. Customers—and that was the one catch: They had to be customers—could put their names on the cards in the cubby's metal label holders. It gave them comfort, a way to connect with people in a world that was so different from the one that had come before.

So, the next morning, after a night of what could only loosely be called "sleep," I picked up the messages and small packages that had been slipped into the slot overnight, and welcomed the handful of Containment agents who'd come by for provisions. Containment fed them, of course, but they'd buy an extra bar of soap or some sugar now and again.

While they perused my inventory, I took the stack of messages to the cubby, began to file them.

One was for me—a note from Gunnar on his own letterpressed

stationery, imported from outside the Zone: "Emme is awake and coping. She didn't see the wraiths before they attacked her, and the attack itself is mostly a blur, so no luck there. Thank you for last night. Love you."

I was glad to hear that she was safe, but disappointed that we wouldn't be able to confirm whether we were dealing with the same wraiths. At least not that way.

The day was absolutely beautiful. I'd propped open the front and back doors to let the breeze move through, put a Preservation Hall Jazz Band CD in an old player. Even Containment agents smiled at the music. It reminded all of us, I think, that there was still something beautiful in the world, even if we didn't see it every day in the Zone.

Unfortunately, jazz wasn't enough to take my mind off Liam Quinn. Last night had rocked me. To come so close to something I didn't even know I'd wanted, then to know that I did, only to have it ripped away . . . I wasn't exactly sure what was going through Liam's head, or what he couldn't "afford" about me. But I had a sinking suspicion. I was a Sensitive—a wraith-in-waiting. I would become a wraith if I couldn't learn to control my magic properly. If I wasn't vigilant enough, or if I made a mistake, I'd become the same monster that had killed his sister, that he hunted. How could he want me when that was the case?

Logic didn't work any better than jazz. I was embarrassed, sad, and getting in way over my head emotionally.

I was at the counter obsessing and organizing the month's receipt copies when Tadji breezed in. Today, she wore jeans and a blousy tank, a worn messenger bag strapped across her body. She looked cool and chic as always.

"It is amazing outside." She plopped the bag onto the counter. She was a welcome distraction.

"I know, right? It would be a beautiful day for a picnic by the river."

She grinned, pushed a curl behind her ear. "If we had wine and fruit and cheese?"

"We have MREs and cheese product. If that's good enough for Containment, it's good enough for us."

She snorted.

"How were your interviews?"

"Good," she said. "One down, two more to go."

She moved aside so I could take change from a man buying a *Times-Picayune*.

I thanked him, waited until the customer had waved his way out of the store. "Tell me about it," I said to Tadji.

"First lady was from a speck of a town halfway to Lafayette. Her son brings her into the city every few weeks to shop for supplies. That's how I heard about her."

"What's her name?"

"Delores Johnson."

I lifted my eyebrows. "She doesn't shop here."

"This isn't the only store in New Orleans."

I humphed. "The existence of other shops doesn't make it right. What did she have to say?"

"We talked about her history, her experiences. The way she thinks about the war and what's come after, about magic, about where she lives." She leaned on the counter, and her eyes lit with purpose. This was my favorite Tadji—because she looked happiest when she was working.

"It's really interesting, actually. She told me she used to be very focused on what came later—on her rewards in the next world, the afterlife, on what would happen to her family when she was gone, that type of thing. She was really focused on the future.

"But now, since magic's here, she talks about 'here' and 'now.' About 'power' and 'making' things, 'doing' things. War seems to have—I don't want to say 'centered' her, because it's war, after all—but maybe made her focus on the now."

"Interesting," I agreed. "She's got, what do they call it, 'agency' now?"

"Yeah. I think that's really where it's going. Is it legit agency? I mean, she's in a war zone. Can she actually do anything, or does she just perceive that she can?" She shrugged. "I don't know. But it's really interesting to watch how the change in language has mirrored the change in society."

"Agreed. I'm glad it was a good interview."

"Thanks. Any word about Emme?"

"Gunnar said she's awake. She apparently doesn't remember much."

"I probably wouldn't want to remember it, either. It's crazy, isn't it? Two wraiths running around for days causing trouble. You'd think Containment would have stopped them."

"It's still a big city, with a lot of places to hide," I said. "And the magic monitors can do only so much." Perversely, I was grateful for that right now.

"I know." Tadji cleared her throat. "Listen, I wanted to tell you, I'm trying to get in touch with my mom. Taking a trip to see them, maybe. It's been a really long time, and—I don't know." She looked up, stared absently. "These interviews just make me want to strengthen those connections."

I didn't bother to hide my surprise. "Really? I thought you didn't know where they were."

"I don't, exactly." She scratched absently at her arm. "But I know where we used to live. I figured that's the best place to start."

"How long has it been?"

"About two years."

"Time flies when you're having fun in a war zone."

She made a vague sound of agreement. "I guess."

I handed a customer a paper bag of goods I'd already packed for her that morning. She ran a tab with the store. I didn't do that for many, but her son outside the Zone sent money every few weeks, and she always paid as soon as she received it.

"Thank you, Mrs. Rosenberg," I said, and she nodded, carried the bag outside again.

Tadji had pulled a notebook out of her bag, was glancing at her notes. She'd broached the idea of her family, so maybe she'd be open to a few more questions. Even if she didn't talk about it much, I wondered if magic was on her mind as often as it was on mine.

"So, your mom, your aunt," I said quietly, although the store was empty. "You said they practiced voodoo when you were growing up?"

Tadji kept her eyes on her notebook. "Yeah."

"When the Veil opened. When we figured out magic was actually a thing. Do you think any of what they did . . . was real?"

She paused, then closed the notebook, put it carefully back in the bag. "I guess that depends on your perspective."

Not exactly an answer. "Where had they lived? They were north of Baton Rouge, right?"

She looked at me for a good, solid minute. "Does it matter?"

The tone in her voice had me standing up again. "Well, no. I was just asking."

She picked up the bag, slung it over her neck, adjusted it. "I should go. Next interview's in a few minutes."

"Tadji—"

But she shook her head. "I should go."

"Okay," I said hesitantly. "Be careful out there."

Tadji nodded, and I watched her leave, feeling like I'd screwed up my second relationship in two days.

I was living two lives—one magical, one nonmagical. And keeping the boundaries clear was getting more and more complicated.

Business was brisk. I was glad to have something else to think about, even if it was hard to concentrate on soap and batteries when my mind was occupied by Containment, Paranormals, wraiths, and now Tadji and Liam.

Half past noon, the door's bell jangled. A man I'd never seen before walked in.

He was tall, with tousled brown hair atop a high forehead. His eyes were green and deep set, crowned by thick eyebrows. He wore a gray suit with a vest, and a button-up shirt. I couldn't remember the last time I'd seen a man in a suit.

I pegged him as Containment. And even though I'd been helping Containment personnel all morning, there was something different about him. He was an unknown—and that scared me.

He walked toward the counter, smiled. "Jack Broussard," he said, pulling out a black leather wallet that held his identification badge.

I glanced at it, nodded, while my stomach clenched with nerves. I didn't think there was a reason for me to be nervous about being a Sensitive—not when we'd taken care of the evidence—but the fact that we'd taken care of the evidence was probably a problem. Still, getting riled up wasn't going to help anything, so I made myself stay calm.

"Claire Connolly."

He put away the wallet again, gaze catching the owl walking stick, still on the counter, still gearless. He ran a thumb over the brass. "This is nice."

"Thanks. It's broken at the moment, but I'll have it fixed soon enough. Are you in the market?"

"Agents can't afford antiques."

"More's the pity," I said. "What can I help you with, Mr. Broussard?"

"Jack is fine," he said "I'm just here to ask some questions— follow up with your interview about the wraith incident Sunday night. You were working at the store on War Night?"

I figured he wouldn't have been in the store if he didn't already know the answer to his question. But there was no point in making things difficult for myself. "Yeah. I was here until about six. I walked in the parade with my friends until about two, then came back to the store and saw the girl being attacked."

He nodded, moved down a few feet to peer into a case that held mostly costume jewelry. "Your father owned this store, and your grandfather before him?"

"And my great-grandfather before him."

"And now you run the store?"

Why is it your business? was what I wanted to say. But I kept my tone light, even though I didn't like where this was going. "I always helped out. But when the war started, my dad started selling dry goods, supplies. I became more involved. And when he died, I took it over."

Broussard nodded. "Are you aware, Ms. Connolly, that there were questions about your father?"

I blinked at him, not understanding the implication. "Questions about what?"

"About which side he was on."

I snorted. "Which side? I think you've been reading the wrong records."

"I take it you weren't aware of your father's paranormal activities?"

"My father wasn't involved in any paranormal activities. He sold antiques, and when the war started, he sold supplies." There was, of course, the little matter of the building's insulation, but I was almost positive that wasn't my father's doing. An accident of war, of magic. But nothing he'd had a part in. If he'd had magic, or was close to someone who had, he'd have told me.

And even if he'd had a paranormal friend who'd insulated the building, there was absolutely no doubt about my father's loyalties. Broussard was just trying to rile me up.

"That's not the information we have."

"Then your information is wrong." I could hear my tone turn snappy but didn't bother to change it. His question was ridiculous and insulting. "My family kept this neighborhood alive during the war. We helped the military get supplies before Containment or Materiel existed. We fed soldiers when convoys were late. We stocked MREs so civilians would have food. My father died because of his war injuries. You want to know which side he was on? He was on New Orleans's side."

"My apologies. No offense meant."

"Really? I'm pretty sure you said it just to gauge my reaction. So I think offense was quite intended."

His jaw tightened. "I'm doing my job."

"Which is?"

"Taking care of this city."

I gestured at the store. "Then that makes two of us."

"I understand you're friends with Liam Quinn."

I felt the blush creep across my cheeks. "I wouldn't say friends." I wouldn't say a lot of things, but "friends" didn't really seem to cover it.

"What would you say?"

Stick to what Containment already knew, I told myself. "As you're probably aware, he's training me."

"You accompanied him into Devil's Isle."

"He thought I'd be a good bounty hunter. He wanted me to see it."

Broussard leaned against the counter. "Being a bounty hunter would be a big change from running this shop."

"I've already fought two wraiths," I pointed out. "And I still run the shop."

"Touché, Ms. Connolly." He straightened, adjusted his suit jacket. "I understand you've seen his apartment."

If the quick change of topic was supposed to trip me up, it succeeded. It figured there'd be cameras in Devil's Isle, but not that Containment would have been interested enough to trace my movements, or his. Still, there was no point in lying, or in elaborating too much.

"Very briefly."

"You know his sister died, and he has an unhealthy obsession with the manner of her death."

I lifted my eyebrows. Had he seen the board, too? Had Containment been in Liam's apartment? "His sister's killer was a wraith. His job is hunting them." I shrugged. "That seems pretty logical to me."

"Does it? Or does it sound like a man obsessed? A man not quite stable?"

I wasn't sure Containment was the best judge of anyone's stability these days. "You'd have to take that up with him. Like I said, he's training me, not psychoanalyzing me, or vice versa."

Broussard nodded deeply, as though he was mulling over important, weighty things. "I could do that. I could talk to him. Wouldn't be that hard to do." He looked at me, considering. "He did mention that he investigated your father? Before he was shot, I mean?"

All the sound in the world dropped away. I'd never stood in silence so immense as the silence that fell around me in the wake of that question.

I'd gone into Devil's Isle with Liam Quinn. I'd met his grandmother. He'd been in my store, met my friends, seen my magic. I'd told him things about me, about my family.

Maybe Broussard was lying. Maybe this was a setup, a trick, to get me to turn on Liam. But maybe it wasn't. And he'd been hiding from me that he believed my father could have been a traitor.

Broussard watched my reaction, could probably see my skin buzzing with sudden and unexpected fury. "I see he didn't tell you. That's curious, don't you think?"

He managed to look concerned, like he actually cared about my reaction, about my possible hurt. But I didn't want his pity. And I certainly didn't want his truth. I had my own to deal with.

I slid the owl closer, picked up a set of tweezers, was proud that my fingers weren't shaking, because it was taking monumental control. "Get out of my store. And don't come back unless you have a warrant."

Broussard held up his hands. "I just thought you should know. In these times, we all have to figure out who to trust. In the meantime, be careful. It's dangerous out there."

I needed space. I needed air. The store felt suddenly stifling, the walls too close, my emotions too high.

I had to get out.

I'd go to the garden, my plot on the top of the former Florissant Hotel. There wouldn't be anyone there, and it was up and away from Royal Street. I grabbed an apron and a canvas-lined garden basket from a hook in the kitchenette, flipped the CLOSED sign on the door, and locked up again.

I walked toward the river, passing the alley where my life had changed so suddenly only a couple of days ago. I passed the front of the abandoned hotel, the restaurant that had taken up a corner of the space completely empty, just like the rest of the hotel. Everything potentially useful had been removed long ago—from the chairs in the lobby to the snacks in the minibars. It had been scary and depressing, but also a little impressive, how carefully people could strip a hotel down to its bones.

I slipped around the building to the fire escape, pulled down to give those of us with plots access to the roof, and climbed the steps. The edge of the building was marked by potted trees and plants that received plenty of water and light on the open-air terrace. A cabana at the far end had once held a poolside bar. It was now the storage room for extra pots, tools, and consecrated earth. There was a compost bin on the far end of the patio.

We'd shored up the rafters beneath the pool, filled it with dirt, and turned it into a garden for small trees and plants with longer root systems. The rest of the patio held raised rectangular planters where we could grow plants of our choice.

I grew vegetables for me, Gunnar, Tadji, and a few other friends who lived in the Quarter, mostly older folks who'd survived the war and didn't have any plans to leave, but also didn't have many resources. I sold any extras in the store.

October was leaf and root harvest time in our little Louisiana garden—kale, collards, spinach, carrots, beets. I put the basket on the ground and tied on the apron. I pulled the few weeds that had snuck into my box, scooped a few ladles of collected rainwater over plants that looked dry, and picked off dead leaves.

When my little plot was tidy, I got to the good part. I snipped spinach and collard leaves, tossed them into my basket. Three carrots, including a white variety that looked like a really creepy finger, and four small beets. Personally, I thought beets were disgusting and tasted like dirt. But they had plenty of fans in the Quarter.

I shook the excess dirt off the beets, put them carefully in the basket so I didn't stain the canvas. Beets stained easily, but made a pretty good fabric dye.

As I thought of the perfectly fucking fantastic ways to use these perfectly fucking fantastic beets, I used a dirty glove to wipe tears from my face, probably smearing dirt across it in the process.

I thought I'd found someone who could relate to what I'd been going through. I felt mortified. And completely and utterly betrayed.

Had any of it been real? His being in my store on War Night? Taking me into Devil's Isle to "help" me? Or was this all some sort of plan? Liam Quinn, bounty hunter, just continuing his work investigating the traitorous members of the Connolly family?

I felt really stupid. And the fact that last night had almost happened—that near kiss—just made the pain keener.

I pulled off the gloves, threw them down, then walked to the edge of the roof and stared out at the city. Slate roofs, black balconies, gaps of broken buildings and rubble that stood out like missing piano keys. And in the distance, the glowing hulk of Devil's Isle, of the prison I was trying to avoid.

Somehow I'd backed right up against it.

I put my elbows on the parapet, watched the river slink by. For just a minute, I let myself indulge in fantasy. I thought of grabbing my go bag and making a real exit this time. Starting over without the Quarter, Containment, Quinn. I'd give myself a new name, maybe cut and dye my hair. My gun was in the safe, extra bullets. I could use that to hunt what game was left, find a place to camp out. Or maybe find some of Nix's friends, a roaming band of "good" Consularis Paras to hang out with, to avoid Containment with.

I sighed, wiped my cheeks. It always came back to Containment. As long as you were in the Zone, Containment would be there.

I stood up again, shook off the self-pity. It wasn't attractive, and more important, it wasn't useful. Running when I didn't think I had a choice was one thing. But right now I had choices.

I also had a few questions for Mr. Quinn.

He walked in at six o'clock, a smile on his face, and even more stubble. He wore a couple of fitted, layered T-shirts today, jeans, and boots. The shirts were snug enough that I could see the bulge of his gun. If I hadn't been so pissed at him, I'd have said he wore the entire ensemble very, very well.

Liam took in the top, skirt, tights, and boots I'd worn today since the weather had cooled a little, offered a friendly smile. "You look nice. You gonna be all right if you get the ensemble a little scuffed up?"

The smile couldn't compete with the tension between us, or my anger. Ignoring the question, I walked to the front door, locked it. I didn't want to be interrupted.

His smile had vanished when I turned around again. "What's wrong?"

"I want the truth. About everything."

Liam put his hands on his hips, frowned. "The truth about what? What are you talking about?" He paused, uncertain for once. "Is this about last night?"

My cheeks warmed. "No, it's not about last night. A Containment agent came to see me today. And he wanted to talk about you."

Liam froze, gaze narrowing at me like a predator ferreting out his prey. Or maybe vice versa. "Which agent?"

"Jack Broussard."

His face didn't register surprise or anything else. "I see."

"Are you going to tell me?"

Liam watched me as silence fell heavy around us.

"Did you investigate my father?"

If I'd surprised him, he didn't show it. But then again, he wouldn't have. And he didn't answer, which only made my fury bloom hotter.

"Was this all a ruse? Your being here in the store that night? Helping me get into Devil's Isle? Are you trying to get information about Sensitives? Is this some sort of sting operation?" My mind spun, trying to make sense of the web he'd woven, the complications, the details.

"*No,*" Liam said, the word forceful enough to snap my gaze to his. His eyes gleamed like hot sapphires. "No, damn it. It wasn't any of that. It's not any of that." He ran a hand across his mouth, jaw. "Sit down, Claire."

"Tell me."

When I stared back at him, he closed his eyes, looked like he was praying for guidance. He wasn't the only one.

Liam pulled out two chairs at the table. "*Please* sit down, Claire."

I sat down, but Liam didn't. Not yet. He walked back to the kitchen, and I heard drawers opening and closing. Dizziness had settled in, just enough to make my hands shake. When he came back with a bottle of cold water, I twisted off the cap, gulped.

He sat down in the other chair, angled it to face mine, and ran his hands through his hair. Then he leaned forward, elbows on his knees, and looked at me.

And he told me his story.

CHAPTER THIRTEEN

"I'm twenty-seven," Liam said. "I was twenty when the war started. A junior at Xavier. I'd planned to go to law school, mostly because that's what Eleanor expected.

"When the house was destroyed, we lost everything that mattered to us. We still had money, but what good would that have done in the Zone? There was nowhere to spend it, and we'd missed the exodus by two weeks, and they'd started closing borders to keep the war contained. So we weren't leaving, and I had to keep my family safe. I walked into the Cabildo—that was when the army was still set up there—and they hired me as a contractor."

"What did you do?"

"We had land, and I liked camping, hunting, was a pretty good shot, good tracker—not as good as Gavin, but pretty good—and knew my way around southern Louisiana. So I did pretty much whatever they wanted that would pay the bills. I escorted convoys, worked as a scout, hunted when a convoy couldn't make it in. This is when I met the gardener—that Sensitive I told you about."

I nodded.

"About six months into the war—this would have been April—

Containment got worried. We'd lost battles at Shreveport and Vicksburg."

I nodded, remembering. We'd had a shortwave radio in the store—that was when stations were still broadcasting in the Zone—and we'd listened to the reports. The reporter had cried when giving the casualty numbers. There were apocalyptic cults carrying signs through the Quarter, promising the end of the world had been coming. I'd been terrified, and barely more than a kid. But eventually the tide had turned, and we'd closed the Veil.

"Containment was aware that I was pretty well-known in New Orleans. Connected, I guess."

"Because of your family? Because you're an Arsenault?"

He nodded, linked his hands together, stared down at the floor. "New Orleans had always loved magic—hell, half the tourism in the Quarter was built on it—ghosts, vampires, voodoo—and Containment wanted to know if any residents were sympathetic to the Paras. If they might do anything that would subvert our defenses, or help the Paras."

He wet his lips, looked up at me. "Do you remember the Hanlon family?"

I frowned. "The ones involved in the cult?" They'd decided the end of the world was coming, and they wanted to be at the front of the line. They killed two human soldiers as a "sacrifice," began funneling food and supplies to the Paras.

"Yeah. I investigated them . . . and then I turned them in." He shifted in his seat. And when he couldn't get comfortable, he rose, walked to the windows in the front of the store, looked out at the city.

"I investigated them because they were on a list Containment gave me." He turned, looked back at me. "Your father was on the list, too."

My heart seemed to stop beating. "So you spied on my father? On me?"

"I kept watch on him," he said carefully. "Containment wasn't interested in you."

That didn't make it any better. "You were watching him because he might have been a traitor. Because Containment thought he might be a traitor."

"We were in the middle of a war."

"Damn it." I stood up, paced across the room, then paced back again. "He died in the war," I pointed out when I was facing Liam again. "Because he was fighting for us. There was *no* reason at all for him to be on any list."

"It's not that simple."

"How isn't it simple? Your investigating my father as a traitor? That seems pretty simple."

"Because I *should* have turned him in. Your father was a Sensitive."

I stared at him. "What? No, he wasn't," I said, my voice barely competing with the roaring in my ears.

"He was. He hid it very well. From you, from everyone."

"No. *No*, that's a mistake." I pointed at him. "You're wrong. He would have told me if he was a Sensitive. We were really close, Liam. He would have told me."

"I'm sure he wanted to protect you. To keep you away from all this. From exactly this conversation we're having right now."

"No," I said, shaking my head. "This isn't right."

But wasn't there evidence to the contrary? "The insulation," I quietly said, staring at the brick wall. "He must have had a friend. Another Sensitive, or a Paranormal."

"Maybe," Liam agreed. "I didn't know the building was insulated until last night. Anyway, I had already begun to learn that not all

Sensitives had to become dangerous. He wasn't the only one I didn't turn in. Containment didn't know that I wasn't turning Sensitives in, of course, because there was no incriminating evidence that any of them were actually Sensitives. But my handler didn't like it. He believed, and apparently still believes, that I was disloyal to the city, to the country. He terminated my contract."

The pieces fell into place. "Jack Broussard was your handler."

He nodded. "He's had it in for me since then."

"Wait, so how did you become a bounty hunter? I mean, if Broussard had it in for you, and terminated your contract, how did you get Containment to pay your bounties?"

"Those family friends in PCC that I mentioned," he said. "As you've seen, Broussard's not especially worried about pissing people off. He hasn't always towed the PCC line, so he has plenty of enemies inside and outside the agency. I had a good record, and there wasn't any evidence your father was a Sensitive. He was extraordinarily careful."

"If he was careful," I said quietly, "how did you know?"

Liam looked at me. "I saw him one night. I was watching the store. The power was out, but I saw a flash of light."

"Candles or something," I suggested.

Liam shook his head. "There was a glow in the air, like a sphere of light. And when he moved, when he walked, it followed him. It only lasted for a few seconds. He was probably looking for something in the store, didn't think about what he was doing."

Something in my heart softened, warmed. "My father could make light?"

Liam nodded. "I get that wraiths are dangerous and any Sensitive can become one. And I saw the result of that. Gracie saw the result of that. But I don't understand why Containment won't *help*

Sensitives. Why they won't acknowledge it can be done. Ignoring it just feeds the problem, puts more monsters on the street."

I flinched at the word.

Liam made a frustrated sound, ran his hands through his hair. "Damn, Claire. I'm sorry Broussard's dragged you into this. I guess he does believe in the sins of the father."

I nodded, walked back to the table on wobbling knees, sat down. I needed to pause, to think. I pressed my fingers against my eyes, like I could block out the world. Like I could change history altogether. But that was an impossible dream. A child's dream. And I hadn't been a child for a really long time.

I heard him move back toward me, felt the air change as he took his seat again. "Why did Broussard come to me now?" I asked, opening my eyes.

Liam shook his head. "I don't know. Containment has seen us together twice, three times if anyone saw us at the Landreaus' house. What did he ask you about?"

"He asked how well I knew you. He said you were obsessed with wraiths because of Gracie."

"He's not wrong."

No, he wasn't, I thought. "Broussard will be back. If he thinks he can use me to get to you, or vice versa, he won't stop."

"You're probably right."

Silence descended.

"I'm sorry," he said again. "I should have been honest with you. I just—I didn't want to hurt you. And if he hadn't told you, I wasn't sure I should be the one."

I nodded, looked up at him. "Thank you for not turning him in. I wish you'd told me—but I'm more pissed he didn't tell me himself. That—that hurts," I admitted. "A lot."

And all my father's talk about keeping my head down. Was that what he'd been doing? Hiding who he was? He couldn't have been hiding completely. Not if he'd known someone well enough to get the building insulated, presumably so he could practice his magic. And knowing that he'd shared himself with someone else didn't help.

Liam made a sound of agreement. "I'm not thrilled with your father, either. Even if he hadn't known you'd become a Sensitive, he could have let you see that side of him. That might have made your last eight months easier."

"I'm sure he thought he was protecting me," I said, but I couldn't muster much enthusiasm. "Just like you did."

Liam nodded. "And we can see how well that turned out. From now on," he said, gaze on me, "no more omissions. We both deserve better."

"Yeah. We do."

I was suddenly exhausted. I wanted nothing more than to climb into bed and stay there for a week. But we still had work to do.

I stood up. "We were going hunting."

Liam's gaze snapped up. "You still want to go?"

"The wraiths who hurt Emme are still out there. And there's no chance Containment is going to change its position about Sensitives if wraith attacks are getting worse. Figuring out what's happening is the only way to ensure that it doesn't happen to me."

Liam stood up. "You're pretty remarkable, Claire Connolly."

"Thanks," I said. *But still, potentially, a wraith.*

On the way toward the door, I grabbed another bottle of water and a granola bar, then stopped at the counter. While Liam glanced back, I opened the safe, pulled out the black handgun my father had given me, confirmed the safety was on, careful to keep my finger away from the trigger.

Liam walked back. "That's the gun?" He didn't need to say it—it was the one I'd killed Paras with.

I nodded, pulled back the slide, checked the chamber. It was empty. I popped out the magazine, checked it. It was full, so I snapped it home again.

"How's your aim?"

"I can hit the side of a barn." I was better with tiny gears than faraway targets. But I was good enough to be safe.

"Can you shoot a wraith?"

I looked down at the gun. "There's no way to bring a wraith back. To make them whole again. So yeah, if lives are in danger, I can." I didn't want to consider whether it would be better to kill it or leave it alive for a never-ending term in Devil's Isle.

I pulled out the waistband holster I kept with it in the safe, clipped it into the waistband of my skirt, situated the gun, and looked up at him. "You ready?"

His eyebrows were lifted in amusement. "I am, Annie Oakley. *Allons.*"

"And once again in English?"

"Let's go."

That I could do.

We locked up the store, walked outside, an entirely new awkwardness settling between us.

I hadn't noticed how Liam had gotten to the store. It wasn't pretty. A mostly rusty pickup truck, the paint that remained a chalky green. It hadn't aged well.

I climbed into the passenger side, slammed the door to close it, and still wasn't entirely sure I'd closed it all the way. "This is quite a vehicle."

"She gets the job done. Outfitted to require as little electricity as possible. But yeah, she's not gonna win any beauty pageants." Liam turned the ignition, and the truck rumbled to life.

"Where are we going?"

"Garden District. That's the last point of contact for the wraiths. I want to see if we can find them again."

I nodded, rolled the window down, letting in the breeze. Liam rounded through the Quarter to get back to Canal, and I watched the sun set behind burned-out buildings and palm trees. There were no people in sight.

Starving, I pulled out my granola bar, peeled down the wrapper. I broke off a chunk, held it out to Liam. "You want some?"

He glanced down at it, then me. "You sure?"

"Positive. But don't get too excited."

He accepted the chunk, popped it into his mouth, grimaced. "Damn. This is not good," he said over a mouthful of stale crumbs.

"No, it isn't," I said, chewing my half. "Probably old," I added, but I didn't dare check the expiration date. We were a little looser with expiration and "best by" dates these days. Most of the time, that was fine. Other times, you ate a granola bar that tasted like glued-together dust.

"Speaking of not good, I think your seat's just about out of cushion." I squirmed, trying to find a comfortable position. It was like sitting on a concrete block covered in marbles.

The truck backfired, bouncing us in our seats and sending a cloud of blue-gray smoke behind us.

"And she's easily offended," I said, then patted the dashboard. "I don't fault you. I fault your lackadaisical owner."

Liam grunted, turned down St. Charles, slowing as he reached the Garden District proper, rolled down his window. The truck wasn't exactly quiet, but without streetcars or planes or the sounds of urban people, we could still hear crickets chirping in the grass, taking advantage of the extended summer.

We passed the Landreaus' house, the lights on and warmly glowing. Gunnar was probably having dinner with them, keeping an eye on Emme to make sure she was all right.

Liam drove slowly, eyes peeled for the wraiths, just in case they'd been nesting near the house. But there was no sign of them.

He turned southeast onto Fourth Street. It was one-way in the opposite direction, but that hardly mattered now.

The houses ranged in size, but most had been well cared for before the war, with wrought-iron or brick or vine-covered fences to separate their kingdoms from their neighbors'. Almost all the houses that remained were dark, the surviving trees and grass overgrown, the batteries in the cars long since dead. The asphalt was cracked, as were the sidewalks that alternated between concrete and brick. It had been a long time since the neighborhood got TLC.

"I used to walk the houses," he said.

I glanced at him. His gaze was on a small carriage house lined against the sidewalk, its door yawning open. "Walk them?"

"The empty ones. I'd let myself in—"

"As you like to do."

He snorted. "The store's door was unlocked. As for the houses, I never went through a locked door. Didn't want anyone looting behind me. But if I had time to kill, and a door was unlocked, I'd walk through. Take a look. See how they lived. What their lives were like."

That was a side of Liam Quinn I wouldn't have expected to see. "And what were they like?"

He frowned, considered. "Some of the houses were completely

empty. They'd taken everything they could. In others, it was like, I don't know, spying on someone's life. There were still clothes in the closets. Magazines on the coffee table. Toys in the kids' rooms. The beds were made up. Lot more mildew, sometimes mold, because of the humidity, but otherwise—they were just houses. I wondered where the people went."

"Did you ever take anything?"

"No, but I've thought about it. Closest I've come was a house in Gentilly. I'd been tracking a wraith, lost him, but saw this house and went inside. Most of it was packed up—you could tell they'd left—but they'd left behind a few things. Big furniture. Mirrors. Some toys and sports equipment. And in one room—looked like the dad's office—there were model airplanes hanging from the ceiling, probably a dozen of them. Lot of work went into them. I thought about liberating one. Seemed a shame all that work was going to waste."

"So why didn't you take it?"

He shrugged. "Because maybe they'll come back one day. Or maybe the kids will. And those memories should be there for them. Should belong to them. Not to me."

I could practically feel my heart melting. "You know, you play the tough guy, but I think you've got a pretty gooey heart in there, Quinn."

Liam snorted, opened his mouth to respond, but didn't have a chance. There was a streak of movement in front of us, a squeal.

"Shit," Liam called out, then slammed on the brakes, throwing out an arm to keep me from flying forward.

The truck ground to a halt with a screech of tires. My heart pounded so loudly I'd have been surprised if he couldn't hear it.

"Wraith?" I whispered.

He nodded and pulled back his arm. Wraith-in-front-of-the-truck being a classic move to get to second base quickly.

He pulled out a flashlight, switched it on, bobbed the circle across the street. There was a *pop*, and the light dimmed, went out, as did the truck's headlights.

"Son of a bitch," he said, thumping a hand on the dashboard. It didn't help.

"Magic and electricity."

"Yeah," he said.

It was dark as pitch, hard to see without any sort of light, especially on streets overgrown with magnolias and crepe myrtles.

"Did you see it?"

"I think it was a girl." I thought I'd seen a glimpse of long hair, maybe a red skirt. But she'd moved fast, crossing the street and stepping into the yard beyond before I'd gotten a good look at her. "She ran away," I said.

"Yeah, I noticed that."

"No, think about it: She only ran because she saw us. What kind of wraith does that? What kind of wraith doesn't attack outright?" She also hadn't seemed to care about my magic, but I was in the truck. Maybe that hadn't been close enough.

Liam stared into the dark. "That's a very good question." He switched off the ignition, popped open the glove box, took out a small black case.

"What's that?"

"Tranqs," he said. "They don't last very long, but if we can get into a position to use them, we can keep her from hurting herself or us."

Since we didn't have a tranq gun, I guessed that "position" meant close enough to punch in a syringe. That was pretty damn close.

Liam looked at me. "Is there any point in telling you to stay in the car?"

"No."

"I didn't think so. The power's out, so the monitors won't be on, nor will the cameras. You can use your magic if you have to, but you should be careful. You may not know when the power's back on."

I nodded. "I'll be careful."

He left the truck running. The starter was probably electric, and if the power stayed out and he turned it off, he wouldn't be able to restart it, and we'd be walking back to the Quarter.

"Follow me," Liam said, then opened the truck's door slowly and quietly. He climbed out, offered me a hand, and I slid across cracked leather and down onto the street beside him. He closed the door just enough to get it out of the way, but didn't bother shutting it. I'd yet to see a wraith who could hot-wire a vehicle. On the other hand, if they were getting smarter . . .

He moved in front of the car, checked the ground. "I don't think we hit her," he whispered, then gestured toward the sidewalk. He looked back at me, put a finger to his lips. I nodded my agreement. I wanted to hear her coming. Staying quiet was the only chance I'd have for that.

We stepped onto the sidewalk, bricks in a herringbone pattern that no longer lay flat, and trod carefully over the uneven surface. There were two houses with a small strip of grass and rocks in between. Probably where the homeowners had parked their cars. One of the houses was a narrow town house. The other was a white two-story house with Greek columns running down the front, and a triangular roof on top.

Liam crouched down, checked the ground, then gestured toward the columned house. He must have seen footprints.

I followed him to the porch, and he took a careful step onto it. Seven years without maintenance could create a lot of problems. When it held his weight, he gestured for me to follow him.

The door was open. He pushed it open a little more, waited in the doorway for any sign of life—or wraith. There was nothing, so he stepped inside.

The wind was picking up, leaves and debris stirring on the porch as I followed Liam into the house. It was pitch-black and smelled dusty. Musty. The humans who'd stayed behind probably would have cleaned it out of anything valuable. But that didn't mean a wraith wouldn't nest here.

We let our eyes adjust to the darkness, until we could tell the house's central hallway split off into rooms on the left and right.

A sound broke the silence—a warbling moan, definitely female. It seemed to come from every room, and set every hair on my body on end.

Was the wraith calling out to us? Or to more wraiths?

"She's making noises," Liam whispered. He was close enough that I could feel the warmth of his body. That comforted me more than it should have.

"Which direction?" he asked quietly.

"I couldn't tell." And now I could barely hear over the beating of my own heart. Facing down a wraith on a well-lit street was one thing. Wandering through a dark and abandoned house in a dark and abandoned city was something completely different. I didn't believe in ghosts; but if I did, I'd have believed they lived here, in this memorial to a different time.

The sound echoed through the house again.

"I'll go left," I whispered. "You go right."

He grabbed my hand. "You'll stay with me."

"We don't have time for that. The house is too big. We go together, we might miss her, and we'll never find her again in the dark."

We stood there in silence for a moment. "If you need me, call my name."

"I will."

And then he stepped away, letting the chill settle between us again.

I moved to the threshold of the first room, walked inside. I could see the silhouettes of furniture, a mirror above a fireplace that reflected only darkness.

I paused, waited to hear movement, or more sounds, but there was nothing. A breeze blew from a doorway on the other side of the room.

I walked toward it, jumped when I ran into a spiderweb dangling from the ceiling, pushed it away.

The next room was a kitchen. A U-shaped set of cabinets with an island in the middle, a small table and ladder-back chairs on the other side of the room. It still looked clean—no piles of empty cans and bottles. Maybe the looters hadn't gotten to it.

She came from out of nowhere. Suddenly, she was screaming and lunging as she tried to claw at me, as if she could dig through skin to get to the magic I'd absorbed. She might have run before, but now we were in her territory. We'd cornered her, and she'd protect herself.

I jumped back, moved around the kitchen island, putting the furniture between us, got my first look at her. She was pale and thin, her hair blond and stringy. But I didn't think she was as far gone as the wraiths on War Night.

"Liam! I found her!"

She opened her mouth, made that sound again. She garbled, part whimper, part moan, part horrible, guttural scream. But I'd have sworn it sounded like an actual word. Something like "context."

"What did you say?"

"*Connnnteshtt!*"

It could have been a word, but I wasn't sure. Couldn't tell.

"I hear you," I said, stepping forward. "I'm listening to you, trying to hear what you tell me."

I put a hand on the gun. Could have drawn it. But I felt too much pity.

Liam had been right. I couldn't do it. Not against someone who hadn't been as lucky as me.

But I had other tools. There was a table and chairs to her left. If I could grab one of the chairs, I could use it like a shield. Maybe trap her against the wall until Liam got here with the tranqs.

I felt around for the magic, began to spin it together, to gather it up.

She screamed again, sensing the gathering of magic, the thing she wanted more than anything else in the world, and she rushed me. She didn't bother going around the island. She vaulted it like an animal, landed on me so we both hit the floor.

Fear tore through me, sharp as her broken and ragged nails. She smelled old and sour, and she looked brittle, but like the War Night wraiths, she was strong, as though magic had concentrated her strength.

She snapped at me, screamed that word—or the sound, or the moan—again and again. I used one hand to try to hold her back, and with the other, I reached out for the chair, pulling power and wood at the same time. But instead of flying toward me, it skittered across the floor, fell over, scraped against hardwood.

She grabbed a lock of my hair, pulled, and yelled again.

"Damn it," I said against the pain, and reached out for the chair again, pushing all my energy into a final surge of magic.

This time, the chair rushed toward me. I grabbed the back with both hands, used the legs to pry her off me and onto the floor. I scrambled to my feet, using the chair legs to pin her to the floor.

Liam appeared in the doorway in front of us, looked obviously relieved to find me mostly upright and the wraith on the floor, although squirming like a fish.

"When I told you about the tranq, this wasn't the plan I had in mind."

I blew the hair from my eyes. "Thank you for pretending this looks like something I planned."

He went down on a knee beside her, opened the case, pulled out a syringe, and pressed it against her neck. A few more seconds of struggling, and she went visibly limp.

He helped me to my feet. "You're all right?"

"I'm fine." I pushed the hair from my face, pulled down the skirt I'd rumpled in the battle, and looked down at the wraith at my feet. "What's next?"

"Now we take her home."

CHAPTER FOURTEEN

We rumbled back to the French Quarter and the Devil's Isle gate, white clouds moving above us. We had headlights again by the time we reached Canal Street. I downed the rest of the water on the trip, along with an ancient stick of beef jerky Liam found in the glove box. It took the edge off the dizziness, but I was going to crash hard later.

I told Liam about the girl, what she'd said, as lightning forked across the sky. A storm was coming.

"If that means anything," he said, "I don't recognize it."

So much for that clue.

He parked the truck near the gate, frowned at me. "You want to stay here?"

I shook my head. "No."

"It might be tough to see—to watch. They'll probably jacket her. And if she wakes up, they'll have to sedate her. She probably won't react well to that."

I could see the war in his eyes. There was always a chance I could end up in Devil's Isle, too. And if I did, he was the one who'd have to bring me here.

If things had been different . . .

But they weren't. There was a big part of me that wanted to say no, to stay in the car and let him take care of this part of it. But that wasn't fair to him, and denial wasn't going to do me any good, either.

"I'll go," I said. "I'm not afraid." It was a lie, but I thought he needed to hear it.

"Okay. Then let's hurry." Liam lifted the girl into his arms effortlessly, walked toward the guardhouse.

The guard, who couldn't have been more than nineteen, kept a nervous hand on the gun at his waist. "Stop," he said, holding up a hand. "Stop right there."

"I'm Liam Quinn, and I'm a bounty hunter." He nodded at the girl. "As you can tell, she's a wraith. And we've got about five more minutes before the tranq wears off. I need to get her to the clinic and in a jacket before that happens."

"I—I need some identification."

"It's in my pocket." He nodded toward me. "Claire. Back right, please."

I nodded, slipped the wallet from the back pocket of his jeans. I pretended not to notice the rest of the architecture.

"Four minutes and forty-five seconds," Liam said as I held the wallet out to the guard for scanning. When he was done with it, I put it back in my pocket. We could settle up later.

"What about her?" the guard asked.

"She's my trainee. Four minutes and thirty-five seconds. I've got a weapon, and you can remove it, or I can keep it on in case she loses it before we get there."

The guard looked nervously at me, Liam, the girl in his arms. "Fine. Okay, fine."

We headed in the opposite direction of Eleanor's house, closer to the Quarter than Bywater this time. And it wasn't as late as the last time we'd come through, and there were more Paras out today.

Mostly adults, a few children. A family of Paras with striking red skin and spaded tails, two children chasing each other on a long stretch of grass that had once been Elysian Fields Avenue. I didn't know enough about the Beyond to know if that was horribly ironic or poetically appropriate.

The clinic was only a few blocks from the gate, but we were jogging by the time we reached it. It was a two-story town house on Frenchmen Street that faced Washington Square. Two pale blue floors of windows with white shutters, a wrought-iron balcony surrounding the top floor.

"It's not very big," I said.

"This is just the first building. They use all the buildings on the block, keep everybody separated."

He reached the door, pushed it open with a foot, maneuvered the girl inside.

I didn't remember the building from before the war, but it looked like an office. The door opened into a small hallway with an empty reception desk and couple of old chairs. Ancient and scarred hardwood floors led down a corridor, with other rooms leading to the right. It was still an old building, and the walls and ceiling were thin. Thumps and muffled voices—some of them very unhappy—echoed through the room.

The girl began to stir.

"Lizzie!" Liam called out, over the din of sound. "I need you!"

There were footsteps, and then a woman appeared on the threshold in brilliant orange. She was slender, a few inches over five feet, with tan skin. Her thick, dark hair was cropped into a bob just above her shoulders and streaked with yellow and orange. Her nose was small and straight, but her irises were the color of flame, and they shifted and shimmered just like forks of fire. There were streaks of color along her neck that disappeared into her top, reappeared below the sleeves to travel to the tips of her fingers. Just like fire, they shifted and moved like flames dancing across her skin.

Lizzie definitely wasn't human. A fire spirit of some sort, by my guess.

She spared me a glance, looked at Liam. "I hope you tranq'd her this time."

"Yeah. And it's wearing off."

She nodded, put two fingers in her mouth, and whistled shrilly. There were footsteps, and two men in scrubs appeared in the doorway. "Get her jacketed first, then get her into a room."

The first orderly came over, his eyes the same burning embers, and let Liam transfer the girl into his arms. They trotted out of the room, down the hallway.

Lizzie pushed a hand through her hair, the fire on her hand shifting as she moved. Like fire itself, it was a little scary, a little awesome. "Haven't seen you this week."

"Long story," Liam said, then gestured at me. "Lizzie, this is Claire Connolly. Claire, Lizzie."

"Hi, Claire." Lizzie looked me over, the fire in her eyes sparking when she reached my face again. I didn't know how she'd done it, but there wasn't a doubt in my mind that she knew what I was.

"Well," she said, smiling, "that's an interesting development."

"I'm being careful," Liam said.

"I certainly hope so. And that she is, too."

"She is," I said, meeting her gaze. I was in the mood for answers. "What happens to the wraiths when they're brought in?"

"They're cared for as best we can. We try to keep them calm, keep them fed, keep them clean. Until someone comes up with a cure, that's all we can do."

"And Sensitives?"

She gestured to a couple of stingy chairs in the waiting area, and perched on the edge of the desk.

"Sensitives are in a separate ward," she said. "Same protocol—calm, comfortable, cared for. But any magical practice—even the regulation of magic—is forbidden here."

"That's ridiculous," I whispered through gritted teeth. "It would keep them from becoming wraiths."

"But it's the Containment way." The flame in her eyes shifted, simmered. "The best bet is to not end up here in the first place."

"Understood," I said, and she nodded efficiently.

"Anything new?" Liam asked quietly.

Lizzie frowned, picked at a stain on her pants, brushed it aside when she realized it wasn't coming out. "Two girls last night."

I guessed she meant wraiths, and it made me feel a little better that she still thought of them as something other than "it."

"Any signs of critical thinking?"

"Not that I'm aware of, but I didn't see them before they were sedated. The girl tonight?"

"Maybe. She didn't attack when she first saw us. Ran instead. And we think she was trying to talk. Kept saying 'contact' over and over again."

Lizzie's eyebrows lifted. "What does that mean?"

"I was hoping you'd know. That have any connection to the Beyond?"

She frowned, crossed her arms. "Not that I know of. Maybe she wants you to contact someone?"

"Maybe. If so—if it's a word, and not just a random sound—that's big. That's the first time a wraith has done that." He glanced at me. "We should go back to the house tomorrow, take a look. Maybe we can find something."

I nodded. "Fine by me."

Lizzie fished something silver from her pocket. It was a stick of gum in its foil wrapper. "Splitsies?" she asked, offering it to us.

Liam declined with a raised hand, and she held it out to me.

I hadn't had gum in ages. For whatever reason, that was one of the first things cleaned out of stores and convenience shops. "Yeah, please."

She broke it in half, tearing through the paper, and handed one to me. I popped it into my mouth, which watered at the sweet bite of sugar and peppermint. "Man, that's good."

She grinned. "Isn't it, though? Found a pack about a week ago. I've been rationing."

"I appreciate it."

Liam rose. "We should go. It's getting late, and it's been a long day."

"Lot of those going around these days." Lizzie hopped off the desk, took a step closer. "There's a lot of talk, Liam. The Paras are getting nervous."

"About what?"

"I don't know. Something feels different."

"The Veil?"

"Could be," she said. "Hard to say in here. We can't actually use our magic to find anything out. But there's something in the air. Something coming. And it's big."

He nodded. "Keep an eye out. You know how to get word to me."

"I do. Stay safe out there."

"I try my best."

"Nice to meet you, Claire Connolly. You be careful, too."

I nodded, and we walked outside, closed the door behind us.

"They let a Para work at the clinic?" I asked.

"As long as she swears not to do magic." He crossed his heart. "She knows the Beyond, was a healer there. Can do the same work here. She's good people."

"She seems like good people. Why are you trying to sell her to me?"

"Because she's a Para," he said. "I'm just trying to broaden your horizons."

Paras didn't lie to me, I thought, but kept the words to myself.

"Let's go to my place," Liam said.

My heart actually fluttered. "To your place?"

"That granola bar didn't do anything for me. You hungry?"

If he had any mixed feelings about my going back to his place, he didn't show them.

This couldn't be a good idea. Not when I was already so close to the edge.

A black cat sat outside Liam's door when we reached the building. I decided I wasn't superstitious, especially when he scratched it behind the ears, and it pressed upward into his hand.

"You have a cat?"

"No," he said as the cat trotted away, presumably looking for greener pastures. "It's a neighborhood cat, I think. I see her every few weeks. I'm pretty sure she thinks she's a guard."

"Cats do their own thing," I agreed.

We walked inside, up the stairs, into his apartment.

"I'm gonna change my shirt," he said. "You want to make us a drink? There's some ice in the fridge."

Maybe coming here hadn't been the best idea, but I wasn't going to turn down a drink right now. Not after the day we'd both had. I walked around the bar, checked out the stock. Rum, bourbon, vodka, rye. A small bottle of bitters, a bottle of Herbsaint. That led to only one conclusion.

I glanced back at him. "Sazeracs?"

He looked impressed by the offer. "Go for it," he said, then disappeared into the bedroom.

I found two glasses, poured in a splash of Herbsaint, swirled it, drained the rest into the sink. It tasted like licorice, and a little went a long way.

I left the glasses on the counter, took a silver shaker to the small refrigerator tucked into the kitchenette at the other end of the room. There was a plastic bin in the small freezer bay that held a block of ice, some of it already chunked into pieces. Functioning electricity at its best. I tossed a couple into the shaker, closed the door again, and stood up.

My gaze passed the doorway to the bedroom, where Liam, clad only in jeans, pulled a T-shirt out of a drawer.

His body was a riot of taut skin over hard-packed muscle, faintly gleaming with sweat. Broad shoulders that curved into strong arms, planks of abdominals that slid into a flat stomach and bridged a lean waist and sculpted chest. Every inch was solid, curving muscle, so that he might have been carved of stone . . . except for the jagged scar across his left arm, a band of puckered skin halfway between shoulder and elbow.

I turned, walked stiffly back to the bar.

Maybe I'd just make mine a double, I thought, adding rye, sugar from a small covered dish, and bitters to the glasses.

Liam walked back into the living room, opened the small refrigerator. He looked inside, took out a glass pan, checked beneath the foil, glanced back at me. "Roasted chicken?"

My stomach grumbled in response, and he grinned. "I'll take that as a yes." He took two small plates from a cabinet, portioned chicken onto each one.

I sat down on a bar stool, slid his drink to the spot in front of the next one. "Where'd you get chicken?" Meat, especially fresh meat, wasn't easy to come by in the Zone.

Liam walked over. "Moses has friends. I bring him electronics every once in a while, and he rewards me. I don't cook much, but I have the skills to roast a chicken. But I do it at Eleanor's. Her kitchen's better than mine."

"I'm surprised Containment lets him keep all that stuff."

"They think he's a hoarder. Which he is," he added, setting a plate in front of me. The portions were small. And when I looked back at the pan, I realized he'd split up the last of it for us.

"But that's not all he is. Just another example of Containment not being attentive to the details."

He picked up a piece of chicken, took a bite, swallowed. "I didn't think to ask—you want a fork?"

"No. I'm good." I didn't need a middleman getting between me and my chicken. I pulled off a chunk of meat, closed my eyes to savor it. "Damn, Quinn. That's pretty good. Thank you for sharing."

"Sazerac's not bad, either," he said, but he was frowning when he put the glass down. "Except that I'm not sure I like Sazeracs. I don't really like the licorice flavor."

I laughed. "Then why did you tell me to make one?"

He shrugged. "It's as prewar New Orleans as you can get. And you seemed pretty impressed with yourself."

I harrumphed, turned back to my dinner.

We ate companionably for a while, talking about Paras, about the war. The things people in the Zone, or at least in the Quarter, always seemed to talk about. So when we'd devoured the chicken, and cleaned up the plates, I tried to switch up the topics.

"So, what do you do when you aren't, I guess, working?"

We'd gone back to the bar. I nursed another Sazerac while he opted for bourbon on ice. "I visit Eleanor. Play cards with her and Victoria or Maria, whoever's on duty."

"Does Eleanor cheat?" I asked, thinking of what he'd said about Moses.

"Not with me." He paused. "At least, I don't think she does."

"Does she win a lot?"

His eyes narrowed as he thought it through. "Actually, yeah. Damn. I gave her a chocolate bar last week."

"Well, that's worth cheating over."

"I can get you one."

I shouldn't have looked as eager as I did. "You can?"

Like gum, chocolate had also been cleaned out of closed stores and empty houses. And what remained hadn't fared well—chocolate, heat, and humidity weren't a good mix.

"Eleanor gets shipments sometimes. One of my cousins—her granddaughter—lives in D.C., sends her things sometimes."

"I wouldn't say no."

"I'll see what I can do." He rose, walked to a small cabinet near the cane sofa.

"You asked what I like to do. I like music," he said. He opened the cabinet, revealing hundreds of vinyl records. He flipped through them, pulled one out, slipped it from its paper, and placed it atop the record player. With two careful fingers, he put the needle into place. As Liam set the record's paper sleeve aside, a man began to sing soulfully about love and desire. His voice was whisky-rough, as if love had done the damage.

Liam turned back to me. "Would you like to dance?"

"I—what?"

He stalked toward me like an Irish warrior, held out a hand, his eyes blazing like jewels. I stared at his hand—the wide palm, the long fingers—then up at him. "Is that a good idea?"

"No," he said with a smile. "But I haven't danced in a long time, and you look like you can move pretty well."

"I was born and raised in New Orleans," I said, hopping off the stool and slipping my hand into his. "Of course I can."

Liam drew me toward him, kept one of his hands linked to mine, settled the other at my waist. Gaze on mine, he began to sway in time to the music. And he was pretty damn good at it. He could keep a beat, had just enough funk to keep the dance from feeling like a seventh-grade cotillion, and just enough self-control to keep it from feeling like a bawdy night on Bourbon Street.

I didn't know how long the song actually lasted—probably no more than three or four minutes. But when I dropped my head to his chest, and his arms came around me, it felt like the song could never be long enough. His arms made a wall between me and everything else in the world.

The song ended, and silence fell like heavy rain. He released me, walked to the bar, put his elbows on it, ran his hands through his hair. He looked like a man in war, in battle. He hadn't said it yet, but it wasn't hard to guess why.

"It's because I might become a wraith," I said. "Because you think I'm a monster."

"*No,*" he said, looking back. "I believe you can learn to control yourself, your magic. That's why I'm helping you. But if anything goes wrong . . ." He paused. "If anything goes wrong, I'd be the man who puts you in prison. And that's not fair to you."

I looked at him for a long time. I was becoming used to the idea that I had magic I could use, power that wouldn't kill me. But in that unfolding moment, I'd have given it up in a heartbeat. I'd have flipped the switch, handed the power to someone else. But that wasn't one of my choices. Frankly, I wasn't sure what my choices were, but I was pretty sure I wouldn't find them here, tonight, while we tortured ourselves with touch and want.

"I should go," I said, and walked to the door. "I can find my way back."

"Claire," he said, following me to the door, but I shook my head.

"I'm a big girl, Liam. I don't break easily, but there's only so much I'm willing to bend."

As I walked down the stairs, I hoped he'd take that to heart.

CHAPTER FIFTEEN

Rain fell through the night. By the next morning, the weather had cleared and the day had blossomed beautifully. Cornflower blue sky with fluffy white clouds, cool temps, a light breeze. If there'd been any tourists left in the Quarter, they'd have filled the streets, the tables at Café Du Monde, the shops along Royal and Bourbon.

I adjusted the clock sign on the front door. I'd told Liam I'd go with him to check the wraith's house, see if we could find anything. I'd guessed we'd be gone for an hour and a half, and I hoped that was right—and that there wouldn't be a run on twine while I was away.

Liam's truck puttered its way down Royal. He sat in the cab like a king, pulled over to my side of the street. His window was rolled down, elbow on the doorframe and one hand on the wheel. He glanced at me, took in the blue and gray tunic and dark leggings I'd paired with knee-high boots. I'd braided my hair, so it lay across my shoulder.

"Hey," he said when I climbed into the truck.

"Hey."

I'd been nervous about seeing him today. The sense that I was nearing the edge of an emotional cliff kept haunting me. Unfortunately, that didn't make me want to see him less—exactly the opposite.

"You sleep okay?" he asked.

"Yeah. Pretty good. I thought about my father a lot." Feeling uncomfortably vulnerable, I looked out the window so he couldn't see the emotion in my face.

We drove through the Garden District and back to Fourth Street to the colonnaded house where we'd found the girl last night.

Liam parked on the street, and I followed up the sidewalk and into the house.

We'd left the door open, and rain had dotted the wooden floor. "You want upstairs or down?"

"I'll go upstairs," I said. "I'll call you if I find something."

He nodded, walked down the hallway.

I took the stairs, which were covered by a thick, carpeted runner. Several rooms led off from the landing.

The first two had been bedrooms for young boys, judging from the paint color and baseball-themed wallpaper border. No furniture, no toys. They'd left in the exodus, probably. Packed everything up, including the children, and gone in search of safety.

There was a small bathroom, covered in old-fashioned pink tile, a pink sink, a pink bathroom. The owners had been into vintage, maybe. Or just hadn't had the chance to upgrade before they'd moved out.

I walked to the third door, pushed it open, and walked into another world. The room had been stripped of furniture and belongings from whoever had lived here before. But the wraith had made it her own. There was a roundish pile of blankets on the floor—probably where she'd slept. Food scraps in another—chunks of rotting vegetables, a few late berries, energy bars, empty water bottles.

I rose and walked to the doorway, called his name. "Liam."

I heard him step into the doorway behind me. He walked in, spun in a slow circle as he surveyed the room.

"She was living here," Liam said. "It's safe, it's secure. Think about the fact that she ran away from us."

"But if she was able to evaluate that—if she could gauge whether she was in danger—why not just go home?"

"Maybe she didn't have a home to go to. Or she thought they'd be in danger from her."

That was depressing.

"Let's look around," he said. "See if you can find anything that will tell us who she is or where she came from."

I nodded, moved to the pile of bedding. That was the nest, the spot where she slept. It made sense that it would be the most secure.

Great theory, but totally wrong. The blankets had feathers, leaves, crumbs. But nothing that wouldn't require forensic equipment to analyze.

I rearranged the blankets—it seemed only fair not to disturb her spot, even though she wouldn't be coming back—and took a step backward so I wouldn't step on it. The floorboard slipped under me with a squeak.

I glanced down. The end of the board was lifted just a little. Accident, or intention?

I got down on my knees, pulled the store keys from my pocket. There was a flat bottle opener on the key chain. As Liam moved silently beside me, I wedged it into the board, pried it up.

Something jumped out. I screamed, jumped back . . . and watched a tiny mouse scurry across the room.

"They don't make wraiths that small, Connolly."

I laughed nervously at the joke. "That scared the crap out of me."

"So I saw. What else is in there?"

I wasn't thrilled about sticking my hand in this time, but I bucked up, reached in, and pulled out a purple Crown Royal bag, the kind with the yellow stitching. I opened it into my hand. There was a house key, a small rock, and a driver's license.

"Hello, Marla Salas," I said, looking down at the picture of the smiling blond girl. She was twenty-three, and her address was only a few blocks from here.

I looked up at Liam. "She hid this stuff, Liam. She put it together, and she put it somewhere she thought was safe. She was *thinking*."

"Yeah," Liam said, standing up again. "She was. And now we've got her address. Let's go see if anyone's home."

The house was a small bungalow with a roofed front porch, dormer windows above it, in a pale pink color. The trim was warm and yellow, and the house was in remarkably good condition. Music was coming from inside. It sounded like Big Band jazz from the 1940s. The music, the cheery paint color, brightened my mood. Someone was making a life there. It was always awesome to see that.

Liam stopped when we reached the porch, stared at the house. "I don't do this often."

I looked at him. "This?"

He glanced down at me. "Make notifications. Someone's in there, probably someone who knew her. That means we'll have to tell them what's happened to Marla."

My mood deflated instantly. I'd been so focused on finding out about her, about the wraiths, that I hadn't even considered what we'd say to her loved ones.

The music stopped, and the door opened. A woman in her early fifties stood in the doorway. She had short gray hair, wore comfortable pants and a shirt. She put a hand on her chest when she looked at us. "You're from the department? You're here about Marla?"

Liam and I looked at each other. The department? Did she mean PCC?

"No, ma'am. We're not from the department, but we would like to talk to you about your daughter, if you don't mind. My name is Liam Quinn, and this my friend Claire Connolly."

"I'm Lorene Salas. I'm Marla's mother. My husband, Paul, is in the garden. Not a lot of produce this time of year, but you make do with what you can."

"I've gotten some pretty good beets," I said with a smile, trying to lighten the mood. And felt stupid for saying it.

She gave us one more appraising look. "Why don't you come inside?"

The house was simple, but tidy. A couch, a chair, a hand-cranked record player. That explained where the music had come from. We sat down on the couch.

"Your daughter's a Sensitive?" Liam asked.

Lorene looked around nervously. "Well, I suppose if you're here you'd already know that. Yes, yes, she is. And a very good one. She's actually helped out the PCC from time to time. That's why you're here, right? You're following up?"

"Following up?" Liam asked.

She went a little wan. "With her disappearance. Some of her friends had worked at the PCC. We didn't talk about it, of course, because her work with them was confidential. But they knew her." Lorene swallowed, worked to keep her composure. "When they hadn't seen her in a few days, they got worried. They came to me to ask questions, try to figure out where she was."

So someone else was aware she was gone, was investigating it. And someone from PCC, to boot.

"Did they leave you a card, by chance? Or some way to get in touch with them?"

"Well, no. They just said they'd be in touch if they found anything out. So I thought that's why you were here today." She swallowed back obvious fear.

"Mrs. Salas, perhaps you'd like to have your husband come join you?"

She went pale as a ghost, moistened her lips. "My Paul has been dead for two years. I say he's in the garden, because you don't know who'll come to the door, what they'll want. It gives some protection. He's not here."

Oh, damn, I thought. She was alone.

Liam reached out, took her hand. "Mrs. Salas, I'm sorry to inform you that your daughter—well, she's gotten ill from the magic. It's hurt her."

"Ill?" She looked back and forth between us. "What does that mean, ill?"

"It means the magic—the infection—overwhelmed her. She's become a wraith."

Knowledge bloomed horribly in her eyes. *"No,"* she said. "No. She was *rigorous.*" She lowered her voice. "She did the 'clearing out.' Kept her magic stable or whatever. She knew how to do that, because she'd worked with the department, you see. She'd never have let herself become—one of them."

Maybe she didn't have a choice, I thought. I could see Liam was thinking about that, too, but he didn't voice it.

"You can't be right," she said.

"I'm sorry, Mrs. Salas, but we are. We found her last night." Liam's shoulders tensed as he prepared himself. And then he put it out there. "We took her to Devil's Isle."

Fear changed to alarm, to anger. "You took her to *prison?*" She stood up. "How dare you! My baby should not be in prison."

"Ma'am, she'll hurt people. That's what wraiths do. I'm sorry, but

I imagine you know that's true. There's a clinic at Devil's Isle where she'll be kept safe, where she won't be allowed to hurt herself or anyone else. That's the best that can be done for her right now."

She looked at Liam, lifted her chin. "I want to see my daughter."

Liam's expression softened. "I'm not sure that's a good idea."

"I want to see my daughter. She's my daughter. She'll be frightened. I don't care what you say about what she is now. She's still my daughter." She sobbed, covered her mouth with a hand. "She's still my daughter."

Mrs. Salas declined Liam's help in getting her into Devil's Isle, said she'd do it on her own.

We climbed into the truck and sat there, both of us staring blankly out the windows, jolted by the scene in Mrs. Salas's house. By the sadness—and the reality check.

Control was an illusion. Even if I managed to control my magic, even if I kept things balanced, something could still go wrong. Horribly, horribly wrong.

Talking to Mrs. Salas had put distance between us again. I could feel Liam pulling away, probably as he imagined my potential future. I didn't have any family left to crush. But there were still people I could hurt. People he'd have to inform.

I shook the melancholy away. That didn't matter. We had to focus on what we could control. "You did what you had to do," I said quietly.

"I don't know if that makes it any better."

"It's not much consolation, but at least she'll know where Marla is. She'll have answers."

"But not all of them." Liam drummed his fingers on the steering wheel. "And we don't have them, either. We're not the only ones who care about this. Someone from PCC is watching out for her, talking to her mother."

"Is that good news or bad news?" I asked. "Do we want them involved?"

"I don't know. Depends on why they were there. We're going to find that out. And in the meantime, I'm going to have Nix come back to the store tonight. You can keep working on your magic. The best way to combat fear is to get to work."

On that, we agreed.

At six o'clock, Liam arrived with both Gavin and Nix in tow. I was still with a customer—someone who'd tried to shop when I was closed and wasn't thrilled about it—so the Quinns made themselves comfortable, Gavin at one end of the cypress table, Liam at the other. Both of them wore the apparent Quinn family uniform— jeans, dark T-shirts, boots.

Nix stood in front of a round vintage candy holder of metal bins around a central pole. I'd filled each one with mismatched odds and ends—spoons, crystal doorknobs, antique hinges. She wore a pale green sleeveless dress, her blond hair in complicated braids. As she spun the holder, checking each bin, it was easy to see her as a stranger in a strange land.

When he wasn't stealing glances at Nix, Gavin looked over the *New York Times* section I'd salvaged from one of the convoy boxes— the pages had been crumpled around bars of soap.

When the last customer was gone, I flipped the sign and locked the door, then walked back to the table. "Please, make yourselves at home."

"Done," Gavin said, refolding the paper.

I put my hands on my hips, looked at the brothers. "I see you aren't punching each other. Friends again?"

"We reached an understanding," Gavin said.

"I'm glad to hear it." I glanced at Nix. "What's on tonight's agenda?"

"Binding."

"Do I need three people to teach me to bind magic?"

"You only need me," Nix said. "But they like to watch."

Her voice was utterly innocent, and I wasn't honestly sure if she understood the implication. But the expression on Gavin's face said he was very, very aware of it.

I guessed that was part of the brothers' understanding—Gavin wouldn't throw a fit about Nix helping if he could keep an eye on her during the training. Or that was what he told himself, anyway, for the chance to be near her again.

"I think your brother's still in love with her," I said quietly to Liam as we took the stairs to the second floor.

"You're nosy, you know that?" He grinned and shook his head, his mood seeming to thaw a little.

"I run a store that's been in the French Quarter for more than a hundred years. I came by it honestly."

"Be that as it may, it's their story, and not mine to tell."

Then, I'd have to convince one of them to tell it.

"Come," Nix said, and sat on the floor on her knees, the skirt of her green dress spread around her. She looked very much like a fairy—I could imagine her in a bayou, moving among the cypresses, floating above the water, faintly glowing as her hair bobbed around her. "Sit down."

I nodded, took a seat in front of her while Liam leaned against a bookshelf and Gavin sat down on the floor, back against the wall, arms atop his knees.

"I want you to go through the entire cycle," Nix said. "First, I want you to move something,"

I looked around at the room and the labyrinth of antiques. "What do you want me to move?"

"It doesn't matter. Pick something. Anything."

I looked around, let my eyes pass the giant star sign, which was still propped against the wall. I mean, I wanted to move it on principle, since we'd started this journey together, but it was a big and lumbering thing. I didn't especially want to impale Nix—especially with Gavin in the house.

I settled on a vintage produce crate with a gorgeous CREOLE LOUISIANA SWEET POTATOES sticker on one end. I could take or leave the crate, but the paper label could actually be worth a lot. Incentive not to bash it against anything hard—like Liam Quinn's head.

"All right. You should probably all get out of the way."

"Why?" Nix asked.

"Because my aim isn't very good." I held up a hand before they could complain. "Keep in mind the context and conditions. And keep an eye out."

The crate sat on the top of a high shelf next to three others. I checked the path, imagined the string that would draw it to me. It would have to go around a chest of drawers with a mirror, then spin sharply back in the other direction to avoid getting snagged on a pink aluminum Christmas tree. Tricky. Not impossible, but tricky.

I blew out a breath, focused on the object. I imagined the room filled with energy, began to pull it together, like a spinning top of magic, of power.

"Good," Nix approved quietly. "Good."

Slowly, I lifted my gaze to the crate, trying to keep the magic together, contained, and began to pull the crate toward me. It bobbled, shook, lifted into the air with a lurch. Bounced against the tin ceiling, sending dust into the air.

"Focus," Nix said. "Reel it smoothly."

"If I could reel it smoothly, I wouldn't need to practice reeling it smoothly," I said through clenched teeth.

I guessed the angles, pulled it forward. It jerked three feet in the right direction, paused, shaking as it hovered in the air. I nodded at it, proud that it had mostly done what I'd asked it to do, and pulled again.

The crate zipped toward the mirror and, as I winced, paused right in front of the glass. The next bit would be trickier—back around the tree and straight toward home. I reached out a hand, imagined fingers grasping the string that connected it to me. I snapped it to the right, then pulled.

The crate zoomed past the Christmas tree, leaving the branches shaking, and whipped toward us like a wooden bullet.

"Shit," Liam said, ducking as it whizzed over his head, only just missing the top of his dark crown of hair.

It flew toward me, and I flicked my fingers up, palm out, forcing it to a stop. It froze, shuddered, and dropped. About four feet from the spot I'd meant for it to.

I let the rest of the magic go, put my hands on my hips, and breathed through my nose, trying to get rid of the dizziness.

"That was not impressive," Nix said.

"I got it here, didn't I?"

Gavin came over, patted my back.

"And barely a concussion along the way."

I glanced at Liam apologetically. "Sorry about that."

"Job hazard," he said.

"Technically, that's not correct," Gavin said. "You keep her from becoming a wraith, and you don't have a job to do."

And wasn't that precisely the problem?

Nix made me immediately try casting again, "because magic isn't always practiced under good conditions."

And without good conditions, it took me twenty minutes to get a tiny dose of magic out of myself and into the box.

"You need to practice," Nix said.

I sat back on my heels and wiped sweat from my brow. The heat had come back with a vengeance, and the second floor was even hotter than the first. I'd changed into loose cutoff jeans and a tank top, but that hardly helped. We'd opened the windows, but kept the curtains drawn just in case. Containment might not have been able to detect magic, but they'd certainly have been able to see it. Unfortunately, the curtains didn't do much to help the already limp breeze outside.

"I'm not trying to avoid practicing," I said. "It hasn't exactly been a slow week. I haven't had time."

"She's telling the truth there," Liam said, glancing at me. "And she understands the consequences."

"All right," Nix said. "You have moved and cast. And now we bind." She walked to the box, which sat on the floor.

"You've put magic into the box. But magic prefers to move. It prefers to live. You must bind the magic into the box, into the wood, or it will return to the world, only to be absorbed by you again."

"Which would make all this work pointless."

"Precisely," she said.

"And how do I bind it?"

"You insist upon it."

She stopped there, as if those four words completely explained the magical process she wanted me to try. Liam and Gavin watched with interest.

"I'm going to need more than 'I ask it to.' "

"I didn't say you asked it," Nix said, walking around the box. "I said you *insisted* upon it." She pounded a fist on the palm of her other hand. "You demand it."

She reached out. "Give me your hand."

I hesitated, then placed my hand in her palm. Her skin was cool, soft, and I smelled the green scent of new leaves as we made contact.

"Magic seeks a home. You only have to give it one." She guided my hand to the box, pressed it there. "Feel what it wants to be, and send it home."

I felt cool, lacquered wood . . . and I felt really, really silly about doing it under the stares of the Quinn brothers.

"You aren't concentrating."

"I feel like I'm in a fish tank right now. Lot of eyeballs, lot of pressure."

"You want us to turn around?" Gavin asked with a grin. "We can do that."

I glanced at Liam. "Can you please control your brother? He isn't helping."

He made a noise that didn't sound especially agreeable. "I haven't been able to control him before. I don't see how I could start now."

"And still, I get by just fine."

"Yeah, we can all see that now, can't we?"

Nix, her hands still in mine, chuckled as the argument heated. "If you hoped to distract them, that was probably the fastest way. Now," she said, pressing my fingers harder against the box. Don't feel the *box*. Feel what's *in the box*. You can close your eyes if it helps with the distraction."

I rolled my shoulders and tried to settle into my hips. I closed my eyes, made myself aware of my fingertips, the sensations of her cool fingers, the wooden box.

At first, there was nothing. It started slowly, a slow vibration beneath my fingers that felt like the humming of a machine. I thought it might be a nervous shake or some sort of trick of my nerves, something I should ignore while I reached for something deeper.

But the sensation only grew stronger, from a soft hum to a vibration that pulsed like a heartbeat.

"Good," Nix whispered softly, like she was trying not to startle me, not to spook me like a nervous animal. "Good. You can feel the magic in the box, in the wood. To bind it, you must unite it. Use your magic to coax it. To push it."

I wasn't entirely sure how I was supposed to do that. So I opted for silent begging. *Hey, little thread of magic. Do me a big favor and ooze your way into the wood, please?*

I paused, hoped for a difference, but the vibrations were the same, and Nix hadn't moved her hand. We weren't done yet.

I assumed this was like trying to do back flips in the pool when I was younger, or like true love. I'd know it when it happened.

The Quinns were still bickering behind me, their words a low murmur of irritation. But that didn't matter. They were not my concern. My concerns were this box, my magic, and my future. And those things were all tied together.

While Nix watched with mild curiosity, I looked down at the box, pressed my fingers against it again, closed my eyes until I could feel the box trembling again.

This time, I didn't ask the magic to move. I made it. Not with words, really, but more like a wish. A really, really strong wish. A demand that it merge itself with the box in which I'd placed it, that they fuse together, be bound together because I ordered it.

The box grew instantly fire-hot.

Nix jerked her hand away, and I did the same, holding my fingers out of reach in case the lid snapped down.

The box shook like it had been electrified, which I guessed wasn't far from the truth if magic was a form of energy. After a few seconds of shuddering, it settled onto the floor again with a heavy *thud*.

The room had gone silent. I glanced over my shoulder, found Gavin and Liam standing beside each other, hands on their hips, staring at the little box. They looked a little bit impressed, and a little bit afraid. That was probably the safest combination for anyone confronted with magic.

And it made me feel spectacular.

I looked back at Nix. "I did it?"

"You did. Not especially elegantly, but you did it."

I didn't care if it was elegant or not. According to Nix, there were two things I had to do in order to avoid becoming a wraith: cast off the magic and bind it to something.

I'd done both of those things. The odds I'd become a wraith went down a little bit more. I just had to hope I had better control than poor Marla.

CHAPTER SIXTEEN

I was getting hungry, so we sent the Quinns downstairs to forage for food while Nix walked me through one more round of casting and binding.

At least the privacy gave me a chance to interrogate her a little. I *was* nosy. Blame it on a lack of television or radio. We had to make our own drama. New Orleans was plenty skilled at that.

I did the casting but made her wait for the binding. "Tell me about you and Gavin. Seems like you two have a history?"

"Binding first," she said. "Talk later."

"History first, or no binding."

Nix sighed, sat back on her heels. "We met during the war. He believed he had feelings for me."

That didn't sound very romantic. Or mutual. "You didn't feel the same?"

"We are not humans. Our emotional lives are different. We are tied to some part of the natural world—of our natural world. For me, trees. There is a connection there. A tether that lasts as long as we do."

She dipped her head, looked at the floor as she continued to speak. "Because of it, commitment is very important to us.

Gavin . . ." Her eyes went foggy as she stared blankly at the floor, eyes tracing back and forth as if she was watching some memory unfold. "He is young, and commitment is not his forte." She smiled a little. "He likes projects, but not finishing them."

"He was unfaithful?" I asked quietly.

Nix lifted her head, laughed charmingly. "Not at all. He is curious. He is brave. He believes he loves me. But he rebels against his family, against his name. Because of that, he is not yet convinced of who he is."

She was being pretty vague, but I thought I had a sense of the picture. "You refused him?"

"I did. The time was not right for either of us. He has much life to lead. And even when he is ready, the time may never be right." She shrugged. "That's the way of things."

It was a depressing way, but since she'd lived a life very different from mine, I didn't think it was fair to judge.

Since I'd gotten my answer, which was much less dramatic than I thought it would be, I bound the magic into the box again, and she finally let me eat.

We made our way downstairs, where darkness had fallen over the Quarter, and prepared to finish off the bread, the carrots, a jar of pickles Gavin unearthed from one of the kitchen cabinets, and a bottle of wine I'd been saving. This seemed as good a time as any to indulge.

We divvied up the food, poured the wine into my mismatched jars, and made a kind-of meal at the cypress table. We skipped the lights for a few dim candles. The less light, the less would be visible to curious people on the street.

"You know what I'd like?" Gavin asked, sipping his wine. "A

steak. A big steak with a baked potato slathered in butter and sour cream."

"You could get those things outside the Zone," Nix pointed out.

Gavin looked at her. "There are a lot of things outside the Zone that aren't here. But that doesn't make that world any better."

Since that comment was clearly meant for Nix—and *about* Nix—and not for our ears, I looked away and caught Liam's gaze. He rolled his eyes with amusement.

"What about you, Nix? What do you miss most about the Beyond?"

She looked surprised by the question. I'd thought about asking if she had a favorite food, but she hadn't really joined the conversation, so I guessed her thoughts were on other things, other memories.

"Everything," she finally said. "I miss everything. It was my home, my heart. Where I came from. I would like to go home again."

"What was it like?" I asked.

"My land was green. Beautifully green, with rolling hills that dropped into the deepest sea, and deep forests so thick and dark that sunlight only barely filtered through to the floor. Crystal blue lakes, snow-covered peaks. It is a land of extremes, but a beautiful and fertile one."

"I'm sorry," I said. It was the only thing I could think to say.

She nodded. "Not all of us feel the same. Some dread the dissension, war, that is probably still waging there."

I nodded, sipped my wine in the silence that had descended heavily again. Probably time to change the subject, I thought, and looked at the brothers Quinn. "We know about the Arsenaults. What about the Quinns? Where did they come from?"

"The bottom of a rum and Coke," Gavin said, and he and Liam clinked glasses.

"Let's just say my mother made a bad choice when she hooked up with a jazz-playin', hard-drinkin' Cajun named Buddy Quinn," Liam said.

"Which Arsenault daughter was your mother?" There'd been five of them, all beautiful girls with dark hair and blue eyes.

"Juliet," Liam said. "The oldest."

I smiled. "I forgot they all had Shakespearean names."

"Thierry Arsenault loved Shakespeare," Gavin said, then held out his hands. "Had one of those big all-in-one volumes of it. Used to read it after dinner. He was a complicated man. An interesting one."

I nodded. The clock chimed, struck ten. We all looked over, watched as Little Red Riding Hood moved through the forest.

"The wolf doesn't come out until midnight," I said when the clock struck ten and she disappeared into the workings again.

"Some werewolves came through the Veil," Liam said. "At least, I'm pretty sure I saw one. I was at the Arsenaults' cabin—one of the last nights I spent there."

"Because of the werewolf infestation?" I asked.

"You joke," he said with one of his surprising, dimpled grins. "Wait until you've seen the horde descending on you."

"They are monsters in both worlds," Nix agreed. "And friends of neither."

That was good to know. I made a note to check the phases of the moon next time I wandered around in the dark.

Liam stood. "We should go. I want to take a look around the Garden District again. We still haven't found two male wraiths."

This time, I didn't offer to go. I needed some space, and Liam and I being in close quarters again wasn't going to help.

Gavin pushed back his chair, rose. "Get some sleep," he said. "You're going to need it after the work you did."

I couldn't argue with that.

Nix followed him to the door, then Liam. I blew out the candles—

I knew the store well enough to move around it in the dark—and met them at the threshold.

There was a small card on the floor in front of the door, apparently slipped into the mail slot. It was a business card. The cream stock was old and worn at the edges. KING SUGAR COMPANY was written across it in tidy block letters, along with an address in Chalmette. That was downriver, and the spot where the original Battle of New Orleans had been fought.

There was a note on the card: LIAM AND CLAIRE, MIDNIGHT.

"What's that?" Liam asked.

"I think it's an invitation," I said, and handed it to him.

Liam glanced at it, flipped it over to check both sides, then passed the card to Gavin.

"King Sugar Company?" Gavin asked, handing the card to Nix. "That's the one along the river?"

"Yeah," Liam said. "It went out of business, but the buildings are still there. I guess someone's decided to start using them again." When Nix handed the card back to Liam, he ripped it in half, then again, then again, and walked back into the kitchen. I heard the water running, and assumed he put them down the drain.

"You don't want to go?" I asked when he came back again.

"I don't know yet," he said. "But I know I don't want someone to find that. Even accidentally." He put his hands on his hips, looked at Gavin. "What do you think?"

Gavin shrugged. "If it's a trap, there'd have been much easier ways to do it. They could have just walked into the store."

Liam nodded, considering, then looked at Nix. "Do you think this is from Consularis Paras?"

"I don't know. There are other Consularis who are not incarcerated. But I don't know of this request."

Liam looked at me. "What do you think?"

"I think we have to go." I wouldn't deny that I was tired, but the card was pretty energizing.

Liam considered. "Unfortunately, I think you're right."

I was starting to get used to the noises and knocks of Liam's truck. But he was much more cautious tonight than he'd been in the Garden District.

Every few minutes, he glanced up, checked the rearview mirror. He wanted to be sure we weren't being followed. I could guess why—to be doubly sure we weren't heading into a trap.

But we were the only ones on the road tonight, and the only humans I saw during the entire trip. Before the war, people would have opened their doors and windows, let fresh breezes push stale and humid air out of the house. They'd sit on porches or stoops, discuss the day or enjoy the night. But there simply weren't that many people left. Those who were left were scattered, and many had been too shell-shocked by war to venture outside their homes unless absolutely necessary.

The refinery was huge—several structures spread over half a dozen acres. Less a campus than a really big Frankenbuilding—a main structure with a lot of add-ons here and there. Lungs of big rusting tanks. Tendons of high, covered walkways that connected the parts together. Mismatched limbs—a building dressed in a complicated brick pattern attached to another outfitted with a completely different pattern. And smokestack feet that punched through the air at the end of it.

A chain-link fence circled the site, or mostly did. It was falling over in some areas, nearly rusted through in some others. Liam found a spot where the link was down completely, carefully drove the truck through.

He moved through the web of buildings, watching for movement, then pulled in front of the largest part of the complex, a hulking rectangle of rusting steel marked with rows of windows. They glowed from the inside. Someone had turned on the power.

"I guess this is our destination," Liam said. He reversed the truck, pivoted until it was facing the exit again. Just in case we needed to haul ass back to the city, I assumed.

We climbed out of the truck, and Liam waited while I walked around to his side. He glanced at me. "You ready?"

"As I'm likely to ever be. Let's meet our mysterious callers."

Quietly, cautiously, we moved inside. The building was empty, but absolutely enormous—a long rectangle of space. The outside wall had windows; the inside wall was made of metal and looked to be melting with rust. Steel girders roughly down the middle of the space supported a spider's web of rusting beams and catwalks overhead and below a ceiling of wooden planks. Lights hung down from the beams. The floor was pitted concrete, marked by pools of bloodred water that had dripped from the rusting wall. It still dripped, sending echoes across the room.

Wings fluttered. Sound filled the room as a flock of pigeons were startled away from a rafter. We ducked as they flew over us, disappearing through broken windows at the other end of the building.

There was another *whoosh* of sound. We both turned back, Liam with a hand at his weapon, a gunslinger ready to fight.

A man had descended in a crouch in front of us. Wings rose high behind him, the arcs above his shoulders gleaming like white silk woven with gold, a strange contrast to the decay around us.

As he stood, his wings retracted, disappearing from sight.

He wore dark trousers and a white button-down shirt, the sleeves folded above muscular forearms. He was strikingly handsome, with a square jaw, straight nose, and strong brow over eyes that gleamed golden. His hair was dark blond and curled into soft waves. I'd have guessed his age as late twenties or early thirties, but Paras were hard to gauge.

A woman emerged from a stairway on the other end of the room, her shoes snapping noisily on the metal treads. Straight dark hair framed a lovely face. Her pinup-curvy body was tucked into rolled-up jeans and a red gingham top, and her eyes were blue behind tortoiseshell glasses.

"Sorry our entrance isn't as good," she said, aiming her gaze at the angel. "Not all of us have wings."

His lips curled with faint amusement. "A pity."

"No need for the weapons," she said to Liam, his fingers still poised on the butt of his gun. "We're all on the same side."

Liam kept his eyes on the angel. "You sure about that?"

"We're sure," another voice echoed across the room from the stairway.

It was *Burke*, descending the stairs in his gray fatigues.

He reached the floor, smiled apologetically at us. "Hey, Claire, Liam."

"I'd like someone to explain what, exactly, is going on here," I said. "Who'd like to start?"

"I'll do the introductions," Burke said. "Liam Quinn and Claire Connolly. This is Darby Craig, our resident biologist, formerly of PCC Research. You know me." He gestured to the angel. "And this is Malachi, a general of the Consularis army."

I looked at Malachi, took in the height, the hair color. "You were at the Landreaus' home. You're the Para I saw in the garden."

He nodded. "Yes. I was watching them."

"Why?"

"I'd been in the neighborhood, walking, keeping an eye out for those who might need help. I saw two Containment vehicles speed by. I followed them, discovered why they'd been called, and wanted a look at the grounds for myself, just in case."

"She said you were a general," Liam said. "You were conscripted?"

"I was."

"And did you fight?"

Malachi's expression remained blank. "I was not allowed to fight. I was imprisoned, used, and for a period, tortured. But I did not fight."

I glanced at Burke, and my expression wasn't friendly. I could respect sneakiness. But not if he'd hurt Tadji. "You're next. Explain."

"I'm a Sensitive, and I've been looking for others. I didn't know your father, but I knew he was a Sensitive. Sometimes it's genetic, so I wanted to check you out."

It was a good thing Liam had told me about my father; otherwise, I'd be finding out here, in an abandoned sugar refinery. "And?"

Burke smiled. "I'm not yet sure. If you've got something, you've been keeping it quiet."

"I am a Sensitive," I said. "Eight months in. I can move things."

"That's handy," Burke said, eyes alight with interest.

"It has its moments." Some good, some bad. But speaking of interest . . . "What's your interest in Tadji?"

His smile softened. It was a pretty good smile. "A beautiful coincidence. I wanted to get closer to you. But I wanted to ask her to dance."

Not entirely a compliment to me, but he looked like he was telling the truth.

"What's your power?" I asked.

"This," he said.

I'd visited a carnival with friends in junior high, had walked through the Haunted House of Mysterious Mirrors on a dare. It wasn't that haunted, and there weren't that many mirrors—three or four that distorted our reflections, so we looked taller or wider or stockier with superlong legs.

Burke's body warped just like that—ripples that moved up and down his legs, torso, and arms as if he were standing in front of a carnival mirror. Except there was no mirror. And then suddenly, there was no Burke.

He'd disappeared.

I stared at the now-empty spot where he'd stood, walked forward, peered into the gap where he'd been. There was nothing there.

And when he grabbed my wrist, I nearly backhanded him. There were more ripples, and then he shimmered back into focus, his hand on my arm, grinning like a maniac.

I just stared at him. "Invisibility. That's pretty amazing."

He let go of my arm, shifted his gaze back to Liam. "It's actually just camouflage on a really detailed level."

"I call it 'nanoflage,'" Darby put in. "Nano-level camouflage. Magic does very weird things to the human body."

"So I see." And since he didn't look weak or hungry, I guessed that wasn't the only skill he'd mastered. "You can cast and bind?"

His smile went serious. This was the business of Sensitives, the most important tools in our arsenal. The things that kept us sane. "I can. You?"

"I'm learning."

"Good," Burke said. "That process will get easier. The goal is consistency."

It occurred to me Burke was the first Sensitive I'd actually been able to talk to about being a Sensitive. It made me feel a little better—knowing I had someone who'd been down the road before.

"How did Materiel end up hiring a Sensitive?" Liam asked.

"Don't ask, don't tell," Burke said. "They don't know. And, speaking of PCC, that's what we wanted to talk to you about—we understand you talked to Lorene Salas today."

So they were the "PCC" reps who'd talked to her family.

"We took her daughter in last night," Liam confirmed.

Burke nodded. "Lorene talked to Lizzie, who told her you were very good with Marla. Very gentle with her."

"We got lucky," Liam said, gestured to me. "Claire handled her, and handled her well. You're Marla's friends?"

"I was," Darby said. "I knew she was a Sensitive, and hadn't seen her in a few days. That's when I went to visit her mother."

"What took you there?" Burke asked.

"We found her nest," Liam said. "We'd gone back to check it out, see if we could find any evidence."

"Of?" Malachi asked.

"Wraith attacks are increasing," I said. "Liam's been tracking them. There have been more, and wraiths seem to be acting more like humans. We're trying to figure out why."

Malachi, Darby, and Burke looked at each other, then at us. "That's quite a coincidence," Burke said. "We're missing Sensitives."

Liam frowned. "What do you mean 'missing' them? As in, they're disappearing from Devil's Isle?"

"Not quite," Malachi said, glancing at Darby. "Perhaps we should start at the beginning?"

She nodded. "So, the Veil was discovered forty-seven years ago."

I didn't let her go any farther. "Forty-seven years? The feds have known about the Veil for *forty-seven* years? How were we so unprepared?"

"It was still closed," she said. "And it's not like we can see through it. At that time, they weren't entirely sure what it was, or what was behind it. That's why Defense created a research team in the first place. When the Veil opened, Defense realized what was happening, what was behind it."

"That's when the Paranormal Combatant Command was created," Burke said, and Darby nodded.

"And the Veil research agency was wrapped into PCC and became PCC Research. War was under way, of course, so Paranormals became the enemy, indivisibly. We didn't know yet about conscription, or the Court, or Consularis."

"And Sensitives?" I asked.

"That was more complicated," Burke said. "Sensitives were too human to be considered true enemies, too Paranormal to be free, and too useful to be ignored. As you know, some were captured, interned. It wasn't, unfortunately, the first time the feds have interned U.S. citizens, and people were afraid of magic, afraid of war. Unfortunately for them, PCC pretty quickly realized they needed Sensitives to close the Veil."

I stared at her. "Sensitives closed the Veil?"

"They did," Burke said.

I looked at Liam. "Did you know about that?"

He shook his head. "Not precisely, but it makes sense you'd have to fight magic with magic."

"Exactly," Burke said. "PCC told the Sensitives they'd recruited that they'd have immunity. That's why so many helped. And because they were willing to ignore the obvious civil rights violations to help the larger goal—human survival. And you know what happened after that. The war ended, and the Magic Act was passed. Anything with magic became verboten. Criminalized. The interned Sensitives weren't released. And the Sensitives who helped didn't get immunity. They went into hiding."

Darby nodded. "We—PCC Research, I mean—tried to get PCC to change its position. We knew about the differences between Paras. We knew Sensitives could manage their magic. We proposed Containment enlist Sensitives and Consularis Paras on a trial basis to track fluctuations in the Veil, help get us prepared in case it split again. But PCC didn't want to hear that. They wanted us to tow the 'enemy combatant' line, and we wouldn't." She shrugged. "That's when I got the ax."

"For Sensitives, Containment thinks magic management is too risky," Burke said, and Darby nodded. "They see *us* as unstable, uncertain. If we don't control our magic, or not well enough, we turn into wraiths. That makes us dangerous."

She looked at Malachi and Burke. "And so here we are, trying to fight the good fight."

" 'We'?" I asked.

"Our allies," Burke said. "Some Sensitives, some humans and Consularis Paras both outside and inside Devil's Isle. We call ourselves Delta." Burke formed a triangle with his thumbs and index fingers. "We're in the Mississippi Delta, and in math, delta means change. That's what we're after—changing Containment's view of Paranormals and Sensitives. Changing *everyone's* view. And right now, finding our missing Sensitives—the ones who helped close the Veil."

"Wait," I said. "If they're in hiding, how do you know they're missing?"

"They're in hiding from *Containment*," Darby said, "but not necessarily from each other. There's a loose network of Sensitives who keep in touch. Not all do, but having that connection is important to some." She glanced at Burke. "We found out about, what, six months ago that one of the 'networked' Sensitives hadn't checked in."

"About that," Burke said with a nod.

"That was the first indication," Darby said.

Liam crossed his arms. "You have a theory about why they're missing?"

"We believe someone is trying to open the Veil again," Malachi said. "And we believe they're using Sensitives to do it."

It was our worst fear come true.

"Why do you think that?" I asked, my voice quiet but still echoing in the large room.

"Because the Veil is fluctuating more than it should be," Darby said.

"Fluctuating?" I asked. "What does that mean?"

Darby pulled a small pocketknife from her jeans, flipped open one of the tools. She crouched, scratched a line through the dirt on the floor.

"This is the baseline," she said. "Normal fluctuations in energy emitted from the Veil look like this." With the tool, she drew a wavy line through the dirt that rose over and fell under the main line.

"Veil fluctuations are common," Liam said. "The Veil is a boundary, a barrier. It shifts and changes."

"True," Darby said. "But there are fluctuations, and there are *fluctuations*." She looked up. "We don't have the full range of monitoring equipment that we used to. But as far as we can tell, and based on some triangulation, the energy currently looks like this." She drew another line, and this one moved wildly above and below the baseline. The rises and falls were bigger, and they looked much more random.

"What would make them different?"

"The Veil didn't open cleanly," Darby said. "It wasn't surgical; it ripped. So closing the Veil meant pulling those ragged ends back together. Seven Sensitives did that, and they encrypted the 'seam' to keep it closed. They used their particular magic to create an encryption—one that consisted of magical keys—that would act as an extra protection against someone trying to open it."

"Which Sensitives did the encrypting?" Liam asked.

"We don't know," Burke said. "No one knows except the Sensitives who did it. That was part of the deal—so the knowledge couldn't be used against them in the future."

"We fear the Veil is fluctuating more wildly because someone has managed to break some of the seals," Malachi said.

"Can you tell how many?" I asked.

"We cannot," Malachi said. "This is the first time in history the Veil was, to our knowledge, resealed in this manner."

"So you think the missing Sensitives and the Veil fluctuations are connected?" Liam asked.

Malachi nodded. "Yes, but we aren't sure how."

"How many Sensitives are missing?" I asked.

"Twenty that we know of," Burke said.

Liam and I exchanged a glance.

"What?" Burke asked.

"Since my sister's death," Liam said, "I've been tracking wraith attacks across the city. They've doubled over the last several months."

"How many?"

"Twenty-four," Liam said. That was pretty damn close to twenty. "Was Marla Salas one of your missing Sensitives?"

"She was," Darby said. "She was a good friend of mine."

"How long was she gone?" I asked, realizing I hadn't thought to ask Mrs. Salas.

"Thirteen days," Darby said. "And she was fine when I last saw her."

Fear bolted through me. Marla had gone from Sensitive to wraith in less than two weeks. That wasn't very much time—and it suggested there wasn't much of a defense to whatever was happening here.

"So could the missing Sensitives be 'missing' because they've been turned into wraiths?" I asked. "I mean, I don't know how that would be possible," I said, really meaning I didn't *want* to know how it was possible. "But the numbers match up."

The Delta folks exchanged glances.

"Not a theory I like considering," Burke said, then looked at Darby. "Is that possible?"

She pursed her lips, considering. "If you denied them the ability to regulate? Or maybe forced magic into them somehow? Increased the absorption rate? I'd have to think through the precise mechanics, but like Claire said, the numbers are awfully close."

On the upside, if someone else had done this to Marla—if it wasn't some sudden failure on her part—there was still a chance I could control my magic.

"So assume you can do it," Liam said. "Why would you want to?"

"So the perps can cover their tracks?" Burke suggested. "You want to open the Veil. You're interviewing Sensitives who might have been involved, and you find one who wasn't. You don't want her talking about the interview, about the questions. So you discard her. If you turn her into a wraith, she can't talk."

"Not to be grim," Liam said, "but why not just kill them?"

"Maybe you don't like Sensitives and Paras," Malachi said. "Letting Sensitives become wraiths, or making them become wraiths, puts more monsters on the street. Proves how dangerous they are."

"Then why open the Veil?" I asked.

"Perhaps to attack," Malachi said. "To be the first through the gate this time."

To initiate war, he meant.

Something occurred to me. "The Sensitives who worked with PCC—they have control of their magic?"

Burke nodded.

I looked at Liam. "Maybe that's why our wraiths are able to think and communicate to a higher degree—because they've kept some of that control. But who's this cold-blooded?"

"We don't know," Burke said. "Someone who wants the Veil open, and who has access to PCC files—they'd need those to identify the potential Sensitives. To find the seven, they'd have to work their way through the list. That seems to be what they're doing."

"It needn't be a human," Malachi suggested. "It could be a dispossessed Paranormal. They aren't opening the Veil to wreak havoc here, but to open their own doorway. And they don't care who they hurt in the process."

"Could be a human cult member," Liam suggested. "There are still humans who think they can prompt the Second Coming by opening the Veil."

Malachi nodded. "There are any number of theories. But we don't have any concrete evidence of who's behind it at this point. That's what we need to find out."

"Can you tell who else they might target?" Liam asked, moving incrementally closer to me, as though he could protect me from harm just by being nearer. I didn't really mind.

"So far," Darby said, "it looks like they're targeting any Sensitives who worked with PCC."

"Surely Containment knows about all this already?" I said. "About the Veil fluctuations? About the Sensitives?" I couldn't believe Containment—Gunnar's organization—would be so clueless.

Burke shook his head. "We've had to be careful what information we pass along, and how we do it. But we've figured out how to share the information with contacts inside Containment and two of its contractors—SecuriCrew and ComTac. They don't think the fluctuations matter. And no one wants to believe there's a risk the Veil will open again, that they'd have to face the trauma of war again. It's easier to say we're overreacting."

They needed help. I'd heard everything I needed to hear. "I want in. I want to help."

They all looked at me. I could feel Liam tense beside me, but he didn't object. He'd have known better by now. Recklessly brave, and all that.

The last few days had changed my circumstances—they'd changed *me*. And it was going to be next to impossible to go back to just selling dry goods in the Quarter.

I didn't know if my father had thought he'd lived a "big" life. I knew he was proud of what he'd done to keep the city fed and supplied during the war. I knew he was glad he'd been able to make a contribution. And yeah, I'd done the same thing, helped keep New Orleans alive, or at least my small corner of it. I'd stayed quiet. I'd worked hard.

But would that be satisfying forever? Now that I knew the truth, or at least some of it, about Paranormals and Containment, I didn't think so. I wasn't sure I could go back to that life.

Yes, it was a life I was thankful for. It was a life that helped me get over loss, and feel less alone when my family was gone. It gave me normalcy and routine, and kept me focused on whether we needed more needles or thread, instead of on what I didn't have.

But it was way too late to honor my father's request that I not intervene; at least I could fight on the right side.

"Why?" Malachi asked, head tilted. I didn't think he was judging the question, but checking my motivation.

"Because if things don't change, if we don't change the way Containment deals with Sensitives, make them acknowledge we don't have to turn into wraiths, I could be next."

"I'm in, too," Liam said. "She just beat me to it. Whoever is doing this has blood on their hands. My sister's. Marla Salas's. And they aren't the only ones."

Burke blew out a breath. "Good. We hoped you'd both feel that way."

"For the record," Darby said, "the pay sucks, because there is none, there are no benefits or sick days, and Containment could be on your ass at any time. But there is a lot of glory in keeping the Veil closed—saving humans from the monsters of the Beyond. No offense, Your Wingedness."

"None taken."

Speaking of His Wingedness, "If the Veil was opened," I said, glancing at Malachi, "you could go home. You don't want that?"

A shadow crossed his perfect face. "I'm a warrior. I lead my battalions, and the fight is not yet done. I did not choose to be here, but the fight has moved into this land."

"Meaning the fight is now against Containment?" Liam asked.

"In a manner of speaking," Malachi said. "It would, perhaps, be better to say that the fight is against ignorance."

"And what's the current agenda?" Liam asked.

"Tracking down the rest of the Sensitives who worked with Containment, even incidentally," Burke said. "But it's a slow process, and we haven't been able to keep up. We're still losing Sensitives."

"We've got a friend in Devil's Isle who has comp skills," Liam said. "If you're good with it, we can talk to him, have him search the network. Maybe he can find something about who might be targeted next."

Burke glanced at Malachi and Darby, who nodded. "Good idea," he said.

"So, how do we communicate?" I asked. "Or know when to meet?"

Malachi whistled. At his command, a milky-white pigeon flew down from the rafters, landed on his outstretched arm. There was a small leather band around one scaly leg. "Carrier pigeon," he said, then gestured to the leather band. "A small message can be placed here."

"I thought carrier pigeons were extinct."

"You're thinking of passenger pigeons," Darby said. "They are extinct. Carrier pigeons are actually a type of homing pigeon, which is not."

I looked at the bird, which turned its head in jerky, robotic movements. War hadn't done much to lower the pigeon count in New Orleans, and since telephones were gone, it was a pretty ingenious solution. Humans had come a long way . . . and sometimes circled right back again.

Malachi nodded. "There's a spot at your store where a bird could land? Where you could receive a message?"

I thought for a moment. "The courtyard windows. They're away from the street, and the other buildings that face the courtyard aren't occupied. There's a flagpole outside the third-floor window. If you can get them to land there, that could work."

He nodded. "When you take the message, you can insert another. The bird will fly back here, where we'll retrieve it."

"What if we need to get in touch with you before that?" I asked.

"Signal us," Malachi said. "You've got a postwar flag?"

That was the flag with gold fleurs-de-lis. "Sure."

He nodded. "If you need to meet with us, hang it on your third-floor balcony. Someone will see it, send a note. And if we need to meet, we meet here."

I nodded. "Easy enough."

"In that case," Darby said with a smile that looked pretty relieved, "welcome to the team."

A warm breeze was blowing outside as we walked across scratching gravel to the truck.

"So, I guess we've joined a treasonous secret alliance."

"That's what it looks like," Liam said as we climbed into the truck. He stuck the key in the ignition, pumped the gas until the truck roared to life.

He glanced at me. "I can't say I'm thrilled about the possibility the Veil will open again—or that we're the only thing standing between war and peace."

"We have to start somewhere," I said.

He looked at me, smiled. "That's one of those things people say that doesn't really mean anything. They just say it to make you feel better."

"Yeah, they do," I said. "And don't you feel better?"

He grunted.

"What are you going to have Moses look for?"

Liam frowned. "I'm not sure yet. It's not like he can search every instance of 'Sensitives' in Containment-Net. That's probably thousands of documents."

I smiled at him. "No. But he could search for 'Marla Salas.'"

He opened his mouth, closed it again. "Damn, Connolly. That's not bad."

"It's pretty damn brilliant, actually."

Liam snorted, swerved the truck around an enormous pothole. "Don't get a big head. I'll talk to him tomorrow."

"If we keep the Veil closed and save the world, do you think there's any chance Containment will rethink its position on Paras?"

"Not immediately. They're too invested in the narrative at this point."

That sounded like something Tadji would say. "Right. Containment lies."

"Put that on a damn T-shirt," he muttered. "But in the long term? Yeah. Public opinion will eventually sway. It always does. And it sounds like we're going to help it along. We just have to keep you safe in the interim. I mean, except for the treason."

"Eh," I said, waving it off. "Compared to saving the world, what's a little treason between friends?"

CHAPTER SEVENTEEN

I found out the next morning, when they blew in like a hurricane—eight men and women in dark gray fatigues with helmets and very large guns, led by Jack Broussard.

He wore a dark gray suit with a pale blue tie, his wavy hair gelled back above his forehead. His badge was on a chain around his neck, and there was a folded piece of ivory paper in his hand.

When he flipped the store's OPEN sign to CLOSED, my heart jumped into my throat. This was not going to be good.

I knew the signs of a Containment raid—agents busting in to look for Paranormals, for prohibited magical goods. There'd been hundreds of them during the war, when Containment decided Ouija boards and tarot cards meant the difference between victory and defeat, and after the war, when they were still trying to round up Paranormals who hadn't yet been driven into Devil's Isle.

I hadn't heard about a raid in the Quarter in years—probably two or three. There wasn't a point to it. There weren't enough of us left, and certainly not enough "implements of magic," as Containment called them, to make raids worth anyone's time—or the bad PR. It didn't do much for morale to bust people who were just managing to get by.

I kept my hands on the counter, forced myself to stay calm, to look bored, even while I was fuming inside. But anger wouldn't do me any good now, and panic would only make them suspicious. Mild irritation might help. Their believing I didn't have anything to hide might get them out of here sooner.

"Agent Broussard."

He walked forward, and the agents fanned out across the front of the store.

"Claire. Lovely to see you again."

"I'm sure. What brings you and your . . . *crew* . . . in today?"

"An inspection," he said. "For potential violations of the Magic Act."

I made myself laugh, but my chest ached with fear. Had they found out about our meeting yesterday? Had we been followed? Had Burke been a plant?

"That's hilarious. Is soap a Magic Act violation now?"

His expression didn't change. I guess the joke hadn't landed.

"You're serious?" I said, with mock surprise.

"Very." He extended the piece of paper to me. I scanned it. It was a form legal document that named me and my store, gave Broussard and Containment "permission" to search the store under the Magic Act. There was nothing to indicate who'd signaled Containment that I might be hiding something . . . except for the Commandant's seal at the top.

Gunnar's name wasn't on it, obviously, but the possibility he knew about this—and hadn't warned me—made my stomach churn with anger and fear. We were going to have a long talk when this was through.

"This paper gives Containment permission to search the store for violations of the Act, tools of magic, and the like."

I leaned forward, voice as fierce as I could make it. "As you damn well know, there are no violations and no tools in this store. There's nothing that *could* be here. Everything I get comes from the ground or a convoy."

"I have a valid warrant."

Fear began to transition to fury. "If you've got a warrant, then use it, and get the hell out of my store."

His smile was thin. "You heard her, folks. Let's use it."

They didn't waste any time. Each agent moved in a different direction, began ripping open drawers, emptying baskets, opening boxes. An agent reached into a vintage Redwing butter crock that was obviously empty. When he didn't find anything, he pushed it over. It hit the floor with a *crack*, sending shards of pottery across the wood. Another agent moved to the stand of walking sticks, pulled one out, rapped it hard against the edge of a bookshelf, shattering it in two. I flinched at the sound, which echoed off the brick walls like gunfire.

"Damn it, Broussard, control your people." My voice was pleading, but Broussard didn't intervene. When I tried to move around the counter to stop it myself, Broussard stepped in front of me. He was close enough that our toes met, that I had to look up at him to meet his gaze.

"If you attempt to interfere with a Containment investigation, I'll have to arrest you."

"This isn't an investigation!" An agent pulled a framed oil painting from the wall—a portrait of a planter who'd owned land on the River Road outside town. The agent, a woman with a square face and cold eyes, ripped away the paper backing, felt around the frame for something that might have been hidden there, which she obviously didn't find. She tossed the portrait away like trash.

"You're destroying my store."

"We're investigating," Broussard said, and made no move to rein in his people. And Paras were the bad guys? Nix had helped me learn how to not become a killer. Broussard was as human as they came, and a bully.

I pulled away from him, afraid I'd give him the kick to the balls he deserved, which would only make things worse for me. I winced as an agent clawed through the small pile of beets I'd pulled from the garden, tossed a couple onto the floor to make his point. That was *food*. You didn't waste food in the Zone, damn it.

"None of this destruction helps you." I looked back at him, pleading now. "If you want something, just tell me."

Broussard pulled a little black recorder out of his pocket, and it blinked green on the counter. "Are you hosting illicit meetings of Sensitives here?"

I stared at him for a moment. He'd missed the truth—if only by a little—which was helpful, because it meant I didn't have to fake an answer. "You cannot possibly be serious."

"You've been seen with Liam Quinn on several occasions. His loyalties are questionable."

"Yes, I know all about your history with Liam Quinn."

For the first time, Broussard's composure slipped. His eyes flashed. "Liam Quinn is a traitor."

"Liam Quinn is a bounty hunter, and as you probably know, he's training me to do the same."

"You expect me to believe that?"

"What, precisely, is hard to understand about that? Surely you don't think a woman can't bring down a wraith. 'Cause I've done it twice now. He's training me because I've seen wraiths and what they can do. I was here during the war, Broussard. I saw people die. I don't want that to happen again." *And I'm trying to keep it from happening.*

The cuckoo clock chimed, and one of the agents moved toward it, reached up a hand to grab it.

Enough, I thought. If I couldn't go around the damn counter, I'd just go over it. It wouldn't be the first time. I braced a hand on the wood, used the shelves like the steps of a ladder, hopped onto the top and onto the floor on the other side.

"Don't touch that," I yelled out, and prepared to move forward, but Broussard grabbed my arm, fingers pinching hard enough to bruise.

"Don't make this more difficult than it has to be." His teeth were clenched.

"I'm not the one making it difficult. Your thugs are destroying my store for no reason. You're going to regret this."

"Is that a threat, Ms. Connolly?"

I managed to wrench myself free, saw the gleam of enjoyment in his eyes. "You're trashing what's left of my family for nothing. But no, Broussard. I'm not threatening you. I'm just telling you the truth."

I tried to wrench away, but Broussard grabbed my other arm, too. And he held them behind me while the agent ripped the clock off the wall.

Tears sprang to my eyes as I tried to jerk forward. "Stop! Just stop, please! Stop!"

But he didn't stop. He ripped off the doors, broke off the girl and the wolf, wrenched away the hands of the clock. He looked inside. Satisfied there weren't any Secret Court of Dawn Plans inside, he dumped the pieces onto a nearby table.

If Containment wanted a war, this was precisely the way to get one.

They went through the front and back rooms, the kitchenette. And then they headed for the stairs.

For the first time, I remembered there *was* something incriminating on the second floor—the go bag I'd tucked back into the armoire after my run-in with the wraiths. There wasn't anything magical in it, but there were copies of my papers, a change of clothes. The purpose would be pretty obvious.

Broussard had let go of my arms, but stood beside me in case I decided to bolt. Like there was a chance I'd leave the store with these people in it.

But when the first agent made for the stairway, I jumped toward the staircase, put my arms against each wall to bar her way. "That's private property, not part of the store."

"Get out of the way," she said. "Or I'll move you myself." She pulled the stick from her belt, adjusted her fingers around the grip.

The bell rang on the door, and we all looked up. Gunnar walked inside.

I didn't think I'd ever been so glad to see him.

There was a pile of wooden-handled brooms in front of the door, spilled from the umbrella stand I'd stored them in. Gunnar looked at them, then the rest of the destruction, the men and women in fatigues, me standing in front of the stairs, arms crossed. His gaze fell on Broussard, and his eyes went ice cold. His jaw clenched, body stiffening, chest rising with indignation.

He strode right to Broussard with fury in his eyes, and his voice was low and dangerous. "What the hell's going on in here?"

"Containment raid," Broussard said. "For potential violation of the Magic Act."

"We haven't actively enforced the Magic Act in three years."

Broussard didn't look intimidated. "That doesn't make it less valid. Just means the enforcement has been lax."

"He asked me if I'm holding secret meetings of Sensitives," I said, my gaze still on the agent in front of me. Oh, how I'd have liked to use my magic to take her down.

Gunnar looked up, found me on the first tread, arms across the stairway, then dropped his gaze to the agent in front of me, who looked like she was ready to tear my arms from my body.

"That's the most ridiculous thing I've ever heard," he said, holding out a hand to Broussard. "Give me the warrant."

"You're not an agent."

"No," Gunnar said. "I'm not. But I'm the Commandant's adviser, and he's your boss. I have no knowledge of this 'raid.' I find it questionable, considering where you are and how many people you've brought."

He looked around the store, met the gaze of each agent. "I don't know what the hell you think you're doing here, but the Commandant does not support the destruction of private property. If you found magical objects here, you take them, you log them, and you turn them in. You don't destroy nonmagicals in the process."

"You've got an obvious conflict of interest," Broussard said, slanting his gaze to me. "She's your girlfriend."

"You are completely oblivious, Broussard. She's not my girlfriend; I'm gay. But she's a private citizen with civil rights. And I didn't ask for your opinion. I asked for the paper." He held out a hand.

Gunnar stared Broussard down with a look that was a mix of fury, irritation, and sheer daring. I wasn't sure if he actually had any authority over Broussard, but he sure looked the part.

Broussard looked pissed, but he pulled the paper from the inside of his coat pocket, handed it over.

Gunnar unfolded and read through it while we waited in silence for his verdict.

After a moment, he looked back at Broussard. "This says the warrant covers the store."

THE VEIL | *249*

"And?" Broussard says.

"The store is here, on the first floor. There's no store upstairs, so you have no right or authority to go up there."

"The warrant—"

"Says what it says," Gunnar said, folding it and putting it in his own pocket. "You had authority for the store, which you've clearly inspected."

"How do I know there's no store upstairs?"

Gunnar rolled his eyes, looked back at the rest of the agents. "Is there a store upstairs? Have you ever bought products up there?"

Silence, until a man in the front shook his head. "No, sir. Not upstairs."

"And there you go. And since you've trashed it, I strongly suspect the Commandant will have some questions about how you went about inspecting said store. And Claire will probably have some thoughts about whether you can ever come back."

"I do," I said to Broussard. "Don't ever step foot in this store again."

Then I lifted my gaze to the agents. A couple looked embarrassed, maybe that they'd let things go so far, maybe because they'd followed Broussard in here at all against their better judgment. Maybe they'd followed tough orders even though they knew better. We'd all done difficult things in difficult times.

Others just looked irritated. For whatever reason, or because of whatever Broussard had told them, they believed I was Public Enemy Number One. And that was fine. They could believe whatever they wanted, no matter how naive.

"If you believe I'd try to hurt this city," I said, "you're not as smart as you think. And you're no longer welcome here."

Broussard directed an agent to pick up the crate that contained the "evidence" they'd gathered. He gestured the man to the door, walked toward me with a piece of paper in hand. "You can come to Containment in forty-eight hours to check the status of your things. They may be retained as evidence in the event further action is warranted, but the clerk will advise."

I scanned the receipt, felt immediate relief. Among other totally innocent things, they were taking a saltcellar, candles, a pearl-handled knife, and a book about nineteenth-century spiritualism. "None of those things are magical," I said, handing the receipt to Gunnar, "and none of them are banned."

Broussard's expression was flat. "These are all goods that could be utilized to develop magic."

He said it like magic was something that could be made from scratch, like baking a cake. Like lighting a candle and saying a few words over the flame could raise someone from the dead or make someone fall in love. Hadn't the Veil proven that what humans knew of magic was just illusion? Just manipulation or coincidence? There was magic, absolutely. But the thing we'd imagined it to be had been only a sickly shadow of the real thing.

"No," I said, suddenly exhausted. "They couldn't. And I'm pretty sure everyone in the room knows that."

"Forty-eight hours," he said, then looked at Gunnar. "Perhaps we should both speak with the Commandant."

Gunnar nodded. "I think that would be best."

Broussard strode to the door, yanked it open, and moved into the overcast day outside.

The door closed silently behind him. They'd even taken the bell off the doorknob. Because that was clearly the key to my improper magical undertakings.

Silence fell as Gunnar and I stared at the remains of my store. No, they hadn't destroyed everything. But they'd tossed over enough furniture, dumped out enough nuts and bolts, that the floor was littered with stuff. It would take hours to put the room back into order.

I walked to the table where the agent had dumped the broken and shattered pieces of the cuckoo clock.

It had taken me a few weeks to get it cleaned and running the last time around. Now it wasn't just about the movement, but the pieces themselves. I'd have to figure out how much of the wood could be glued back together, or figure out a way to get new pieces cut. It would take months if I was lucky. I stood up Little Red Riding Hood, put the wolf upright beside her. And hoped I'd be lucky.

"I'm sorry, Claire," Gunnar said.

I nodded. But I couldn't stop to think about regret or how presumptuous Broussard had been, how sorry he should have been, and probably never would be. That would only enrage me even more, and Containment wasn't exactly on my good side right now.

The damage had been done. It was time to clean it up.

Gunnar offered to help before heading back to Containment, and I accepted. We worked in silence, started with the furniture. Turning over chairs. Righting tables. We put drawers back in their homes, piled their contents on top of tables. Together, we got the stand for the walking sticks upright again, began slotting them back into their spaces. They'd broken three of them—one basic cane, a stick with a brass monkey on the end, and a stick that held a small sewing kit. They'd left the broken slivers of wood, but taken the sewing kit. Because a couple of old needles, a bit of string, and a thimble were clearly the keys to my evil plan.

I put the pieces of the sticks on the counter, looked back at him. "I didn't ask you why you came into the store."

252 | CHLOE NEILL

Gunnar was putting antique silverware they'd upended back into its box. He smiled. "I came by to give you an update—Emme's doing better. Her fever's gone, and she's been up and around the house."

"Good," I said. "That's good. Any other sign of the wraiths?"

He shook his head, divvied up forks and spoons into their slots. "No. But there was another pair sighted in Mid-City last night. They didn't harass anyone that we know of, but the monitors are farther apart out there."

I nodded. "Why would Containment authorize the warrant?"

"Specifically, I don't know. Broussard must have made a case."

I had to ask. There just wasn't any way around it. So I gathered up my courage, looked at him. "I need to ask you something."

He looked up at me, brows lifted.

"I'm sorry, but I have to know: Broussard questioned me about Liam. Did you tell them I've seen him since the night of the wraith attack? That he's been here?"

Gunnar froze, a serving spoon in hand. I could see the hurt in his eyes, the set of his jaw. "Excuse me?"

"I'm not saying you'd have done it on purpose, but is there something you could have said that would make them suspect me of something?"

He put down the spoon, turned around to look at me. "Let's start with logic, Connolly." He only called me "Connolly" when he was angry. That wasn't a good sign.

"Containment interviewed you and Quinn in here after the Quarter wraith attack. You walked through the gate with him, were verified by the Containment guards. And when Solomon's men attacked you both—which you also didn't tell me—agents responded. You also admitted to Broussard that you knew Liam."

I guess he'd read that report, too. "I had to ask."

"Did you, Claire? Did you have to ask if your best friend played the snitch?"

"Someone told them something," I said. "You and Burke are the only people I know in Containment." I could have been wrong, but I had a pretty good sense Burke wasn't talking.

"Are we?" Gunnar's expression chilled. "Liam Quinn works for Containment."

"He's a contractor. He doesn't really work for them."

Gunnar's expression didn't change. "The paychecks come from the same place either way." He crossed his arms. "You started acting different the second he walked into your life. You sure this isn't about him? Are you sure you can trust him?"

How could I be sure anyone right now was trustworthy? In a matter of days, everything I knew about the world had been turned upside down. The splitting of the Veil had proven that magic existed, and it was no fairy tale.

"Are you sure Containment is trustworthy?" I asked him.

"Of course not."

I stared at him. "What do you mean 'of course not'? You work for them."

Done with the silverware, he closed the cloth-lined box. "People always say it like that. Like Containment is a unified thing, a force against evil." He looked back at me. "Containment is just people, Claire. It's made up of people, some good, some bad, most in between. Just like any other organization in the world, it's only as trustworthy as the people who are in it."

"I didn't know you felt that way."

He made a harsh sound. "It's not exactly a popular opinion. And it doesn't help people very much. They need to believe there's good and evil in the world, and that the dividing line between them is very, very clear. That's how we made it through the war, Claire. Because in the midst of tragedy and violence and death and worse, for all that evil, there was still good. There was still a good guy."

Now, that sounded like the Containment I knew. But Gunnar wasn't saying that the world really was black and white—just that people needed to believe it was. I couldn't really argue with that.

"I'm sorry," I said.

Gunnar grunted.

"For what it's worth, I didn't want to believe you had any part in it, even accidentally. But there aren't a lot of options."

"Again, I offer Quinn."

I shook my head. "He plays it close to the vest, but I think he's got a good heart." Not that I'd ever tell him that. "He may be paid by Containment, but I don't think there's any love lost there."

Gunnar walked toward me at the counter. "He told you about his previous employment? About his work for Containment?"

I nodded. "Ya. And that Broussard's got it in for him. Do you think that would motivate Broussard?"

"I didn't know." This time, there was regret in this eyes. "I'm sorry. I know how much the store means to you. How much all of it means to you. But I swear, I didn't know. Warrants shouldn't even go through the Commandant without going through me first."

I sat up a little straighter. That was very interesting. "They shouldn't?"

"No. Which means someone avoided me. I wouldn't have thought Broussard had the chops for this, but who knows. I checked him out around the office after you said he talked to you. The man's like a dog with a bone. And he's got it in for Quinn over that last contract."

"But surely that's not enough to decide that I'm hosting Sensitive tea parties. That's a pretty specific accusation."

"You aren't, are you?"

He was grinning, which meant we were okay. "No. But only because I can't find any tea."

Gunnar smiled. "Don't think about the world as good and evil, Claire. Those are labels that don't mean anything. We assign them out of fear. Think about what is objectively right, and what is objectively wrong. That's how I stay employed in Containment. Because I understand the difference between those things."

God, I wished I could tell him about everything. I knew I couldn't—it would put everyone at risk.

He looked at the wreckage of the store with his hands on his lean hips. "I work for Containment, Claire, because it helps New Orleans. That's what I was born to do. But that's not all I am. For now, let's do what we can. Let's get back to work."

Gunnar was a good man. And sooner or later, I was going to have to do right by him. I was going to have to tell him the truth.

It was well dark when I locked up the store, turned off the lights, headed up the stairs. I was too exhausted to do anything but fall into bed.

I reached the second-floor landing and made the turn . . . to see light streaming down the stairs. I'd turned off the light—I remembered doing it, always made sure that I did it in order to conserve what energy there was.

Someone had turned it back on again.

Was it Liam? Had he found out what had happened, come to comfort me? It didn't make sense that he'd not have used the front door—he had such a fondness for it—but nothing else made sense, either.

And God, I would have liked to see him tonight. He'd become an axis—a stable, center point that all the crazy traveled around.

I put a hand on the railing, began to pull magic just in case it wasn't him and I needed to use it against whoever was trespassing in the store. I took the stairs one at a time, each creak sounding like a gunshot in the quiet. I stepped onto the landing and looked inside.

He stood in the middle of the room, a lock of dark blond across his forehead, wings folding at his back, disappearing. The window was open, the curtains thrown back. Moonlight streamed across his body and sent shimmering light through the room.

Malachi.

There was an angel in the third floor of my French Quarter town house, looking as relaxed as any average and casual visitor from the street. Which he most definitely was not.

I walked into the room. "If someone saw you come up here, reported you, we'll both be in trouble."

"No one saw me," Malachi said, with utter self-assurance.

"What are you doing here?" I asked, still a little wary.

"I introduced a pigeon to the flagpole, fed him. It's part of their training process."

The pigeons. Of course.

I walked to the window, moved the curtain aside. A gray pigeon blinked round eyes at me from the flagpole outside my window.

"Cool," I said, then dropped the curtain again.

Malachi smiled. "He'll fly back home again shortly. Next time you see him outside, give him a bit of grain. With time, he'll learn to return here should we need to get a message to you."

I nodded.

"I also came to see if you were all right."

"You heard about the raid?"

He nodded. "In a manner of speaking. I wanted to see your store for myself, had planned to check on you when the sun went down. I waited nearby—there are ways that I can be very discreet. I saw them come in." Guilt etched in his face. "I am sorry that I didn't intervene."

I wouldn't fault him for that. "They'd have arrested you on sight."

"Likely," he said. "But that's no excuse for standing by. You're not hurt?"

"I'm fine. We've started putting the store back together."

"We?"

"My friend Gunnar helped."

He crossed his arms. "Why did Containment come?"

"They believe I'm holding secret meetings of Sensitives here."

His eyebrows lifted. "Where did they get that idea?"

"I don't know. Probably from someone who wants them focused on me, instead of on the Veil opening again."

"That's a reasonable strategy. And apparently a successful one."

"Yeah."

Malachi walked forward, cast his gaze on the ceiling. I'd hung an assortment of stars there—some crystal, some glittered, some old-fashioned mercury glass. They caught light through the window, swirled it across the across the floor. Some nights I'd lie on the daybed and watch them spin, watch the light turn and shift. It usually helped me calm down.

Malachi looked up at them. "Those are beautiful."

"Thank you."

"You know angels, as you'd call us, prefer high ground."

I nodded.

"My home was near the top of a mountain. And when darkness fell, it seemed every star in the universe was visible. There aren't nearly so many stars here."

I smiled. "Not below sea level, no. But more stars now than before the lights mostly went out."

He nodded, looked back grimly. "I remember seeing the glow of the city—an orange haze. I didn't come here—it wasn't allowed by the Court soldiers who'd conscripted me. But I could see it in the distance."

"New Orleans was a wonderful place. Complicated. Rich. Sometimes awful. Sometimes wonderful. It's like that today, too. Just in a different way."

He watched me speak, nodded. "I can see that. Well," he said, "it's late. I should go and let you rest."

He walked to the window, glanced back. "Good night, Claire."

And then he was gone.

opened the store the next day, right on time. We'd gotten almost everything upright and off the floor, but every shelf and table was covered with things that needed fixing, organizing. I could have asked folks to shop somewhere else until everything was clean and tidy again. But that would hide what Containment had done. And there was no more hiding. Not anymore. Not after this. I didn't have family they could come after. But I had my store, and my friends. They'd already screwed with part of that. I wouldn't give them a chance to screw with the other.

Broussard might not have liked me very much. And Containment might not have trusted me. But the Quarter liked me a lot—and more, they liked Royal Mercantile. It was an institution. Part of the Quarter, part of New Orleans, part of the Zone. It had helped them through lean and leaner times. And when they discovered Containment had taken its wrath out on this cornerstone of their lives, they were pissed.

They came in slowly, one at a time, then groups of three or five as word spread through the Quarter and uptown. I sold out of batteries, combs, hammers. I doubted anyone needed any of those things. But today they were shopping in solidarity, not in consumption. I even managed to sell two slightly warped walking sticks. Heavily discounted, of course.

Mrs. Proctor brought in a bowl of what she called "mock pie"—a mash of powdered biscuit mix and canned fruit. (She hadn't bought any butter, but she'd ended up borrowing half a stick from a neighbor.)

I wouldn't fault the agents who were following the chain of command, who probably thought they were doing the right thing— keeping an eye on a dangerous element. Containment agents still came by the store throughout the day, although none of them had participated in the raid. But they still wore apologetic looks.

It was late afternoon when Liam appeared on my threshold.

He'd skipped shaving again, and the scruff seemed to make his eyes even more brilliantly blue. He also looked tired. Maybe he hadn't slept any better than I had.

"What happened in here?" he asked, surveying the store.

"You should have seen it before we cleaned it up. And I'm not being sarcastic."

He walked toward me, looked me over. It was warm out, and Liam smelled like hard work and clean sweat. "You're all right?"

I looked at him, tried to sound totally nonchalant, which was definitely not how I felt. I was relieved, more than I should have been, to see him standing there. "I'm fine. Your favorite Containment agent came by yesterday with a warrant to search for Magic Act violations. Seems to think I've been having secret Sensitive meetings here."

Liam's eyes narrowed. "Where'd he get that idea?"

"He wouldn't tell me. Gunnar didn't know, either." I looked around. "He helped me get things cleaned up. It doesn't look like we made much of a dent, but we actually got quite a bit done."

"Is it possible someone saw us at the refinery?" Liam asked.

"Maybe? My best bet is that it's someone who wants to open the Veil and is working really hard to keep Containment distracted. And Jack Broussard, who is most definitely a tool, is a very good tool for that. I didn't see him today. Maybe he's cooled off."

"I'm sorry, Claire."

I nodded. "What about you?"

"I've been hunting," he said, and I realized there was a faint shadow on his left cheekbone.

He hadn't asked me to go. It didn't surprise me to learn he'd wanted space. Hell, right now, even though part of me wanted him around all the time, I needed space. I wanted that beach scene Burke had mentioned, and a few hours of sunlit oblivion. I wasn't sure either of us was having very good luck with that.

"Caught me with an elbow," Liam explained. "Male wraith in Irish Channel."

That was between the river and the Garden District. "He was one of Delta's Sensitives?"

"He was. Lizzie's got him now."

I nodded. "Best place for him," I said, but knew that wasn't saying much.

"Speaking of Delta, do you want to go see Moses?"

"He found something?"

Liam nodded. "I'm not sure what, but I got a message he had something he wanted me to see. I'm headed back to Devil's Isle, thought I'd see if you wanted to go with."

I grimaced, gestured toward the still-disorganized store. "Do you think it's safe for me to go in there right now?"

Liam considered. "You're also supposed to be my trainee." He pulled out a laminated card. "And I got you a transit pass."

I took it, checked the print on both sides. It looked legit. "How did you manage this?"

"Like I said, I have friends in PCC. I didn't know about the store—about what Broussard did—but I think going proves you aren't afraid of Containment, or of being in Devil's Isle. That says you've got nothing to hide from Containment or anyone else. I think that's our strongest defense."

"And how do we explain our visit to go see Moses?"

Liam smiled. "I'm a bounty hunter; he's got information. We're still trying to figure out where the wraiths are coming from, which is completely legitimate."

"You've got this all figured out, don't you?"

"My good looks are exceeded only by my brains."

"And your humility."

He grinned. "I've got no need for humility."

He had me there.

Since organizing literal nuts and bolts didn't sound any better, I opted for the field trip.

I served a few last customers, then closed the shop a little early and locked it up. We walked down Royal. There were a few strollers out tonight, men and women that I recognized from the neighborhood or the store walking in the same direction as we were. The reason rang through the air the closer we got to Jackson Square.

"Memorial in Song," Liam said as we reached the wrought-iron fence. We walked to the gate, looked inside. A hundred people stood in the Square singing "Over in the Gloryland."

It had taken four days after the Second Battle to arrange for a memorial for the folks who'd died. Every year, just as we celebrated the victory of War Night, New Orleanians gathered in the square four days later to mourn those who were lost. They'd sing hymns until darkness fell, and then they'd light candles and sing until the wicks burned down, until the square was left in darkness again.

It had been so crazy since War Night, I'd totally forgotten about the memorial. I couldn't carry a tune, but I loved being so close to something so beautiful. It made me feel, just for a little while, closer to my dad.

"Can we stand here for a minute?" I asked, closing my eyes and letting the voices wash over me. "Just for a minute."

I could feel Liam's gaze on me, looking, questioning. And then he settled in beside me. "Of course we can," he said, and he began to hum along.

As it turned out, Liam could sing pretty well. We listened for two more songs, swaying to the music before we turned back to our task.

Hawkins was at the gate again. If there were standing orders to look at me sideways, he didn't act on them. He scanned our IDs without comment, and didn't say anything until the warning speech.

The streets of Devil's Isle were unusually quiet. "Where is everyone?" I asked.

"It's memorial day for them, too," Liam said quietly. "They have their own dead to mourn."

I felt stupid and insensitive for not realizing they'd need to grieve, too.

We walked to Moses's shop, found him deep in an argument with something he kept trying to hit with an old-fashioned flyswatter.

It buzzed through the air toward us, zooming right into my face, pausing long enough for me to get a look at a curvy green female with wings like a dragonfly's, and probably twice as big as one.

She looked me over, flipped me off, and flew out of the store through a flapping pet door.

"Charming. Peskie?"

"Peskie," Liam confirmed. "And a very unhappy one by the look of it." He walked toward Mos, smiled. "Who'd you piss off this time?"

We walked to the back of the store, where Mos worked on what was left of his hair with a small plastic comb.

"No one. She wants unacceptable terms, she can get her electronics from somewhere else. Keeps messing with my hair."

"I think you look devastatingly handsome."

Mos looked up at me, blushed. "You shitting me or trying to get information?"

I grinned at him. "Telling the truth. Plus the information thing."

He looked at Liam. "I like her."

Liam made a vague noise that probably could have gone either way. "I got a message you have something for us."

"I do," Mos said. He spun in his chair, used the dark monitor behind him to check his reflection, finish his hair, then tossed the comb away. And then his hands were on the keys, and he was moving through layers of security like a knife through butter.

He got to a document, sent it to an old-fashioned printer that whirred back and forth across paper with holes on each edge.

"You are the master of technology," Liam said.

Moses grunted. "Don't I know it?" When the pages had printed, he ripped it off the printer, ripped away the edges, slapped them on the counter in front of us. "Poked around a little in the Containment files searching for the name you gave me, then moved into the files of some of those businesses they hired to do their work. This one belonged to a contractor called ComTac."

Liam nodded. "Some of our acquaintances talked to them."

We looked down at the page. It was clearly a list, but that was about all I could tell. They used the English alphabet, but the words themselves didn't make any sense. Just jumbled bunches of letters.

"I don't know what I'm looking at here, Mos," Liam said.

"It's a list of persons of interest," Mos said. "Says so right at the top."

The top said nothing of the sort.

"But not so you'd get that at first glance," Mos said. He flipped over the pages, folded it once longwise about a third of the way across, then again. When he turned it back, he folded the flap again, hiding some of the letters in the middle.

"Cheap way of encrypting," he said. "Effective if you don't do print." He grinned with sharp teeth, turned the list toward us again. "But ineffective if you do."

It became readable. And it became a list of three columns: name, location, power.

"Oh, damn," I murmured through the horror. "It's a list of Sensitives. Probably the ones who worked with PCC during the war."

"Yeah," Liam said. "Their persons of interest." He flipped to the second page, reoriented the folds so the names lined up, scanned them. "I count forty-three names in total. And they've been working through the list."

He was right. The first two dozen names had lines through them; they'd been marked off the list. Marla Salas was right in the middle, her name struck through. And we knew what had become of her.

"Damn it, Liam—she wasn't saying 'contact.'" I looked at him. "She was saying 'ComTac.' She was trying to let us know. She was *communicating* with us."

Liam's eyes widened, and he stared down at the paper. It was the first proof we'd had that wraiths really were capable of communication. "Damn," he said quietly. "ComTac is trying to open the Veil.

They have to investigate each one. Eliminate them one by one to find out if they had the encryption keys."

I looked back on the list, scanned through for names that looked familiar, as if I'd somehow be able to match up the wraiths I'd seen with the Sensitives on the list.

And on my second pass through, I saw it.

"Oh my God."

Liam's gaze snapped to mine in alarm. "What?"

The names had been crossed out in order—one after another. And the next two names on the list, the ones that hadn't yet been crossed out, were frighteningly familiar. I knew them.

Phaedra Dupre	Chenal	Conduct magic
Zana Dupre	Chenal	Call animals

"This is Tadji's family," I said, looking up at Liam. "Her mom and aunt. Is Chenal in Acadiana?"

"Yeah. Pointe Coupee Parish, I think." He frowned. "Why?"

"She said she wasn't sure where they were—that they moved around a lot—but she told me she grew up somewhere in Acadiana."

"That a friend of yours?" Mos asked.

"My best friend." I turned to Liam. "We have to warn her, and we have to get them out."

It only took Liam a moment to realize the implication, what they were in line for.

"We're going right now," he said, and put a hand at my back to guide me to the door. But he looked back at Moses.

"Take care of yourself, Mos. If this is ComTac, or even if it isn't, they're willing to hurt people. I don't want you to be one of the people hurt. Hell, we've probably put you in danger just by coming in here."

"People come in, come out, all the time. You're no different." His voice was gruff, but I saw the understanding in his eyes. "I'll be careful like I always am. You take care of yourself and Red. And you let me know what you find out."

We left Moses to his store and ran for the gate.

Ten sprinting minutes later, we were back in front of my store, where Liam had parked his truck. We climbed back in and flew toward Tadji's cottage.

It was a traditional New Orleans Creole cottage—a small, boxy front, with two long shuttered windows in between two narrow doors, a small porch in front. The house was painted a pale, cheery green, the trim and porch white. Tadji sat on the porch in one of two rocking chairs, notebook and pencil in hand. Surprisingly enough, Burke sat in the other chair. I wasn't entirely sure how I felt about that. Glad that we'd be able to loop Delta into what we'd found out. But I didn't like to see Burke hanging out with Tadji under what might have been false pretenses. Did I think he needed to tell Tadji the truth about who he was? Absolutely. But did she need to find out here? Right now, and from me? I was fuzzier on that.

"You take her, and I'll take him?" Liam asked.

"You read my mind."

Tadji and Burke stood when we climbed out of the truck. Burke smiled, at least until he saw the expression on our faces.

I saw the instant flinch of concern in Tadji's eyes, but she stayed composed. "What's wrong?" she asked as we crossed the small strip of grass in front of the house.

"I need to talk to Tadji about a family matter."

Burke's eyebrows lifted, but he didn't budge. Instead, he looked at Tadji. He was worried about whatever this was, and he'd take his cue from her. "Tadj?"

She watched us for a moment, eyes narrowed. It was clear she was suspicious, but she had to know we wouldn't make such a weird request unless there was a good reason for it.

"It's fine," she said finally. "I'll talk to them."

Burke smiled, squeezed her hand. "All right," he said. "But I'm holding you to that lemonade you promised."

She nodded, watched as he walked down the couple of porch stairs to the sidewalk. He stopped when he reached Liam.

"Let's go inside," I said. She stood there for a moment, not sure what to do, before nodding and opening the door.

The interior of the cottage was as original as the exterior. Old oak floors, brick walls, simple, pretty furniture. The house smelled of antiques and peonies, but it was a little stuffy. Probably why she and Burke had been sitting on the porch.

"What's this about?" Tadji asked. She put the notebook and pencil on a small table, crossed her arms.

"Your mom and aunt might be in danger. We need to find them."

"What? How could they be in danger?"

"Because they're Sensitives."

She froze. "How would you know that? Is this because of those questions you were asking me the other day? Because you were trying to find out where they were?"

"What? No. Oh God." I put a hand on my chest, horrified that she'd had to worry I was trying to rat out her family. "Is that what you thought? That I was trying to get information about your family? No. I mean, I was curious, but not because I wanted to get your family into trouble." I swallowed. "It's because I'm a Sensitive, too."

She looked stricken, like I'd slapped her.

"Let's sit down," I said, gently taking her arm and moving her to a chair. When she was seated, I took the chair opposite her.

"Tadji, I know you don't like magic, and I know you don't want to talk about it. But I think it's better just to get it all out there, okay? So that's what I'm going to do." I moistened my lips.

"Someone is trying to open the Veil, and they need Sensitives to do it. Your mom and aunt are on a short list of those who've been targeted for information. The people who are doing this—we think it's a defense contractor—is turning the Sensitives into wraiths to cover their tracks. We need to get to your mom and your aunt before they do, and we need to go now. I wouldn't bring this to you if I didn't think it was necessary. If I didn't think there was a chance they were in very real danger."

Her gaze stayed steady on me. "You're sure about this? You're positive?"

I nodded. "I'm sure."

"They're my family," she said quietly. "Magic or not." She cleared her throat nervously. "Right now they're in Chenal. I knew where they were. I didn't tell you, or anyone else, because . . ."

"Because they're Sensitives," I said gently. "Because they're fugitives. I understand."

She nodded. "We can go now?"

"Right now," I agreed, standing, and offering her a hand. "And we'll get there in time."

Days like this I really missed telephones.

I considered, before we left town, going to the Cabildo and dragging Gunnar into the truck. But like Tadji and Burke, I wanted to ease him into whatever was going on here, not throw him into the deep end. We'd get Tadji's family safe, and then we'd talk to Gunnar.

It would take about two hours to get from New Orleans to Chenal, and we'd pass what remained of Baton Rouge along the way.

We hurried down I-10, the six-lane divided freeway that would get us past Baton Rouge to the Mississippi River.

Louisiana's former capital had taken too much damage, and was closed after the war—the humans relocated, the Paras shipped to Devil's Isle. Louisiana didn't have a functioning capital anymore. The entire state was within the Zone, a "conflict community" under the Magic Act, and that made it Containment's territory.

The city looked like a ghost town. The downtown had been almost completely destroyed in the Battle of Port Allen. Containment blew the levee to shift the momentum in the fight. It turned the tide, literally, but flooded the city. The capitol building's former tower, four hundred and fifty feet of limestone, had fallen, and now spread across the ground in a long pile of vine-covered rubble.

Neighborhoods not blighted by war and magic still stood empty, but like the tower, nature and time were taking them back. Where the soil was still good, vines and grasses had crept in from the edges, threatening to overtake streets and bridges, and the asphalt had buckled in areas Containment hadn't bothered to fix.

Liam slowed as we prepared to cross the New Bridge that led across the river. It wasn't really new anymore, but the name had stuck.

"What's wrong?" Tadji asked.

"Just want to take it slow," Liam said, eyes scanning left and right. "You can never really tell about bridges—how well Containment's kept them up."

Tadji grabbed my hand, squeezed, and, just as I'd done when I was younger, I tried to hold my breath as we drove beneath the bridge's steel ribs, and the river roiled beneath us.

"Look," Liam said as we reached the crest of the river. A black bear ambled in the opposite lane, two small cubs trotting playfully behind her.

Humans were no longer in control of Louisiana, if they'd ever been.

We passed the cities, entered rural areas where there once had been long fields of rice and sugarcane. Some areas were still scorched by the magic. Shrubby trees were beginning to cover the fields that hadn't been, because there was no one left to farm them. In another few years, it would be impossible to tell a field had ever been here.

"Why?" I wondered, staring at a strip of land that was still black and devastated so many years later. "Why does magic do this to land?"

"Salt."

Liam's answer was so quick, so simple, I glanced back at him. "What?"

"'For they have destroyed the offenders and salted the earth beyond them, so that nothing else shall grow there,'" he quoted. "Magic is power. Power effects chemical and physical change. And where earth is concerned, it tends to make salts."

I nodded, recognized a dark box on a pole near the road. "Magic monitors?"

Liam glanced out the window, nodded. "Yeah. Not nearly as many out here as closer to the cities. And the farther you get out, the fewer the markers."

Along with the magic monitors, billboards dotted the landscape. They were peeling or shredding now, but they'd been long forgotten by whatever company had hung them. They advised people to save water, to GARDEN FOR VICTORY, and BEAT MAGIC WITH MIND AND MUS-CLE. The letters were big, the pictures simple. The messages a little depressing, even now.

As twilight fell, scorched land turned to swamp and both sides of the narrow road dropped into murky water dotted with duckweed, cypress trees and their knobby roots peeking through like tentacles. Liam turned off the AC and rolled down the window. The scent of the bayou washed in—green things, wetness, decay. It was an earthy scent, not totally unlike the smell of New Orleans after a heavy rain. It was all swamp one way or the other.

Other than the occasional scorched tree, there wasn't much evidence of war here at all.

"The battles didn't often reach the bayous," Liam said. "Too messy, too wet, not enough line of sight."

Tadji nodded. "And when they did, the impact was often covered with a few feet of muddy water. Turn here," she said, and directed Liam to turn the truck onto a bumpy gravel road, the swamp lapping at the edges. If the water had been much higher, the road would have been impassable.

The house sat on an empty rise surrounded by magnolia trees and palmetto plants, and was absolutely gorgeous. We weren't far from the river, and the house, two stories with porches that extended the length of the building, sat on brick columns to keep it dry in case of flood. Both floors were lined with windows and haint blue plantation shutters. The house looked old, but was in perfect condition.

A car was parked beside a boat on a trailer in the driveway beside the house, and a pirogue leaned against one of the columns. Transportation for any conditions.

Tadji opened the truck door, hopped down into the grass, wiped Quinn Truck Residue from her pants. I followed her.

Liam circled around, and we glanced at each other while she looked at the house.

"You all right?"

"No," she said. "I'm nervous, and my palms are sweating, and my stomach is in a knot."

"You can do this," I said. "We'll go in, get them out, and go."

"Let's be quick about it," Liam said, and gestured to the stairs. "Shall we?"

We took the steps to the first floor, and Tadji knocked on one of the double doors, also haint blue, before pushing it open. She walked inside, and we followed.

The interior was lovely, and beautifully French. Ivory walls climbed to an olive green ceiling, which met the painted wooden mantel of a fireplace. The floors were dark wood, mostly covered by a faded rug. The furniture was simple, and probably as old as the house. Ladder-back chairs, a table that held a hobnail vase of flowers, a low sofa.

We walked through one parlor and then a dining room, also pretty and outfitted with antiques, and then into the kitchen.

A woman stood there, stirring a pot that sizzled on the stove.

"Hervé? That you? I thought you were bringing the propane tomor—" She turned back and glanced at us with eyes the same deep brown of Tadji's. The resemblance didn't end there. Her skin had the same dark depth, her limbs similarly long and slim. Her hair was a short cloud of tight curls, the fingers around the spoon elegant and slender.

When she recognized Tadji, she froze, looked from her daughter to the strangers she'd brought with her. Fear crept into her eyes, and the spoon clattered to the floor.

CHAPTER NINETEEN

"Tadji. What are you doing here? You're not supposed to be here. It's too dangerous. And you aren't to bring strangers into the house. Are you all right? Is everything all right?"

Her words were fast, panic clearly seeping in.

"They're friends," Tadji said, taking a step forward, "and they're here to help. Things are happening, Mama. Big things. You need to be prepared."

Her eyes narrowed. "What kinds of things?"

"We should talk to you and Aunt Zana together. It affects both of you."

She picked up the spoon, turned off the stove. "Zana," she yelled. "Come in here, please."

We stood in awkward silence in the kitchen until floorboards began to creak in another part of the house.

Zana came through the doorway in a pale pink dress, looking much like a ghost in this very old house in this very old bayou. She could have been Phaedra's twin. She had the same long bones and wispy figure, but her face was a little longer, her mouth a little rounder.

Her eyes widened when she saw Tadji in the kitchen. "Tadji. What are you doing here? Has something happened?"

"Hi, Aunt Zana. This is Claire, and this is Liam," Tadji said, pointing to us. "We need to talk to both of you. Is there a place we can sit down?"

Phaedra took Zana's hand, walked into the living room linked to the kitchen. They sat down on one couch while Tadji and I sat down on the other. Liam stayed on his feet, arms crossed and ready to move. I hoped we had more time than that.

"What's this about?" Phaedra asked.

"It's about you and your magic," Tadji said.

The sisters looked at each other, linked their hands again.

"What about it?" Phaedra lifted her chin defiantly.

"Someone's trying to open the Veil," Liam said, "and they're looking for Sensitives who can help them. They have a list of Sensitives, people who they're interrogating to get that information. And we think they're making them wraiths so they can't report about that interrogation."

Phaedra's brows lifted. "I don't see what this has to do with us."

"You're both on the list," he said. "We think you're next."

The words fell like thunderclaps in the quiet room.

The sisters' fingers tightened. "We haven't left the bayou in years," Phaedra said. "We couldn't be on any list."

"We've seen it," Liam gently said. "You're on it."

Tadji stood up. "It's too dangerous for you to be here without help, without support. They could come for you, and no one would know it. You could come back to New Orleans with us." She looked at me and Liam.

"We have friends you could stay with," I said. "You'd be safe there until we can make sure the threat is gone."

Tadji nodded. "Yes. Exactly. The three of us rode down here together. I can drive back with you in the sedan."

"Nonsense," Phaedra said, crossing one leg over another. "That's nonsense. We've done no one's business but our own for years."

"But you did someone else's business at one time, Mrs. Dupre?"

All eyes turned to Liam.

"You helped Containment during the war. And when you discovered they lied about immunity, you disappeared. Maybe after that, you've done favors for friends, used your magic. Become known as women who could help?"

Phaedra's chin lifted again in that proud, defiant way. She was definitely Tadji's mother. "It's a difficult life out here. You work hard for it, and you get to know the folks who help you. We've done right by our neighbors. It's what anyone would do."

Liam sat down on the arm of the chair, his eyes fixed on Phaedra. "I don't doubt that one bit. But when you help, word spreads about who you are, about where you are, and about what you can do. The fact is, you're on the list, and they know where you are."

"Even if what you're saying is true," Phaedra said, "we aren't going anywhere. This is our home. We aren't going to leave it."

And then, suddenly, they didn't have a choice.

It started as a low throb of sound, a drumbeat in the distance. And then it grew louder. *Thuck. Thuck. Thuck. Thuck.*

You didn't often hear air traffic over the Zone—it was too risky to fly when you could suddenly lose power—but I remembered what a helicopter sounded like.

I stood up, my heart pounding as loudly as the rotors. I thought, hoped, that we'd managed to get here in time. It didn't look like that was the case.

"Stay here," Liam said, and walked to the window, used a single finger to slip back a curtain and looked out. He let out a low, growling curse as it passed over the house, and then he looked back at me, nodded.

Liam shifted his gaze to Phaedra and Zana. "It's a ComTac copter. That's the defense contractor we think is trying to open the

Veil—the ones who have the list with your name on it. They'll look for somewhere to land, and then the operatives will come here, and they'll come for you."

Phaedra's eyes and expression had gone flat. "They'll get the encryption over my dead body."

"The encryption?" Tadji asked, glancing between Liam and her mother. "What does that mean? I don't know what that means."

"Damn," I murmured.

"It means your mother's not just a Sensitive," Liam said. "She's one of the seven Sensitives who closed the Veil. ComTac wants her to help get it open again."

Tadji's eyes grew large, her gaze jumping from Liam to her mother and back again.

"We'll get into the details later," Liam said, "when everyone is safe. But for now we need to get out. We don't have much time."

"We don't need protecting," Phaedra said, standing. "The sun is setting. We can get into the bayou, hide. We've got provisions there." She looked at her sister, who nodded. "We stored them, just in case. They won't be able to find us."

Liam looked at Tadji, who looked completely out of her element. And for good reason—this was precisely the element she'd been trying to avoid for years.

But it was too late for regrets or questions. We had to move.

"Let's go," Liam said, gesturing toward the door. "Lead the way, Mrs. Dupre."

Back to the porch, down the stairs, around the house to the back. The bayou began about fifty yards away, with stubbly grass and a small shed in between. With Tadji in front, Liam behind, we ran for the shed.

The yelling started just before we dodged behind old wood.

Either they'd found a landing spot for the copter and hurried from it, or they'd had vehicles on the ground, too. ComTac wanted its Sensitive. And ComTac was prepared.

We peered through the worn wood at the house. Operatives in black fatigues spilled like termites around each side of the house, carrying very large weapons. They formed a human barrier on both sides, preventing us from running back the other way and toward the cars. It was the bayou or Devil's Isle. And that was only really a choice if we assumed they wouldn't follow us through the swamps. Unfortunately, these guys—and they were all men—looked like hard-bitten warriors. Big muscles, lots of ink, faces that seemed to have taken plenty of abuse from Paras or otherwise. They wouldn't just let us go.

"We seem to have a problem here."

A man stepped through the line of men, walked toward us. He was tall, probably in his late sixties. He had closely cropped hair in a military style, wore fatigues in the old brown and green camouflage style the military hadn't used in a decade. His face was long and haggard, jowls sagging on each side of his face. And there was hatred in his eyes.

"Come out, come out, wherever you are." There was a Southern lilt to his voice.

Liam looked at me, and I shook my head. "Don't even think about it," I said.

"No other choice," he said, pulling the keys from his pocket and pressing them into my hand. "You can drive?"

I nodded.

"Get them to the truck. They'll be followed through the swamp. Get them to New Orleans, to Gunnar or to Gavin. That's your best bet."

"No," I said, grabbing his arm. "You are not going out there."

"I am," he said. "ComTac killed Gracie. ComTac might not have held the weapon, but ComTac built it. It's time they acknowledge what they've done. What they've started."

We looked at each other. His eyes blazed with fury and rage, but behind them was grief. He was haunted by Gracie's ghost, and needed to help her now in the only way he could.

"Be careful," I said, knowing that he needed to fight this battle.

His eyes widened with surprise, that I hadn't tried again to stop him. He looked at me for another moment, then stepped out from behind the shed, hands raised.

Terror speared through me, sharper than any Valkyrie weapon.

"You're trespassing," Liam said, his voice utterly calm.

"At the home of suspected enemy combatants," the man said.

Phaedra's lip curled, and she opened her mouth to protest, but Tadji clamped a hand over it, shook her head fiercely. *"Stay quiet."*

"I didn't get your name," Liam said as we watched.

"You can call me Rutledge." He gestured back toward the operatives. "These are my men." He tilted his head. "And you're Liam Quinn. Former Containment contractor. Now a bounty hunter, with all the glamour of that particular job."

"More bounties these days," Liam said. "More wraiths. But you already know about that, don't you?"

It was a test, to see if this had been the man who put the plan in place. And when Rutledge's features drew tight, I guessed we hadn't been far off the mark.

"My sister was killed by one of your wraiths, Mr. Rutledge. She was seventeen when she was attacked. Her death was needless."

Some of the soldiers around Rutledge exchanged glances. They might not have known about the collateral damage.

"Civilian casualties are unavoidable. I regret the necessity, but not the operation."

Liam's eyes hardened. "We aren't in a war."

"Oh, but we are." He took a step forward. "The war didn't end, Mr. Quinn. The war was *paused*. Do you think there's any chance the Paras won't come back again if the Veil splits? Do you think they aren't planning to try to break the encryption? And do you think we'd be prepared for a surprise attack? Or that the Paras in Devil's Isle wouldn't rise against us if that happened? Don't be fooled, Mr. Quinn, by the theory some of these monsters are our friends. They are not."

"So you think forcing the Veil open is a better option?" Liam asked. "Forcing war again, when it nearly destroyed the South the first time around?"

This time, Rutledge looked surprised. He hadn't expected us to have gotten so far, to have understood so much. "Better to be proactive than to wait for certain death. Don't dismiss what you don't understand, Mr. Quinn. Now, we're here to speak with the Misses Dupre. If you could request they come out from their fairly obvious hiding space, we can all be on our way."

"They are humans, and you have no right to detain them."

"We have the right to retain enemy combatants, including Sensitives, which they are. And if they come out now, we'll promise not to kill the daughter."

Phaedra slipped out of Tadji's grip, and she was moving before we could stop her. She stepped next to Liam. Fury seemed to swirl around her like a queen's cape.

"You touch one hair on my daughter's head, and you will regret it for the rest of your very short life."

Go, Mrs. Dupre. And she meant business, too. I could feel the tendrils of magic moving past me, blowing my hair as she spindled her magic and prepared to strike. I knew from the list she could "conduct magic," but I had no idea what that actually meant, or how to plan for it.

Hatred bloomed across Rutledge's face in ugly red splotches. "You are tainted with magic. And since we have considerably more numbers than you, and better weapons, I suggest the rest of your friends come forward now so we can all go about our business."

"You'll need to recalculate your numbers," said a voice behind us, and we all looked back.

They emerged through the trees like spirits—a dozen Paranormals with weapons in hand. There was no gold armor this time. Instead, they wore what looked like worn and discarded human clothes.

Half of them were angels—tall and uniformly beautiful men and women with skin in a rainbow of shades, from ghostly pale to gleaming brown-black. Their eyes gleamed gold, just like the tips of their wings, which disappeared as they silently touched the earth.

The rest of them were an assortment of creatures. They were a small and self-made army, clothed like humans, but very definitely Paranormals. And they stood behind Malachi like his dedicated troops. Burke had gotten word to them, thank God.

Rutledge took in the sight, and his eyes gleamed. "This isn't your fight."

Malachi stepped forward, stood beside Liam. "Since you'd wreak hell upon us all, of course it is."

Malachi's voice dropped. "Disable and disarm the operatives," he said quietly to his battalion.

He raised his bow, which gleamed gold in the falling darkness.

I was struck blind by memory, of a glint of light off the armor, the weapon, of the Valkyrie who'd come to kill me. Of the red-brown stains across her mouth and lips, and the hunger in her eyes. For death, for blood. I'd never been afraid like that—I'd never experienced fear that had slunk through my muscles and bones like freezing water, leaving me staring at her, my heart racing, pounding in my ears.

I'd had nightmares as a child that a stranger stood at the end of my bed. I'd seen him, but couldn't scream. I was terrified, but had no voice. I felt just as defenseless when she stared me down.

Sound rushed back like a wave. "Claire. Claire."

I looked down, found Liam's hand on my arm, the gripping fingers white with effort. He and Phaedra had moved behind the shed again.

I looked back. The Paras were rushing forward on one side of the wall of men, weapons raised for battle. They'd funneled together on the left, forcing the operatives to regroup, and leaving the right side of the yard open for us. If we could get around the house, we might have a chance to get out alive.

ComTac began firing. Gunshots sang through the air, zipping past the angels and zinging off their weapons. They launched their own onslaught of arrows.

"Let's move," Liam said, and pulled me toward the other side of the house, the Dupres behind us.

My adrenaline surged, but my body wanted nothing more than to hunker down until the fighting was over. But I wasn't seventeen anymore, I reminded myself. I was an adult, with my own power.

We ran for the house, edged to the side of it, and neared the front yard. But Liam stopped short, held up a closed fist to make us stop, too, as he evaluated our options.

He looked back at me. "I'm going to have to draw them off. Wait until I've gotten them away from the truck, then run to the vehicle. Get them to New Orleans. And no heroics."

"I'm not going to just leave you."

His expression was fierce. "Yes, you are. Do what needs to be done, Claire."

And then he was gone. He ran past the truck, and two ComTac operatives who'd been assigned to watch gave chase.

Damn. I didn't want to leave him, but I didn't want to waste his bravery. And I had to get the Dupres to safety. I had to keep the Veil closed.

I looked back at Tadji, handed her the keys, looked at her mother and aunt. "On three, we run to the truck." The fighting was loud, and I had to shout for my voice to be heard over gunshots and the clang of weapons. "Tadji drives. Phaedra and Zana in the front. I'll get into the truck bed. Okay?"

That, I hoped, would let me use whatever power I might be able to gather if someone chased us. Could I move a helicopter? Didn't know. But I might need to try. And it seemed safer to do that from the back of the truck than from the front.

"I don't want any of this," Tadji said. "I don't want any of this."

I looked back. Tadji's eyes and pupils were wide. She was getting shocky. I had to keep her calm.

I snapped my fingers until she focused on me. "Tadji, I know you're freaked out, but right now we have to move. Okay?"

She swallowed thickly, nodded.

"On three," I said again. "One . . . two . . ." I made like a sprinter, crouched and ready to run—but then Zana Dupre screamed.

I turned back, found a black-clad Containment operative, face smeared with camouflage, holding her arm, a bowie knife in hand.

"You've got the wrong one," I said. "I'm the Sensitive."

He looked at me, was just unsure enough to hesitate. Zana kicked him in the shin, and the surprise put him off balance. He stumbled a few feet away but got his balance again and lunged at me, leading with the knife. I dodged, then kicked up at his elbow to get him to drop the weapon.

It actually worked. He yelped, and the knife slipped from his hand. He fell to the ground to retrieve it. But Zana was faster. She got to it first, kicked it into the underbrush.

The man realized his error fast enough. He pulled out his gun, aimed it at the Dupres, prepared to fire.

Not on my watch, I thought, and began gathering magic, moving toward him to close the distance, improve my aim.

Unfortunately, I hadn't noticed Phaedra Dupre doing the same thing. She aimed the burst of magic at the man just as I stepped in front of him.

Her shot hit me with the heat of a thousand suns.

The shot would have knocked out a human. But I was a Sensitive. My body absorbed magic, wanted magic, all the magic it could find. And it had found the mother lode. I guess this was what the list had meant by Phaedra's ability to "conduct magic."

I rolled away, arms and toes curled in pain. Every inch of my body—from head to fingertips to toes and everything in between—felt on fire. This was bad.

"Go," I said to Tadji, voice hoarse and suddenly parched. "Go. *Now.*"

I wasn't fine. Wasn't close to fine. But I couldn't fix myself and take care of them. Tadji looked at me, made a decision, and pulled her mother and aunt toward the truck.

Fire balled in my stomach, tears springing to my eyes. This was what being a wraith felt like, I thought, and knew I had to get rid of the magic. I moved to my knees, searched for something I could funnel it into. To my left, there was a stand of tangled trees, a finger of the bayou that edged the back of the property. And on the leading edge, the stump of an ancient cypress, long since cut down, maybe to build the house, maybe for firewood.

I crawled toward it, one excruciating knee at a time, my arms and legs shaking with the effort, sweat pouring down my back, shots firing in the distance. I reached inside, began pulling the magic together one hot and miserable thread at a time. Every time I thought

I'd managed to corral all the magic that had buried me, I found another hank of it hiding in a dark corner of my psyche.

Just as the magic had rushed me, it poured out again. Cold surrounded me, seeped in where the magic had vacated. I felt like I'd been thrown from the equator to the Arctic Circle, my teeth and hands chattering with the sensation.

I coughed, and my throat felt parched. But I had to bind the power. I had to bind it or my body would seek it out again, and I'd be back at the start.

I put my hand on the cypress, begged the magic to bind itself, to sink in and find its home. But the buzzing continued, a hornet's nest inside my head.

Tears of frustration slipped from my eyes. I flexed my fingers again, put my palm back on the stump. I couldn't ask it; I had to *demand* the magic be bound.

I imagined the conversation I'd like to have with Rutledge, what it might feel like to push a little magic into him, let him feel what it meant to be "contaminated" or "tainted" with it.

That was close enough to a demand for the stump. The magic filtered into the wood, and the world finally stopped vibrating.

"Thank God," I said, and hit the ground.

CHAPTER TWENTY

I woke in the truck. I was nestled against the door, the vehicle bumping along the road. The world was quiet and dark, no lights across long lots of former farmland.

I put a hand on the dashboard, tried to sit upright. My head spun like a tornado. "Oh God," I said, and put my other hand on my head as nausea swelled in my belly.

"Don't toss your cookies," Liam said, handing me a bottle of water. "Drink this."

I uncapped it, drank until I was heaving for breath. "Are the Dupres all right? Tadji?"

"She's fine. They all are. They're in the car behind us. How are you?" He put a hand on my head. "Your temperature feels a little better. You were freezing."

I glanced back to check the headlights, but my stomach rumbled with objection. I turned around again, put a hand on the dashboard, waited for the world to stop spinning. "I think I had all the magic at once. And then I got rid of all the magic at once."

"Phaedra said you'll heal, although that tree stump will never be the same. It's mulch at this point."

My head felt five or ten pounds too heavy for my neck, and I was only barely keeping it from rolling off onto the very dirty floorboard. I put my head back on the seat, closed my eyes, breathed quietly until I could sit upright without wanting to hurl. "What happened?"

"Since you survived the first war," Liam said, "it will not surprise you to learn that even guns are often not a match for Paranormals with a point to make. The operatives had been planning on taking the Dupres without any trouble. So when the Paranormals advanced, they retreated pretty fast."

"Maybe that will make Rutledge think twice before pushing further. Before taking a shot at the Veil."

"Or he'll just come with more firepower next time. A man like that doesn't just abandon his plans. He tweaks them." He drummed his fingers on the steering wheel. "We're taking the Dupres to Gavin's. He's a less obvious target than Gunnar. And Gunnar's house is too big, with too many people. That assumes his father would even let us in anyway."

"Okay," I said.

He glanced at me. "But I want you to tell Gunnar what happened here, about everything. He needs to get Tadji and her family under protection, warn the Commandant about Rutledge."

My heart hiccupped. "But you, Moses, Eleanor—that would put everybody at risk." *And me,* I thought.

Liam glanced at me. "There's no help for it now. Rutledge has seen us, and he's alive. Our asses are already on the line."

Once again, being imprisoned in Devil's Isle became a very real possibility.

I folded my arms, suddenly freezing. "He may not be able to do anything."

"We have to try." He winced as the truck hit a pothole, bounced. "We don't have a better option at this point. I just hope to God he's worthy of the trust you've put in him."

"He is," I said without hesitation. I believed it. I just hoped I was right.

"I notice you did not get into the car and drive away. What happened to 'no heroics'?"

"Recklessly brave?" I offered with a small smile.

Liam chuckled. "Jesus, Claire. You are absolutely terrifying."

I decided that was a compliment.

Pain in the ass or not, when we got Tadji, Phaedra, and Zana settled at Gavin's, Liam drove me back to the Cabildo.

War or not, the Cabildo was still beautiful, if lonely without its neighbors. Two long stories of arches and windows, another row of windows below a mansard roof. And at the very top, a cupola that still gleamed white and silver.

I walked inside to the security desk, waved at the guard. She shopped at the store, knew me, and knew that Gunnar and I were friends.

She probably wouldn't have appreciated the irony that she'd just waved a Sensitive through the front door of Containment HQ.

I took the staircase to the second story, where the floors were gleaming dark oak and the walls were crisp white. The Commandant's staff had desks in the long hallway in front of a bank of windows that faced the Square. The desks and chairs were mismatched, pulled from the remains of the Presbytère.

There weren't many agents left at this late hour. But Gunnar sat at his desk in the row, next to the doors that led to the Commandant's office. He was back in his dark fatigues, head down as he flipped through a binder of notes. At the sound of my footsteps, he glanced up, his eyes widening with concern.

He got one look at me at the end of the hallway, came toward me at a run. "What the hell happened to you?"

"It's a long story that you don't want to hear in this particular location."

He glowered.

"I swear, Gunnar, I'll tell you as soon as we step foot out of this building." I caught other agents rising from their desks, watching us with suspicion.

"All right," he said. "Let's go."

We walked downstairs, climbed into the truck, sat there for five minutes while I told Gunnar the truth about everything. About being a Sensitive, the wraiths, Devil's Isle, the Veil opening, all of it.

By the end of it, he was fuming. "I want to talk to Tadji."

"We don't have time for that," I insisted. "Rutledge could be trying something else right now."

Gunnar ignored me, looked past me to Liam. "I verify before I report. Gavin's place."

Liam didn't argue, and Gunnar didn't talk at all for the rest of the trip.

"Stay here," he said as soon as Liam had given directions to Gavin's unit but before Liam had pulled the truck to a complete stop. He climbed out of the truck and slammed the door closed before I could object.

He stayed in the building, a warehouse turned condo building, for fifteen minutes. We waited in silence. Our situation was precarious, so we skipped discussion for staying inconspicuous and keeping an eye on the streets around us.

When Gunnar climbed back into the truck and shut the door, it was a solid minute before he spoke.

"Richard Rutledge is the CEO of ComTac," he finally said. He must have been familiar with the organization. "It's privately held, and he's the principal shareholder. He has a lot of money."

"So all that talk about protecting humans?"

"Some of it could be true," Gunnar said. "Right now he doesn't have an army of his own nearly big enough to fight the Paranormals. At least, not that your tax dollars have funded. But if the Veil opens again, if we have to wage a war again, the feds would probably give him plenty of money to build one."

"So he wants the cash?" Liam asked.

"And the power," Gunnar agreed. "I'm going to get guards on Gavin's apartment, just in case."

"Gavin won't like that," Liam said.

"I've already convinced him." Gunnar's tone was dry. "Will you take me back to the Cabildo? I need to talk to the Commandant."

Liam gestured toward me. "And her?"

"She goes back to the store, where she'll stay until further notice."

I hated his presumptiveness, but I'd rather be in the store than anywhere else, so I didn't bother to argue.

He had a right to be miffed at me. Better, I thought, to let him power through it. He ran as hot as Tadji ran cold. I ran somewhere right down the middle. Probably one of the reasons we were such good friends. Or had been until one man's greed tore us apart.

By the time we got back to the store, it was past midnight and my body ached all over. I wanted to crawl into bed and hibernate for a month or two, but that wasn't in the cards.

Liam and I sat at the table in the store's backroom, waiting for Gunnar to arrive.

He'd crossed his arms, crossed his ankles on top of it, staring out the front door. I sat in the chair beside him, arms on the table, head on my arms. I closed my eyes, jumped back to consciousness when Gunnar came back in.

I sat up, pushed the hair from my eyes.

"You shouldn't have let me fall asleep," I said as Gunnar crossed the room.

"You looked exhausted," Liam said.

I looked at him. The bruise on his cheekbone was darker, and he looked tired, too. "I think we could both use a nap."

He half smiled. "Soon as we save the world."

"What happened?" I asked.

Gunnar pulled out a chair, which squeaked in objection across the floor. "The Commandant approved the Chenal operation. He thought Rutledge was planning to bring in a rogue Paranormal. Rutledge is already back, had already talked to him. He told the Commandant the operation was sabotaged."

Ice water ran down my spine. "He gave the Commandant our names?"

Gunnar shook his head. "No. According to the Commandant, Rutledge didn't give any names. He stuck to his 'rogue Paranormal' story."

Liam frowned. "Why not give us up? He had to know we'd go to Containment."

"Why would he?" Gunnar asked. "He doesn't know that Claire has a connection to the Commandant through me, or that I knew about Tadji's family, the missing Sensitives, the entire deal. And I didn't at the time. He'd have thought it would be too risky."

Liam held up a hand. "So if he didn't tell the Commandant about us, who'd he blame for the operation going bad?"

"He said there was a conspiracy against Containment that originated in Devil's Isle—and a Para with a lot of computer equipment."

His words were soft, full of regret. But they echoed through me like a gunshot.

My heart sank like a stone. "Moses," I said, my voice barely a whisper. "He got to Moses."

We hit the street running.

Liam got us through the gate, and we ran without stopping toward Moses's store in clothes still streaked with dirt and sweat from the last battle.

A fire truck was parked in the middle of the street, firefighters still pouring water onto the smoldering ruins of what had once been "Moses Mech."

The store was gone. There was nothing left but a heap of bricks and twisted bits of metal and wire in a pile. Shards of electronics were everywhere, plastic snapping underfoot or melted into big globs and piles. Water ran in little rivers through the debris, collected in the gutter and poured down the street.

"Oh, Liam." It was all I could think so say. Nothing else seemed appropriate. And even that didn't come close to being enough.

I didn't know what had happened, what had turned Moses's store into rubble, but he couldn't have survived this. Not if he was inside.

I knelt down, picked up an "M" key from an old gray keyboard, rubbed my thumb over the faded letter, and put it in my pocket. It would be my memory of him, this man I hadn't known very long, but who'd been nicer to me than a human deserved.

"They did this because of us," I said, rising again. "Because he helped us."

"*They* didn't do anything," Liam said. "Rutledge did this. Rutledge arranged this. That piece of shit must have found out Moses accessed their file, decided he was the easiest person to hit. He's in

Devil's Isle, after all. Less than human." He swallowed hard. "I will see that asshole in the ground if it's the last thing I do."

"Containment wouldn't have blown up the building, would they?" I asked quietly. "Not when it would have endangered the neighborhood, the grid, whatever."

"Containment didn't."

We turned back. Hawkins stood behind us, hands stuffed into his pockets.

He seemed shorter than I remembered, probably because he wasn't standing in his security station.

"They didn't?" Liam asked.

"Agents came for him—but it was ones who work for ComTac."

Liam frowned. "Did they take him out of the building?"

"Don't think so. I mean, I didn't see anything."

I looked at Liam. There was a strange look on his face. "Thanks, Hawkins. I'm gonna get her home."

I was completely confused but let Liam take my arm, guide me away from the rubble. "All right," I whispered. "I know you know something, but I don't get it. You're going to need to fill me in."

"Moses didn't want anyone else to get his toys, so he rigged it to blow."

"Fuck yeah, I did."

We stopped, glanced around, but saw nothing but darkness.

"Mos?" Liam whispered. "Where are you?"

"I'm in heaven, genius. Where do you think I am?" A thick hand poked out of a narrow gap between the two buildings. Not big enough to be a full alley. Just big enough for him to squeeze into. He moved forward into the light, still hidden from view from the rest of the street. "I'm right here. Bastards got to my shop, so I blew it."

Liam looked utterly relieved. "You scared the shit out of us."

"You're not the only one. I didn't survive war to get taken out by some assholes with a death wish."

"It was ComTac?" I asked.

He nodded. "Decided to use me as a scapegoat, I hear. Fortunately, I got a couple friends in Containment yet. They got the word out."

"I'm sorry you had to blow your store. Do you have a place to stay?"

He snickered. "I've got the tunnels, Red."

I looked between him and Liam. "The tunnels?"

"That's a story for another time," Liam said, looking at Moses again. "You need anything?"

"Not right now. Let me get settled first."

"Tunnels?" I asked quietly again as we walked back toward the gate.

"*Tête dure.*"

"I'm not hardheaded."

"And that's exactly what a hardheaded person would say."

I didn't have an argument for that.

We found Gunnar at the table, elbows on the tabletop, head in his hands. The store was dark, the candles lit. The power must have been out again.

"Hey," I said, putting the pilfered "M" key onto the tabletop. "I didn't expect to see you here. I figured you'd have gone back to the Cabildo."

"I'm on leave."

I pulled out the chair beside his, sat down. "Wait. What?"

He lifted his head, linked his fingers together. "I'm too close to what's happened, the Commandant needs to evaluate the informa-

THE VEIL | 295

tion regarding the various parties and determine if I've been derelict

tion regarding the various parties and determine if I've been derelict in my duty."

"Were you?"

"Of course not."

"Well, there you go. The Commandant will figure out what actually happened and get you back in your position."

He nodded. "What did you find in Devil's Isle?"

I glanced at Liam. I wasn't sure how he'd want to handle that part of the truth.

He pulled out a chair, took a seat at the table. "Let's just say Rutledge didn't accomplish what he set out to accomplish. Body count is lower than believed."

Since the body count had been one, that meant there were no casualties. Without him coming out and saying it, of course.

Hope blossomed in Gunnar's face. "You're serious. You aren't just playing with me?"

Liam's smile went bland. "I rarely play."

I was pretty sure that was meant for me.

Gunnar blew out a breath, sat back, ran his fingers through his hair. "Oh thank God."

"None of this was because of you, Gunnar—just like Liam told your father. This is about Rutledge. And it sucks."

"It's a miracle," Liam said. "She is capable of listening."

"You're hilarious as always." I looked at Gunnar. "And I'm sorry to you, too. I waited to tell you because I didn't want to put you in a horrible position—"

"And you weren't sure about my loyalties."

"And I wasn't sure about your loyalties," I confessed. "But we've already been through all that. Can we agree we both did what we thought was right in the moment? What we thought would hurt the fewest number of people?"

Gunnar dropped his hands, put his palms on the table. "Agreed."

I nodded. "Good. Good." Because I didn't need to be fighting with everyone I knew right now.

"Listen, would you mind staying the night? There's a bed in the back room, and I'd feel better if someone else was here." That was absolutely the truth, but it would also keep Gunnar nearby. He was very much defined by his job, and he wasn't done talking this through.

"I think that's a good idea," Liam said. "I don't think Claire should be alone. Not until your boss pulls his head out of his ass and shuts Rutledge down."

"I was always the smartest man in the office," Gunnar said.

"And, like Mr. Quinn, ever so humble."

"Mr. Quinn should get going," Liam said, rising. "I want to go see my grandmother." He clapped Gunnar on the back. "You did the right thing. Hopefully, Containment will recognize that. If not, they're idiots."

Gunnar nodded. "Appreciate it."

Liam gestured toward the door, motioned for me to follow. The night was still, humid, quiet. The memorial songs had all been sung.

"I want to check on Eleanor," he said. "Just in case. I have some favors I can call in for extra security, and I think it's time to do that. I want to make sure she's protected."

"Favors?"

He blew out a breath. "I'll have to ask Solomon."

I winced. "There's no other way?"

"Not after tonight. And his price will be high. But there's no avoiding it." He glanced back at Gunnar. "He'll be all right?"

I nodded. "I think so. He'll adjust, or the Commandant will come to his senses when Rutledge causes more trouble. That seems pretty inevitable." And that reminded me. "Be careful in Devil's Isle. He could still have friends."

His gaze softened. "Are you worrying about me now?"

I let my gaze linger. "I know you can take care of yourself. But I might have heavy furniture that needs lifting. So it's always good to have muscle around."

He grunted a laugh. "Hilarious as always."

"I'm trying," I murmured as he walked away. Because I wasn't sure what else to do.

CHAPTER TWENTY-ONE

The smell of rich coffee wafted upstairs. I came down in a robe, my hair pulled into a bun, to find Gunnar and Liam sitting at the store table. They held mismatched mugs, and there was a carafe in the middle of the table. I paused on the stairs, waiting until I'd composed myself.

"*Bonjour*, Claire," Gunnar said. "Liam is teaching me some Cajun French."

"Oh, good. Now both of you can mutter under your breath in a language I don't speak." I pointed at the carafe. "Is that coffee?"

"The real deal," Gunnar said. "Courtesy of Mr. Quinn."

"Thought we could all use it," Liam said.

So he thought he could woo me with coffee. I poured coffee, held the warm mug in my hands, and closed my eyes to enjoy the steam that drifted up. I took a drink. It was hot, strong, black. I felt better almost immediately.

All right, it was a good play. "God, I miss coffee."

"You *sell* coffee." Gunnar pointed to it. "It's over there."

"Since we don't get it very often, I didn't want to get used to it. And besides—it's never as good as when someone brings it to you."

I looked at Gunnar. "You seem to be feeling better."

"I did what I could," he said. "I'm not going to sit around because they aren't handling it well. I'll give them time to investigate, and then I'll make my case. I've got a friend, a colleague, who I've asked to keep me updated."

"Good," I said, and glanced at Liam. "How's your grandmother?"

"Fine. No incidents."

I looked at Gunnar. "And Tadji? Her mother?"

"Good. No incidents for them, either. Bigger picture, I don't know what that means. Maybe that Rutledge is retooling. Hopefully, that he'll give us a little time before he moves again."

"Time to get Containment in line?"

"Exactly," Gunnar said.

I nodded, sipped my coffee. "He'll make a move. Rutledge, I mean. Why wouldn't he, after all this planning?"

"Agreed," Liam said, refilling his cup. "The only issue is—"

"Where, when, and how well you're prepared for it," I finished, rising from my chair.

Liam looked at me with surprise. "That's twice in a row that you've listened to me."

"Veil fluctuations," I grumbled, and headed upstairs.

I got dressed and came downstairs again to find Gavin rushing in through the front door. Since he was on guard, it was quickly obvious that something was wrong.

"What the hell are you doing here?" Liam asked.

"Tadji's mom. I left when the Containment guards relieved me half an hour ago. I verified their ID, then went to the store to grab a few things—food, water. When I got back, the guards were dead. They took Phaedra."

Fear blossomed like a crimson rose. "Tadji?"

"My next-door neighbor's a former marine. She and her aunt are with him for now. That was the safest place I could think of."

"They didn't take Zana," I said, and looked at Liam. "They figured out Phaedra locked the Veil?"

"Or she told them to protect her sister."

I hadn't known Phaedra long, but that sounded like something she'd do.

Liam's eyes narrowed at Gavin. "How'd they find out where you live?"

"I don't know," Gavin said, looking completely stricken. "I don't know who could have told them."

"Rutledge must have connections," Gunnar said. "Which means he won't have any doubts now that Containment is onto him."

"He'll try to open the Veil now," Liam agreed with a nod. "Even if he doesn't have all the Sensitives, he'll know he only has one shot. Hell, the way the Veil's been fluctuating, he could already be close."

"We have to tell the others," I said. "We have to go to the refinery. That's the meeting spot."

If I was really, really lucky, there'd be a pigeon outside my window, ready to take a message to the rest of our allies.

"How are we going to get there?" Gavin asked. "I'm guessing there are more people than us who need to go, and I'd really prefer not to ride in the backseat of that piece-of-shit truck again."

"It's not a piece of shit."

"It's piece of shit enough."

"Children," I said quietly, and looked at Gunnar. "There will be more of us. Can you get us a ride?"

He nodded, and there was a gleam in his eyes. "Give me ten minutes," he said, and set off at a run toward the Cabildo.

I'd been prepared to raise the flag to signal Delta, but it wasn't necessary. There was a gray pigeon, its feathers shimmering iridescent in the light, perched outside the window.

It had a note already, and it seemed our friends were thinking the same thing: DISCUSSION RE: BAYOU AND NEXT STEPS AT USUAL PLACE. NOON.

It was nearly noon. I gave the pigeon some feed. While it bobbed its head at the grains, I scribbled out a small reply, tucked it into its pouch. I kept it short and sweet: RUTLEDGE HAS PHAEDRA DUPRE. MEET ASAP.

By the time I made sure the pigeon was in the air and made my way to the first floor, tires were squealing outside. Gunnar pulled up in a white van with CONTAINMENT in black block letters along both sides and the back.

Liam, Gavin, and I rushed outside. I locked the door behind us, followed them into the van, which had plenty of windows and three long bench seats.

"She isn't sexy," Gunnar, "but she'll get us where we're going. Which is where?"

"King Sugar Company Refinery," I said. "And step on it."

That van could move. Like most postwar vehicles, it had been stripped of nearly everything electrical. No radio, no AC, but at least it moved. So we drove toward Chalmette like schoolkids on a field trip.

Gunnar's eyebrows lifted when he drove over the broken fence to enter the property, but he followed us inside without comment.

Malachi, Burke, and Darby already stood inside the giant space. Malachi carried his immaculate golden bow, which seemed so out of place in this rusting hulk of a building.

Their eyebrows lifted when Gunnar and Gavin walked in behind us. I decided I'd head off any argument.

"Malachi, Darby, Burke, this is Gunnar Landreau. Formerly the Commandant's senior civilian adviser, and my very good friend. He's on our side. Well, NOLA's side, anyway. And this is Gavin Quinn, Liam's brother. He's a tracker, and he was with the Dupres when Phaedra was taken."

There was silence for a moment while they considered the rest of my crew. They must have decided they were okay.

"That's good enough for me," Malachi said.

Darby nodded. "Agreed. Let's get to it."

Gavin stepped forward. "The Dupres were at my condo. There were two guards with them—both experienced Containment agents. Both had IDs that I personally verified with Containment. I went downstairs to the market for water, food."

I could hear the guilt in his voice, wanted to reach out and soothe him, but didn't think this was the time for it.

"When I came back, the guards were dead, and the operatives were taking Phaedra. I gave chase but wasn't able to catch up. I got Tadji and Zana out of the house, got them safe."

Gunnar took over from there. "The Commandant's been apprised, but he knows only what he needs to know about what happened yesterday and what Rutledge has done. Containment can scramble jets and prepare ground support once we know where to send them. But PCC first-response jets come in from Tyndall, which is in Florida. Even when we know where they're going, it will take time to get the jets in the air, and then here. We're on our own until then. We have to keep the Veil closed until the cavalry arrives."

Liam looked at Darby. "Where will they go? Rutledge and his people?"

"Talisheek," she said. That was the location of the war memorial.

"The Veil crosses at Talisheek," Malachi said. "That's where the majority of Paras came through."

"Is there a way you can get a message to Containment?" Gunnar asked. "Some way to warn them where it might happen?"

"I can arrange it," Malachi said. "It's easiest for me to get in and out of the Quarter unseen."

Wings notwithstanding.

"How does the encryption work?" Liam asked.

"Only Sensitives who worked the encryption have the full details," Darby said. "But I understand there's a box that holds the encryption; it's stored in the base of the war memorial. Each Sensitive has to apply his or her magic to the box to unlock one of the seven locks. The locks are keyed to their magic."

"We don't know if Rutledge has all seven of the Sensitives," I said, thinking of what Liam had said. "But this will be his one shot, so he'll do what he can with what he's got."

Burke nodded. "He could have all the Sensitives now, or he could have had each of them at some time, and he's been unlocking the encryption incrementally."

"He'll bring more people this time," Gavin said, rubbing his chin with his thumb while he considered. "Not enough to beat back a first wave of Paras through the gate—he doesn't have that many people—but enough to keep him and his people safe so they can get out of there and warn Containment more troops are needed."

"Actually," Burke said, "we don't think Rutledge believes the Paras will be waiting to come through the Veil. We managed to grab one of the ComTac operatives. Rutledge operates from what's called the 'power loss allocation' theory. It's popular in military circles. Basically, it supposes Paras used all their available resources to get the Veil opened and send troops through the first time. And they sent all the good warriors through for the attack, so anyone left in the Beyond would be easy to battle. Not the types to be lined up at the door."

"So," Gunnar said, "he basically thinks he'll open the door, and no one will be there?"

"Exactly," Darby said.

"That matched what he told us in Chenal," I agreed. "He thinks he's being proactive."

"That's absolute nonsense," Malachi said. "It doesn't reflect what actually happened or the remaining population of Paras in the Beyond."

"Which Rutledge would know," Darby said, "if he or anyone else in PCC listened to anything a Paranormal had to say."

"But since they didn't, he'll get the Veil open and be the first at the gate to bill the feds for all the defense services he can provide," Liam said, obviously disgusted.

"So, what's the plan?" I asked.

"Claire and I will take the Veil," Burke said, glancing at me and making my heart chill. "We'll do what we can as Sensitives to keep the locks closed. And if some of them are open, to close them up again."

"Okay," I said, and I could feel Liam's worry blossoming beside me.

"Have you ever been near the Veil?" Burke asked. "Actually close to it?"

I shook my head.

"As we've discussed, it's not just a line on a map. It's energy and magic that moves like a ribbon; it undulates. You're sensitive to magic. That means you'll be sensitive to the Veil. You'll be able to feel it if it gets too close."

"Is that good or bad?"

"It's the doorway to *all* the magic," he said. "Unless you want all that magic at once, stay away from it."

Solid advice.

"The rest of us will take the operatives," Malachi said, glancing around.

"You'll be seen again," I said, thinking of the consequences.

He looked at me, smiled gently. "There's no help for it. We have to fight as long as we can. The Veil cannot open again." He looked back at everyone else. "Is everyone prepared?"

Everyone nodded. I'd brought my gun, but as we'd seen when chasing Marla, I still wasn't thrilled about using it. Not that magic was much better.

"In that case," Burke said, "I suggest we move."

It was an hour-long drive to Talisheek, although Gunnar's driving like a maniac sped it up somewhat. Since Malachi could get around on his own, he promised to meet us there after he got the information to Containment about the location of Rutledge's operation.

We were mostly silent during the drive, thinking about the battle, about Paranormals, about each other. I hadn't talked to Tadji since the battle at Chenal. She'd been freaked out then, and I could only imagine she'd been even more freaked out now. Rutledge certainly wasn't doing much to make her believe that magic was anything but a cancer. And after all this, I didn't know where our friendship would stand.

There hadn't been much to Talisheek before the war—just a grocery store and post office, a few houses. The landscape had been mostly trees, with parcels scraped down to earth to plant crops. Now spots of forest and the char of battle covered the ground like a checkerboard. No one lived in Talisheek now.

Gunnar parked a quarter mile away, down a long-abandoned gravel road, and we crept in silence toward what was left of the brick arch that marked the front gate. We reached it and slipped behind brick to watch the action on the other side.

Most of the lawn where the battle had raged was still black, although grass had grown through in small patches that magic hadn't managed to kill. And in the middle of that parched earth, the monument to war—two angular, forty-foot-tall concrete wings that soared into the air. The statue's shape had been controversial—wings weren't exactly popular with humans. But they made for a perfectly haunting reminder of what had happened here.

There was about ten feet of space between the wings. That area was paved with bricks carved with the names of the units that had fought at Talisheek.

Two military vehicles were parked near it. And there were three dozen operatives on the ground and around the monument. Rutledge stood near the base of the wing on the left, with two other people in nonmilitary gear.

One was Phaedra Dupre. I didn't recognize the other one—a shorter man with dark skin. If he was a Sensitive like Phaedra, did that mean there were only two locks left?

Wings fluttered, and Malachi landed behind us. "He has already unlocked some keys."

"How do you know?" Liam asked.

"We are close to the Veil, and its fluctuations are obvious. It is wilder now, like a flag held by a single thread in a fierce wind. We must keep it closed."

Rutledge opened a panel in the wing, pulled out a large gray box that glinted with gold. I guessed that was our prize.

There was a woman with Rutledge in green, but her back was to us. But when she turned, she looked much too familiar.

"Oh, damn," Liam muttered.

It was Nix. Green dress, her magical mask thrown away to reveal her pointed ears, her faintly green skin, a golden staff in hand.

She stood beside Rutledge. He was telling her something. As though he was emphasizing his point, he turned, reached out, caressed her shoulder. She didn't show any reaction to his touch. But longing was clear on his face.

"Double damn," I murmured as the memory of her at the table in the store struck me. "She said she wanted to go home. He's helping her open the Veil so she can do that."

"Is she using him, or is he using her?" I wondered.

"Probably both," Malachi said. "She has information and expertise, and wants to go through for personal reasons. He has personal feelings for her, but wants to open the Veil for financial and professional reasons. It is mutually beneficial."

"And mutually repugnant," I said, thinking of the trust we'd all put in her. "She put Broussard onto me," I realized, and felt fury light inside my gut.

"Probably so," Gavin said morosely.

I looked at him. "I'm so sorry."

"It's done," he whispered fiercely, his features set and hard as ice. I'd seen Liam do the same thing—shut down his emotions. The Quinn boys were good at it.

"She is fallen," Malachi said. "She is a traitor. Let it be heard and remembered."

I reminded myself never to get on his bad side.

"The refinery isn't safe," Liam said. "She knew we were meeting there. We'll need a new location."

"We'll discuss that after," Malachi said. "For now, let's focus on the task in front of us. He won't know that Containment is on its way yet." He walked forward, looked at me and Burke. "We have a few allies moving forward from Bogue Chitto, should the worst happen. But there are not many, and they may not be enough. We can't wait."

"So 'hurry' is what you're saying," Burke said.

Malachi nodded. "It would be best."

"We've waited long enough," Darby said. "Let's do this," and she pulled a handgun from a shoulder harness and held it like a pro.

"Gunnar, Gavin," Malachi said. "Pull the outside guards right and away. Darby and I will take Rutledge and the operatives at the wing."

"And Burke, Claire, and I will take the box," Liam said.

Malachi nodded. "And may God have mercy on us all."

Gavin and Gunnar began with a scream, a long and haunting yell as they emerged from the gate, immediately banked right, drawing off a couple of the guards. Darby and Malachi ran straight ahead toward Rutledge. He screamed out orders while Nix looked momentarily shocked, but then threw the male Sensitive to the ground toward the box, trying to get him to hurry.

I'd always thought there was something off about her.

"That's our cue, kids," Liam said. "Burke, you wanna work your magic?"

"On it," he said, and his image fluttered and disappeared.

"Right up the middle to the box," Liam said, talking to the spot where Burke *probably* was. "We're right behind you."

"On my way!" Burke said, and the only things that remained of him were the impressions he left in the grass.

We followed at a run, Liam at my side, gun drawn and shooting at operatives, as he kept an arm around me. I was, I thought, supposed to be saving my magic for whatever awaited me in that box. So I didn't try to rip the weapon out of anyone's hand, although I would have enjoyed seeing the look of magic-induced panic on their gun-wielding faces.

"I've got Nix," Liam said, and I could hear that little revengy thread in his voice. He wasn't just fighting for humans; he was fighting for his brother.

She met Liam with a bansheelike scream, thrusting her staff at him. He dodged it with a kick, aimed a punch at her side, which missed.

Burke came back into focus on his knees in front of the box. "Focus, Claire," he said, snapping my gaze back to him and the terrified Sensitives.

"Phaedra. Tom. Good to see you again. Rutledge brought you here?"

The guy, who must have been Tom, nodded. "He wants to open the Veil. He threatened to kill our families—to hurt them. He's already turned so many into wraiths."

"We know," Burke said, inspecting the box. It was made of pale gray marble. There were seven golden dials that looked like watch gears scattered across the top, golden hinges along the edges, golden keyholes along the front. Six of the gears were popped up. One was still nestled in its slot in the marble.

"He's unlocked six so far," Phaedra said. "He's been bringing them here, one at a time, making them work the encryption. And when they don't do it, or can't do it, he lets the Veil break them."

"I already gave him my key. I'm so sorry. So sorry." Tom was sweating, crying, nearly feverish with magic that poured off him. I knew the feeling. Understood it well.

"Don't sweat it, Tom. We're going to get you some help, okay?"

"Just hers," he said. "It's the only one left."

"It may not matter," Phaedra said. "It may not take unlocking the last one. The Veil is wild."

Burke put his hand on one of the locks, blew out a breath, and concentrated. His image flickered like an old, broken television, but nothing on the box changed.

Phaedra screamed. I looked back. Nix had grabbed her arm; Liam was on the ground a few feet away.

I guessed it was down to me and the treacherous bitch. "Let go of her," I said.

"I'm sorry, Claire. You know I can't do that," Nix said.

"I know you lied to me, and Liam, and Gavin. Were you using us the entire time? Getting information about Sensitives, or just trying to keep us preoccupied so we wouldn't interfere with your little plan to use Rutledge to get home?"

"You don't know what it's like to be a pariah. To live in hiding."

"You're right," I said, voice dry. "Sensitives have no clue about that, because we're welcomed with open arms. You're Consularis. You're not supposed to be our enemy—you're supposed to be our friend. And that's what you've been telling us. But here you are, trying to unleash hell all over again."

I'd had just about enough of bad behavior today. I reached out, wrenched the spear from her hands. I'd surprised her, which was good, but the weapon was so heavy I could barely hold it upright. But at least it was out of her hands.

Nix's lip curled. "You cannot handle that weapon, Sensitive."

I caught the sound of fluttering wings, realized I had a plan. "Don't need to," I said. "Malachi!" I called out, and using all my strength, and a good bounce on my toes, tossed it above my head into Malachi's hands.

He landed a few feet away, Nix's weapon at the ready, and faced her.

I ran back to Liam. A cut on his forehead was bleeding. I patted his cheeks. "Liam? Liam! Wake up, lazy. There's a near war going on here."

"How badly do you need me?"

"Pretty bad," I admitted, relief flooding me when he opened one eye and winced. I managed to pull him into an upright position.

"She beaned me on the head," he said.

"I got her spear. Gave it to Malachi."

"Good girl. Gotta get up." He stood up, blinked, shook his head. "Headache tomorrow. War today."

There was a scream behind us. Rutledge, bleeding from a cut on his arm, was up and running.

I stuck out a foot, which he caught with his ankle. He went flying, landed five feet away on his face in the dirt. And damn, was that satisfying.

Suddenly energized, Liam climbed to his feet, stalked toward Rutledge, kicked him hard in the side. "That's for my sister, you asshole, and for all the other lives you've taken. Destroyed."

"Claire!" Burke yelled, a warning. "I need you!"

I glanced back, but before I could run, something hot and heavy lapped at my back, making me instantly dizzy. I lurched forward, had to put my hands on the wing to stop from hitting it.

Tom screamed, hit the ground, clawing at his clothes. Sweat was pouring off his body.

"Burke," I said, forcing myself to get up, to move to Tom. I dropped beside him, trying to grab his hands before he ripped through fabric and skin. "What the hell was that?"

"The Veil waving closer," Burke said. "That was the magical equivalent of water lapping at your toes." Which meant the real thing would take us down altogether. "We've got to get Tom and Phaedra out of here."

He whistled, an earsplitting sound that had me covering over my ears. Within seconds, an angel descended, his dark skin a gorgeous contrast to ivory wings. He glanced curiously at me, then Burke.

"These are the Sensitives," Burke said. "They need to get to safety, away from Rutledge."

The angel nodded, and without hesitation plucked Phaedra from the ground and spirited her into the air, wings flapping to keep them aloft.

"Damn," I said quietly, watching them fly away. I'd seen angels in combat. But I'd never actually seen an angel fly. It was beautiful and haunting, for all that it was still completely terrifying.

Another angel descended, grabbed Tom.

"They'll be safe?"

"They're Consularis," Burke said. "I called with a war whistle, something we worked out during the last go-round. We don't command angels, but we can ask for their help to keep people safe. That's how we do it."

I nodded, and movement caught my eye, and I glanced back across the field, where a woman slipped toward the woods.

She was tall and slender beneath the ComTac fatigues, with long straight hair that fell nearly to her waist. And it was vibrantly red. She turned back, looked in my direction. Her skin was pale, and her eyes, just like mine, were green. The tilt of the nose, the curve of her lips, the long almond shape of her eyes—also like mine.

I hadn't known my mother. Didn't have a single memory of her, red hair or otherwise, because she'd died when I was two, the victim of a flu strain that had swept southern Louisiana.

Or so I'd been told.

"Claire!"

My mind racing, I looked back at Burke, who frowned at me, hands on his knees. "Are you all right?"

I nodded vaguely, switched my gaze back to the woman, but she was gone, probably disappeared into the bayou. "I'm fine. There was a woman with red hair. Did you see her?"

Burke's eyes widened. "No. You're the only redhead I've seen around. Get down here with me, Claire."

I wanted to follow her, to obsess, to work through who she was. But I didn't have time to think about it, or her, right now. That was for later. I dropped to my knees beside him.

"Put your hands here and here. We need to cast magic into the box, okay? I think that will reinforce it enough to keep the Veil from splitting. And we need to do this now, because I don't think it's going to hold."

I heard the soft *pop* before the *zing* of sound reached me. Burke froze, then looked down at the spreading blossom on his chest. He'd been shot.

"Oh, damn. Oh, damn." I pressed a hand to the wound, which was warm and wet with blood. A lot of blood. I pushed harder, applying pressure and trying to stanch the bleeding. But there was so much blood.

"Malachi!" I called.

Flutters, the movement of air, and then he was on his knees beside me, eyes wide and lips parted as he looked at Burke.

"I think this is my last battle," Burke said, coughing.

"Not today," Malachi said, a promise, and lifted the man into his arms without so much as a wince. He rose into the air, hovering, wings beating against gravity, and looked back at me.

"You have to do it, Claire. You have to close the locks. We don't have much time."

"Okay," I said, wiping sweaty hands on my jeans. "Okay," I said again, and blew out a breath.

I put a hand on the box, closed my eyes, tried to ignore the screams, the crashes, the *pops* of gunfire around me.

Sweat rose on my back as the magic in the air grew fiercer, hotter, but I forced myself to concentrate.

It's a box, I thought. *It's just a box with parts and bits. I know how to move parts and bits. I can even do it with my mind.*

So, technically, it was the perfect task for me. If I could make my magic work.

I closed my eyes, felt my magical way through the box. Each of the seven locks was different. There were springs held by tension, and pins that weren't physical—not really. They were magical. Each tensioned for the Sensitive's magic, so that only their magic could be used to slip the pins into place, to let the top gear turn into the appropriate slot.

I opened my eyes, concentrated. I didn't have their magic. But I had mine. And maybe that would be enough.

Instead of large handfuls, I imagined gathering tendrils of magic, thin and gossamer, filament-fine. I pulled them from the air, and, ignoring the sounds of battle, worked to slide them into the locks. It took two tries, my remembering to imagine that the locks were enormous and the magic was small, and fitting them together.

Once it was inside, I concentrated on the movement of the pins, the snap of each spring. One lifted, paused. I offered a jog of magic to the right, and the pin slid home. One of the locks reengaged.

I was getting it, I thought.

I managed two more before the Veil moved again.

Magic flashed over me with blinding light and heat. For a moment, in that blaze of power, I could see the Veil. It shimmered with iridescent color like a soap bubble as it rippled across the ground, back and forth like the line Darby had drawn on the floor of the refinery.

And then I could see *through* it. I looked through to the other side, past the shimmer, and into the Beyond . . . where they waited.

Thousands of them in long columns, battalions of Paranormals prepared for war. They wore the same gleaming armor as the Paras we'd fought before, and that was enough to send my heart racing.

A woman on a black destrier, her skin lustrously pale, her long black hair tied into a tail wrapped with gold that wound across her shoulders, stood in front of her army. Both woman and horse wore golden armor, and she sat like a queen as the horse moved impatiently beneath her.

She froze, snapped her head to mine like she could tell she was being watched. She snapped the reins, moved the horse forward, one shaggy hoof at a time, toward the Veil, her eyes on mine.

She could see me, too. She grinned horribly, shouted something to her troops that I couldn't hear, and raised her golden spear into the air.

The thousands of troops behind her did the same, sunlight spearing off their golden weapons and leaving spots in front of my eyes.

And then the barrier passed over me again, releasing me to the ground.

I hit my knees, sucked in air, tried to steady myself in the world. It hadn't killed me, but it certainly didn't feel very good. The Veil had coated me in magic, and my body had sucked it up like a tempest on desert sand. My hands were shaking with exhaustion, with magic that boiled beneath my skin. I could feel the anger growing, my skin burning with irritation. I'd have to cast it, bind it, if I had any hope of avoiding the agony Tom had suffered, much less getting the rest of the locks engaged.

Or did I?

Maybe I didn't have to cast it off. Or not the usual way. Maybe there was a way to use the power . . . like a magical locksmith. If I could do one pin at a time with a little bit of magic, couldn't I do all the remaining pins with all the remaining magic?

I put a hand on the box. It was hot as an oven, and I yanked my fingers back, stuck my fingertips into my mouth to cool them. But I was hot and parched, too, and it didn't do much good.

Human bodies were not made for magic.

I pulled my sleeves down to protect my fingertips. It hardly helped, but there wasn't much else to do. This had to get done. That meant I had to do it.

When I was little, I'd fallen down a staircase, and I'd been horribly afraid to climb one again. But the size of the staircase didn't matter, my dad had told me once. You took one step at a time either way, so you focused on each step.

That's why I made plans. Because he'd taught me to take fear and break it into tiny little parts. It was easier to beat back the parts when they were small. So that's what I did.

Step one: Gather the magic.

I had more spinning magic inside me than I needed. But I still didn't think it would be enough for this. Fortunately, with so many Paranormals in battle, the air was alive with it, and the Veil was right behind me. Great strands of power hung in the air like party streamers—millions of them, waiting to be plucked. And that's just what I'd do . . . and I'd hope it didn't kill me in the process.

I grabbed them by the imaginary handful, pulling one swath of thread after another toward me, braiding them together as I pulled.

Step two: Use the magic.

Slowly, gently, I moved the magic toward the box, let the tendrils slink inside like water, gently searching, gently questing for the pins that would pop the remaining locks back into place. I imagined it was like playing the piano with one hand—each finger had to press a certain key at a certain time, then another key a moment later. Or, perhaps, two or three keys at once. It was the order, the tune, that mattered.

Heat washed against my back as the Veil moved again. Sweat dripped into my eyes, had dampened my shirt as the sun bore down. I'd never been so hot, not even in the bayou, with Phaedra Dupre's accidental magic running through me. I wasn't sure I'd ever be cool again. But if that army came through because I hadn't locked the Veil, it wouldn't matter.

"Lock," I said, and felt springs engage, pins move. I pulled them toward me, all five fingers pushing keys with more speed, with more finesse, as the song rose to its ultimate crescendo. The tumblers clicked, and there were soft whispers of metal against stone as the gears popped into place.

One more tumbler, then two, then three.

And then the Veil was locked again.

The tension in my shoulders eased. And since I didn't need the magic back, and didn't want it spilling and releasing the locks again, I ordered it to *stay*. The box seemed to sigh as magic settled in.

But I didn't have long to relax.

Now locked and reencrypted, the Veil snapped back along its meridian. But all that kinetic magic had to go somewhere. The earth began to shake, to rumble, and then it began to split. The pavers between the wings began to draw apart as a fissure split the earth down the middle, drawing a gap between the wings.

"Claire!"

I heard Liam's voice behind me, watched in horror as the earth began to disappear beneath my feet. I turned onto my belly, grabbed at grass and pavers as I scrambled away from the edge, as my feet kicked at air. I finally got purchase, scurried to my feet just in time to watch the fracture reach the box, which began to tumble into the maw in the earth that all that excess magic had wrought.

"No!" I screamed out. I was nearly empty of magic, but I used what tendrils I could find to grab the box, pull it one sweating inch at a time back into the air. It flew ten feet above my head, set down with a thud ten feet away.

The locks still perfectly in place.

"Jesus! Claire! Claire!" Liam fell to his knees beside me, rolled me gently onto my back. And then his hands—so gentle compared to the panic in his voice—were on my head, my shoulders, my abdomen, checking me for injuries.

His hands settled on my face, cool against hot and flushed skin. "Claire. Come back to me, Claire. Come back to me, baby."

I opened my eyes, stared into seas of roiling blue water. "I'm all right."

His lips were parted, his breath rushed, and his eyes tortured. The moment stretched, filled to encompass us both, staring at each other from a magical battleground.

"The Veil? Did it reopen?"

He smiled. "It's closed. You locked the Veil. And you split the earth. You were amazing."

I nodded. I lifted my gaze to the impossibly blue sky, watched a pelican drift across it, completely oblivious to what had happened here on earth.

Fixing that damn owl was going to be a cakewalk after this.

CHAPTER TWENTY-TWO

Malachi escorted Darby into Bogue Chitto to keep her away from the Containment troops who'd nearly reached us.

We ran back to the van, drove a few hundred yards away, close enough to watch Containment troops arrive on the scene. They'd dragged out the few remaining ComTac operatives—and Rutledge's body. Malachi had taken Nix as well, and there'd been a look of grim determination on his face when he'd carried her away. I didn't ask what he'd do with her; I didn't think I wanted to know.

Gunnar, Gavin, Liam, and I reconvened at the store. We were still in muddy clothes, still tired from battle. And since we all either had magic or were magical sympathizers, we were fugitives at worst, in legal limbo at best. I still had the redheaded woman on my mind, and I hadn't looked into my father's magic yet. But I'd have to deal with both later.

Everyone else was lying low. We'd gotten a pigeon message that Burke was all right. Tadji, Phaedra, and Zana were back at Gavin's CBD condo with Darby as guard.

We debriefed with Gunnar so he could talk to the Commandant and try to make the best of the situation. And then we let Gavin vent.

Yeah, he and Nix hadn't technically been together anymore. But she'd hinted even to me that she hadn't given up on him. And her betrayal was pretty harsh.

"I should have known," Gavin said, knocking back another shot of good Irish whiskey from the bottle Liam had pulled from his personal stash. "Her name was 'Nixon,' for God's sake."

I opened my mouth to ask the obvious follow-up, but Liam shook his head. "It's what she named herself when she first came through the Veil."

"She said she saw a Nixon bumper sticker on a car ditched in Bogue Chitto," Gavin said. "She thought it sounded pretty."

Grief darkened his eyes. "I knew she wanted to return, that she never really felt comfortable here. But I didn't think she was capable of betraying us in order to get back through. She knew how bad it had been to come through in the first place."

I sighed. "Speaking of how bad it had been, I need to tell you something."

The room went silent, all eyes on me.

"What is it, Claire?" Gunnar asked.

"When we were on the battlefield, the Veil moved over me." I paused. "And when it did, I could see through it."

I figured there'd be some oohs and aahs after that, but there was nothing. I looked at Gunnar, since the next part was especially for him.

"There were a lot of Paranormals. Several battalions in a field, in columns. It was an army waiting to fight, more than I've ever seen together at once. And there was a woman on a very big horse in front of them. She had long dark hair. Very pale. She carried a spear. She looked like she was in charge."

"Wait," Liam said, holding up a hand. "You saw through the Veil?"

I nodded.

"That's . . . amazing," Gavin said.

I didn't want to be amazing. I wanted to be inconspicuous. "Maybe every Sensitive can do it," I said. "I mean, how many times have Sensitives been standing right inside the Veil?"

Liam lifted a shoulder. "I honestly have no idea."

"The army," Gunnar said. "The woman on the horse. Does it mean the Court's won? That they've conquered the Beyond?"

It took Liam a moment to answer. "I don't know. We'll have to tell Malachi."

I nodded. "The soldiers were prepared to fight. They had weapons, armor. She called to them. I couldn't hear what she'd said, but she called to them, like she was getting them ready to charge."

"The army is assembled," Gavin said.

"They're going to try to open the Veil again," Gunnar said, standing. It was time for him to see the Commandant.

"Yes," Liam said, and we all knew that worse things were on their way.

Gunnar left to make his report. Liam went back to Devil's Isle to get a shower and a clean change of clothes. That left me and Gavin in the store.

It wasn't fair of me to push my drama onto him, but I had the sense he'd like the chance to talk about something else. "Can I ask you a question?"

He looked up at me. "Go for it."

"Why did you punch your brother when you first walked into my store?"

"He kissed my fiancée."

After a moment of stunned silence, I asked, "Did he know she was your fiancée?"

"He did, yeah. Technically, she kissed him. He just happened to be there. Her pitiable bad judgment, since I'm obviously the handsome one."

"Obviously. Is she why you left the Zone?"

Gavin's expression shuttered. "She was one on a long list of reasons. Nix being one of the other ones."

"Yeah."

Gavin cocked his head at me. "And what's going on with the two of you?"

"We're friends. Kind of." It was becoming my stock response.

"No, but you're a crappy liar. He brought you into the District, into his apartment, and to meet our grandmother. He's become part of this saving-the-world quest at least in part to impress you. And I've seen the way he looks at you. I'd say his interest is more than 'acquaintances.'"

"He's decided he can't have me."

He rolled his eyes. "What ridiculous theory supports that?"

I looked at him. "I'm a Sensitive. He's a bounty hunter. He could wield too much power over me, and it wouldn't be fair."

Gavin snorted. "He's got plenty of alpha male in him. Plenty of protectiveness." He leaned forward over the table. "Can you take care of yourself?"

"Of course."

"Are you going to become a wraith?"

My voice was flat. "No."

"Then this is *his* problem." He sat back, grinned as he slung an arm over the back of his chair. "You know what your best move is here? You let it stay *his* problem. You just keep being your sexy redheaded self."

I smiled. "Thank you."

He held up a hand. "Don't get too excited. I'm taking myself off the market right now."

"Because of the utter betrayal."

"Because of the utter goddamn betrayal."

"I think that's a good decision."

He finished off his drink. "Damn right it is." He looked up at me, grinned. "Watching my big brother get his comeuppance is going to be a lot of fun, Connolly. I look forward to it."

I thought I did, too.

And it made a really nice change from worrying about the end of the world.

It was nearly ten when Gunnar walked in, back in his fatigues. Liam, Gavin, and I sat up straight, waiting for the verdict.

"No one's going to Devil's Isle."

I breathed a little easier. But my palms were still sweating.

He sat down, pulled out a chair. "The Commandant does not know about anyone's magic. As unfortunate as Nix's involvement was, she gives us a very good scapegoat. He thinks Rutledge was obsessed with her, decided to help her open the Veil so that she could go home again."

"That's the truth," Liam said. "If not all of it."

Gunnar nodded. "And since Rutledge is dead, he can't exactly contradict the story. We'll have to keep an eye on the remaining ComTac operatives. They don't have any incentive to rat you out— even if they knew who you were. That's not clear, since their mission was to open the Veil."

"What about the raid on Claire's store?" Liam asked.

"Broussard maintains he got an anonymous tip. Not hard to imagine that was Nix."

It could have been Nix, sure. It probably had been. It also could have been Rutledge, or someone else entirely who wasn't a fan of me. That was something I'd have to ferret out later.

I leaned forward. "What about Phaedra and Tom? Their roles would have been obvious, since the Veil was locked."

"They've gone back into hiding, just in case," Gunnar said. "They've worked out a way to communicate with Tadji. Places they can meet, leave messages for each other."

Not an ideal solution, but it was the best way to keep all of them safe.

"The Commandant wants to try to match security images of the recent wraith attacks against the list of folks suspected of being Sensitives, especially anyone Rutledge might have focused on. I'm going to try to get medical care for anyone who needs it. We don't know if there's a treatment for wraiths. But the Commandant has gotten a new appreciation for Sensitives, so we've got a better opportunity to look now." He looked at me. "I'd still recommend you stick with 'don't ask, don't tell' at the moment."

"I won't be telling," I assured him. "What about you?"

He smiled. "I'm back on duty and out of the magic game. My job, as far as I see it, is to keep Containment on the straight and narrow."

"Says the Commandant?" I asked with a smile.

Gunnar grinned, sat back, crossed his ankles on the table. "Exactly. And that, lady and gentlemen, is a full day's work."

There wasn't much we could do with that right now. For tonight, at least, the Veil was closed. Tomorrow would bring what it would. We'd talk to the rest of the group, figure out a plan.

But that was for tomorrow. Tonight, I had other plans. So when the door opened and Tadji walked inside, I scooted them all out.

"All right," I said. "She's here. Everybody out."

I'd known she was coming, had already warned them they'd have to give us some space when she arrived. Some time to talk.

She'd asked for the meeting, and I was ninety percent sure I knew what was going to happen.

Tadji had been through hell, and she had walls higher than Devil's Isle. She was going to talk about magic, about how she couldn't deal with it—or by extension, me.

"Hey, Tadji," Gunnar said as he and Liam rose from the table. "We're just leaving. Gonna go home, maybe crack open a beer."

I loved Gunnar, but he wasn't an actor. And he didn't sound even slightly convincing.

"Okay," Tadji said. "Thanks for the heads-up?"

They walked out, leaving us alone.

"Hey," I said, standing to give her a hug. "How's your mom?"

"She's okay, all things considered."

"You wanna sit down?"

"Yeah," she said, and pulled out a chair.

We sat in silence for a moment. I missed the ticking of my cuckoo clock. It would have given me something to focus on.

Might as well cut to the chase, I thought, and make it easier on both of us. "Are you breaking up with me?"

She half laughed, half sobbed, as tears began to flow. "I don't know. I had this entire speech prepared—you know me and words— about how I need to take a break. About how I don't know if I can do this. If I can live with all this magic."

I nodded, made myself stay quiet, let her get it out.

She wiped away tears. "Growing up was hard, Claire. Being surrounded by the magic, the expectations. It was too hard, and it took so long for me to get away from it. I hoped New Orleans had gotten free of it. But it's not. Is still here, and it's messy." She looked up at me. "It suffocates me."

Wasn't it strange that I'd had exactly the opposite experience? A father who'd had magic but had hidden it from me.

326 | CHLOE NEILL

I wanted to tell her not to worry, that it wasn't a big deal, that it would all be fine. But I didn't know if that was true, and it wasn't fair to minimize what she was feeling.

She sighed. "Burke told me who he was. What he was."

Good. God knew, I supported honesty in relationships.

"I just—this isn't the life I imagined. All this damn drama. All this damn magic." She looked at me. "Angels, Claire. Angels in my backyard. In my bayou. The thing is, though? I don't know what I'd do without you."

I brushed sudden, sharp tears away. "I don't know what I'd do without you, either. I need someone smart and logical to deal with all this nonsense."

"It is a lot of nonsense, isn't it?"

"It is. It really, *really* is. And I'm not just saying that because I need you to keep me apprised of your dating situation."

"And speaking of, let's talk about Liam."

I didn't think that was entirely necessary. But I owed her one.

When the store was empty again and the night was quiet, I realized sleep wasn't going to come anytime soon, not with my mind spinning with Big Questions. So I walked back downstairs.

I flipped on the lights, smiled at the familiar buzz of electricity. Such a human thing. And today, I found that very comforting. I sat down at the counter and pulled over the owl, which still waited with unseeing eyes to move again.

I picked up a silver tool and got back to work.

Stay quiet. Work hard.

Because sometimes, when the world was shifting and changing around you, that's the best thing you could do.

Turn the page for an excerpt of the first novel in
Chloe Neill's Chicagoland Vampire series:

Some Girls Bite

CHAPTER ONE

THE CHANGE

Early April
Chicago, Illinois

At first, I wondered if it was karmic punishment. I'd sneered at the fancy vampires, and as some kind of cosmic retribution, I'd been made one. Vampire. Predator. Initiate into one of the oldest of the twelve vampire Houses in the United States.

And I wasn't just *one* of them.

I was one of the best.

But I'm getting ahead of myself. Let me begin by telling you how I became a vampire, a story that starts weeks before my twenty-eighth birthday, the night I completed the transition. The night I awoke in the back of a limousine, three days after I'd been attacked walking across the University of Chicago campus.

I didn't remember all the details of the attack. But I remembered enough to be thrilled to be alive. To be shocked to be alive.

In the back of the limousine, I squeezed my eyes shut and tried to unpack the memory of the attack. I'd heard footsteps, the sound muffled by dewy grass, before he grabbed me. I'd screamed and kicked, tried to fight my way out, but he pushed me down.

He was preternaturally strong—supernaturally strong—and he bit my neck with a predatory ferocity that left little doubt about who he was. What he was.

Vampire.

But while he tore into skin and muscle, he didn't drink; he didn't have time. Without warning, he'd stopped and jumped away, running between buildings at the edge of the main quad.

My attacker temporarily vanquished, I'd raised a hand to the crux of my neck and shoulder, felt the sticky warmth. My vision was dimming, but I could see the wine-colored stain across my fingers clearly enough.

Then there was movement around me. Two men.

The men my attacker had been afraid of.

The first of them had sounded anxious. "He was fast. You'll need to hurry, Liege."

The second had been unerringly confident. "I'll get it done."

He pulled me up to my knees, and knelt behind me, a supportive arm around my waist. He wore cologne—soapy and clean.

I tried to move, to give some struggle, but I was fading.

"Be still."

"She's lovely."

"Yes," he agreed. He suckled the wound at my neck. I twitched again, and he stroked my hair. "Be still."

I recalled very little of the next three days, of the genetic restructuring that transformed me into a vampire. Even now, I only carry a handful of memories. Deep-seated, dull pain—shocks of it that bowed my body. Numbing cold. Darkness. A pair of intensely green eyes.

In the limo, I felt for the scars that should have marred my neck and shoulders. The vampire that attacked me hadn't taken a clean bite—he'd torn at the skin at my neck like a starved animal.

But the skin was smooth. No scars. No bumps. No bandages. I pulled my hand away and stared at the clean pale skin—and the short nails, perfectly painted cherry red.

The blood was gone—and I'd been manicured.

Staving off a wash of dizziness, I sat up. I was wearing different clothes. I'd been in jeans and a T-shirt. Now I wore a black cocktail dress, a sheath that fell to just below my knees, and three-inch-high black heels.

That made me a twenty-seven-year-old attack victim, clean and absurdly scar-free, wearing a cocktail dress that wasn't mine. I knew, then and there, that they'd made me one of them.

The Chicagoland Vampires.

It had started eight months ago with a letter, a kind of vampire manifesto first published in the *Sun-Times* and *Trib*, then picked up by papers across the country. It was a coming-out, an announcement to the world of their existence. Some humans believed it a hoax, at least until the press conference that followed, in which three of them displayed their fangs. Human panic led to four days of riots in the Windy City and a run on water and canned goods sparked by public fear of a vampire apocalypse. The feds finally stepped in, ordering Congressional investigations, the hearings obsessively filmed and televised in order to pluck out every detail of the vampires' existence. And even though they'd been the ones to step forward, the vamps were tight-lipped about those details—the fang bearing, blood drinking, and night walking the only facts the public could be sure about.

Eight months later, some humans were still afraid. Others were obsessed. With the lifestyle, with the lure of immortality, with the vampires themselves. In particular, with Celina Desaulniers, the glamorous Windy City she-vamp who'd apparently orchestrated the coming-out, and who'd made her debut during the first day of the Congressional hearings.

Celina was tall and slim and sable-haired, and that day she wore a black suit snug enough to give the illusion that it had been poured onto her body. Looks aside, she was obviously smart and savvy, and she knew how to twist humans around her fingers. To wit: The senior senator from Idaho had asked her what she planned to do now that vampires had come out of the closet.

She'd famously replied in dulcet tones, "I'll be making the most of the dark."

The twenty-year Congressional veteran had smiled with such dopey-eyed lust that a picture of him made the front page of the *New York Times*.

No such reaction from me. I'd rolled my eyes and flipped off the television.

I'd made fun of them, of her, of their pretensions.

And in return, they'd made me like them.

Wasn't karma a bitch?

Now they were sending me back home, but returning me differently. Notwithstanding the changes my body had endured, they'd glammed me up, cleaned me of blood, stripped me of clothing, and repackaged me in their image.

They killed me. They healed me. They changed me.

The tiny seed, that kernel of distrust of the ones who'd made me, rooted.

I was still dizzy when the limousine stopped in front of the Wicker Park brownstone I shared with my roommate, Mallory. I wasn't sleepy, but groggy, mired in a haze across my consciousness that felt thick enough to wade through. Drugs, maybe, or a residual effect of the transition from human to vampire.

Mallory stood on the stoop, her shoulder-length ice blue hair shining beneath the bare bulb of the overhead light. She looked anxious, but seemed to be expecting me. She wore flannel pajamas patterned with sock monkeys. I realized it was late.

The limousine door opened, and I looked toward the house and then into the face of a man in a black uniform and cap who'd peeked into the backseat.

"Ma'am?" He held out a hand expectantly.

My fingers in his palm, I stepped onto the asphalt, my ankles wobbly in the stilettos. I rarely wore heels, jeans being my preferred uniform. Grad school didn't require much else.

I heard a door shut. Seconds later, a hand gripped my elbow. My gaze traveled down the pale, slender arm to the bespectacled face it belonged to. She smiled at me, the woman who held my arm, the woman who must have emerged from the limo's front seat.

"Hello, dear. We're home now. I'll help you inside, and we'll get you settled."

Grogginess making me acquiescent, and not really having a good reason to argue anyway, I nodded to the woman, who looked to be in her late fifties. She had a short, sensible bob of steel gray hair and wore a tidy suit on her trim figure, carrying herself with a professional confidence. As we progressed down the sidewalk, Mallory moved cautiously down the first step, then the second, toward us.

"Merit?"

The woman patted my back. "She'll be fine, dear. She's just a little dizzy. I'm Helen. You must be Mallory?"

Mallory nodded, but kept her gaze on me.

"Lovely home. Can we go inside?"

Mallory nodded again and traveled back up the steps. I began to follow, but the woman's grip on my arm stopped me. "You go by Merit, dear? Although that's your last name?"

I nodded at her.

She smiled patiently. "The newly risen utilize only a single name. Merit, if that's what you go by, would be yours. Only the Masters of each House are allowed to retain their last names. That's just one of the rules you'll need to remember." She leaned in conspiratorially. "And it's considered déclassé to break the rules."

Her soft admonition sparked something in my mind, like the beam of a flashlight in the dark. I blinked at her. "Some would consider changing a person without their consent déclassé, Helen."

The smile Helen fixed on her face didn't quite reach her eyes. "You were made a vampire in order to save your life, Merit. Consent is irrelevant." She glanced at Mallory "She could probably use a glass of water. I'll give you two a moment."

Mallory nodded, and Helen, who carried an ancient-looking leather satchel, moved past her into the brownstone. I walked up the remaining stairs on my own, but stopped when I reached Mallory. Her blue eyes swam with tears, a frown curving her cupid's bow mouth. She was extraordinarily, classically pretty, which was the reason she'd given for tinting her hair with packets of blue Kool-Aid. She claimed it was a way for her to distinguish herself. It was unusual, sure, but it wasn't a bad look for an ad executive, for a woman defined by her creativity.

"You're—" She shook her head, then started again. "It's been three days. I didn't know where you were. I called your parents when you didn't come home. Your dad said he'd handle it. He told me not to call the police. He said someone had called him, told him you'd been attacked but were okay. That you were healing. They told your dad they'd bring you home when you were ready. I got a call a few minutes ago. They said you were on your way home." She pulled me into a fierce hug. "I'm gonna beat the shit out of you for not calling."

Mal pulled back, gave me a head-to-toe evaluation. "They said—you'd been changed."

I nodded, tears threatening to spill over.

"So you're a vampire?" she asked.

"I think. I just woke up or . . . I don't know."

"Do you feel any different?"

"I feel . . . slow."

Mallory nodded with confidence. "Effects of the change, probably. They say that happens. Things will settle." Mallory would know; unlike me, she followed all the vamp-related news. She offered a weak smile. "Hey, you're still Merit, right?"

Weirdly, I felt a prickle in the air emanating from my best friend and roommate. A tingle of something electric. But still sleepy, dizzy, I dismissed it.

"I'm still me," I told her.

And I hoped that was true.

The brownstone had been owned by Mallory's great-aunt until her death four years ago. Mallory, who lost her parents in a car accident when she was young, inherited the house and everything in it, from the chintzy rugs that covered the hardwood floors, to the antique furniture, to the oil paintings of flower vases. It wasn't chic, but it was home, and it smelled like it— lemon-scented wood polish, cookies, dusty coziness. It smelled the same as it had three days go, but I realized that the scent was deeper. Richer.

Improved vampire senses, maybe?

When we entered the living room, Helen was sitting at the edge of our gingham-patterned sofa, her legs crossed at the ankles. A glass of water sat on the coffee table in front of her.

"Come in, ladies. Have a seat." She smiled and patted the couch. Mallory and I exchanged a glance and sat down. I took the seat next to Helen. Mallory sat on the matching love seat that faced the couch. Helen handed me the glass of water.

I brought it to my lips, but paused before sipping. "I can—eat and drink things other than blood?"

Helen's laugh tinkled. "Of course, dear. You can eat whatever you'd like. But you'll need blood for its nutritional value." She leaned toward me, touched my bare knee with the tips of her fingers. "And I daresay you'll enjoy it!" She said the words like she was imparting a delicious secret, sharing scandalous gossip about her next-door neighbor.

I sipped, discovered that water still tasted like water. I put the glass back on the table.

Helen tapped her hands against her knees, then favored us both with a bright smile. "Well, let's get to it, shall we?" She reached into the satchel at her feet and pulled out a dictionary-sized leather-bound book. The deep burgundy cover was inscribed in embossed gold letters—*Canon of the North American Houses, Desk Reference*. "This is everything you need to know about joining Cadogan House. It's not the full *Canon*, obviously, as the series is voluminous, but this will cover the basics"

"Cadogan House?" Mallory asked. "Seriously?"

I blinked at Mallory, then Helen. "What's Cadogan House?"

Helen looked at me over the top of her horn-rimmed glasses. "That's the House that you'll be Commended into. One of Chicago's three vampire Houses—Navarre, Cadogan, Grey. Only the Master of each House has the privilege of turning new vampires. You were turned by Cadogan's Master—"

"Ethan Sullivan," Mallory finished.

Helen nodded approvingly. "That's right."

I lifted brows at Mallory.

"Internet," she said. "You'd be amazed."

"Ethan is the House's second Master. He followed Peter Cadogan into the dark, so to speak."

If only Masters could turn new vampires, this Ethan Sullivan must have been the vamp in the quad, the one who bit me during round two.

"This House," I began. "I'm, what, in a vampire sorority or something?"

Helen shook her head. "It's more complicated than that. All legitimate vampires in the world are affiliated with one House or other. There are currently twelve Houses in the United States; Cadogan is the fourth-oldest among those." Helen sat up even straighter, so I took a wild guess that she was also a flag-flying member of Cadogan House.

Helen handed me the book, which must have weighed ten pounds. I centered it in my lap, distributing the mass.

"You won't need to memorize the rules, of course, but you'll want to read the introductory sections and have at least a passing familiarity with the content. And of course you can refer to the text if you have specific questions. Make sure to read about the Commendation."

"What's the Commendation?"

"The initiation ceremony. You'll become an official member of the House, and you'll take your oaths to Ethan and the rest of the Cadogan vampires. And speaking of, payments typically begin two weeks after take the oath is taken."

I blinked. "Payments?"

She gave me one of those over-the-glasses looks. "Your salary, dear."

I laughed nervously, the sound strangled. "I don't need a salary. I'm a student. Teaching assistant. Stipend." I was three years into my graduate work, three chapters into my dissertation on romantic medieval literature.

Helen frowned. "Dear, you can't go back to school. The university doesn't admit vampires as students, and they certainly don't employ them. Title VII doesn't cover us yet. We went ahead and removed you, just to avoid the squabble, so you won't have to worry about—"

My pulse thudded in my ears. "What do you mean, you removed me?"

Her expression softened. "Merit, you're a vampire. A Cadogan Initiate. You can't go back to that life."

I was out the door before she was done talking, her voice echoing behind me as I rushed to the first-floor bedroom that served as our office. I wiggled the mouse to wake my computer, brought up a Web browser, and logged into the university server. The system recognized me, and my stomach unclenched in relief.

Then I brought up my records.

Two days ago, my status had been changed. I was listed as "Not Enrolled."

The world shifted.

I went back to the living room, my voice wavering as I fought through the quickly rising panic, and faced Helen. "What did you do? You had no right to take me out of school!"

Helen turned back to her satchel and pulled out a sheath of paper, her manner irritatingly calm. "Because Ethan feels your circumstances are . . . particular, you'll receive your salary from the House within the next ten business days. We've already arranged the direct deposit. The Commendation is scheduled on your seventh day, six days from now. You will appear when commanded. At the ceremony, Ethan will assign your position of service within the House." She smiled at me. "Perhaps something in public relations, given your family's connections to the city."

"Oh, lady. Wrong move, bringing up the parents," Mallory muttered.

She was right. It was exactly the wrong thing to say, my parents being one of my least favorite topics. But it was at least jarring enough to wake me from my daze. "I think we're done here," I told her. "It's time for you to leave."

Helen winged up an eyebrow. "It's not your house."

Brave of her to piss off the new vampire. But we were on my turf now, and I had allies.

I turned to Mallory with an evil grin. "How about we find out how much of the vampire myth is actually myth? Don't vampires have to have an invitation to be in someone's home?"

"I love the way you think," Mal said, then went to the door and opened it. "Helen," she said, "I want you out of my house."

Something stirred in the air, a sudden breeze that blew through the doorway and ruffled Mallory's hair—and raised goose bumps along my arms.

"This is incredibly rude," Helen said, but yanked her satchel up. "Read the book, sign the forms. There's blood in the refrigerator. Drink it—a pint every other day. Stay away from sunlight and aspen stakes, and come when he commands you." She neared the door, and then, suddenly, like someone had flipped the switch on a vacuum, she was sucked onto the stoop.

I rushed to the doorway. Helen stood on the top step, glasses askew, staring back at us in disheveled shock. After a moment, she straightened her skirt and glasses, turned crisply, and walked down the stairs and toward the limo. "That was—very rude," she called back. "Don't think I won't tell Ethan about this!"

I gave her a pageant wave—hand cupped, barely swiveling.

"You do that, Helen," Mallory dared. "And tell him we said to fuck off while you're at it."

Helen turned to look at me, eyes blazing silver. Like, supernaturally silver. "You were *undeserving*," she sniped.

"I was *unconsenting*," I corrected and slammed the heavy oak door shut with enough force that it rattled the hinges. After the *scritch* of rocks on asphalt signaled the limo's retreat, I leaned back against the door and looked at Mallory.

She glared back. "They said you were on campus by yourself in the middle of the night!" She punched my arm, disgust obvious on her face. "What the hell were you thinking?"

That, I thought, was the release of the panic she'd suffered until she learned that I was coming home. It tightened my throat, knowing that she'd waited for me, worried for me.

"I had work to do."

"In the middle of the night?!"

"I said I had work to do!" I threw up my hands, irritation rising. "God, Mallory, this isn't my fault." My knees began to shake. I moved the few steps back to the couch and sat down. Repressed fear, horror, and violation overwhelmed me. I covered my face with my hands as the tears began to fall. "It wasn't my fault, Mallory. Everything—my life, school—is gone, and it wasn't my fault."

I felt the cushion dip beside me and an arm around my shoulders.

"Oh, God, I'm sorry. I'm sorry. I'm freaked out. I was so scared, Mer, Jesus. I know it's not your fault." She held me while I sobbed, rubbed my back while I cried hard enough to hiccup, while I mourned the loss of my life, of my humanity.

We sat there together for a long time, my best friend and I. She offered Kleenex as I replayed the few things I could remember— the attack, the second set of vampires, the cold and pain, the hazy limo ride.

When I'd sobbed my body empty of tears, Mallory stroked the hair from my face. "It'll be okay. I promise. I'll call the university in the morning. And if you can't go back . . . we'll figure something out. In the meantime, you should call your grandfather. He'll want to know you're okay."

I shook my head, not yet ready to have that conversation. My grandfather's love had always been unconditional, but then again, I'd always been human. I wasn't ready to test the correlation. "I'll start with Mom and Dad," I promised. "Then I'll let word trickle down."

"Tacky," Mallory accused, but let it go. "The House, I guess it was, did call me, but I don't know who else they contacted. The call was pretty short. 'Merit was attacked on campus two nights ago. In order to save her life, we've made her a vampire. She'll return home tonight. She may be dizzy from the change, so please be home to assist her during the first crucial hours. Thank you.' It sounded like a recording, to be real honest."

"So this Ethan Sullivan's a cheapo," I concluded. "We'll add that to the list of reasons we don't like him."

"Him turning you into a soul-sucking creature of the night being number one on that list?"

I nodded ruefully. "That's definitely number one." I shifted and glanced over at her. "They made me like them. *He* made me like them, this Sullivan."

Mallory made a sound of frustration. "I know. I am so effing jealous." Mal was a student of the paranormal; as long as I'd known her, she'd had a keen interest in all things fanged and freaky. She put her palm to her chest. "I'm the occultist in the family, and yet it's *you*, the English lit geek, they turn? Even Buffy would feel that sting. Although," she said, her gaze appraising, "you will make damn good research material."

I snorted. "But research material for what? Who the hell am I now?"

"You're Merit," she said with conviction that warmed my heart. "But kind of Merit 2.0. And I have to say, the phone call notwithstanding, this Sullivan's not a cheapo about everything. Those shoes are Jimmy Choo, and that dress is runway-worthy." She clucked her tongue. "He's dressed you up like his own personal model. And frankly, Mer, you look good."

Good, I thought, was relative. I looked down at the cocktail dress, smoothed my hands over the slick, black fabric. "I liked who I was, Mal. My life wasn't perfect, but I was happy."

"I know, hon. But maybe you'll like this, too."

I doubted it. Seriously.